DAYS OF BLACK THUNDER

DAYS OF BLACK THUNDER

Herman Lloyd Bruebaker

To order additional copies of this book, contact:
Xlibris Corporation
1-888-795-4274
www.Xlibris.com
Orders@Xlibris.com
32878

Other novels by Herman Lloyd Bruebaker
(Published by Author House)

Pharaoh's Promise
The Lost Jewels
Tomorrow Afternoon we die
Treachery in the Night
Red Star Rising
Blood on Winter Snows
Feast of the Black Phoenix

(Published by Xlibris)

Some Dreams Best Forgotten
Passage from Limbo

"Today, every inhabitant of this planet must contemplate the day when it may no longer be habitable. Every man, woman, and child lives under the nuclear weapon of Damocles. Hanging by the slenderest of threads, capable of being cut at any time by accident or madness. The weapons of war must be abolished before they abolish us."

John Fitzgerald Kennedy, President of the United States
(1961-1963)

CHAPTER ONE

Tales over the years would different why that Bolshevist nuclear thunder came crashing down on a unprepared terrified population. Some claimed hell and brimstone came after the globe turned away from God and this was his punishment. Others scoffed the short vicious exchange was due to electronic problems aboard a Soviet submarine off the coast of Southern California. No official reasons were posted because nobody knew why. But the how was well known when a submerged Russian sub fired its first missile launching a war with no turning back. In those few hours the world went crazy. After that another new enemy emerged once the explosions stopped. This was when Mother Nature made herself savagely known. In the next twenty-six days mankind's insanity sent civilizations crumbing into nuclear waste. Where many cities once stood now only deadly radiation graveyards stained the soil with their unmarked and forgotten graves. But today was greeted with doubt and little enthusiasm by the emaciated world's dark nightmarish terror. Another Dark Age was within sight.

All of this was unconsciously acknowledged by a solitary figure dressed in battle camouflaged clothing. He was thoughtfully standing on a low knoll overlooking the raging Pacific Ocean. In 1520 the Portuguese navigator Ferdinand Magellan named this body of water pacific. In his native tongue this meant peaceful. But four hundred and seventy-nine years later it certainly wasn't living up to its name. For long minutes the warrior stared at those choppy waters crashing upon sandy beaches.

He hadn't heard another man come up from behind and silently study the choppy waters that were near impossible to travel. "I can remember when people crowded this beach soaking up sun and swimming in cool waters." There was a short pause followed by a chuckle. "During my college years I sure found some nice babes along here."

"I didn't know you went to college."

"Yeah, I graduated from the university at Santa Barbara. That's where I met my wife."

The warrior nodded before looking over his shoulder at the slender marine reliving his past memories. "Yeah, I remember when this highway was bumper-to-bumper with automobiles. Now there's only rattling wrecks when the wind whistles through them." Businesses and residences along this once sunny paradise now lay in blacken ruins. Casualties in the opening hours of this nuclear carnage were incredibly high. Looking at the gray skies restricting much of the sunlight he mumbled. "But damned do we need rain. Maybe it would wash away that blasted soot in the atmosphere."

This marine known as Billy Bob shook his head. "It hasn't rained since this war began."

"It'll rain sooner or later."

"It better be soon. Have you noticed the grasses and trees are dying everywhere you look? And what about that little garden we planted? Nothing is coming up. We got to have sun and rain. That's all there is to it."

"Yeah, I know." the officer moaned. "Well, for now we can't do anything about it. So let's get back up the beaches and join the others."

They carefully made their way back up to the highway overlooking this winding stretch of beaches. There he greeted thirty more warriors standing about two armored personnel carriers. The men were eating cold rations and drinking the last of their beer. After World War III broke loose California received the initial nuclear missiles from underwater Soviet submarines. Hoping to neutralize this Pacific region Moscow was stunned by their results. If they had doubts about justifying the attack it was too late to turn back. Allies nations launched their war toys and the war President Kennedy warned about became reality. One marine grabbed a beer from a bucket and tossed it to his commander. Catching the bottle the lieutenant twisted off its top. When food was offered the tall man shook his head. After raising the dark brown bottle, the naval lieutenant saluted his comrades then drained its contents without pause. Throwing down his empty bottle he momentarily looked at the fading gold label and frowned.

"Hey, lieutenant," a marine corporal yelled from the carrier. "Chief called several minutes ago. Said to tell you we got company back home."

"Did he say who?"

"He didn't say."

"O.K. Call back and say we should be home in another three hours."

The rugged man standing in at six feet and three inches looked back at the choppy waters. After scanning the region his brown eyes saw no threat. The chattering marines looked sloppy security wise, but that was a disillusion. There was a dangerous alertness in these men serving in the nuclear wastelands. Lieutenant James Blackmore and his marines walked cautiously, otherwise, they didn't survive. Their bodies were padded by thick winter clothing that provided some warmth against the coldness cloaking the area. Their weapons were carried for immediate use. There was no proven way of recognizing friend or foe. Their assiduous attention to these desolate surroundings wasn't taught in classrooms, but from battling insurmountable odds.

Billy Bob after finishing his nature call joined James on the knoll's edge. "The Chief said some companies from 345th Infantry were shuttled to posts between San Diego and Riverside. So when do we get help? Over the last two months we have lost thirty-six men and Yuma hasn't sent one marine to fill our dwindling ranks." He dubiously added after a short silence. "We're stretched pretty thin, lieutenant."

After nodding his agreement the officer was silent. James Blackmore was commanding officer of Mobile Radar Station Ten Delta, one of four such stations scattered from San Diego to San Francisco. For the last six days they had been on reconnaissance patrol. He ran a gloved hand across the making of a short black beard. This thirty-one year old Apache pilot was aboard a large aircraft carrier when the war broke out. Nine days later the flattop was sunk off the Philippines by a Soviet submarine. He was in the water for forty-nine hours before rescued by another carrier that was sunk a few hours later. The war's nuclear phase ended when supposedly all thermonuclear warheads were expended. Then the conventional warfare began and existed to that day. Battle lines were drawn and savagely fought along the Canadian/American borders.

Walking over to the command vehicle James asked its radio operator. "Any update on that task force Yuma reported coming down from Alaska?"

"Nothing yet."

Removing his heavy combat helmet James thoughtfully looked around. "You can't hide a damned task force." His almond brown eyes showed signs of frustration after six days of fruitless searching. Naval Headquarters was quartered in Yuma after Washington, D.C. was destroyed by missile attacks during the war's first minutes. It was vital Russia's last known naval task force be stopped. "When did you last talk with the Chief?"

"About twenty minutes ago. He said all radar stations up North have reported in. Not a whiff of the damned communists." The young marine private scratched his ear then asked. "When we do find them what the hell are we going to do? That's a damned surface task force we're talking about. We only got two helicopters. The last I heard our only two destroyers in the Pacific are off Mexico."

"I don't know." He shrugged. "Maybe a miracle would help. All I know, private, is we're to find the ships then notify Yuma."

Wanting to strike a blow at the Soviet Union, these men volunteered for the newly organized Western Outer Perimeter Defense Forces. This military group manned the isolated early warning radar systems for the battered United States. The former super power was reduced to thirteen states with their national capital in St. Louis, Missouri. Without even knowing it James accepted another warm beer and unscrewed its top. For the last six days they had monitored the coastal regions between Los Angeles and Santa Barbara. Civilians reported seeing Soviet spies in the area but they hadn't found them.

Billy Bob enlisting the same time as James became good friends with the lieutenant. After the tall black man's wife died during Soviet missile attacks on San Diego, he devoted all of his energies toward killing Soviets. Though they hadn't found the enemy, evidence was strong they were discreetly circulating about the area. Billy Bob had a large nose and thick lips with a quick laughter that was rare these days. The private always carried a short-barrel shotgun and was quick to use it.

"Maybe these ships don't exist," he cynically suggested. "Maybe it's another Russian misinformation tactic?" The marine leaning against the carrier frowned. "Hell, the bastards have been good at that since Stalin's days."

James shook his head. "No, they exist. There have been too many confirmed sightings since leaving their Bering Sea by the way of Alaska. We just can't find them. But it is damned important we find them before they slip down the coast and into Mexican waters."

"Then why haven't we found them? Look at those devilish waters. How the hell does a bunch of ships escape detection when they have to cruise so close to land?"

"Lately the Russian Navy has been known to snatch some pretty reckless successes. That's why they're beating the hell out of us in the Gulf. We got to locate them because our own navy can't afford another surprise slipping into the Gulf of Mexico." Glancing over his shoulder James asked the radio operator. "What about updates on that new storm front blowing across Canada?"

"Yuma's last update said it was due sometime tomorrow."

The marine leaned out of the carrier's window to get a better look at his commanding officer. His face was smeared with an oily lotion soothing his dark skin's irritation from the many airborne pollutants. This four year veteran marine was stationed at San Diego when missiles demolished the West Coast naval installation. There wasn't much left of the city after the smoke cleared. Galvin Harper was one of three radiomen assigned to Ten Delta. His short, skinny frame had a deep scar running down the right cheek and it was still healing. Galvin got this disfigurement when running into a burning building to rescue his trapped colonel. "The Chief said this one was going to be a bastard."

"Aren't they all?" Draining his beer James hurled the bottle into the choppy waters. Debris and sooty smoke from the numerous fires was making each day more like a heavy gray overcast winter day. It was getting worse each day. In the last three weeks the temperatures dropped another eight degrees. "Would you sail those waters?"

"Are you kidding? That's a stormy nightmare out there."

"But the Russians are doing just that." James growled. After a few moments of cold silence he looked at Billy Bob. "Our only challenges are two old destroyers cruising off Mexico. The battered remains of our navy are blockaded in ports up and down the Gulf. Their only hope is our buying them time to repair their ships and make ready to face the growing Russian threat out there. How do we it . . . I don't know. But I don't have to remind you the United States isn't doing very good in this war. We're being defeated on every battlefield and it's not going to get any better in the weeks to come. Not only does our problem lie on the battlefields, but also at home. Our civilians are suffering serious morale losses."

"You don't have to lecture me on that crisis."

After the attacks stopped five months ago, Billy Bob was among those marines rounding up dazed citizens for relocation to the mid western states. But many people electing to salvage their wasted dreams stayed. That's when America's real troubles began. There were occasions when marines were forced to fire into disgruntled crowds of looters or angry people denied their former land holdings. It was after his third massacre of crazed citizens that Billy Bob requested a transfer to Outer Perimeter Defenses.

"Flame thrower!" a marine anxiously yelled.

There were disgusted moans as two of their number carefully made way down the sloping rocky bank. While James and Billy Bob quietly watched from above, flames quickly consumed four bloated bodies that were washed ashore. After satisfied there were no remains, the two marines climbed up the slippery embankment, deposited their weapons in the carrier, and grabbed a beer. They angrily gulped down the liquid after doing what no man liked, but knew had to be done to control the outbreak of diseases. Bodies were constantly washing ashore. Even inland it fell to their lot to burn all corpses found. It was an emotional drain all men shared including the CO. After hearing another vehicle pulling up, James gave the ocean a last scowl then walked over to the new arrival.

*   *   *

"Find anything new?" he asked the crew dismounting from their NIMDA Shoet II armored carrier.

Most of them shook their heads while passing. For the last two days they patrolled independently of James' probe. The six men wearing red-cross armbands were grimy and sour-mannered. Three other heavily armed marines climbed from the Israeli built vehicle and gave their commanding office a slow nod in passing. Their beer ran out last night. Seeing a sharp dent on its side James ran his gloved hand over it.

"Ran into some civil resistance yesterday over by Taiguas." reported a short black staff sergeant. On his twenty-fifth birthday he spent all day burning decaying bodies. Hailing from Hattiesburg, Mississippi this man had stood before marine disciplinary boards more than once. In other times he would have being cashiered from the Corps. But in these chaotic days marines with nasty tempers were in great demand. Dennis Carter, better known as Chatterbox, liked the naval lieutenant's fair way of commanding.

"Was it serious?"

"Not really, but we saw more evidence those damned gangs are operating around here. Found couple Mexican families ruthlessly slaughtered near some church ruins with their women raped. As if these people don't have enough trouble we have Mexican punks running around raping and looting." He angrily shook his head.

The lieutenant thoughtfully studied this marine needing a rest away from the carnage they daily witnessed. "We'll have such people around until civil order can be returned."

"And when will that be?" There was a curt defeatist tone in his husky voice.

There was a short pause. "I really don't know. But I do know to mentally survive this get use to telling yourself it's only a bad nightmare."

"How often do you tell yourself that, lieutenant?"

There was a short pause then his voice became bitter and distant. "Thousands of times a day and I still have nightmares at night. But what you see is what we have, sergeant. The United States we were borne in is no longer around. You either cope with it or you die. That's the only way you'll get through this, Chatterbox. Millions of people died in those attacks leaving nothing but devastation. I have been watching you these last few weeks and Bro you're losing it. Get a grip on your emotions or we'll be burying you out here." There was another short pause. "Do you understand that, marine?"

After a few moments the staff sergeant slowly nodded with little conviction in his response. "Yes sir."

"Good. Now continue with your report. Did you find any sign of Soviet activity?"

"No. We saw a lot of new violence, but it was from our own people gone whack go. But there was something else. On several occasions we discovered decaying bodies with a sticky green substance eating away at their bodies. I have never saw anything like that before. And I sure as hell didn't study it in med school."

"Were there any particular areas?"

"We saw the largest number of these bodies around Refugio, but I don't think it has anything to do with that region. The sticky bacterium smells like hell." After James wanted to know more, Chatterbox continued in a slow thoughtful manner. "This green stuff eats away the flesh. At one place we found dead animals after having feasted on the infectious flesh were bloated and seeping that junk. About ten miles from here we found a white woman of middle age having died several days previously. Performing a battlefield autopsy I discovered her kidneys, liver, and heart were wasted by the greenish slime." When one of his men brought over two beers the men gladly accepted them with strained smiles.

"Did that kill her?"

"No, that's the strange thing about this slime. Her skull was split open probably by a sharp object. It was following her death that the wasting began."

"Civil disorder?"

"Probably, though I'm certain she didn't have this ailment before death. The cerebrum and cerebellum were mushy from this substance." He shook his head before uneasily muttering. "I have seen some wild stuff in my time, lieutenant, but nothing like this."

Though Chatterbox only finished three years of med school he was Ten Delta's medical doctor. James stood in the chilly wind sweeping in from the ocean pondering over what he had said. Below them the crashing waves sounded like thunder.

"So what do you think?"

"I don't know for sure."

"Then give me your best shot. It's been months since the nuclear attacks. Is this an illness generated by excessive radiation? Or do we have a new plague on the loose?"

"It could be radiation related. I did random radiation monitoring and found a gradual deceasing." Reaching into the SHOET he pulled out a folded map. After spreading it on the ground both men knelt while Chatterbox continued his briefing. "Here at Edwards along the Southern Pacific rail line, we found scattered bodies with bacteria infections. And along the coast we found more infected bodies." He studied the map for a few moments then nervously suggested. "This may very well be the advance outbreak of a plague. We sure as hell have the foundations for such a happening."

James stared at the map then stumbled to his feet. "Aw shits, that's all I need. As if you haven't notice the temps are falling. If we don't get rain soon that sooty debris curtain above the earth will worsen then we have a full fledged greenhouse affect." He paused. "O.K. let's mount up and go home. You ride with me so we can talk more." James briefly looked at the skies. "We need rain real soon or we're done for."

CHAPTER TWO

As the three vehicles cautiously drove along the coast back toward their home base, James viewed the devastation with increasing depression. It was easy to tell Chatterbox to bear the situation, but harder to do it. They saw scattered bunches of people along the way. While some waved at them others remained stony silent. The war's devastating shock was still strong among the survivors. He seriously doubted if that whiplash trauma would ever be completely healed

"I don't think I'll ever get used to seeing this," Chatterbox bitterly groaned while passing through what used to be a small town along the coast.

"You probably won't."

He thoughtfully glanced at the weather conditions that were growing worse. "While checking out Santa Barbara this time one of my men visited the college campus he attended before the war."

"Who was that?"

"Private Shaker. Well anyhow, there wasn't much left to brag about the campus that was a bunch of wasted buildings. I shouldn't have allowed him to visit the site. That was a bad move on my part." His face twisted that wretched expression when having looked on death too often. "Shaker was away for the weekend when the attacks came. His girl friend was in their dorm room studying. He wanted to find something salvageable." Feeling tears trickling down his face Chatterbox shook his head to drive away the hideous emotions. "We buried his girl friend's remains."

It was a while before James asked. "How is Shaker?"

"Last night I gave him a shot to soothe his emotions. But he's doing better today. It was just the shock of walking among the debris and finding your girl friend's burnt remains. They were going to marry after graduation." Slapping a balled fist against his thigh Chatterbox moaned. "I hope every damned Russian alive dies in Hell for what they did."

Laying his hand on Chatterbox's shoulder, James sympathetically said. "I'm sorry about Shaker. I know if the same thing happened to me . . . I probably would go off the deep end. But we got to cope with this or go down ourselves. I'm sure every man in Ten Delta has similar emotions waiting to explode. But still we have to cope because it's not going to get any better for awhile." For a moment he stared at the thunderous waves crashing across twisted boat wreckages that were gradually pushed ashore. "I don't have the answers about our future, Chatterbox. I doubt if anybody does. We just have to struggle with each day. I don't have to tell you the future looks bleak. The United States is down to thirteen states with most of our country wasted and millions of dead. The last I heard we aren't doing worth a damn along the Canadian border. But with faith we'll make it. That I promise."

"Well, I don't see how it can get any darker. Most civilizations were vaporized in the first hours. Hundreds of millions were killed with untold numbers later dying from radiation poisoning, rotten foodstuffs, lack of medical care, and not to mention those civil disorders raging across the planet. Only God knows when this nightmare will end." He shrugged his broad shoulders before saying. "Maybe he doesn't even know when. Now we have another new problem and this one is scaring the shit out of me."

"You mean that green stuff?"

"No, not that but that's a damned nightmare by itself. I'm referring to another situation promising to create some pretty bad political headaches. More frequent during this patrol we saw Mexican flags planted everywhere."

"What about them?"

"There are rumors among the people."

"Chatterbox, you're talking in circles. We too seen the scattered flags, but right now I don't see a problem with that. California had millions of Mexicans so they're trying to cope with the crisis. Everybody has different ways of doing that."

"Then let them cope that way in Mexico. California is American soil. If they want to plant flags then make sure it's the Stars and Stripes." He paused for a moment before somberly adding. "Lieutenant, those rumors are serious. We're hearing talk Mexico intends to annex California. Those militant Mexicans we have fought the last few days are supposedly advance elements of that political effort. It's a new political group that doesn't even have a name."

"What about the Mexicans in our area? What do they say about this group?"

"They're worried about it."

*   *   *

The lead vehicle suddenly swerved to miss something in the highway. About that same time an explosion erupted nearby. The three armored cars stopped in defensive positions while their marines rapidly dismounted. Bullets whizzed passed while James scrambled to some rocks then with his glasses scanned the area. The hostiles were well hidden in building wreckages. Counting the gun flashes James estimated ten terrorists. One man carelessly firing his weapon showed too much head and a marine ended his life with a well-aimed shot.

"Chatterbox," James ordered. "Take a squad around those rocks over there and eliminate that hostility in the building ruins to our right."

While his marines darted through the ruins James observed the enemy's firing. Judging from their reckless gunfire the attackers weren't military trained. They were probably another group of bandits causing Ten Delta numerous problems these days. But within twenty minutes the fighting was over. While James and Chatterbox carefully examined the dead men other marines were smashing their few weapons.

"These men are bandits," the staff sergeant speculated while moving among their bodies. "They don't have the slightest idea about ambush positioning. And another thing, lieutenant, they're all Mexicans."

"Think maybe that's because this region is mostly Mexicans?"

A marine walked up and handed over two folded flags removed from a dead body's backpack. Chatterbox stared at the cloths for a moment before mumbling. "Russian colors." He thoughtfully looked at James. "This isn't good, lieutenant."

"All right, when we get home I'll notify Yuma of your suspicions. But I hope you're wrong on this one. Let's burn those bodies and get back on the road."

*   *   *

While the burning took place James walked a few feet from the armored carriers and studied the darkening skies. Thoughts of the war's opening hours rushed forward. Russian penetrations never seriously affected the mid western states. After Washington D.C was destroyed, the government smoothly transferred through the chain of command. With the White House and Congress totally wasted leadership fell to the Chairman of Joint Chiefs. Admiral Jonathan Washington survived because he was away in the Ozark Mountains hunting wild boar. Now tucked away in his St. Louis capital, the silver haired admiral struggled to hold together a battered collection of war-shocked states. The soft-spoken man's armies were failing to achieve victories along the Canadian borders where most of the fighting was now confined.

After Chatterbox called out James walked over to where he was staring at some bodies. "Some of these civilians have the green bacteria."

"You're right that they smell," James mumbled while holding a gloved hand over his nose.

"The victims all have common connections. You apparently must be alive to contact the bacteria. None of those dead bodies we burned these last few weeks had this illness. From what I loosely deduct this plague seems to be spreading, lieutenant."

*   *   *

At Tailguas the camouflaged vehicles turned off the badly damaged highway onto a surface road meandering along the shores. The crashing waves were only several hundred feet away. Southern Pacific Railroad repair crews once checked their rails using the one lane paved road. While the armored cars made their slow cautious drive toward the radar station some miles away, James settled back pondering over what Chatterbox had said. Along this road were a series of ravines carved into the ground by waters flowing down from Los Padres National Forest to the ocean. They would soon stop at the one known as Arroyo Hondo.

"How many Mexicans do you think lives in California?"

"God, I don't know. I remember our last census listed them as the largest ethical group."

"And you really think Mexico wants to annex the state?"

"Yeah and this isn't a new political cause. The Mexicans have always wanted this state returned to Mexico."

"We would never let them get away with that." James stubbornly argued.

Chatterbox frowned. "And who's going to stop them? St Louis is too preoccupied with the fighting in Canada. The only real military presence in California is our scattered radar stations. Even Thomas's infantrymen are too busy rounding up citizens for relocation. From a legal standpoint it looks as if we're abandoning the state."

"That's because this coast is too dangerous to live in."

"Well, either way the Mexicans are going to cause us plenty trouble."

"You may be right." After a short silence James looked toward the ocean. "But for the moment that problem will have to wait. There's a Soviet task force coming down this coast and that's our main concern. If those ships reach the Gulf our unprepared Navy will be blown to Hell. That's not going to happen if we can help it."

Chatterbox pointed at the burning detail finishing their gruesome task. "What about those diseased bodies?"

"We'll notify Yuma and see what they can come up with."

Chatterbox made a bitter expression. "Yuma doesn't give a damn what happens out here, lieutenant."

*   *   *

Later when the Israeli-manufactured armored cars noisily braked to a halt, James was snapped from his troubled reflections of their traumatizing situation. They were at Arroyo Hondo. Several marines quickly dismounted to establish security perimeters. Getting too close to the cold ocean was exceptionally unfriendly and in their early days three marines was sucked under by the large cresting waves crashing ashore. With everything as it was being careless was dangerous.

As James dismounted he glanced at Chatterbox. "What's our major medical problem right now?"

"Depends if it you mean our command or the civilians?"

"How about our men," James asked while observing the staff sergeant rechecking his automatic weapon. That was done every time he left the armored vehicle.

"We have increasing numbers of psychological cases." There was a short pause then a deep frustrated sigh. "In med school I never got into psychosis."

"Are you saying our men are going crazy?"

Chatterbox shook his head. "Right now they aren't. But if some of them aren't removed from this nightmare, we may have future serious problems."

"That's a pretty harsh medical opinion."

"But true. But then again what can you expect from the men? Every day Ten Delta is faced with horrific situations that would have only months ago driven a man insane. Good God, now we're faced with an approaching enemy task force and there's not much we can do to stop it. Then there are all the makings of a possible plague about to break out. To make matters worse, we have an increasing hostile situation with the Mexicans. To make this even more bizarre the government expects us, a mere 59 men, to handle the situation. If all of this won't drive a man crazy I don't know what will." He threw his hands up. "We find all of this entertaining in a damned movie but damn it we aren't in a movie. This is all too real."

"Things are bad all around and we have to do with what's available. I don't know what else to tell you."

Seeing two marines scouting down where the arroyo dumped into the ocean, he motioned for the sergeant to accompany him. James' mood was just about as unfriendly as the waves crashing ashore. The heavy assault rifle was slung over his shoulder by its leather strap. Their bad emotional six-day patrol was beginning to strain his physical reserves. All he wanted was a hot shower, clean clothes, shave, and climb under his sheets for a long uninterrupted sleep. But what he saw in the sands promised to delay those desires. Salty mist drenched his face while staring at the tracks.

"What do you think happen here?"

The squatting black man studied the crushed rocks where patches of dried mud encased large tire tracks. "Multi-wheeled vehicles came ashore not that many hours ago. This mud hasn't caked that hard. They proceeded up that rocky incline to the surface road. These invaders wanted their landing kept secret. But they must have been in a hurry and missed these three patches of mud." For a few minutes he stared at the tracks. "This is an unusual tread pattern but I have seen them."

"They were landed from the ocean. See where the ramp crashed down on the rocks. Maybe the Soviets put ashore a scouting party?"

Chatterbox agreed. "That's the only people I know who would have that capability. But that means the task force isn't too far away." He was silent for a moment. "This confirms what Juan Lopez told me yesterday." Waiting until a camera was brought from the lead armored car he kept talking. "Remember the Lopez family?" When James didn't recognize the name he kept talking. "Their ten year old son fell from a building he was playing in. Now you remember, right? He stopped us yesterday and gave the base two cases of Jack Daniels Black Label." The sergeant smiled. "Every time we pass their settlement they give us something to take back. Well, anyhow he told us about a ship he saw cruising pass in the night. Didn't know what it was except it was large."

"We don't have ships down this way." James replied. "Hell, take a look at those waters. The weather is so screwed up after the nuclear war ships can't sail no further than ten miles off shore or the turmoil will sink the ships."

After finishing photographing the landing site Chatterbox put the camera back in its case. "That's why he mentioned it." While climbing the loose rocks up to the surface road, the sergeant glanced at his CO. "You still haven't made your peace with God, have you?" Reaching the summit James took out a cigarette and lit it. Chatterbox refused the offer after quitting three months ago. Half way through the war's nuclear phrase while fighting Soviet marines in the Far East, he became a Born Again Christian and was always trying to bring James back into the folds.

Exhaling the smoke James thoughtfully looked at Chatterbox. "Still trying, eh? But you're wasting your time. I don't accept all that crap about the war. God didn't cause this crisis. Mankind did with his toys and arrogance." Pointing at the thunderous fires sweeping through the Los Padres National Forest miles away he frowned. To their northern direction other fires consumed the Santa Ynez National Forest with a wrath that was terrifying. "There's part of nature's punishment. All of that damned smoke and drifting debris will be our deaths if we don't find a means to halt their spread. Those fires are nature's way of saying you destroyed my earth far too long and now it is payback time. That enemy task force and the Mexican threat are political. God isn't involved in this problem at all." James stopped talking and solemnly watched the drifting smoke. "No matter where you are fires in Asia, Europe, South America, and North America are massive geographical monsters raging out of control. That's our primary threat and it has nothing to do with God. Mankind made this happen and mankind will have to find means to stop it."

"But God will . . ."

James suddenly became defensive. "What will God do? Look, Chatterbox, I'm not interested in converting to your religious theme. I'm sort of biased by what has happened. All along this coast there are church ruins with decaying bodies who prayed their God would stop this senseless slaughtering. But his ears were turned away. Those people died asking for help that never came. You don't seem to understand God didn't cause this devastation and he isn't going to repair it." He briefly studied the black man's stern expression. "I respect your religious beliefs. That's your right, but I don't subscribe to them. We have massive problem coming at us from all corners of his coast. It's there we have to concentrate our efforts. If you want to pray that's your business, but please do it on your own time."

He was used to James' refusals. About to climb into his SHOET Chatterbox paused. "What do we do about Lopez's report?"

James thought over it for a moment. "With everything considered he was probably right. After you have rested take the identification manual and see if he can identify the ship." There was a pause before the lieutenant walking back to his own armored car swung into the passenger's entry.

After the convoy was on the move James thoughtfully studied the black gathering clouds. This weather was going crazy. Earth desperately needed rain to wash sunlight soaking debris from the air. Only then mankind might have a decent chance at surviving. Prior coming to California he was shown top-secret photographs taken from their orbiting space station. They confirmed all the major world capitals were in radiation ruins. Those painful memories caused his face to grimace. It took mankind only twenty-nine days to destroy what took centuries to build. The rumbling convulsions of exploding missiles, raging fires ignited by falling bombs, deadly clouds of poisonous gases released by Third World Powers all contributed to civilizations' demise. Each missile programmed for specific targets went astray after electromagnetic fields embraced the earth. But soon it didn't matter if their missiles fell on designated targets or not. Simply falling promised death and destruction and after all that was their objective.

CHAPTER THREE

Some time later the column slowly passed the Can del Molino ravine which was only ten miles from Ten Delta. That was when the lead car suddenly swinging to the side stopped and marines scrambled from its rear. James' driver cursed while sharply whipping to their right to avoid a collision. Even before they halted James was grabbing his rifle and stepping from the vehicle.

"What did you see?"

"Movement," Chatterbox said while pressing binoculars against his eyes. While scanning the ravine dropping forty feet into the nearby ocean, he felt the icy winds that were getting stronger. James joined him with his glasses. Down below in the ravine were battered metal sheds rattling in the wind. "Whoever it was sure hot footed it into the clutter down there."

"Could be people finding shelter from the storm?"

"Then they aren't friendly. People around here know us and don't run like damned rabbits."

Chatterbox's infra-red glasses pierced the darkened ravine. His suspicions something wasn't right down there became stronger.

James nodded agreement then whirled about. "Two marines with assaults down there to scout. I want a mounted machine gun positioned here for fire support." As he yelled marines were already scrambling down the gradual decline scattering loose dirt and rocks. Turning about again the lieutenant shouted. "Third SHOET . . . face our rear for fire support."

Once again tension cloaked this small column as marines with heavy assaults quietly moved through the damaged sheds. One by one they thoroughly searched the structures before announcing they were hostile free. About to climb back up the twenty foot incline a marine stopped and picked up a gray can. After handing it to James they joined the established defenses. The lieutenant rolled the chicken soup can around in his hand. It was processed in St. Petersburg, Russia.

Looking at Chatterbox he rolled his eyes. "Well, that seals any doubts. The Soviets are ashore."

"I wonder how many?"

"They couldn't have landed too many back there. It was probably an advance scouting party?" He observed James looking to their rear. "Want me to take a party back and see if we can pick up their tracks?"

"No, it's too late for that. Take a gander at those damned clouds. That storm is rapidly coming in from the ocean." James said. "We better get our butts back to the base."

Chatterbox started to walk away when stopping. "Oh yeah, I forgot to tell you that we saw Thomas' teams at Santa Barbara. He said to tell you hello."

"What's he doing down this far? I thought the 356th was finished relocating people from around here?"

"Yuma wanted a last swing through and this time they signed another four thousand people for Kansas resettlements. The relocates are camping at Chumash and this time they'll be airlifted to the Mid West. I guess there's too much lawlessness on the rails and highways to safely travel."

"There aren't enough troops for patrolling between Yuma and California so that figures. All right, let's get this show back on the road. I'll ride with you in the lead. We need to discuss this situation."

As their column rumbled over the gutted road leading to their hidden radar station in Gaviota, James thought about what they had found at the ravine. That only confirmed what Yuma had warned them about. He briefly wondered how the Army's 356th Specialized Regiment was handling the relocation crisis. They had a lousy job of uprooting the defiant people. He didn't blame the people for not wanting to leave their homes.

They were perhaps six miles from the coastal town of Gaviota when the lead driver swirled to miss something on the highway. About that time an explosion erupted dangerously close to the vehicles. Three armored cars halted in defensive positions as their small cannons rotated. Bullets were whizzing about as marines scrambled from the vehicles and began firing at their aggressors. Running to some nearby rubble James flopped down while bullets raged above his head. The hostiles were well concealed among the rocks. Counting the gun flashes James estimated maybe twenty hostiles. This number was reduced when one terrorist carelessly raised his head and a marine sharpshooter ended his life.

"Chatterbox," James ordered. "Take a squad around those rocks and eliminate the damned punks." Judging from their bad ambush tactics the hostiles weren't military trained. A few minutes later after the gunfire stopped James cautiously walked among the bodies. Four marines collecting their weapons smashed them on the rocks. Walking over to where Chatterbox was examining a dead terrorist the lieutenant mumbled. "Are they Mexicans?"

The staff sergeant ripped open the dead man's backpack and removed two folded flags. "Russian and Mexican colors," he angrily said.

*   *   *

The Russian destroyer stayed close to the wretched Californian shore line even though the tricky maneuver was exceptionally dangerous. Unpredictable high crashing surf coming in from a hostile Pacific Ocean made it necessary to do so. Further out tumultuous weather conditions were too rough to chance their few warships. Night rapidly rolled over the region as that Soviet warship plowed determinedly through excessive choppy waters. The five hundred foot warship rolled dangerously while plunging in and out of the crashing waves. Senior Naval Captain Karl Voronov had over the last twenty days struggled through the hostile ocean. His ship flying the red banner with gold hammer and sickle was the first enemy ship to cruise this region after the United States Pacific Fleet was smashed in battles off the Philippines.

"Steady on course," the captain barked. This weather tested the skills of his many years in uniform. When his helmsman showed signs of weakening the captain stepped to his side and whispered. "Steady, comrade, the ship will go wherever you want it to."

This enlisted man from the town of Tatshchevo was a good seaman if given the chance. Failure in what was left of the once mighty Red Navy wasn't tolerated. That was the dark side of his crew. None of them were wanted by the Naval High Command to fight the more important battles taking place in the Gulf of Mexico. Thus his ship was manned by castaways rejected by High Command. However, under his strong iron hand the men were shaping into a decent fighting bunch. Captain Voronov was also disgraced when losing his heavy cruiser in battle off the Philippines. Even with a serious shortage of competent naval captains he was lucky to get another ship.

Satisfied with his helmsman's performance the captain crossed the reddish illuminated bridge to sit in his elevated chair bolted to the deck. From there he studied the falling darkness. Reaching for a phone attached to the bulkhead the captain asked. "Navigation, what's our estimated time of arrival?" He wanted to drop anchor in a protective cove and wait out this storm.

"Three hours, Senior Captain Voronov."

This didn't make him happy, but what else was there to do? It wasn't his men's fault they were behind schedule. Weather along this western coast possessed an evil of its own. When a rating brought a cup of weak flavored tea he smiled. Their orders were simple. Cruise the Californian coast and eliminate without mercy all known military installations. When their assembled task force arrived on station within an unspecified time, the coast must be cleared of all military threats. There wasn't much left to waste. Supposedly along the coast were seven mobile radar stations manned by the newly organized Western Outer Perimeter Forces. Having yet to lock horns with this group, Captain Voronov assumed they were manned by inexperienced crews? Why would the Americans position their best troops along this nuclear wasteland? The decisive battles were being fought in the Gulf of Mexico and along the Canadian borders.

When the ship's fog horn sounded everybody aboard grabbed for something solid to hold onto. That was the signal their 7900 tone destroyer would be plunging through another huge swell. After the skadrenny minonosets (Russian for destroyer) emerged from its icy descent her crew smiled. The old ship was a grand lady despite what their High Command said. When first reporting to this ship commissioned in the '80s Captain Voronov groaned his disgust. But after months aboard her the captain developed a special bonding with this veteran of savage battles whose scars were many.

Captain Voronov was not a handsome man no matter how the subject was approached. Facial burns weren't fully healed after his cruiser sunk during a fierce battle in the war's early stages. A prominent nose twisted at its end seemed out of place on the moon shaped face. But his slightly overweigh body was impressive in the dark blue uniform. Brown eyes checked various electronic instruments scattered about the cramped bridge. Most of them still operated even though heavy electromagnetic interferences lingered after the nuclear explosions. His thin brown hair the color of worn leather was with sprinkles of gray. The ship took another sharp plunge through crashing waters. He calmly grabbed his chair for support. His facial expression was troubled. This mission should be handled by special trained Soviet troops in the task force and not the Navy. It was crazy patrolling these waters, but orders were orders. The obedient captain always fulfilled his orders no matter how much he distrusted their political content.

After snorting his displeasure at having to plow through endless parades of crashing waters the captain awkwardly left the bridge. He heard the senior officer on duty assuming command while he was gone. Minutes later he entered a compartment crowded with communications equipment. He impatiently waited while a junior officer decoded another message from the task force's flagship.

"What do they want this time, comrade lieutenant?" he bitterly asked after the specialist handed him a single page.

"Just more information on Ten Delta's commanding officer." the petty officer solemnly reported. "Lieutenant Blackmore was a helicopter pilot before his carrier was sunk off the Philippines. It's strange their military would put a low ranking lieutenant in charge of an important facility."

The captain shrugged his indifference. "The Americans are critically short of commissioned officers same as we are." He dropped the page in a basket for future study. "Don't the fools know by transmitting such useless data they may be tracked by radar? I already know Ten Delta is commanded by a lieutenant. The fact he was a navy helicopter pilot doesn't make a difference"

"Maybe they believe EM interferences will hinder the enemy's radar?"

"Those random interferences affect our own systems just as well. What they should be considering is these coastal radar stations have a better chance at tracking us. Then all they have to do is call the info to their Yuma headquarters. It's that simple." He held onto a cabinet top as the ship rocked its way through another huge swell. "What about the latest on our marines put ashore?"

"Not since they landed sixteen hours ago have we heard from them." Observing the captain's troubled expression he said. "But they are operating under strict radio silence, Comrade Captain."

"What about your grid search for Ten Delta?"

"It's still negative."

Still holding onto the cabinet for support as the ship splashed through icy swells, the captain thoughtfully speculated. "The other six radar sites aren't hidden, but Ten Delta is. Don't you find this rather unusual?"

The communications specialist nodded. "It tells me this Lieutenant Blackmore is clever. He conceals his station while the others operate without camouflage." The junior petty officer paused for a few moments then continued. "I have scanned this coast for hours without success."

"And why is this?"

The man solemnly rubbed his chin. "Either the EM interference is stopping us from tracking him or . . ." After thoughtfully analyzing his theory he somberly said. "This American is cunning. His station goes on line for a short time then shuts down before we can identify his originating point."

"Then how is he watching the coast?"

"I have a theory about that. During World War II the Americans used coastal watchers to track the Japanese. It's very possible Blackmore is doing the same thing. This way he keeps his radar time down to a minimum while maintaining a tight intelligence belt along the coastal waters."

"Then we're dealing with a fox, but even foxes make mistakes. We have to be ready when that time appears. We still don't know how many men Blackmore has or what kind of weapons they possess. If he works in the shadows then hopefully our marines can find people willing to tell us what we need."

Captain Voronov bid the man good night and went to his cabin. There opening a bottle of vodka he poured half a glass. Thoughtfully flopping in a chair, the senior captain sipped the clear liquid while condemning this war cruise that had been bad from its very start. What good was it to conquer a nation already blasted to hell? He smiled as the groaning ship emerged from another neck jerking submerging. For days they had searched for Blackmore's hidden Ten Delta Radar Station. The evasive station was a painful thorn in his side. As a young midshipman in June of 1963, Karl witnessed many startling changes ripping across the Soviet Union. He was promoted to senior captain just before the communist nation crashed in 1990. Then came those unpopular democratic reforms pushed on a people raised on cradle-to-grave welfare. But the Russian people had been under total rule for too long and the reforms didn't set well. The next few national leaders couldn't set the troubled nation on a true course. That's when Victor Kossier stepped from the shadows screaming anti-Western slogans and recklessly making promises only a communist would do. While the United States and Great Britain were fully developed in their Middle Eastern wars, the Russian nation slipped back into communism. The red banner reappeared two years ago without opposition from the Western World. When that happened Karl knew it was only a matter of time before war torched the earth. But nobody thought that hostility would destroy everything mankind had worked for over the centuries. Once those missiles roared into the skies there was no turning back for either side.

Before long the weary captain climbed onto his bunk and was fast asleep. Dreams of what used to be crowded his thoughts.

*　　*　　*

While the Russian warship neared its safe haven at Isla Vista, weary United States Marines were home after six days on patrol. Sixteen cases of bandits raiding the civilian settlements were tried with James as judge and jury. The guilty were punished with death by firing squad. Since Ten Delta resources were limited brutality was matched with equal brutality. On the lighter side Ten Delta treated one hundred cases of illness and injuries. This kept Chatterbox busy most of the time. Fourteen marriages were bonded by James. While searching for communist spies and evidence of the approaching enemy task force, James made certain the dazed civilians were cared for. These marines became the symbol of their nation's isolated outposts.

Ten Delta's executive officer Chief Petty Officer Timothy Hickman was glad to see the overdue patrols back. Though against the CO leading patrols, his arguments fell on deaf ears. Right after the group arrived at the camouflaged underground base, the chief sensed the grimness shared by their ranks. Something was different about these men. James immediately went to his quarters and showered then visited the dining area. The Chief watched the lieutenant wolf down scrambled eggs and bacon chunks with little talking while eating. After smearing globs of blackberry jam on bread, the commanding officer accepted a coffee refill and leaned back in his chair.

"What about the latest news from our battle zones," he asked. Before the Chief could reply he pointed at the bread and jam. "This taste good after eating those damned Iranian War rations."

Chief Hickman grinned. "Then you better enjoy because our supplies are pretty low. It's about time for another salvage hunt. But with everything coming down as they have the last few days I couldn't spare the men."

"It's that bad, eh?"

"Yeah, Thomas stopped by yesterday to report increasing interference from Mexican bandits. They're now calling themselves freedom fighters."

"Freedom fighters for what?"

"They're freedom fighters for the return of California to Mexico. They claim we took it illegally."

"Illegally, that's bullshit. Mexico lost it in the Mexican-American War. If I remember my history they're lucky we didn't take their whole damned country."

"Well, whatever, but they're posing an increasing serious threat. Sooner or later we'll have to face the issue."

"For right now we have other problems." In the next several minutes he discussed finding the landing spot of those alleged Soviet troops. Timothy's report that last night several vigilant civilians claimed foreign troops were along the coast was disturbing. "Well that confirms our suspicions the Soviets are mobilized and ashore. Tomorrow morning we'll send out patrols and I'll take the two Apaches to search from the air."

"That might have to wait. Yuma reports a serious storm front rolling our way."

"Ever since that nuclear phase ended we have had storms on a regular basis." The CO nursed his coffee for a few moments then said. "We found corpses with a green sticky substance oozing from their bodies?"

"What is it?"

"We don't know yet. Chatterbox believes it may be the making of a plague."

"Isn't that rather immature?" a voice asked. Turning around in his chair, James observed an average height woman with short clipped black hair approaching their table. Sitting without invitation she opened a thick briefcase laid on the table. "I'm Major Savannah Davidson, Marine Headquarters Staff." The woman handed over a stapled set of orders." Her unfriendly voice caused James to study the dark blue eyes with a sharp curiosity. Her tunic carried no ribbons or medals meaning this woman had no combat exposure. "As those orders states I'm attached to your command for thirty days as an observer."

"What exactly are you observing?" James curiously asked.

"Why this particular coastal region hasn't been subdued and her civilians relocated." Seeing his stern expression she continued. "The northern regions are already classified subdued."

James handed her orders to Hickman. After reading them the chief signed as Ten Delta's second-in-command. "As I understand those northern units has doubled my manpower and received considerable support from Yuma." He had already decided this major wasn't his favored woman. She wasn't a model in a physical sense, but Savannah Davidson wasn't unattractive. Her finely etched features on the aquiline face showed facial bones. "Tell me, major, what is exactly your specialized field?"

"Applied medical research."

"And what does that mean?"

For a few moments Savannah stared at her cup before speaking. "Up north we have been found corpses with an unidentified bacterium."

"The green substance?" he curiously asked.

"Yes."

"It's down here also." James noticed she found this information disturbing. Deciding this woman looked very much like the actress July Garland, James approved her looks, but disliked her arrogance. "We just came off a six day patrol and found several of those bodies. One of my men, a pre med student before the war, is quite disturbed about that bacterium."

"What did you do with the bodies?"

"Burned them just like the other bodies we find."

She was quick to say. "You can't burn them. They must be buried with layers of lime poured over them. At the present we know little what this infection is all about. But we do know once airborne it quickly infects others within a small circle."

"And where do we get this lime? Home Depot isn't exactly available at the moment."

She removed a sheet from her briefcase. "This is the address of National

Chemical Storage and Sales located in Santa Barbara. We have reliable information their underground storages survived the bombings."

"And this is all we do about the bodies?"

"That's how you dispose of the dead infected with this green slime. My job is to determine where it originated from, how deadly it is, and last of all find a means to stop the spread. I will require your assistance." She frowned then sarcastically added. "With your spare time this should pose no problem."

"What spare time?" James curtly asked.

"General Paulson told me Ten Delta has lots of free time."

"And General Paulson can blow it out of his ass. My men are running their butts off patrolling and monitoring the citizens still in this region. And we do have an enemy task force supposedly coming down the coast . . ."

"Forget about that task force. General Davidson believes the ships have turned back." she confidently said.

For a moment James scowled at this woman then slowly said. "Then the General had better get off his fat ass and reevaluate the situation." Her sour expression turned serious when James added. "Today we found evidence the Soviets have motorized units ashore. Adding to this there have been reports of a foreign warship cruising our coast at night. No, the General is wrong and why not? He has been wrong on many occasions. That mysterious naval force is coming down this coast. When is the main question?" His temper let loose while Hickman quietly observed the female major with increasing interest. "People like General Paulson sit in their gilded offices and refuse to recognize political danger signs. They did this in 1990 when the Soviet Union crashed. Instead of helping the fallen Russian people stand tall again they made great speeches, but nothing else. When the United States stormed into Iraq the world condemned us and wouldn't help. When that Russian bastard snatched power nobody did anything. When that damned red banner again flew above their warships Washington and the UN didn't protest. Then because of their gross indifferences we again had the same communist threat."

"That's an unfair political assumption."

"Yeah, you tell me how it's unfair. We have millions of people dead or dying. Along the Canadian borders we're getting our ass kick in every battle. Most of the country will be nuclear wastelands for centuries to come. Did you take time to notice those fires while flying in here? They have been burning out of control for months. How long do you think it'll be before a greenhouse effect wipes out the human race?"

"It won't come to that?" she stubbornly argued. "The government will find a way to stop it?"

James stood then glared at the naïve woman for a moment. "If you believe that then a rude awakening is rapidly coming. Now if you'll excuse me I'm going to bed. The last six days has been chaotic." When she started to protest he looked at Hickman. "Assign her a place to sleep and I'll see you two tomorrow morning."

CHAPTER FOUR

After James left the mess hall Savannah looked at the Chief and thoughtfully asked. "Is he always that nasty?"

"He just came off a six day patrol. That'll make anybody nasty."

"So what's the problem? According to General Paulson this region is subdued for the most part."

The chief petty officer chuckled. "Is that what the General claims? Then the General needs to come down and check out the situation. The grid starting at Santa Barbara and running down to San Diego is a politically hot zone. During their six days out they buried over two hundred bodies and medically attended another five hundred people. And this was done while fighting bandits threatening to overwhelm this area. In their spare time our marines searched for that task force and fought off increasing presence of Mexican nationals vowing to annex California." His voice became harsher. "Now we have the possible makings of a plague. But other than those few annoying situations this is a peaceful zone." He paused for a few moments. "Major Davidson, I don't care what that fat ass General lies about in his daily summaries to St. Louis. This isn't a peaceful countryside. We have serious problems that General Paulson ignores."

The Chief couldn't decipher what she was thinking. Turning about she briefly studied the marines coming and going in the dining area. "This is an unusual facility?" she indifferently remarked.

"That it is and we're proud of it. Ten Delta is the fourth radar station in a chain scattered along the Californian coast. We're on the outer boundaries of Gaviota's city ruins. These underground chambers were part of the Johnston Tool and Die Corporation. As your helicopter came over you probably saw what remained of the Gaviota State Park. Not far away to our rear is the Los Padres National Forest. But since last year most of its one million acres of pine forests have burned." He drank some coffee while wondering if she really understood the widespread devastation. "Did you know within the Dick Smith Wilderness was the last home of the Californian Condor bird? Those fires killed the last bird of that species." Frequently during his many depressions, Chief Hickman compared the fate of that bird to mankind. They too were heading toward the same extinction.

"How did you find this location? All I saw was rubble and ruins."

"One of our men formerly worked for the British owned company. These underground chambers were storage areas and emergency shelters for their six hundred employees. We have our own electrical and waters sources. A nearby exploding missile destroyed the structures above ground, but didn't disturb these subterranean spaces. We have an amazing group of marines in this command. It took three weeks to create a radar station that's difficult to locate and well protected by electronic monitoring." He drained his coffee. "If you would like I'll give you a fifty cent tour."

Walking down a long hallway with rooms on both sides she asked. "Why was this city bombed in the first place? It doesn't seem to be a strategic spot."

"The Soviets learned this was the mustering area for our National Guard. Gaviota took a nuclear missile within two days of the war's beginnings." He stopped talking for a minute. "The unexpected attack caught many people in the open. This manufacturing facility was working that day so civilian and military causalities were awful high." The hallway opened into a large high ceiling chamber. "This was their main storage area. It took our working parties one week just to clear out the materials. As you can see it's now our helicopter hanger. We have two Apache attack machines and one Huey transport." For a few moments he observed the activity around the helicopter from Yuma that was being prepared for its return flight. "The aircraft touches down in the walled compound above us then an elevator brings it down here for storage."

"Clever," she coldly praised. "But why aren't the other sites hidden. I understand they're in plain sight."

"Their commanders believe there's no real danger."

"And obviously you don't share their feelings?"

"I don't. Their indifference is crazy and I don't understand any of it. Most of our people are dead and the country blown away. We're losing our war along the Canadian border. It's becoming only too obvious Mexico intends to annex California. If the Soviets take this coast they will have an uncontested beachhead to land troops and supplies. But our senior military commands ignore the dangers." He angrily shakes his head.

"The country still is in a state of shock." she casually admitted.

Departing the underground hanger by way of a flight of steps, they were in a courtyard surrounded by huge piles of rubble and high warped beams. The winds were icy cold while semi-darkness cloaked the devastation that was unnerving.

"Well, they better snap themselves out of that shock. Time is running out."

"I think you're failing to see the overall picture." she somberly charged.

"And what is the overall picture, major?" Timothy crisply asked. "In California we only see the suffering, death, bloodshed, and disillusions of a beaten nation struggling to stay afloat."

"Of course, I can't tell you any details, but there are future campaigns that hopefully will turn back the tide of this ugly war." Savannah cautiously replied. "The populace doesn't know how devastating this war really has been. There are even those who believe this war was local and not global. This is because global communications are gone. Another reason is too many people refuse to accept a war that developed into this nightmare. But I can assure you all over the world dazed people are staggering from the rubbles of their cities. And just like us they're trying to pull together their devastated countries." They walked into the compound's middle where twisted steel beams reached four stories above them like menacing guardians of this havoc. "Where are your radar antennas?"

Timothy pointed at a warped third storied beam and said. "Attached to that is our main dish. With all of that twisted debris around it the dish is practically impossible to detect." He turned about and pointed at another collection of mangled beams and rubble. "Up there is our guard post. Its height allows our sentries to see not only around us, but up and down the coast. We operate the radar as little as possible so to reduce the enemy's painting our radar's radiation. Anyhow with all of the EM interferences caused by the nuclear warfare surveillance is restricted."

"Very clever."

The Chief grinned. "That was another of James' doings."

"You sound pretty proud of the lieutenant?"

"He's a good man and a damned good commanding officer."

Savannah didn't comment, but quietly followed him back into the underground complex. She didn't object when escorted to a small comfortable room set aside for her quarters. Judging from family photographs on the walls a marine had been moved out for her occupation. After undressing and climbing under the warm blankets she was fast asleep. She knew General Paulson's headquarters was corrupted with misinformation, but she was startled at the deception's depth.

*   *   *

For the last two hours Captain Voronov stayed on the enclosed bridge as his ship battled the crashing waves. The moaning and groaning destroyer stayed together as her captain knew she would. Karl tried seeing through the water splashed windshield. The wipers were going full power without providing a clear view. Why they were even cruising this time of night through heavy waters was against his wishes. If he had his way they would drop anchor at Isla Vista until morning. But those orders were recklessly countermanded by the ship's political officer and there was nothing he could do about it.

He stopped pacing the bridge and ran a hand through his unruly hair. Sighing softly when the ship plunged through another crashing wave, he grabbed a railing for support. With a roaring defiance the destroyer shot from the waters like a frightened child. His troubled facial expression revealed his displeasure in risking the ship. For long hours the warship cruised close to the coastal lines searching for Blackmore's evasive Ten Delta. It was vital these radar stations be eliminated before the task force arrived. When a crewman brought a cup of steaming tea he smiled. It tasted good going down his throat.

Suddenly the ship's fog horn began blaring and everybody responded.

Their engineering officer had devised that warning signal when the ship was about to plunge through another dangerous barrier of stormy waters. Karl dashed to the windshield and what he saw scared him. With many years at sea never had he seen such a high wave. He yelled to increase speed then the captain did the only thing left to do. He grabbed hold of a railing running around the bridge and held on for dear life. While he watched the monstrous wave crested then charged the lonely warship with roaring defiance.

When icy waters violently rushed over the tossing destroyer it was like a raft charging down a raging river. Though lasting only a short time the deluge seemed like hours. Karl heard a terrified scream as those rumbling water passed over the ship. For seconds they seemed to be completely submerged. The ship was tightly secured for rough weather so there was no internal flooding. The first thing Karl noticed after the danger passed was no quartermaster standing at the wheel. Dashing over to the spinning wheel he fought to control it until another sailor rushed over. Breathing heavily the elder man leaned slightly over until his heart stopped furiously pounding. Then the senior captain stood straight and evaluated the situation. He had injured men on the bridge.

Grabbing the phone he rapidly ordered. "Medical watch to the bridge on the double! Damage Control make reports. Deck forces check lifeboats!" Slamming the phone on its cradle he checked his men. One had a broken arm. Several suffered cuts and bruises but not serious enough to relieve them.

Minutes later the phone rang. Wrapping his bleeding hand with a clean rag Karl cradled the phone between his neck and shoulder. "Captain here, what's our damages? That bad, huh?" His face became very distressed. "Very well, do your best." He pressed the disconnect button. After a short pause he rang the political officer's cabin. There was no answer. Ringing another number he instructed his security officer to check on the man and have him report to the bridge without delay. "Navigation, this is the captain. Set course for Isla Vista. Flank speed."

Hanging up the phone he walked over to the medical team now working on his quartermaster. The man was a mess. A slight head shake from a medic warned him the man was dying. During the tidal wave his quartermaster was thrown against the spinning wheel crushing his chest. He walked to the windshield to hide his tears. The veteran seaman serving under him for years was a good man. Karl softly cursed. When would this insanity stop? There could be no victor in this war. The United States was crushed with thirteen states struggling to keep their colors flying. Thirty-seven states had perished during the initial nuclear phase. Most of the new Soviet Union was in flaming devastation. Now both countries struggled to crush the other with rapidly depleting forces, but his government never entertained the thought of a truce. They wanted to totally destroy the United States.

The senior medical rating came over and sadly informed him their quartermaster had died. Karl accepted the news with a grim expression. Standing at the windshield he watched the destroyer plowing through more rough waters. After the waves passed, the ocean calmed a little before working up another terrifying watery invasion. Hearing the engineering officer's gruff voice he turned.

His face was unhappy. "I have bad news, comrade captain. Damages experienced from that last plunge are far more serious than expected. We have oil leaks in the aft steering compartment. Minor damages on our radar mast have blacked out all communications for the time being. The forward gun mount has problems. Deck lieutenant reports four life boats damaged beyond repair." He sighed deeply from frustration.

"We're heading back to Isla Vista," the captain replied. "There we can make repairs."

"Hopefully we can make repairs. Our spare parts are very limited. Those oil leaks worries me the most." The engineering officer grinned. "Somehow we will make it, comrade captain. We always have in the past."

After the man left his bridge Karl thoughtfully stared at the distant reddish glow caused by forest fires. He wouldn't relax until his ship was safely inside that haven. Isla Vista was located between Coal Pit Point and Goleta Point. There the ship would make repairs and bury their dead.

The short man standing at five feet and five inches wasn't an impressive man by any standards. Stopping at the windshield he studied those burning mountains and thought about his past. He never regretted leaving his birthplace of Vladivostak. At an early age Karl went to the capital city of Primorsky Kray in Far Eastern USSR. There he spent his teens laboring in the city's shipbuilding facilities. Being the terminus of the Trans-Siberian Railroad he was introduced to life's darker secrets. After the region's harsh winters arrived Karl worked as a deck hand on the icebreakers. Karl eventually accepted his family's offer of financial aid and attended the university. After graduating with an engineering degree Karl entered a life at sea. Not until his marriage did promotions in the Soviet Navy come swiftly. Sadness settled on his face as memories of his lovely wife charged back. Maria was visiting their daughter when American missiles buried Moscow under millions of radioactive tons of rubble. After a few moments he forced back the grief. He had men aboard who now looked to him for encouragement. This ship had become his mistress.

Captain Voronov faintly smiled. The ship was now gracefully taking on the rough waters since that tidal monster passed. Her long, cold-business like profile was painted a mixture of gray and darker gray hues. Her hull and superstructure glistened from the crashing ocean waters. He walked about the crowded bridge. Several times stopping Karl talked to his young seamen. This was important to their fragile morale. Many of these young men were away from home for the first time and now that the war had erased their anchoring places, the ship became important to their existence. Two electronic ratings working on damaged instruments looked up and grinned. The warship again plunged through the unruly Pacific as icy sheets crashed over her main deck. He glanced at his watch noticing the arrogant political officer hadn't shown up. Walking back to the two ratings he removed his hat and scratched the itching scalp. It was important they get this system working.

"How bad is the problem?" he asked.

"We can't find the problem. Though the radar dish is damaged it shouldn't affect this responder. They operate off different frequencies." a young repairman explained. While replacing his circuit tools the man kept talking. "We have experienced stronger EM interferences over the last several hours and this may be causing our problems. But without the proper troubleshooting instruments there's no way to know."

"Why don't we have such instruments aboard?"

"We did. But while in our last dry dock the political officer loaned them to another ship. When we were leaving that ship wouldn't give them back."

"Why didn't our officer demand their return?"

"He said we wouldn't need them and refused to press the issue."

He grunted his disapproval of the political officer's interferences, but there was nothing he could do to countermand those orders. Informing the bridge he was leaving Karl heard the duty officer take command. The destroyer's NATO classified Top Steer radar system was old and should have been replaced years ago. Only the newer ships received their latest generation of surface-and-air search systems.

Entering the cramped radar compartment Karl first let his eyes adjust to the reddish glow again. "Find anything new on your search?"

The young man seated before his monitor replied in a husky voice. "No, comrade captain, we haven't found one clue on the station's whereabouts." Vadim was only eighteen years old when his last ship was blown up during battle. Coming from Georgia's rich farmlands he knew the regions received little damages from enemy missiles. But chemical warfare accidentally launched by their own army killed millions including his family. The Communist Party publicly blamed the Americans for this terrible accident, but those in the military knew otherwise. Karl trusted this tall lanky kid from Russia's farmlands. "If they are out there we'll find them. They will broadcast sooner or later then we got them."

Lightly patting Vadim's shoulder Karl said. "You're a good Russian comrade, my friend. One day this will be all over and we can go home."

*　　*　　*

As they walked down the hallway Timothy suddenly looked at Savannah and asked. "Have you had an opportunity to eat since arriving?"

"No."

"Then please join me in a late night meal." He chuckled. "I'm afraid it will have to be scrambled eggs and bacon."

"Sounds good to me," she gratefully accepted.

After collecting their food on metal trays they slowly ate and discussed the war. She looked around for James but he wasn't inside. Savannah noted the marines from Ten Delta's last patrol were with tormented expressions. When looking at the petty officer she saw he was short with more weight than needed. But after twenty years in the Navy he still ran five miles on the treadmill.

"So how's the weather in Yuma?"

She shrugged. "Much better than here that much I will say. We don't have your cold temperatures because of our distance from the ocean. But we do have the same gray overcasts. Do you have family?"

It was a few moments before he shook his head. "They died when Soviet missiles reduced San Diego to rubble"

Savannah regretted asking that after detecting his hatred when mentioning the enemy. In a few minutes she analyzed this older man who was popular judging from the marines' warm greetings in the halls and mess deck. His weathered skin strained tight brought attention to the high cheek bones and rugged appearance. She would later learn he had five ships blown out under him during the war's early months.

"I'm sorry," she awkwardly said.

"You learn to live with it," he mumbled then quickly changed the subject. "Since you're from headquarters what do you think about this weather?"

"Depends on what you mean."

"We have heard if there isn't rain before long we may have a greenhouse affect?"

"There's one underway."

"What about this mumbo jumbo about the earth freezing?" While talking Timothy's thick mid western accent was noticeable.

"Your weather here and what's experienced in the western states is quite different. I noticed out here trees and grasses are dying from the lack of sunlight. Of course those dying trees are fueling the mountain fires raging out of control. Since the war began burning forests are quite common throughout the world. But you are right, Chief. If rain doesn't come soon we'll be facing much worse conditions than defeat on the battlefield. We desperately need rain to clean the air and put out those fires."

Savannah saw James come into the mess hall, fetch a cup of coffee, stop and talk with several marines then come over to their table. "I thought you were going to sleep all night?" she casually challenged.

"The duty officer woke me up with bad weather reports."

The Chief nodded. "That front hit thirty minutes ago with heavy lightning and thundering accompanied by fierce winds."

"What about rain?"

"Nothing."

"Yeah, we couldn't be that lucky. What about the tower?"

"I closed it down when the winds became too dangerous up there."

"All right, but after this storm passes get men back up there on the double. Right now with no tower watches and radar shut down we're running blind."

"I would like to talk with your medical specialist regarding the bloated bodies." Savannah asked.

"There will be time for that tomorrow, major."

She spoke with a testy tone. "I wish to talk with him now."

Sitting his coffee cup down James glared at the woman. "Tomorrow you may talk with Chatterbox, but not before then. He just came off a six day patrol and is sleeping. You're not about to wake him up." His voice was harsh. "Tell me something, major, how many hospitals are there in Yuma?"

"There are four."

"And are they fully equipped?"

"Yes," she said defensively. "But I fail to see how that relates to my request?"

"It has everything to do with it. Chatterbox is our only medical specialist for nearly four thousand people in this general area. He does this job with medical supplies salvaged from buildings because Yuma doesn't send us medical supplies or additional personnel. My man is tired and frustrated. He needs his rest and you aren't going to disturb him." Standing the lieutenant looked Timothy's way and spat. "I'll be in operations planning tomorrow's activities." Without looking at Savannah he left the chamber.

It was a short while before Savannah commented. "He definitely has a short temper."

"Only when he's pushed into a corner," Her expression relayed her doubts so Chief Hickman continued. "The lieutenant has more on his shoulders than he should. Yuma continually challenges our intelligence reports so we end up fighting impossible situations with fewer men and no support from Yuma. Now we have an enemy naval force coming down this way and Yuma doesn't believe it."

"I already told you intelligence has confined the ships turned back."

"And we have proof that they haven't. The Soviets are doing another smoke and mirrors job on Yuma. Their problem lies with the fact they're too far inland to know what's going on. We on the other hand evaluate things differently." He quickly held his hand up. "You don't have to say it. The General thinks he has all the answers, but he doesn't."

"I strongly disagree. General Paulson has a very qualified intelligence department providing him with daily updated briefs. If they say the enemy task force has turned around then that's what we accept as fact."

CHAPTER FIVE

The fact Captain Voronov's destroyer safely made it to Isla Vista was testimony to his seamanship under very adverse weather conditions. They reached it just in time as the storm's eye swept down the coast. Naval High Command warned these disturbances were because of the increasing greenhouse affect cloaking the globe. After several trips to communications the captain became worried. Contact with their landing parties was hours overdue. Unable to sleep Karl stayed on the bridge waiting out this storm. After his initial briefing on this ambitious campaign Karl still remained unenthused about its chances of success. Along this Californian coastline the scattered American military was weak and disorganized. Risking their few ships on this objective was foolish. He was for bypassing these few radar stations and heading for the Gulf of Mexico where naval campaigns were about to break loose.

Standing over in the corner was another officer who didn't share Captain Voronov's popularly aboard the ship. He was a colonel in the KGB. That alone was enough to discourage trust by the crew, but they weren't stupid enough to challenge his presence. After the Soviet Union collapsed in 1990, the Komitet Gosudarstvennoy Bezopasnosti was replaced by another less ruthless Federal Police. But once Kossier became Russia's sole leader the KGB was reinstated. Their brutal hand with unlimited powers was once again entrenched throughout the Russian political and military agencies.

Karl studied the list of damages caused by the storm. There were few that couldn't be repaired after the storm passed. Their major problem was radar would have to be repaired at their British Columbian naval port. Sitting in his bridge chair the captain thoughtfully watched the frenzied activity aboard his anchored ship. Motor boats shuttled back and forth from the shore where security was established. Working parties were frantically repairing damages with the help of floodlights since it was night. Waters inside the cove were choppy, but nothing like what existed beyond Isla Vista.

"Why wasn't I consulted before you ordered the ship here?" Mikhail Karsavin curtly demanded.

"I sent messengers to your cabin several times," Karl replied. "When you didn't respond I had to make decisions fast because of the approaching storm."

The political officer angrily said. "That is no excuse. We have been in storms before so why is this one any different?"

Captain Voronov gave the army colonel a short cynical scowl. "Comrade, this ship can not cruise through storms much less darkness without functional radar."

"What's wrong with our radar?"

"Before we got inside the cove our radar mast was damaged."

The political officer walked to the windshield and looked down on the ship's activity. Power lights were strung about the rocking main deck as work crews labored at various tasks. For a couple of moments he watched several seamen rigging lines to the tall super mast where their radar dish was positioned. The cold strong winds smashed waves noisily against the hull. This supposedly safe haven wasn't his choice. The ship's violent motions made him terribly sick. Escape from his illness was found in a glass bottle. When earlier summoned to the bridge he was unable to move from his bunk. If Mikhail thought his drinking was a secret he was wrong. Clasping hands behind his back he turned to the skipper.

"How long will these repairs take?" he curtly asked.

"Hopefully by late afternoon we can be underway."

"You don't sound too confident."

"My technician isn't certain the radar can be repaired before returning to port."

"That's completely out of the question. I expect this ship to be underway by late afternoon and no later. Is that understood, Comrade Captain?" he sharply demanded. Sensing the attention shown their talk he turned about. This was sufficient to cause crewmen to scramble about their duties. Turning his anger back on the captain he said. "It's best we understand one another. I was ordered aboard this ship to ensure our mission is successful." He sighed deeply. "Soon there will be other ships coming down this coast. But before this happens, those American radar stations must be destroyed. Naval High Command feels Ten Delta is the most dangerous."

Mikhail wondered what was going through this popular officer's mind. Karl seemed to be listening though Mikhail was doubtful. The skipper was unaware Mikhail knew about his secret dealings with the former Party Chairman Boris Yeltsin. Those were dangerous times while Boris struggled to become a major power broker during Premier Gorbachev's time in office from 1985 through 1991. Boris expressed trust in Karl who repeatedly refused political appointments. He was satisfied commanding warships, but not manipulating political schemes behind closed doors. While the political officer spoke the gray haired veteran sipped hot tea brought over by a glavnyy starshini. The senior petty officer didn't offer tea to Mikhail knowing how he disliked the beverage. When 1993 challenges against the government threatened civil war, Karl flew to Moscow with the Navy's loyalty tightly ensured for Boris. Later when hard line communists clashed with the Russian Orthodox Church, Karl quietly defused a bitter battle affecting 60 million faithful.

Mikhail was no fool and knew this man could be a valuable ally, especially now he was far away from his communist cronies back in Russia.

The political commissar knew it was time to brown nose this stubborn captain. "It is most important our mission is successful. Ever since the foul capitalists brutally murdered our Presidium, we have been waiting for an opportunity to deliver a dagger strike. That time is now upon us. What I'm telling you is highly classified but I feel you need to know. The American naval forces blockaded in their Gulf ports can not leave without our warships sinking them. We have reliable intelligence the Americans are planning a breakout shortly, but they don't know we know this. When they realize what's happening we'll have a surprise for them. That's why our task force must reach the Gulf before this happens. Once our task force links up with warships already in the Gulf, we'll deliver a decisive blow against the capitalistic Americans." His rough husky voice gained excitement. "With their naval forces defeated, the Americans won't be able to stop our future landings." Shrugging he boasted. "This will be the end of that capitalist devil."

Karl didn't say anything for a few moments. "Have you ever fought the Americans?"

"No."

"Then my advice is don't count victories until they're firmly in your hand. The Americans traditionally has a knack for changing fortunes both politically and militarily." the captain warned. "I have seen them pull victories out of certain defeat."

"That's treason . . ." Mikhail muttered.

"No, it is treason when a man recklessly walks into a risky situation arrogantly disillusioned. If we expect to win this cruel war it must be with cunning and awareness our enemy is equally cunning." Captain Voronov frowned then turned away from the furious political officer. After hearing the colonel stomp from the bridge the skipper mumbled. "What a stupid asshole."

*　　*　　*

The Soviet Union embraced a long relationship with the KGB. It was their ruthless arm which eliminated everybody opposing the Communist Party. Once Kossier strong-armed his way into power, KGB was the first agency restated with full uncontested powers. Months after the first missiles flew their murderous flights it was learned the Russian Premier was murdered by his own government. But it was too late to charge KGB with his murder. The globe was already burning. When the chief of Glovnoye Razvedyvatelnoye Upravlenieye (GRU) Vicktor Kossier became the ruling power, it was obvious who ordered the smoking gun. Early in the war it was clearly a Soviet victory, but with time that became a gamble. Russian planners often grossly underestimated their opponents. Following their advice Kossier directed his commanders to fire chemical agents among the opposing NATO forces. When some Russian field commanders refused KGB squads killed them. Even though Karl Voronov wasn't in the inner political loop, he suspected there was foul political activity behind the scenes. After signing another engineering report the skipper leaned back in his chair.

"What do you think is going on, my friend?" Karl asked the engineering officer.

Lieutenant Commander Bogdanov frowned showing two chipped teeth in the front. These men had served together for several years and trusted each other's opinions. "Some dirty laundry is being dragged through our power corridors. Those incompetent admirals in power can't see pass their assholes."

"Do you think finding those radar stations is that important?"

"No. Our surprise element was lost long ago." Pausing he thought about something then said somberly. "I remember reading about a battle in the Americans' history books. It pertains to a Mexican emperor named Santa Ana back in the Eighteen Hundreds. The Texans' rebellion was causing the man serious troubles. He could have easily bypassed the Texans' resistance at the Alamo and probably caught Houston without a trained army. But instead, he chose to besiege the old mission for thirteen days. During that time hundreds of his veteran soldiers were lost in senseless battles. Of course, the Alamo fell but General Houston had that extra time to prepare for his next battle."

"You think we have an Alamo here?" Karl curiously asked.

"Yes, I do. Over the years I have studied their military history and find the Americans a remarkable people. They have waded through some pretty bad times, but each time victoriously emerged against all odds. Wasting time along this coast is costing us valuable time that should be spent cruising to the Gulf." His expression was solemnly cold. "Karl, I know these people. I have read about their depressions. Before you can blink they change their fortunes on the battlefields. Premier Kossier boasts how they are defeated, but that's a lot of bullshit. When they are down on their knees and everything looks bleak, that's when these stubborn people work their best."

A communications specialist came onto the bridge and looked about. After handing the captain a message he left. Karl read the dispatch then grunted. "The task force admiral is complaining about our incompetence in finding these stations. He refuses to wait until they are destroyed."

"When are they arriving?"

"Sometime day after tomorrow," he skeptically replied.

"What about our marines we landed several days ago? Maybe they have found something that will help?"

"We haven't had contact with them for several hours. I'm not sure if they are dead or merely running radio silence. But either way they're silent."

"Major Darkanbayev is a competent marine officer. Maybe this Lieutenant Blackmore is a clever man, but our major is also cunning as a fox. Those two should be an interesting match."

*   *   *

Five hours after the patrol's return a marine on guard duty complained of stomach pains. Chatterbox was called to their sick bay where he treated the man. Appearing to be the start of a gastrointestinal ulcer the soldier was confined to bed for eight hours. Unable to sleep Chatterbox volunteered to finish out his watch post. There was no mediation for the ailing marine. Chatterbox knew he should have an endoscopy, but that was out of the question at Ten Delta. Chief Hickman was advised the man needed to be flown to Yuma. His gastrointestinal bleeding wasn't going to heal itself.

Once the winds died down the tower watch was reopened. Ten Delta's main observance post was cleverly concealed atop a heavily damaged clock tower. Whenever their radar was malfunctioning, which was most of the time, two marines with binoculars manned this lofty post scanning for trouble. Once daylight passed that post became extremely uncomfortable as icy winds charging across the Pacific pounded the ruins. However, this was Chatterbox's favorite place because of its isolation. The second marine asked for a sip from his thermos. The sergeant handed the coffee container over. Though the hot liquid didn't totally ease the chill it helped. After two long sips the marine handed back the thermos.

"Thanks, Bro," Corporal Smith said in a scratchy voice. With a soft frustrated groan he put the night enhancer glasses against his eyes. "What did the Chief say about those stiffs ya'll found?" This black marine raised in Riverside, California was tall and chunky thought little was fat. He was a big boned man. At least that's what his Momma said when kids joked about his size. After Arlington High School he graduated from college with an engineering degree. Ebenezer Smith was by far the best educated man at Ten Delta.

"He didn't say much."

"That doesn't mean anything. The Chief is a quiet man." The machine gun specialist scanned the darkness. "Though the damned storm was a pisser it didn't compare with Yuma's warnings."

Lowering his glasses after studying those raging fires atop the nearby mountains, he said. "Any storm these days are hard to predict. But if you look down the coast you can see it tore the hell out of those ruins." Chatterbox turned about checking the immediate zones down below without finding any threats. "What do you think about that broad?"

"She is pretty, smart, and arrogant as hell. Sure as hell don't get along with the CO." There was a brief silence. "I heard tomorrow the Chief and you are going out with her to find some bloated corpses?"

"Yeah, so I hear. That should be interesting."

*   *   *

While crossing the main deck Mikhail paused after observing the captain and engineering officer conversing even as water banging against the hull sprayed them. A frown crossed his face. They were probably scheming against his authority. The two officers were that treacherous type. The KGB never was politically confident with the Navy whose Party membership was low. He unconsciously grabbed a railing as the ship roughly rocked and after looking at the darkened skies knew there was another storm brewing. Once back in the new Russian capital Mikhail would file charges against the arrogant captain. Naturally the Naval community would close ranks around him, but that was to be expected. The captain was a serious threat. Giving the men a last cynical glance he walked away without them knowing he had been there.

The grim faced colonel awkwardly made his way down a narrow passageway. More than once losing his balance he crashed to the metal decking. Fortunately for his strong pride there were no seamen around to see this. He often cursed this old eskadrenny minonosets. Reaching his cabin he staggered inside and quickly took the vodka bottle from a bulkhead safe. Not bothering to fetch a glass he hurriedly drank from the bottle. The ship's constant pitching was upsetting his stomach. Satisfied he had enough courage; the bottle was locked up before calling the captain to his cabin.

"Did you wish to see me?" Karl asked after knocking and entering. The smell of vodka was strong.

Belching didn't soften Mikhail's stomach's sourness. Sitting on his bunk he fought back another urge to vomit. Handing the captain a blue folder he asked. "Do you know an American scientist named Earl Craver?"

Accepting the classified folder he shook his head. "No, should I?"

While the ship rocked against pounding waves Mikhail wondered if the captain smelled vodka on his breathe? "He's very influential with President Washington. We have reason he's on the way to Ten Delta."

Karl solemnly stood in front of the KGB colonel. There was a tiny speck of vomit on the brown uniform that Karl didn't mention. "Do we know why he's coming?"

Not stopping the foul smelling belch Mikhail refused to look at Karl's sharp disapproval. "No, but the Naval Command wants to know. Their request was received a few minutes ago. Major Darkanbayev should be able to find out. Contact him."

For a moment Karl just stared at the drunkard commissar. "We have not heard from the major for several hours."

After this the colonel groaned while holding his stomach and passed out. Karl disgustedly stared at the army officer's vomit smeared tunic. Throwing a blanket over the man he left.

*   *   *

By early morning hours the storm had passed Ten Delta on its way down to San Diego. James and his executive officer walked the compound checking guard posts for cracks in their security. Physically and mentally the four hours of sleep had done wonders for James. It was basically dark while moonlight tried passing those heavy debris layers in the skies. From the seaward side these ruins appeared just that with no evidence a radar station was contained within. Timothy hoped the Soviet warship didn't have heat sensors that could detect the underground facility. Ten Delta recorded dropping temperatures warning of another incoming storm.

"Did they get that dish working again?" James asked.

"No. It's the same primary enhancer tube that's been acting up for the last two weeks." the chief wearily informed. "Hell in the last two weeks it has been down sixty percent of the time." When James gave him a questioning glance Timothy said. "The tubing is old and needs replacing. That's the bottom line."

"Is there any way we can jump start it until Yuma sends a part?"

"Maybe Tyler can fix it, but I wouldn't hold my breath."

They stopped at a staircase smashed beyond recognizance. Disappearing into the rubble it was difficult to see after some twists and turns it came to a shaft fitted in the ruins. This was an ascending passage that via a ladder entered the tower above them. The wind became stronger swirling loose sooty dust and tiny bits of debris about as if house cleaning.

"What do you have against her, James?"

"I don't have anything against her. Why do you ask?" There was a short silence before he chuckled. "Forget it, there's no way that's happening. Not in my time."

"But she's pretty and intelligent."

"And she's arrogant as hell. No, forget it. I have enough trouble as it is."

"We'll wait and see," the Chief said as a smile crossed his beefy face. After waving at the lieutenant, he returned to the underground facility whistling an old fifties' rock and roll tune.

*   *   *

James shivered as icy breezes swept in from the Pacific. Within the last four hours the temps dropped to a nasty 37 degrees. He knew an increasing enhancement of solar ultra-violet radiation, caused by the earth's damaged ozone zone, was introducing another danger for the battling planet. He moaned his frustration at those things not controllable and entered the narrow tunnel. After climbing a steep iron ladder he was inside the tower.

He greeted the two sentries. "See anything?"

"Nobody is crazy enough to be out in this damned weather."

"I sure agree with that," James said. "But you can never tell about those damned Soviets. They do crazy things when you least expect it."

Down below the tower was tons of twisted rubble after flames and explosions destroyed the manufacturing facility's surface structures. This was the secret of their survival. Nothing about this consortium of ruins suggested the presence of inhabitants. When viewed from the ocean the only thing conspicuous about this twisted site was its isolation blocking the waves crashing ashore. Ten Delta went deep into its bowels with their helicopters, guns, and electronic systems. What Yuma didn't provide was salvaged from numerous coastal ruins. Without close scrutiny it was impossible to find the large camouflaged door opening into the underground complex.

"On the way back we found evidence the Russians landed a party." James thoughtfully said while scanning the terrain with an image intensifier tube giving him a greenish glowing view. "The ocean is pretty rough so we assume the enemy put into a safe haven for protection." The two marines gave him their total attention. "Still we must keep our vigilance at a peak. There's no doubt the Russians outnumbers us." He smiled at these marines whose youth made him wonder what they were doing before this war.

"When will it rain?" one asked after accepting the enhancer James handed back.

"I hope real soon." Though the burning mountains weren't that close they gave the horizon a strange brightness. He studied Corporal Thorton for a few moments. "I heard you had another run in with Sergeant Tyler?"

The black marine slowly admitted in his thick southern accent. "Yes sir." The tall, wiry framed, brown skinned marine knew this wasn't a friendly chat with the commanding officer.

"What was your problem this time?"

"He gets under my skin." the native of Georgia bitterly groaned. Cold winds howled through the ruins. "His problem is he thinks he's a better man than me." He shook his head. "He's a damned nigger and nothing more." Nervously shuffling his feet Thorton didn't like it when the lieutenant glared at him. He fingered the NVS-700 starlight scope in his hand for something to do.

Several times in the last four months Corporal Thorton stood before James on charges. He was a borne trouble maker and should be doing brig time back in Yuma. But beneath this rebellious spirit was a good marine. All Thorton had to do was find that evasive spirit. He was the best explosive man in the unit. In battle Corporal Thorton and his gun were bonded. But tempers raged when around he was around his sergeant for too long.

James' face became hard and unfriendly. "Regardless of your personal feelings, corporal, Tyler is your squad sergeant and as such he will be obeyed. Now I don't know why there's bad blood between you two, but I do know it stops today. If not I'll have your ass on the next chopper to Yuma. There you can sweat off your rebellious moods in their brig." When the big man snapped to attention James demanded. "Do I make myself clear on this issue?"

Staring straight ahead Thorton loudly snapped, "Yes sir."

"Yes sir what?"

"Yes sir, I understand fully."

James replied while still frowning. "I hope so, corporal. We got a serious mess on our hands and only a good bunch of marines can make it go away. You're a damned good marine. Getting along with your squad leader is part of being a good marine." Walking to the ladder he paused. "You two carry on."

CHAPTER SIX

Ten Delta had the older NVS-700 night enhancer scopes. The newer advanced models were issued to their battered divisions along the Canadian borders. Thorton's kept flickering because its batteries were depleting their energy. A cold wind whipping through the ruins crashed loose debris about or rattled useless dangling power lines against steel beams jutting from the rubble. The corporal sadly remembered how this coastal stretch used to be crowded with beach lovers. He came to California from Georgia to attend college but soon left because of low grades. That was when he enlisted in the Corps.

Ebenezer lowered his scope. "How does it feel when the Old Man reams you a new asshole?"

"Not good."

"What the hell is between Tyler and you?"

"Nothing big."

"Like hell it is." The marine slowly swept his designated grid with the scope. "The Old Man is really pissed this time, Bro. You better get your shit together or find your black ass in the brig. I hear tell that damned hellhole is no place to be."

Thorton reaching for the thermos in the darkness nearly knocked it over. Catching the wobbling container he unscrewed its top and poured a cup of coffee. After putting the lid back on, the marine carefully put his container out of the way. The coffee felt good going down this throat. The weather was whipping up another storm. Aiming his scope down the beach line, he watched the crashing waves coming ashore then rushing back into the ocean. "God, I'm glad to be here and not out there." he mumbled softly. Laying aside his scope the marine finished the coffee while studying the distant reddish glow. A few minutes later his enhancer went black. Cursing he slapped the instrument hoping to kick its power back on. It worked in the past, but this time the instrument was dead.

"What's wrong?" Ebenezer asked after lowering his enhancer.

"Batteries are dead."

"Go get another scope."

"There isn't another. The others crashed, remember?"

"Oh yeah, I remember now." Ebenezer raised his scope and started scanning again. "All we get out here is shit." From the compound ran a one lane paved road that ended at the highway two blocks away. It was a cluttered drive through the mess.

While Thorton messed with his malfunctioning device Ebenezer kept surveying his grid. They still had another two hours of watch. He thought of the scrambled eggs breakfast and smiled. Cold air coming from the raging ocean snapped his wandering reflections. Then suddenly the corporal stiffened. Quickly adjusting a knob for greater clarity he whirled to glance at Thorton.

"We got company!" he coldly announced.

Thorton was already reaching for the phone. "Hostile? Friendly?" he asked. "Watch commander, this is Post One. Intruders confirmed." He slowly provided coordinates. "Sector one-four-nine, repeat, sector one-four-nine. Three unidentified males armed with automatic weapons." He mentally pictured the explosion of activity produced by his phone call. Confirmed hard data was transferred to a large plastic board. Master Sergeant Tyler stood before the plotting board sternly watching additional information penciled in by a private. "Hostiles are now moving away from immediate ruins. Shit these dudes are armed with one LAW and assault rifles."

Ebenezer calmly adjusted his instrument while relaying information to Thorton. His attention was drawn to the one who seemed to be their leader. He was carrying a small black box in hand. What he saw caused a sour explosion in his stomach. "Oh shit!" he groaned. "Let me have that phone. This is Ebenezer," he rapidly said. "Do not activate perimeter scanners! I repeat do not activate scanners! Intruders has electronic detection device!" He heard the phone talker at CIC (Combat Intelligence Center) anxiously relaying his warning. After his message was acknowledged Ebenezer mumbled that was close. The detection device would have pinpointed their scanners and there would be hell to pay. After handing the phone back to Thorton he again focused on the intruders.

He thoughtfully watched the hostiles leaving their area without finding Ten Delta. These men dressed in summer camouflage uniforms were easily identified as military. "The intruders have left our immediate region. Seven males accounted for. Hostiles' vehicles are parked one block away. Ford light truck with canvas rear. Six hostiles have loaded into truck. Two armored cars have pulled up. CIC, I confirm red stars painted on their doors." Ebenezer carefully detailed the intruders' progress. The scope's enhancer powers cut through the darkness like a knife. "Hostiles' direction of departure is southeast to highway." He waited a respectful period before lowering the scope. His eyes always ached after using the Starlight. The stomach growled from the intense tension caused by this intrusion. "Inform them the intruders are no longer visible."

Thorton grinned. "Good job, Bro."

Both men turned their attention to the closed trapdoor. The sound of pounding boots on the ladder rungs caused them to aim their weapons until the password was sounded. After unlocking the trap plate Thorton stepped aside as a frowning Chief Hickman propped back the heavy door and climbed up.

The chief was panting hard as he pulled himself up. "Damn it, I got to lose weight. Those ladder rungs are murder." He looked at each man and asked. "What do you have for me?"

"Seven hostiles confirmed as Russian marines and armed with automatic weapons." Ebenezer reported. "They're carrying assault weapons strapped to their backs. That's standard operating procedures for Soviet marines."

"What do you think they were doing?"

"They were definitely searching for our compound," Ebenezer was quiet for a moment. "No doubt about that." The marine looked at their surroundings. "And there's another thing, Chief. Those men were from an elite unit judging how they conducted their search."

"If they're that good why didn't they find us?"

"Because we're so cleverly camouflaged among these damned ruins a rat would have trouble finding us. Hell, I know where we are at and several times when walking down that road at night I had a hard time finding the base. But if CIC had activated their scanners the communists would have located us. They were carrying an electronic scanner." The marine thoughtfully stared at the darkness before speculating. "We were lucky this time, Chief."

The chief petty officer nodded. "And as marines we know luck eventually runs out."

*   *   *

Coming back into the hanger, Timothy saw Sergeant Tyler and James discussing something near the Apaches. Being the largest chamber down below it housed their two Apaches, the Huey, and another chopper Savannah had came in. Their land vehicles were parked against the southern wall. The chief waved at them in passing. He wanted to make certain everything was smoothly operating in CIC. Unlike outside temps the facility was warm. Running from the central hub were eight rooms and two hallways allowing passage. Ten Delta converted the drab spaces into livable spaces with oil paintings taken from abandoned homes in the area. Timothy greeted those marines met in the hallway and headed for CIC directly across from the mess hall.

Not long afterwards James joined his executive officer in CIC. Positioned on one wall were four consoles with various blinking colored lights and five television monitors. This was Ten Delta's main board of surveillance sensors that closely monitored the four directions from their compound. At the moment none of the lights were red or yellow. Green lights meant no intrusions. One marine seated in front manning the grounds' watch looked up acknowledged the CO then continued his scanning.

"Those marines were probably from that landing party. The question is how did they narrow down their search to Gaviota so quickly?"

"They must have an informer."

"Could be," James thoughtfully replied. Standing in front of a Californian map he was quiet for several minutes. "According to our visitor Yuma intelligence claims the task force has turned around. But the appearance of those Soviet marines disputes their evaluations." After pulling up a chair he sat while crossing his legs. "If Yuma believes there's no danger then they aren't sending any help. That means we're on our own and that's scary."

"What can we do, James? Hell, we're only a handful of men. Ten Delta wasn't put here to stop a naval task force."

"Then we better find a way or our friends in the Gulf may get their butts kicked."

"But what and how?" the chief petty officer was frustrated over their impossible prospects.

James smiled. "I have confidence in your cleverness. Why don't you draw up a rough outline and we'll discuss it later tomorrow. But our immediate problem is those Russian marines. Obviously they're running with local intelligence that we must quickly plug up. After dawn see if you can rustle up some information from your civilian contacts." At the door he stopped and looked over his shoulder. "Where is that woman?"

"She's probably sleeping."

Making a curt expression he complained. "That's all I need right now—a nosy arrogant bitch on my tail."

Chief Hickman grinned. "I don't know if that assumption is totally right. After you stormed out the cafeteria we talked at some length. She really isn't that bad. Maybe she's used to getting her way, but that's all." He shrugged and added. "That's no crime. We all do it at one time or other, right?"

Walking to his quarters James couldn't discard a nagging feeling Ten Delta was about to catch hell. He knew the Chief was right. Ten Delta wasn't equipped to contest a naval task force. But if that enemy task force got pass their friends in the Gulf would suffer. There had to be a way to slow those ships. In his room after pouring a glass of Scotch he sat. Were the Russian marines ashore to find them or were they searching for garrison sites? Either way they were an immediate threat.

The lieutenant thoughtfully looked about his small room. His men had found a dark blue carpet in a nearby store then painted the walls a light blue. Two very valuable paintings hung on the walls. This was where he came when needing to be alone. He was mentally exhausted with no time to relax. Another sharply worded message to Yuma probably wouldn't produce any action. Sipping the golden liquid, James thought about when there were no nuclear wastelands reeking of death and promising little future.

The phone rang. "Yeah, Chief, what's up?" There was a short silence. "All right, I'll be there in a minute. Meanwhile, get a confirmation on it."

The petty officer looked up when James hurried in. "Maybe we're having natural interferences?"

"I don't think so. If one radar site didn't respond that could be natural causes. But none of them are answering our calls. That spells trouble for the radar chain." James studied the wall map for a bit. "If we have enemy soldiers then they may also have them. What about San Diego?"

"No communications for the last ten hours."

One of the communication specialists brought over a decoded message. James read it before paling. "It's a Code Red Zero Bravo from Five Baker. They're under attack."

"We got to help them," Timothy anxiously recommended.

It was a few moments before James shook his head. "We can't."

The Chief was staggered by his reply. "What?" he stammered.

"If we launch our choppers the Russians will know Ten Delta's location. That can't happen. First, we have to take out those marines. And that we can't even do until daylight." He looked at Hickman's anger and coldly stated. "We don't launch a response until those Soviet bastards are found, do you understand? We can't put Ten Delta in harm's way, at least not right now." The weight of what he was doing was heavy as James glanced at the piece of paper then said. "Get hold of your informers at the first crack of dawn. See if they know anything about Russian soldiers coming ashore. We eliminate that threat and then go to San Diego."

Timothy protested. "But they'll be dead by then."

"Chief, get a hold of yourself. Five Bravo is probably destroyed by now. Most likely the other stations are out of commission. That's why they aren't answering our calls. That means Ten Delta is the only station on line." Handing the paper to the petty officer James ordered. "Notify Yuma all other stations are off the line. Give them what few details we have about the communists. Then get ready to survey your network. We don't have much time to waste since we're their primary target." Walking to the door James said while passing. "I know you have friends at Five Bravo and so do I. But we can't help them. We have Ten Delta to worry about."

*   *   *

For the last two hours Karl Voronov hadn't left his bridge chair after weather conditions started deteriorating. In all of his years at sea never had he witnessed such crazy climates. Another cup of hot tea was brought to the commanding officer. He momentarily thought of the drunkard political zampoli passed out in his cabin. Colonel Karsavin was totally immune to this insanity. Maybe that was how to cope with it.

Commander Bogdanov came on the bridge after checking progresses on their repairs. "Everything is coming along perfectly."

"Good. Will we be ready to sail by late afternoon?"

"There's no reason we shouldn't be. But the radar system won't be on line. There's too many things wrong with it. Maybe our base can repair it, but we can't."

Karl frowned. "The colonel won't like that."

The engineering officer hated the political commissar and didn't hide it. "Well, to hell with his asshole. Unless the drunkard bastard knows how to retool burnt out parts he hasn't a choice in the matter."

Karl grinned. "Forget about him. I'll handle him after his vodka wears off." He turned away for a brief spell. The distant burning mountains fascinated him in a weird sort of way. "Communications received acknowledgements from our other teams. The radar stations were put of commission as planned. Only Ten Delta remains on line."

"I'm certain Darkanbayev will find that base." There was a faint doubt in his voice while looking at the distant reddish glow. "Every time I look at those mountains I sense the insanity of this war. I fear KBG is dragging our countrymen through the muck of history. And if we win this war then what's left to conquer? Everything is either destroyed or burning." His voice was soft spoken though nobody on the bridge condemned him for those treacherous words. "The whole damned world is burning and for what? So those KBG thugs can brag they conquered the evil master—America?" He paused again. "But tell me, Karl, who is the evil master? I'm a little confused."

"History will record the truth. It always does."

The lieutenant commander frowned. "Depends on who is writing it."

While the engineering officer read some updated progress reports, Karl thought back to those days he commanded the heavy cruiser. Her glory days came to an explosive halt while battling superior numbered American and British warships. The two day surface battle was savage. Karl knew their invasion forces heading for Borneo and Malaya should never have contested the Americans. But they did with devastating results. That was KGB's first major blunder in speculating what the Allies would do. That day Karl saw the first crack widening in their naval structure. As the war proceeded he silently watched in alarm as the split became wider. Regardless what their countrymen were told the Navy knew they were losing this war. Now anchored off the coast of California, once considered the Pacific's golden jewel, he watched the state burn while its cities lay in ruins. Karl softly cursed the KGB.

His starpom looked around. It was good those glavnyy starshini ratings were friendly to the captain and not that political asshole snoring in his stateroom. The common seamen were loyal to their captain. He glanced towards the hatchway to see a senior petty officer quietly standing there. The signals glavnyy starshini would warn the bridge when threats, such as Mikhail, came close.

"Why don't you get some sleep," the engineering officer suggested. "Everything is running smoothly. We have another two hours of darkness. I'll wake you if anything turns up."

"This war is wrong, my friend." the captain softly denounced.

"Every man aboard this ship knows that, but we aren't in a position to do anything about it."

CHAPTER SEVEN

Twice in the last two hours James wandered into the deserted compound to look at the skies. With layers of sooty debris shading out the stars and moon he felt even worse. If rain didn't come soon it wouldn't matter who won the war. Life was going to simply cease. A short time in CIC finished his final planning for their two morning missions. By six o'clock and no acknowledgements from the other radar stations, James knew they wouldn't be answering.

When entering the mess hall James was solemnly greeted by his marines. News about their other radar sites was already circulating among the men. James walked through the food line watching food heaped upon his tray. It was his orders all participants in today's missions eat a hearty meal. Scrambled eggs piled with well cooked bacon slices crowded one side of his tray. Hash browns and canned fruit was dumped on the other side. With a large cup of coffee the commanding officer walked to his reserved table in the rear.

A few minutes later Chief Hickman and Sergeant Tyler joined him.

The chief petty officer looked at the food and chuckled. "Think they gave you enough?"

"I guess the cook thinks I need to gain weight," James said while chewing a couple of bacon slices. Though canned the salty bacon still tasted good. Glancing at Tyler he asked. "Is your detail ready to go?"

"We'll ready as ever."

"And you understand your orders?"

"We're to search for signs of an enemy warship's anchorage. Our mission is only seek-and-report. We aren't to engage the enemy unless forced to."

"Good. Make certain you follow those orders to the letter. Right now we're not in a position to challenge them. If you do find that ship, look for any weakness that may help us later."

"What are you thinking to do?" Timothy asked.

"I dunno. But I once had an admiral tell me every weapon has its weak point. I'm hoping that's true in our situation. Now let's talk about your mission today, Chief. I don't want your squad too far away from Gaviota because Russian reconnaissance teams are somewhere in this vicinity. Try and find the major some bloated bodies then maybe she'll go home?"

"What about the other radar stations?"

James sighed before saying. "We have to assume the worse and let it go at that. As I see it we're about to fight for our own survival. Concentrate on that." He disapprovingly glanced at the mess hall door. "Chief, your friend is here."

*   *   *

In the hanger Sergeant Tyler inspected his squad for the last time then looked at two marines leisurely carrying assault rifle ammo boxes. "Hey, you damned jarheads, what do you think this is—a damned picnic? Get the lead out of your ass and climb aboard. I don't have all day to piss around." He waited until they were in the armored vehicle. Tyler was about to follow when seeing Chatterbox hurrying into the hanger. He was carrying his black leather backpack with medical supplies.

Before climbing in, Chatterbox looked at his sergeant. "Did you hear the news?"

"You mean about the battle along Canada's Churchill River?" Tyler sadly nodded. "Yeah, I heard. Sort of got our ass kicked there, didn't we?"

"We lost seven hundred dead with eleven hundred wounded or missing." The marine exhaled as if hoping the ugly news would fade away. "We can't keep this up much longer. This country needs a real ass kicking victory to snap their morale from the dumps. Otherwise, we're going down the tubes."

The master sergeant only nodded and closed the door. For the last few weeks all news from the battlefields was bad. He knew the government wasn't telling the public their real situation. Back during World War II after the Japanese bombed Pearl Harbor, the United States was in a similar crisis. But this time it was different. Millions of Americans were buried beneath radioactive rubble. If Ten Delta couldn't slow down that naval task force their crushing defeats would be even worse.

As their armored vehicles passed through the opened door and into the cold early morning hours, Tyler looked at his squad. "All right, listen up and heed what I'm telling you. Our assignment today is locating that enemy ship's anchorage. This is a seek-and-identify mission . . . nothing more. You jarheads understand that?" There was a unified 'yes sir' sounded.

As the vehicle rumbled over the terrain heading for Lompac, Sergeant Tyler stayed up front with his driver. The twenty year veteran was fighting his third war. His black face was long and narrow. Immediately upon eye contact another person knew this man was all Marine Corps. Everything about the man borne under the Sagittarius sign tended to be large. His muscular trunk was large. The hands were overly large possessing legendary strength. Tyler boxed for the Corps and never lost a match. On the firing range he easily qualified on every weapon from both American and Soviet inventories. Those large brown eyes once sparkled with a love for life.

But Sergeant Tyler lost everything when enemy missiles rained down on Oakland, California. After that he rarely smiled.

Though it was daylight their vision was restricted because of the sooty skies. The two Israeli built NIMDA Shoet vehicles carefully wound their way through fallen debris or missed craters created by exploding bombs. The General Motors six cylinder engines weren't exactly quiet, but with those howling sleuth wasn't a factor. Multi-colored camouflaged painting amalgamated with the devastation around them. The Shoet similar to Russia's BTR-152 was an all steel welded body promising some protection against small arms gunfire. Behind Tyler sat fourteen marines solemnly quiet with their thoughts. With the coming of daylight winds would lessen somewhat, but the temperatures weren't tropical as before the war.

In the following two hours the ugly square-shaped war machines slowly found their way through debris-cluttered ruins crowding the ocean's shores. Tyler frequently patrolling this area noted the green terrain was rapidly disappearing. Miles away the sprawling Santa Ynez Mountains was bathed in a glowing reddish haze as fires furiously burned out of control. Two days ago one of their Apaches flying over the area said it was turning into a blacken scar. Every man in Ten Delta knew what a greenhouse affect meant.

Chatterbox was seated behind him studying a folded map. "What are you doing?" Tyler asked.

"Trying to figure out where a ship would seek haven." he answered without looking up. "The ocean is too rough to stay out there. If their captain is smart and I don't see why he wouldn't be, that ship is anchored inside a cove. And there aren't that many around here."

"Got any suggestions narrowing down our search?"

There was a short silence. "Two places come to mind." Chatterbox said. "If I was seeking a haven from those rough waters, Isla Vista would be one place."

"And the other?"

"Cojo Anchorage, but I prefer Isla Vista."

Standing behind his 7.62mm NAG machine gun mounted over the enclosed cab, Lance Corporal Truman Lincoln Thorton cautiously observed their slow progress through the ruins. They had seen only handful of people who quickly disappeared into the ruins. The twenty-six year old marine from North Carolina unconsciously felt his heavy camouflaged jacket checking if his small box of pills was still there. Nobody knew he popped drugs that relaxed his depressions. As the vehicle bumped noisily over the rutted highway running along the ocean he kept a sharp lookout. Thorton suspiciously regarded each overturned burnt automobile as a possible ambush sight. Some thirty feet behind them followed the second vehicle. Thorton heard the sergeant talking with Chatterbox. He remembered the lieutenant's threat of brig time if he didn't straighten up and fly right.

All of this devastation easily wore down a person's sanity. Each marine at Ten Delta had his own way of handling the mental crisis. Thorton used his racist thoughts in explaining the war ravaged countryside's grisly attachments of death. James was always stressing positive outlooks. But what did the lieutenant know? He came from a well-to-do family in San Francisco. The man probably never missed a meal in his life. Thorton bet he never woke up four in the morning to do a newspaper route then go home for household chores. This was all before a skimpy breakfast then off to school. Because the school district wouldn't send a bus out to where he lived, Thorton walked six miles to a boring school that didn't want him. The brown skinned man looked cautiously about while they rumbled through soot covered grounds. At sixteen Thorton began having sex with his younger sister. One day his thirteen year old sister announced she was pregnant. When the school discovered this she was taken from their home by the social services. The drunkard father beat his son so bad he couldn't walk for days. During that time his hatred for the abusive father increased thrice fold. Later when his father was found dead in a muddy ditch nothing was thought of it. That was when Thorton enlisted in the Corps. He wasn't the best all around marine material, but in combat he was a raging bull. In this war that was what the Marine Corps needed.

Attached to the Shoet's long hood was a small revolving apparatus. Inside the cab Tyler held a black box the size of a cigarette carton. A small screen blinked with wavy green and yellow lines. Tyler wasn't concerned with those colors, but when red lines appeared they had trouble. This British made instrument extensively used in Vietnam detected warm blooded beings within a three hundred feet range. Ten Delta regularly used the instrument on their patrols.

"Stop!" Tyler anxiously ordered. He was staring at the screen now showing four red dots moving steadily towards them "We have confirmed targets bearing three o'clock. Dismount and establish firing perimeters until targets are identified." He heard marines noisily jumping from the stalled vehicle. "Chatterbox, stay close to me." As he dismounted Tyler shouted. "Thorton, keep a sharp eye and open fire on any suspicious movements."

It was a few minutes before four civilians wrapped in blankets for protection against the bitter winds appeared from the rubble. They abruptly halted when seeing the weapons pointing their direction. The shabby figures were too hungry and cold to be worried about the soldiers' unfriendly acceptance of their arrival.

"Identify yourself," Tyler curtly demanded.

"I'm Bobby Benson and they're my family."

"Drop your blankets so we can see if you're armed or not." the sergeant rapidly issued orders. "Do you have identification cards?" After satisfied they were unarmed he told them to reclaim their fallen blankets. They were a pathetic sight in the dirty ragged clothing. "What are you doing here? Why haven't you surrendered to the army for relocation?"

"We lived in the mountains," the lanky sickly looking man said while Tyler examined his California driver's license. "I thought there was hope staying in the mountains until this was all over."

Handing the wallet back to the old man, Tyler suspiciously asked. "What changed your mind?"

"We ran out of food days ago and the coldness drove us down."

"Chatterbox," Tyler instructed. "See if we have extra food."

The Benson family sitting in a small circle quickly wolfed down the rations given to them. Still standing their defensive lines the marines watched this familiar sight with heavy hearts. A marine stayed in the warm cab monitoring the heat detector and chewing on a candy bar. When the food was gone Tyler gave each a bottle of beer. Their appreciative smiles were enough to soften even the hardest of emotions. Sitting on the ground bundled in their torn blankets, the family nervously waited to see what the black sergeant would do next. The winds blew loose sooty debris around in dancing tunnels. These war dazed civilians sat clutching their blankets and wishing the carefree days were back.

"How long have you been wandering around?"

"We got here six days ago. Some other people told us marines were down here."

"What are your plans?"

"Try to find that army group gathering people for relocation. There's no hope for survival around here. No food or water. We barely missed getting killed by Mexican bandits on three occasions."

"Well, stay close to the shore until passing Gaviota only twenty miles and you'll find an army assembling camp. They will relocate you from there." Tyler grinned when the old woman muttered a prayer for their deliverance. "During your wandering by any chance did you see anything out of the ordinary?"

"Only that ship . . ."

"What ship?" Tyler asked the old woman.

"It was two days ago we saw a ship off the coast. We frantically waved at it hoping they would rescue us." she fearfully mumbled.

"Then what," Tyler sternly asked.

"We ran for the ruins."

Tyler was puzzled. "Why?"

"We saw a Russian flag on its mast."

"Do you think you could identify the ship?" When the old woman reluctantly nodded, Tyler told Chatterbox to fetch the naval identification manual from their Shoet. "Now I want your family to carefully look through these pages and identify that ship." The sergeant looked over his shoulder. "One of you men grab those candies from the car."

Sergeant Tyler impatiently paced about while the family thoughtfully searched the pages for the ship they saw. Chatterbox leaned against the armored car amused at how fast they ate the sweets. After a while he cautiously walked the general area surveying the damages. At times he wanted to angrily scream curses on the Russians for what they had done to his country. When Tyler yelled his name Chatterbox knew the ship had been identified.

Handing the manual to him Chatterbox looked at the ship listed on that page. "The KONSTANTANTINOVICH, hell I thought she sunk off the Philippines last year." He gave Tyler a thoughtful glance. "I wonder how many more ships we thought were sunk are cruising out there." The marine turned to the family. "Are you certain this is the one you saw? This is very important."

The mother nodded. "That is the one . . . I'm sure of it," she confidently stated.

"Why are you sure?"

"Because there were lots of barrels stored on deck and I saw the number 306 painted on its side."

After the family continued on their way Chatterbox was the last to climb back into the Shoet. Inside the armored carrier he continued staring at the manual's page showing the KONSTANTANTINOVICH. She was a mean looking destroyer. Once Tyler looked back and saw his intense study of the ship without saying anything. The two Shoets slowly made their way along the shore detouring after the service road became too wasted to follow. Finally, after passing Canada de las Panochas, Tyler struck up a conversation with Chatterbox seated behind him.

"What do you know about that ship?"

"Not much, except she was supposedly sunk off the Philippines last year." Chatterbox exhaled his frustration. "This manual defines her weaponry as four 130mm twin turrets and four 30mm Gatling guns. Those alone could waste us. This manual lists her missile capabilities as eight SS-N-22 quads on either side of the bridge and a helicopter deck with 44 missiles."

"You mentioned a helicopter pad?"

"Yeah, she carries one Helix chopper."

"That's strange," Tyler said. "Wonder why we haven't seen it airborne?"

"I don't know."

"What else does it say about her?"

"Well, she's a big one nearly 156 feet long. The ship carries a 320 man crew with cruising range of 6500 miles while maintaining 20 knots speed. It states her turrets are fully automatic and water cooled." There was a short silence. "This is interesting. Her missiles only have a range of 70 miles. Its missile control system is the last generation, but still capable of illuminating us."

"Maybe those damned EM fields are giving it trouble?"

Chatterbox shrugged. "Perhaps, but why hasn't it affected our radar?"

"I dunno. Where the hell did you learn all of this?"

"I took a course in Russian weaponry while at communications school."

*   *   *

After passing Arroyo El Bulio the going became easier. Driving along the shore Tyler thoughtfully watched the crashing waves with a growing uneasiness. Not long after that the two vehicles pulled into what was known as San Augustine. It was here some months ago a famous battle took place. Ordering the Shoets to halt the master sergeant wearily climbed out and cautiously looked around. Though the Shoet's semi-elliptical springs and rubber AAOM springs needed replacing such spare parts weren't available. Above them the sun tried filtering through sooty debris drifting high above the land.

"Sergeant Tyler," a marine called out. "You better get over here."

With M-16A2 in hand the sergeant charged over the brown grassy knoll where the actual confrontation took place. Some marines were already running with their rifles ready for firing. Chatterbox quickly posted perimeter guards before running after the sergeant. Corporal Thorton spun his machine gun around its allowable rotation. After hearing the marine yelling he expected the worse. Behind them the sounds of waves washing shore reminded this small patrol how isolated they were. The howling winds were cold and unfriendly. Sergeant Tyler's large form disappeared over the small hill before Chatterbox reached him.

Tyler halting on the other side held his weapon tightly while cautiously looking about. It was easy to see a battle once unraveled here. A burnt car was overturned with two enemy tanks nearby in their blackened vigilance. Everybody in the Marines Corp knew how the last ten defenders made their final stand behind that bullet riddled auto. From the nearby woody area Russian soldiers had rushed the weak position. Over one hundred American men, women, and children bravely fought the invaders. The youngest was seven years old. Legends told how he manned a machine gun jerked from a dead Russian. The oldest was ninety six years old. This near blinded man killed many enemy soldiers before falling. When Apache helicopters arrived the defenders were dead. The story of this valiant fight was repeatedly told in their schools. White crosses arranged in neat rows encircled the battlefield. In its middle was a metal flagpole with a flag. When he hurried over the others parted a passage.

For a moment Sergeant Tyler stood looking down at the sooty soil. "Damn it!" he growled. Like all Americans the national colors represented their determination to crush the communists. The torn flag lay trampled on the ground. Kneeling down the large black man picked up the cloth then looked at the broken rope swinging back and forth in the wind. "Repair that pole!" he shouted. When his men didn't move fast enough the sergeant angrily screamed. "Get the lead out of your ass! I want that cloth flying in ten minutes or I'll nail your damned worthless hides up there!" Handing the dirty cloth to a marine he stomped away.

Chatterbox stood close by when his sergeant rushed pass to sit on the knoll's crest. Never had he seen the man so violently upset. For a few moments he silently observed the rough ocean's salty spray drifting their way. Looking over his shoulder, Chatterbox saw marines repairing the flagpole while another rope was attached for the flag. One marine was over at a nearby creek washing away the flag's grime.

"What's wrong, man?" Chatterbox finally asked.

"Nothing," Tyler groaned.

Chatterbox gave the sergeant a disturbed look. "Like hell. Hey, Bro, this is Chatterbox. I have known you for three years and know your damned changing moods better than your mamma. So do me a favor and stop the shit. Something really hit you back there." His disposition went sour even though Tyler was his senior sergeant. "I want to know what's rubbing you the wrong way. The whole troop has a right to know. We're on a critical mission and you're not about to let your emotions go astray. So drop the shit and talk."

Tyler frowned. "You're lucky I don't jam my fist down your throat?"

The staff sergeant grinned. "I know. So c'mon, Bro, what's wrong?"

"What do you know about this place?"

"I know a bunch of angry Americans fought some Russian marines and got their butts killed. It became known as the Battle of Arroyo San Augustin. Some pretty emotional stuff here." He watched the torn flag pulled up the flagpole while marines sharply saluted. He was always curious why during devastating times mankind found patriotism. "What am I missing?" he skeptically asked.

Tyler expressed his surprise. "Where the hell is your pride?" Shaking his head the sergeant moaned. "Sometime I think your heart is cold as a chunk of ice."

"What's that got to do with this place?"

"The Battle of Arroyo Augustin was fought by black people, Chatterbox." After seeing his surprise he continued. "That's right, smart ass. Every man, woman, child who fought and died down there was black skinned. They didn't have to do it. A motorized Marine unit was on the way. But they did it anyhow. When an enemy soldier fell his weapon was picked up by our brothers and sisters."

Chatterbox wasn't impressed. "So why isn't this told in schools?"

"Our people are doing everything they can to cope with this devastating nuclear nightmare? Millions of our people are dead while their homes are in ruins. I guess the races in America have finally come together to work it out. With all of your intelligence you're still overlooking that bonding. You're trying to see things as they once were and that's not the case now. Today race and different religions are working as one to see that our nation survives. That's why our brothers and sisters died over there. They were trying to preserve their freedoms."

Tyler knew he wasn't getting passed Chatterbox's stubbornness when he asked. "Who do you think desecrated the monument?"

"You didn't hear one word I said, did you?" Tyler curtly asked.

"Look, I appreciate what you're saying, but right now I have too much on my mind to buy that stuff. Things really haven't changed that much. Just look at Ten Delta. Yuma has written off this post because most of us are blacks. We're just black niggers to their white asses—nothing more." He frowned. "I'm more interested in surviving, but it'll be because of our cunning and not because of that stupid ass General Paulson."

Their conversation was interrupted when a marine yelled for the sergeant on the double.

Tyler disgustedly looked at Chatterbox before trotting down the slight hill to the summoning marine. For a couple of minutes after kneeling down Tyler studied the tire tracks. Concern was registered in his eyes. "Military tread that's for sure. They're something like the lieutenant found further down the coast. This 30.00X18 tread is used exclusively on heavy military vehicles."

"How long ago," Chatterbox asked.

"They're probably no more than a day old." When standing the salty air dampened his face. "I saw this tread pattern while with NATO. They're used on the PSZH-IV armored car, a favorite Russian reconnaissance unit." He slowly turned around. "We definitely have visitors out here." Motioning the marines' return to their vehicles Tyler and Chatterbox followed. "Radio Delta and inform the lieutenant of our find."

CHAPTER EIGHT

Captain Voronov wasn't in a good mood after learning the underwater repairmen discovered additional damages from their tidal waves challenges. Though working parties labored hard at their tasks some couldn't be repaired. After informed their radar was to be used only in times of extreme emergencies the political commissar was furious. The main enhancer rod was rapidly wearing out and could only be replaced in their shipyard off British Columbia. To make matters worse communications with that naval port was cut off. Colonel Karsavin insisted they keep trying. Captain Voronov's arguments that broadcasting permitted more opportunities to locate their ship fell on deaf ears. The KGB colonel boasted all Americans were stupid farmers, but the ship's crew knew otherwise.

At ten thirty that morning Captain Voronov was shocked after Mikhail came on the bridge ordering the ship to set sail. "But our repairs aren't finished."

"They will have to wait."

The captain seeing it was foolish to argue reluctantly asked. "What course headings, Comrade Colonel?"

"Your navigator has the coordinates. We're sailing to Santa Barbara."

Commander Bogdanov rushed onto the bridge minutes after Mikhail left. "What the hell is going on? My damage control teams are trying to work down below."

Karl frowned. "The commissar wants to visit Santa Barbara."

"Does he know we have repairs underway?"

"He doesn't give a damn. Speaking of repairs what about that number two shaft? Is it serious?"

"It's damaged enough I wouldn't recommend making way through rough waters like last night." the engineering officer reported. "You got to talk with the man. We're endangering the ship by leaving before finishing the major repairs."

"He won't listen, commander. The fool has no idea how a warship functions. Argue with him and you'll hear that spill about commanding tank regiments."

The commander angrily shook his head. "What about my workers on shore?"

"We'll leave them. Have the marines stay with them. We're coming back after Santa Barbara. If you have jobs that can be fixed while we're underway keep them working."

"This is sheer insanity," Bogdanov grumbled.

"You better believe it," Karl complained. "But there's not one thing we can do unless you want the KGB down our throats."

The engineering officer walked to the windshield and thoughtfully observed his working parties ashore retooling needed parts. It was a makeshift affair, but aboard the unstable ship it was impossible to grind exact measurements. Looking at the skies layered with smoke and debris from global fires he exhaled. "We're able to marginally operate our radar because of atmospheric interferences. Now the commissar wants us to illuminate when its primary parts are fast wearing out. This is crazy."

Karl shook his head. "Long as the bastard is aboard we have to put up with him. You'll have to do what I'm doing—endure the bastard and hope for the best." Karl stopped talking for a moment. "I have instructed the navigator to plot a course one mile off shore. Yeah, I know that's putting the ship under unnecessary strains because of the choppy waters. But maybe we can avoid detection by the Americans."

"Then we will have to make way at ten knots and no more. The damaged shaft won't endure much more banging around."

They had been underway for no more than two hours when the commissar came on the bridge. He wasn't happy with the slow speed. Only after going down into the hot engineering spaces and hearing the grinding shaft did Mikhail approve the slower knots. After that Mikhail disappeared again. Karl hoped he was enjoying his vodka breaks since that kept the fool off his bridge. Refusing to leave the enclosed bridge Karl ate his lunch of a meatless sandwich and hot tea. He was satisfied with lettuce and tomato stuffed between thick black bread. Engineering called every fifteen minute reporting number two shaft was noisily grinding away. Strong winds sending waves splashing over the main deck soon cancelled all work there. Each time the screws were lifted out of the waters by high waves Karl gritted his teeth when hearing the noisy protests.

Karl was hanging up the phone when Mikhail came on the bridge. After checking their coordinates with the navigator, he walked over to the captain seated in his elevated chair. "You seem overly concerned about something, Comrade Captain?" he indifferently asked.

"Engineering reports increased friction on number two shaft." Karl curtly advised. "Every time the shaft turns it's grinding into its casing." He glared at the army colonel standing before him with folded arms and an arrogant frown. "That's the thunderous noise you hear and the shaking we feel. Any time that shaft will snap."

"Then you'll have to nurse the shaft." The political commissar impatiently exhaled. "Senior Comrade Captain Voronov, it may surprise you that at one time I commanded a company of tanks along our Mongolian frontier. There were many times we needed spare parts for the tanks, parts that weren't available. We didn't whim about our shortages, but cleverly used what was on hand and went forward with our missions." Mikhail's face turned dark with anger. "And that's what you shall do, captain."

For several moments Karl angrily stared at the overly confident zampoli. "May I remind the Comrade Colonel that KONSTANTANTINOVICH isn't a tank, but, instead an 8000 ton warship."

Mikhail grinned. "The same principle applies. Now you have your orders, captain, please see to it they're carried out."

The commissar gave the acrimonious captain a parting scowl then walked over to the enlisted sailor manning the wheel. "Maintain steady course," he sternly advised. Then loud enough for everybody on the bridge to hear he said. "No course change without my express approval." Walking to the hatch he paused then turned and spoke directly to Karl. "It's important we find Ten Delta as quickly as possible. Our task force is speeding this way. The fate of our glorious Motherland rests squarely on our shoulders." Before the captain responded, the colonel in his tailored brown uniform departed the bridge.

Mikhail thoughtfully walked onto the open bridge wing and looked around. The ship plowing through crashing waters at a slow 10 knots was sharply disapproved. But a friendly glavnyy starshini from engineering assured him number two shaft was truly troublesome. Icy winds ripping across the churning ocean dampened his unprotected hands and face with a salty grime. The wasted Californian coast was only one mile off their course this mid morning with skies a gloomy gray overcast. He smiled. It was fate the once mighty United States would fall under Russia's armies.

Captain Voronov stepping from the bridge hatch saw Mikhail and was going back inside, but the commissar invited him to stay. With no other choice the skipper nodded. KGB officials had argued strongly against Karl Voronov commanding this warship. If this had being the Red Army their demands would have swiftly seen the free thinker Karl thrown into prison. However, the Red Navy jealously protected their senior officers. But Mikhail knew this would change once victory was achieved. There would be many sweeping reforms in the Soviet military. Mikhail looked at the man's large crooked nose turning red from the chilling winds.

"May I inquire why we're going to Santa Barbara?" Karl asked.

"We're picking up a special team of intelligence agents dropped there last year."

Karl was flabbergasted. "And they have survived that long?"

After seeing his surprise the commissar was quick to arrogantly reply. "They did because army intelligence agents are smarter than your naval ones." After a short silence dropped between them the colonel boasted. "The team was inserted last year to gather information for our future occupation of the Californian wastelands."

*   *   *

The morning hours sluggishly passed for the men of Sergeant Tyler's patrol. They occasionally picked up more evidence of enemy reconnaissance teams. Homeless Americans like the Bensons provided bits and pieces of information. When woven together a vague picture of what the Russians were planning began emerging. The two Shoets parked among some ruins for protection from the winds. The marines ate cold rations and discussed the war's nightmares. Chatterbox and Tyler quietly studied a regional map.

"Those two Russian armored cars drove along the coast until reaching El Capitan State Beach. It was there they murdered some transients. We then lost their tracks until Juan Martinez's family warned us about two military vehicles with red stars on their sides."

Chatterbox took the map from Tyler. "Remember we speculated the ship would seek shelter from the storms at Isla Vista?" he mumbled.

"Yeah, I remember that."

Pointing at the map the staff sergeant said. "These armored units are heading for Isla Vista. It isn't that many miles down the coast."

"So you think they're heading back to the ship?"

"I think so."

"All right, let's say you're right. So why did their captain pick Isla Vista for anchorage? That place seems to me to be a poor choice."

"Actually there are few places along the Californian coastal lines offering good anchorage from the storms. Especially ones like we have been having. Studying the map I would think Channel Islands National Park in the Santa Barbara Channel would be better suited. This weather has everything screwed up."

Tyler stared at the map with a deep thoughtful expression. "You can't hide a destroyer. So when reaching Isla Vista we should see the ship?"

"Yeah," he mumbled. After deeply exhaling the staff sergeant reached for his opened can of peaches and ate some. "With luck we should kill two birds with one stone. We'll see the Russian warship and maybe along the way take out those PSZH-IV armored cars."

Later the two Shoets were driving over Highway 101 winding along the coast. In places it was near impossible to drive because of numerous abandoned or burned vehicles. Four miles from Isla Vista they left the high profile highway and made slow progress through wrecks crowding the local road. Their security alertness became tensed with the possibility of finding the enemy near that anchorage. Goleta was a fairly large township of ruins that Tyler chose to detour around. Though this cost time he felt it was worthwhile. After reaching Goleta's outskirts Tyler parked his vehicles among some rubble and took stock of their situation.

* * *

James was in the hanger checking maintenance progress on their Apache helicopters. The machines would shortly be airborne and everything had to be right. The mechanics looking up from their work acknowledged the grim faced lieutenant. Word had spread throughout the facility about the other radar stations. Nothing was kept from these men for very long. Chief Hickman's patrol in Gaviota ended unsuccessfully and returned one hour ago. Major Davidson was furious no bloated corpses were found.

The chief joined James in the hanger but neither man spoke for several minutes.

"While I'm thinking about it," the Chief somberly said. "Pretty Face is in the cafeteria if you want to talk with her."

"Why would I want to do that?" James sarcastically replied. "I have enough troubles as it is."

Timothy smiled his foolish expression. "Well, for one thing she can brief you on what's happening in rest of the world. Some of it may surprise you. I bet if you gave her a chance you may find the woman fascinating, James. She's a very smart person even if she's a woman."

James walked around the chopper checking the weapon pods. "I'm certain she's smart, Chief. Otherwise she wouldn't be holding that cushy staff post in Yuma." He fully trusted his chief mechanic to make certain everything was functional. But right now he needed something to take his mind away from that woman. "While you were gone Yuma radioed their concerns about the lost of our other radar stations."

"When are they going to reestablish the sites?"

"They're not."

"But why," Timothy anxiously asked. "Hell, our system can't do the job. We have enough trouble keeping our radar on line. Not only that, but its range is terribly limited." Frustrated he threw his hands up. "For god's sake, James, the unit is over thirty years old and badly in need of overhaul. And I'm not even sure if that's going to improve its performance. It's an old piece of machinery needing to be thrown into the junkyard."

James stopped his inspecting and frowned. "Even so, chief, it's all we have. And probably all we'll get." Ten Delta was isolated by nearly one thousand miles of hostility and destruction before friendly secure territory was reached. "Our nearest touch with organized military commands is Yuma and god knows that's loosely defined. General Paulson may not be the smartest asshole on the block, but he has his problems. Poor communications caused by sooty atmospheric conditions, smashed transportation grids between there and the coast, and serious lack of adequate manpower allotments adds up to serious problems down the line. And we're the last on that line. The other radar sites aren't going to be replaced because there are no spare radar units. What we have are being used on the battlefields."

"So what did they say about the enemy warship presence?"

"Maybe at first they didn't believe us, but now they do." James said after pausing by the chopper's Hellfire rocket launchers. "But the bad news is there are no resources to lend us. Bottom of the supply barrel has been tapped."

"What about those two destroyers off Mexico? Why can't they be transferred down this way?"

"I suggested that, but never got an answer from Group Intelligence."

"Meaning we won't. Why don't we take a break in the cafeteria? It'll give you an opportunity to discuss the war with Savannah."

Though not enthused with the suggestion James went along. The cafeteria wasn't busy as most marines were running security details. The lieutenant after grabbing a cup of coffee joined Timothy and Savannah at a table close to the door. The major thoughtfully studied his rugged body and firm jaw line. He noticed she seemed more relaxed in the camouflages than her dress uniform. Briefly appraising her while walking to the table James suspected there was more to this woman than met the eye.

"What was Central Command's reaction when you told them that task force would pass here within two or three days?" she curiously asked.

"They didn't believe me at first."

"I'm sure it stirred up a hornets' nest. About the other radar stations I'm sorry. That's a bad break for coastal security."

James gave her a dirty look. "It's even worse for those men dying at their posts."

"Maybe they aren't all dead. They may be prisoners."

"Neither side takes prisoners out here, major." James soberly replied with a deep frown.

Savannah didn't speak for several moments. "I have been here only a few hours, but during that time I have heard repeated slurs about Yuma Central Command. Your men gripe about the lousy supply chain and constantly complain that these stations are seriously undermanned."

"They don't see too many things around here that changes their minds."

"You may believe this region has been forgotten by St. Louis and Yuma, but it hasn't. Not by a long shot. I realize you're not in the loop of highly classified info. So I'll brief you on what I can. Maybe that will help explain what's going on back home. To start off our war has taken a serious turn for the worse. We aren't doing that well on the Canadian battlefields and that's where our primary clashes are taking place. As you probably already know what's left of our Navy is blockaded in their ports. The enemy sails along the Gulf States doing just about what they want to." She stopped talking to angrily observe his skeptical expression. "Whether the war was accidentally started or not doesn't matter now. But once it broke out the Soviets knew exactly what they needed to hit. Our industrial centers were taken out within hours. Military warehouses were blown up either by missiles or bombers. They went for our throat and removed government structures. Missiles caught the Senate and House of Representatives in session. The White House was demolished by a nuclear missile while the President and Soviet ambassador were at a state dinner." She paused for a moment. "Our Navy was practically destroyed in those first hours and during later massive surface battles. The Air Force was flattened for the most part on their airfields. Armies were seriously hit in the weeks to come. After Washington was destroyed our capital was moved to St. Louis. To summarize this, the United States of America is crippled and vastly outnumbered. Your men moan and groan they're forgotten and badly supplied. I have news for your men. So is every other military unit, but they're still fighting the enemy. Our country in the days to come will either emerge as a victor in this terrible war or they'll go down in a vicious bloodbath. That's the dark cloud hanging over our country at the moment."

"It's that bad, eh?" Timothy asked after a short tensed silence at the table.

"It's far more complicated."

When the public address system summoned the lieutenant they quickly left their table. Going into CIC James went over to the monitors that were still black.

"Update," the CO demanded.

"We have an unidentified helicopter inbound over the Santa Ynez Mountains."

"Is it on radio silence?"

"Every fifteen minutes the words 'Ride sunset' is broadcasted."

"It could be an enemy aircraft?" Timothy suspiciously suggested.

Savannah's challenging smile took James by surprise. "Maintain radio surveillance until it starts broadcasting 'Dawn arising.' Then send the words 'Come down' in short bursts." She looked at James' dim refusal in his eyes. "The aircraft originating in St. Louis is carrying Earl Craver, the Presidential scientific advisor."

James curtly demanded. "What's going on here?"

"Gentlemen," Savannah sharply announced. "Ten Delta is about to take part in an unusual operation. That's all I can reveal until Earl arrives."

"Then you're not here to analyze bloated corpses?"

"No, that's not entirely right. Though part of my job is determining if this green matter is contagious or not. But Earl is coming here for a totally different issue." She listened as the radio receiver recorded another broadcast. Though not on the line, their equipment still evaluated coordinates and distances of each interception. "Has your patrol called in?"

"No."

"Then recall them."

"Why?" James curtly asked. "They're looking for the ship's anchorage and those missing Russian marines."

"The KONSTANTANTINOVICH is anchored at Isla Vista."

"How did you know that?" James suspiciously wanted to know.

"We have known that since she sailed from their British Columbia naval port. The ship regularly sends coded messages back there. We have a clandestine interception station in the Humboldt National Park region. The Russian destroyer has a political commissar who isn't too smart. Not only does he broadcast a lot, but their radiomen never changes frequencies."

"How long has that station operated?" James asked.

"For the last nine months they have intercepted heavy communication activity from the British Columbia naval port."

"Then your station should have known about the radar station raids?"

Savannah briefly looked at James' accusing expression before turning to the radiomen and removing her ID wallet. Flipping it open the major showed her ID to the enlisted marine. "Recall the team now." she ordered. When the radioman glanced toward James for confirmation she bitterly declared. "Marine, you have been given an order. Do it now or I'll have you up on charges for disobedience. Now do it!"

After they left CIC Savannah paused in the hallway. "Lieutenant, perhaps it's best if certain rules are understood. When I give an order it'll be obeyed without questioning. This covert will have top priority over anything you may be doing." After the two naval types nodded their reluctant agreement she forced a weak smile. "Now while we'll waiting for Earl's arrival, I need to see your daily security logs."

"What are you looking for?" Timothy asked.

"I'm looking for daily temperatures that are drastically changing, references to dying vegetation, storms' active lengths, and observances of large fires. I'm particularly interested those in the mountains." When they looked at her with puzzled expressions Savannah grinned then shrugged.

CHAPTER NINE

For the past two hours Sergeant Tyler's patrol stayed concealed among some jungle like trees. Their tensed attention was focused on a camouflaged Russian armored vehicle parked among some piles of rubble after two large buildings collapsed. Lying amidst chunks of crumbled concrete and twisted steel frames Tyler watched three Russians cautiously walking about the deserted road. Chatterbox mentioned the winds were getting stronger. A glance toward the nearby ocean caused him some uneasy moments. The water was becoming choppy with ten foot waves splashing ashore.

"What do you think they're doing?" Chatterbox asked after flopping alongside Tyler.

"I dunno, but they don't seem to be in a hurry."

"We don't have much time to screw round. Those skies don't look that good. I think we may have another storm on the way."

When debris suddenly started flying through the air, Tyler ordered his men to scramble into whatever protective coverings they could find. Giving the Russians a last glance he saw they were running towards their armored car. The master sergeant barely made it to an underground cavity before powerful winds started whipping through the ruins. Such destructive storms abruptly coming out of nowhere was a constant threat. They usually lasted only a short while then everything was normal again. Their haven made when the buildings crashed down provided enough room for ten marines. The remaining men were cooped up in their vehicles. Chatterbox quietly timed the storm and noticed with a deep frown they were lasting longer.

"Where are the damned Russians?" he asked the sergeant.

"I saw them running for their vehicle when the storm hit."

"You think they're buttoned up like us?"

"I would think they're inside their armored hunks waiting out the storm just like us." Tyler studied his pinched facial lines before asking. "Why? What are you thinking?"

"Oh, I don't know. I was thinking we know this area around El Capitan beach. God knows we have patrolled it enough. We're buttoned up right now because of the storm. I bet my best Sam Cooke records the damned communists don't know the terrain. At least, I bet not good enough to be wandering around blind in the storm."

"So?"

"This is the best time to take them out."

"Our orders are not to engage the enemy."

"But we may not get another opportunity like this? I'm sure the jerks have codes and radio frequencies in the armored cars."

*   *   *

After anchoring off Point Castillo in the Santa Barbara Channel, Captain Voronov sent his working parties back on those priority jobs needing completion before their entry into the Gulf of Mexico. He uneasily walked the bridge finding their high profile very foolish. Colonel Karsavin impatiently waiting for his contacts didn't seem concerned. As usual the commissar underestimated the Americans. Karl frequently called engineering for status reports. Pulling on a heavy overcoat the captain walked the open bridge wing watching his damage control ratings work. Finally, the man went back into the warm bridge.

"This turbine," Mikhail curiously asked. "Can it be repaired in the Isla Vista cove?"

"No."

"You seem confident it can't be replaced." the commissar charged. "Maybe you agreed too fast? When I was with tanks it was damaged cannon barrels that couldn't be repaired in the field. But in time that was proven wrong."

"The difference between a tank's cannon, Comrade Colonel, and a ship's shaft is several tons." the captain somberly advised finding it difficult to suppress his anger.

When the political advisor left his bridge in a sour mood Karl didn't mind. Men such as Mikhail Karsavin were a cancerous germ eating away at Mother Russia. For a short time following the successful overthrow of communism in August 1991, there was hope for his crippled country. Following the climax of their Second Revolution nourished by Mikhail Gorbachev the prospects were hopeful. Propelled by the thunderous forces of democracy the gigantic country entered the Western World. One major reform in the military was swift removal of all political commissars. However, the old Soviet Union wasn't ready for the laborious struggle to solidify their freedoms. As the years slowly passed nobody noticed the old Party slowly regaining its lost powers. While the United States was hopelessly entangled in their Middle Eastern wars, the communists forcibly assumed full power. That was when a cruel revolutionist named Vicktor Kossier toppled the rightful government without protest from the Western World. After that it was a short walk to this devastating global war.

Later the KGB colonel strolled about the bridge wing confident his overdue contacts would soon signal from the shore. Occasionally, Commander Bogdanov passed him with a sour expression, but Mikhail didn't object. He intended to enjoy this brief lull from the storms. His headache throbbed no matter what medications were taken. Since the captain wasn't on deck, he sat in the elevated chair and propped his feet against the bulkhead. Years ago he visited Santa Barbara finding the city bursting with a love for life. Now it was a wasteland of toppled ruins where winds constantly howled through. From that chair he could see the U.S Naval Reserve Training Center ruins. Though the Santa Barbara Yacht Club burned its flagpole still fluttered their tattered banner. He didn't have to consult charts about this region. Up the coast was the giant Vandenberg Air Force Base while off shore was the Navy's Pacific Missile Range. Soviet missiles from a Yankee submarine blasted both facilities into rubble. The commissar indifferently watched those raging fires on distant mountains. It didn't bother this cold hearted man that hundreds of millions died before the global war focused on the Canadian frontiers.

Finally walking back on the open wing, Mikhail thoughtfully watched seamen laboriously pushing fifty-five gallon drums on the slightly pitching decking for securing. They were involved in a very important task. Those drums contained fuel for aircraft aboard their principle ship. This became a priority after six oil tankers were sunk last year. With only four tankers left in the Soviet Navy, they were careful about their sailings. Two of those ships were in the Gulf of Mexico feeding their hungry warships. Another one was safely anchored at their British Columbia port.

Suddenly those deafening winds died down followed by a strange silence. Mikhail quickly looked about seeking the source of this uncanny situation. About that time the ship's collusion alarm began sounding. Whirling around Mikhail heard the duty officer screaming into the public address system a huge wave was heading their way. A horrified mask charged across Mikhail's face while tightly grabbing the life railings. There was no time to flee into the bridge. When thirty foot waves crashed against the ship Mikhail didn't let go of his death grasp until the groaning eskadrenny minononosets stopped shaking. The crashing waters rushed through open hatchways and swept brutally across the main decking. During all of this chaos Mikhail caught a glimpse of fuel drums being ripped from their lashings and tumbling over the sides. After the danger passed the commissar stood there heavily panting and afraid to let go of the railing. Those waves were unlike anything he had ever seen. This meant the weather was rapidly changing for the worse.

Captain Voronov was on his bridge immediately after the storm's fury passed inland. "Engineering!" he shouted into the phone. "Damage reports on the double." His face turned pale as a tremble ran through his heads. "Very well, see to it necessary repairs are made." He looked at the drenched shivering colonel. "The storm caught us totally off guard. Opened hatches flooded two gunnery compartments. Some damages in weapons storage. Repair teams are on the job."

"I saw drums being washed overboard."

"We lost sixty drums."

Mikhail anxiously ordered. "We need to find them. That fuel is increasingly hard to find ashore."

"My lookouts are searching the waters, but they aren't to be seen."

"Where the hell did they disappear to?" Mikhail curtly demanded.

"Those waves may have washed them inland. The waves were high enough. Or they may have been swept out when the waters rushed back to sea."

After the hatchway was pulled open by a senior rating, he struggled inside and tried coughing up the salt waters swallowed when caught outside. His face was pale and wretched. Karl stepped across the compartment to stand before the frightened seaman.

"Take your time, Iva. Take your time."

Mikhail was about to angrily degrade the petty officer when he hacked a last time and straightened up, but didn't when Karl gave him an angry scowl.

"We lost the drums, Comrade Captain. We weren't through securing them when the waves came."

"I know about the drums. There was nothing you could have done to save them." Karl replied.

"No," Mikhail interrupted. "The drums are gone and they were your responsibility." The petty officer snapped to attention. "You gave failed the Party! Do you know how long it took this ship to collect that fuel? Way too long. Because of your stupidity some of our planes will not fly. You have done our country a great disservice!"

The commissar's face turned red from his anger. When the petty officer started to say something, Karl watched in horror as the colonel whipped out his pistol and fired twice. Terrified pain crossed the startled petty officer's face. The captain's angry protests seemed far away as he collapsed on the decking. Red stains quickly distorted the salty water at his feet. The petty officer gave his captain a last pleading look for forgiveness then darkness closed over his numbed body.

Holstering his revolver Mikhail turned to scowl at Karl's temporary numbness. "I won't tolerate failures aboard this ship, Comrade Captain Voronov." he harshly warned.

Karl once regaining his clear thinking turned to the stunned engineering officer. "Prepare his body for burial."

"No!" Mikhail sharply interrupted. "There's no place for blundering fools aboard this ship. Throw his body over the side then hoist anchor and sail back to Isla Vista!" When Karl hesitated he stared his furious expression. "Do as I say, Captain Voronov or I shall have you thrown in the brig!" Only when the captain finally nodded and gave the orders for leaving port did Mikhail's hand drop from the holster. "I want to talk with the electronics specialist about the radar."

"I'm afraid that's impossible, Comrade Colonel," Karl's words came out bitterly harsh.

"Are you challenging me?" the commissar spat.

"No, that isn't my intention, but we have only one electronics specialist aboard the KONSTANTANTINOVICH," the skipper groaned.

"So," the colonel nearly shouted when finding his patience snapping. "Have him report to the bridge on the double!"

"I can't. You just murdered him."

*   *   *

Savannah impatiently watched the radiomen tracking Earl's incoming helicopter. "What's his ETA?" she asked.

"Thirty minutes unless he changes course again."

Marines manned their battle stations as a thick tension settled over Ten Delta. With majority of their personnel on patrol the station was critically shorthanded. Even so everybody was performing at their peak. While thoughtfully rubbing his chin James quietly stood behind one radioman. He was uneasy with these developments rushing upon Ten Delta without warning.

"Does Craver have our coordinates?" James asked after a short spell of silence. "Yes."

"Then why the hell is he taking a sightseeing tour?" the CO blasted. "The longer he stays in the air it's that easier for Soviet spies to track his ass."

"I'm certain Earl has his reasons." Savannah defended.

"I sure as hell hope so." Turning to the chief he asked. "Have you heard from Tyler?" Timothy shook his head. James looked about the compartment crowded with radio and electronic equipment that was off the line meaning they were totally blind, except for their watches posted in the tower. It was a few minutes before he made up his mind. "Chief, activate our electronics. There's too much happening for us to stand here with no eyes."

After the monitoring equipment came on line James quickly studied the screens. All lights were green meaning no intruders. But they had problems in another sector. Savannah stepped aside as James and his chief quickly evaluated the new threat.

"We have an incoming airborne bogey," announced a short light-skinned Negro seated in front of his radar console. All attention was quickly turned upon the short staff sergeant. His finely etched facial features made him look like a movie star playing out a role. Benton Wakefield borne in Oakland, California had never left until enlisting in the Corps. His crisp voice was calm even when stressed out. "Estimated speed is 45 miles per hour with a steady southern course maintaining close proximity to the coast line. Unidentified target emitting weak signals."

"What the hell is it?" James anxiously mumbled while watching the radar tracking.

Sergeant Wakefield shook his head. "I have never seen anything like it, sir. It's traveling 60 feet above the surface and is too small to be a helicopter."

"Go to Defense Alert One." James looked at Timothy. "Recall Tyler's group." Absorbing the raw data coming into CIC, the lieutenant paced back and forth behind Wakefield. There was a cold calmness in his voice. "What about Craver's flight?"

"Still on his irregular course."

"His flight's ETA?"

"Fifteen minutes."

"O.K, let's concentrate on that unidentified target. Chief, go the tower. You may be able to visually check it out there." Studying the short range radar he added. "We can't be certain if it's friendly or unfriendly. So let's assume it's unfriendly."

*   *   *

Powerful winds raged through the coastal region like angry gods bent upon smashing whatever was left standing. Timothy pulled his fur collar tightly against his neck before hurriedly climbing the ladder. Its metal roof loudly pounding up and down was threatening to rip loose and go crashing down into the compound. Secured on a table was a small radar unit removed from their wrecked truck sitting in the yard's corner like banished child. One marine was hunched over a small screen watching the green dot moving along the coast. When a thunderous explosion unexpectedly sounded Chief Hickman jumped. The other marine grinned and said it was only a nearby building collapsing then went back to studying the object being tracked.

Timothy cursed. "Damned I wish we had visual capabilities." The green dot would often time stop and slowly rotate before continuing. "It's too small to be a helicopter."

The operator was quickly adjusting a set of knobs. "It's maintaining irregular speed and directional bearings."

"The damned thing is on a seek-and-identify mode," the chief hissed. "It's looking for something."

"Yeah, probably us," the marine moaned. "I first picked it up off Sacate." He was anxiously trying to obtain a better fix. The video screen didn't present images but only color lines designating speed and bearings. While observing its changing colors, the marine shouted to be heard above the roaring winds' increasing howl. "No radiation emitted. UFO probably has a small propulsion system . . . possibly battery driven."

They frequently ducked as debris sucked up by powerful twisting winds charged over the tower. Visual contact was now limited to forty feet and reducing rapidly. Whirling dust prompted Timothy to lower his goggles for protection from the blinding storm that erupted almost without warning. Horrifying noises generated by this storm was deafening. Objects larger than men were hurling through the air. Twisted beams, weakened by past storms and explosions, swayed in the bitterly cold winds until crashing to the ground. Those waves thunderously rolling ashore sent misty clouds into the unfriendly skies. The tower was swaying dangerously to the right then to the left. They grabbed railings to hold on. One marine was clutching a metal railing while screaming this was crazy. The other marine shielded their radar equipment with his body. The tower suddenly gave a series of groaning noises. It was then Timothy knew the tower was about to come crashing down.

Their approaching target was forgotten when seeing a large twisting object hurling toward the tower's crumbling structure. "Hit the deck!" he shouted.

Timothy's warning was heeded right before a long steel beam about the size of a car sliced through the tower like a chain saw. The first marine dropped like a bag of dirt while clutching the railing for safety. The second marine tried heroically to protect the radar set. All Timothy heard was a single terrified scream and afterwards that terrible ripping sound. Minutes after the storm charged pass Timothy pulled himself up on the wobbly cluttered platform. There was only destruction greeting his startled survey. There was no radar set on the tower. Where the railings used to be was now a gaping hole. Quickly looking about Timothy didn't find the second marine.

Though the storm's fury was gone the smashed tower was threatening to topple over. Timothy whirled about when hearing the surviving marine's panic-stricken cry for help. The unstable platform had tossed the injured man over the side, but he caught a loose railing. Timothy reaching out grabbed his clawing hand and slowly pulled his trembling body onto the platform. Another stone sector gave way and fell crashing down forty feet to explode in their compound.

"We got to get down!" the chief yelled. "This thing is going down!"

Hell broke loose atop that tower as other groaning sections started breaking off. The two men were knocked about by bitterly cold winds carrying sheets of water sucked up by the whirling tunnels. Both men desperately hung on for life as the tower swayed even more. Another section of stone roughly broke off and crashed downward. With everything erupting like it did they didn't expect help from their comrades. They probably didn't even know the tower was breaking up. They were on their own.

"Grab my hand," Timothy shouted to the frightened marine clinging to a loose railing that was about to break apart.

It was a deadly struggle crawling inch by inch across what remained of the tossing platform. The chief knew they had to reach that ladder before it too came crashing down. Twice they lost ground and had to laboriously regain those few inches. The chief felt the tower giving way to the damages burst upon it by that storm. Reaching the ladder they both scrambled down even as the platform broke loose. Dodging falling debris the men swung open the door and ran inside Ten Delta as the tower gave its final groan.

*　　*　　*

After sending the injured to their sick bay Timothy rushed into CIC. That was James' first knowledge their tower was gone. "Are you hurt?" he quickly asked the drenched man in his torn camouflaged clothing. Several bruises and minor cuts trickled blood down his face.

"I'm all right. Billy Boy is in the sick bay." Timothy paused to bitterly suck in his breath. "But we lost Manny when an iron beam tore through the tower."

"I'm sorry we didn't know. Are you certain nothing is seriously wrong with you?"

"I'm O.K. What about that helicopter?"

"It'll be here in about ten minutes. He's on a steady course now."

The chief petty officer walked over to Wakefield. "What about that UFO, do you have an identity yet?"

"Nope, that damned storm caused heavy interferences."

Before further discussion was possible color monitoring screens came back on line. They saw an orange tube-like object hovering off shore rotating in a slow searching mode. Its eye pointed toward the ruins where Ten Delta laid hidden.

Wakefield stared at the torpedo shaped UFO before muttering. "That's a rotary-wing unmanned pod we used for short range probes." He gave James a quick glance. "They haven't been used since Iraq."

Without taking his attention from the threatening shaft James asked. "Are you familiar with them?"

"I worked with them several years ago in Poland." He studied the hovering spherical module painted a rough orange and sporting one small red star on its frontal plate. Three-blade counter rotating propellers kept it steady during the short pause above unfriendly choppy waters. "That single electronic eye pointing our direction is confused. See how it keeps irregularly spinning?" He touched the screen. "This bent antenna probably has its visual system cut off." There was a short silence before adding. "It has an S-band FM/TV data link electronically hooking it to the originator."

"That Russian destroyer," James inquired.

"That's my guess."

"Do you think it illuminated us?" Timothy asked.

"I don't think so. See how the machine rotates. It's confused. If the machine had painted us it would have pulled out of range. It's only a seek-and-identify unit without weapons."

Without hesitation James ordered. "Take it out now."

The marine ordered to shoot down the module raced down the corridor and then outside. He dodged falling debris disturbed by powerful winds, but climbing over loose stones was another problem. Nearly reaching the top their sharpshooter would helplessly slip down again. Finally finding an ideal shooting spot the sniper scooted closer to the rubble's crest and peeked over. Hovering only sixty feet away the module was suspicious of the ruins. Its small red light indicating searching mode was often blotted out by the sooty debris. The shoulder fired missile was already primed and ready for firing. When the trigger was pulled its Javelin rocket shot toward the revolving object. There was a loud explosion then the orange module simply disappeared as burning parts fell into the ocean. After that the sniper ran like hell across the compound dodging falling debris from the sucking winds.

CHAPTER TEN

Tyler's plan of slipping upon the buttoned up Russians was cancelled when another unexpected storm suddenly swept over their area. Huddling inside the dust filled cavity they waited out the thunderous crashing noises. After the violence passed they crept from their concealment and cautiously approached where the Russians were parked. Tyler and Chatterbox stopped when seeing the vehicles were gone.

"You want to explain this?" Tyler skeptically suggested.

"The bastards tore out during the storm." Shaking his head the staff sergeant moaned. "They sure have balls driving in those damned storms. Hell, you can't even see the tip of your hood." Looking about he mumbled. "Boy, this one was a killer. It tore the hell out of these ruins. I don't even know where the street runs anymore."

A marine trotted over. "Sergeant, we got a recall."

"Wonder what's going on?" the master sergeant asked after nodding his acknowledgement. "C'mon, let's get the hell out of here. No telling where those bastards are roaming."

Moving north up the coast the patrol was passing what remained of Refugio State Beach when Chatterbox in the lead Shoet yelled to stop. While Tyler was jumping from the second armored car, the staff sergeant ran over to some decaying bodies lying alongside the road. Reaching Chatterbox the master sergeant remained standing with his weapon ready for firing. Vision was sharply reduced by swirling debris created by explosions from the war's early days.

"What do you have?" Tyler harshly asked. Where they had stopped was in the open and easily detected if the winds died down.

"These bloated bodies have that green oozing bacteria," The marine leaning over poked at the one corpse with a stick. "This is interesting."

"O.K. but get your examination over with and let's get the hell out of here. We're too high profile out here."

"This is strange." he muttered after several minutes. "I know this man. His name is Manson."

"Where do you know him from?"

"Two days ago we stopped him for field interrogation in Gaviota. He used to have a home near Lake Cachuma."

"Are you certain of that?" Tyler curiously asked after his interest was drawn to the old man's wasted body sporting a shabby beard.

"Definitely positive because I clearly remember our long discussion about the evils of war." Chatterbox straightened up. "Two days ago he was healthy as a bull. Now he's dead and bloated from this mysterious bacterium."

"Is this important?"

"Could be. Until discovering these bodies we didn't know how long the infectious process took. Now we have a dateline and that's pretty frightening. His decaying is progressing at a rapid speed." Chatterbox used his stick to pull back Manson's dirty shirt slimy with that creeping green substance." Tyler stepped back to escape the horrible smell of decaying infected flesh. "Now that I'm seeing its initial stages this tells me something. Their deaths have all the symptoms of radiation poisoning." He groaned. "I wished there was a dosimeter handy to confirm my suspicions."

"If it's radiation poisoning then what's all the mumbling about. Hell, man, these areas took nuclear strikes." Tyler lost interest after Chatterbox confirmed radiation poisoning was a problem they regularly encountered.

"No, that was only the foundation for these deaths. Take a closer look. Manson has all of the classic symptoms contributed to radiation exposure. Loss of hair is our first clue. Then there's dried blood about his nose and chin that probably came from nose bleeds, another sign of radiation dosages."

"All right, that's enough. We have established these bloated bodies died from radiation exposure. That's nothing new around here. Let's get the hell out of here before we're caught by the Russians."

Chatterbox impatiently held his hand up. "Hold on. There's something else not connected with radiation exposure." With the stick he gently touched some gross burns on the face and arms. "Have you ever seen this type of burn? No, well I have in medical educational films."

Tyler gave him a curt look.

"What do you know about the Vietnam War?"

"Not that much. I was too young to enlist, but my uncle fought over there."

"What did he do?"

"I don't know for sure, but I think it had something to do with helicopters. As a young kid I remember him talking about a ranch or whatever."

Chatterbox frowned. "Was it Operation Ranch Hand?"

"It sounds familiar. But can't we talk about this while going back?" Tyler suggested. "This isn't a good place to hold a medical lecture, Bro."

Minutes later the Shoets were rapidly driving back to their base. "The bloated bodies have all the signs of radiation. In the past when we found them radiation burns and dried up bleeding had covered the new sign." Chatterbox quit talking when passing where their evidence of landing Russians was found. "Some of his boils were about the size of silver dollars. The skin's membrane became awfully thin and that's what allowed the greenish pus to seep out. I remember that medical class only too well. Most of us students nearly puked. We were watching documentary films on American defoliating agents used in Vietnam. Actually the formulas were created to use against the Japanese during World War II. According to those films there were over 1200 different compounds. In Vietnam they were narrowed down to four agents. One was shipped in 55 gallon drums marked with an orange stripe. That's how the name Agent Orange came about."

Tyler grimaced. "I heard old timers talk about Agent Orange and supposedly it was nasty stuff."

"Agent Orange was our all-purpose defoliant during that war. One of its elements was arsenic agents."

Tyler sat quietly while Chatterbox briefed him. Remembering Manson's body covered with those festering green boils was enough to gag him. Over the last few months Tyler had burned some pretty badly decomposed bodies, but these were the worst he had seen. After Chatterbox asked how his uncle had died, Tyler was silent for a moment then said it took three years before his uncle painfully died.

"Sounds as if your uncle died after being extensively exposed to arsenic acids. There was one defoliant agent used in Vietnam whose main element was arsenic. It was called Agent Blue. Its solution of cacodylic acid and 54% arsenic acid made a horrible defoliant."

"How does all of this come together? I once read those agents were safely stored away in a secret site."

"I don't know. None of this makes sense. Maybe that major back at base can explain this."

Not far from Gaviota the Shoets turned onto a Southern Pacific surface road running along the shore. Tyler thoughtfully sat in his lead car bumping over the rough road wasted by crashing waters coming in at high tide. This new development bothered him. He was certain whatever Chatterbox had stumbled across wouldn't benefit Ten Delta. The sergeant didn't like the stormy looks of those dark rolling clouds barely seen through the sooty atmosphere. They needed rain real soon, but Lieutenant Blackmore said as long as those debris layers stayed in the air there would be no rain. What they needed was a miraculous break, but lately divine intervention was avoiding the battling United States. Then suddenly he sat up when hearing something that wasn't friendly.

"Into that gully!" he shouted at the driver.

As the first Shoet drove into a deep gully alongside the road the second one obediently followed. Jumping out before the vehicle stopped Tyler was yelling at his marines to throw camouflage netting over the cars. After lots of practicing this tactic was quickly done. For all practical purposes the two vehicles became invisible. The marines were dismounted with readied weapons. Remaining beneath the light netting they patiently waited for whatever Sergeant Tyler had heard.

Tyler didn't say anything while suspiciously looking up at the skies. His face was strained from worrying. Dressed in camouflages the soldier wore two bandoliers with ammo packs for his Sig 550 Swiss assault rifle. This became a favorite at Ten Delta because its trigger guard when folded to the side allowed its gunner to fire with gloves on. Down his back on its canvas strap hung a Lthaca Stakeout 2 gauge shotgun. Squatting some feet away Chatterbox thoughtfully watched the master sergeant. Tyler was a mean mother in battle. Strapped to his leg was an ugly double-edged four inch knife. Chatterbox looked through the thin netting at those black clouds rolling like hundreds of huge basketballs. God, it had been too long since he made a few baskets with friends. Then Chatterbox sadly realized his friends were all dead.

"There at eight o'clock approximately five hundred altitude." Tyler shouted.

Following his directions it was easy to see the Soviet Kamov helicopter following the coast line toward Santa Barbara. The twin turbine aircraft was obviously searching the coastal regions. Tyler knew it was foolish to engage it. The chopper's four-barrel Gatling gun would easily take them out. After the NATO codenamed Helix B faded from sight, Tyler cautiously waited another twenty minutes before ordering his armored cars back on the road. This was the first time they had spotted a Soviet helicopter and that wasn't good.

"That's another clue the Russians have arrived." Chatterbox sarcastically warned.

*   *   *

When the message was delivered Mikhail hesitated to open it. The duty radioman smartly saluted then quickly left the commissar's cabin. The smell of vodka was very strong both in the room and on Mikhail's body. The coded message required a manual for deciphering, but it was several minutes before the political officer unlocked his bulkhead safe. The ship was encountering rougher than normal waters on its way back to Isla Vista. After that storm at Santa Barbara, Mikhail doubted if he would see another storm as bad as that one. By now his stomach was getting used to the ship's tossing and pitching. Sitting on his bunk he slowly deciphered the short message.

When his spies didn't show up at Santa Barbara the commissar knew something had gone wrong. Sometimes when facing serious problems he sought Captain Voronov's advice. Not because he was to be trusted, but because Karl Voronov would do everything in his power to protect his ship and crew. Calling the bridge he instructed the captain to join him in the stateroom.

The knocking senior captain entered only when summoned. After motioning for him to sit, the commissar studied the weary commanding officer while handing over a glass of vodka. "I just received this message from the admiral." While Karl read the decoded communication Mikhail paced the pitching deck as the ship plunged through rough waters. After the message was handed back he frowned. "For the last five months our ships in the Gulf managed to keep the American Navy blockaded in their ports. But this you already know. But what you don't know are recent intercepted messages suggests the ships are planning to break out." The worried political officer stopped pacing. "These aren't rumors. Reliable information indicates they will do so within the next few days and that must not happen. This will be our final opportunity to smash the bothersome American Navy. Because of this the admiral was instructed to move forward our plans to move into the Gulf. The ships we have discreetly assembled over time will be here sometime tomorrow afternoon."

"What about Ten Delta," Karl questioned. "Are they to be bypassed?"

"No. Central High Command feels the radar station must be eliminated least it becomes a rallying point for the Americans. We are to waste all military installations. That includes the Army's 365th Regiment known to be operating in this area."

Karl was shocked. "I fully understand destroying Ten Delta because they're a combatant unit. But why attack the 365th? They're a medical group relocating displaced citizens to their Mid Western states."

Mikhail suspiciously stared at the captain. "You find displeasure at killing the 365th. Why is this?"

"Because 365th is a noncombatant unit without tanks or artillery. All they operate are trucks and ambulances. I'm unaware of any incident where our military has interfered with such missions. Did Central Command give thought if we attack this group, the Americans may treat our own noncombatant commands with the same hostility?"

"The matter is considered closed, captain. As Russian officers we're expected to obey our orders and not question them." Forcing a faint smile he said. "The matter is closed. Now let us discuss other issues. Do you have any news on that missing module?"

"It's believed the machine was lost during the storm."

"Any possibility Ten Delta shot it down?"

"It would only be a remote chance."

*   *   *

After the incoming helicopter radioed for instructions, James reluctantly gave permission for its landing. If there were Russian agents in the Gaviota area they would now know Ten Delta's location. After leaving CIC in charge of a husky black sergeant named Richards, James walked to the hanger. Accompanied by the chief petty officer Savannah walked to the busy hanger. By the time they reached it a large door had slipped open allowing a small tractor to pull the large chopper inside. The iron door closed with a loud thump. All of this required little over ten minutes.

Earl Craver smiled his best when approaching James. He was handsome with rugged features rivaling that of a professional football linebacker. Gray eyes the color of gun metal gleamed with a faint cold indifference as he thoughtfully appraised the well organized hanger. Noting how this man in the expensive tailored gray suit walked with bold confidence James wasn't impressed.

Extending his hand the man greeted in a pleasant voice. "Earl Craver, Lieutenant Blackmore." He handed a sealed envelope to the distrustful officer. "My secret orders from the President, sir."

James regarded this calm mannered man before opening a colored envelope having the new White House logo embossed across it front. He slowly read the orders before handing them to Timothy. Savannah standing several feet away observed this meeting with concealed reservations. "Welcome to Ten Delta, Mr. Craver. Though presently we're involved with a series of disturbing issues, Ten Delta will do everything possible to assist." He gestured at the chief. "May I present my executive officer, Chief Petty Officer Timothy Hickman. Major Davidson recently arrived from Outer Perimeter Command at Yuma." James curiously looked at Craver's helicopter. "Chief Hickman will show you to your quarters. After you're settled in we shall discuss your needs."

"I prefer to discuss those needs now."

"I'm afraid that isn't possible. I have a patrol coming in that requires debriefing. And there's a Russian destroyer off coast we need to find. And to make matters worse, we discovered a Soviet marine unit is covertly operating in our district. All of these I must attend to." Giving the annoyed civilian a loose salute he walked away.

Savannah smiled to herself. That was probably the first time Earl Caver was ever denied a request. While leaving the hanger she saw the lieutenant stopping at the specially equipped large chopper. After twice circling the machine with admiration, James patted the fuselage with the same loving care a lover showed his girl friend.

A tall lanky light complexioned man stepped from the chopper and when observing James' interest came over. "Lewis Lindsay United States Air Force." He held out his hand in a warm gesture. "A real beau, isn't she?"

"That she is, captain," James while shaking his hand. Afterwards running his hand over a white weapons' pod he muttered. "God, she is something else."

"There's not another one in the entire Air Force." Lewis boasted with a wide smile. "She's mean as a dog in heat, aggressive as hell in the air, and armed to the teeth." He patted the rocket pods attached to the side.

James was quiet for a moment. "I assume this flight wasn't an impulse?"

"No, it has been six months in planning."

"And Craver is the cog?"

"He definitely is." When James started to further his questioning Lewis held his hand up. "Mr. Craver will brief you later. I'm just the driver."

"Then perhaps you can tell me why you flew that wandering course." James' voice became harsh. "That was really stupid, captain. You let every damned spy in this area know you were coming. And to boot probably told them where Ten Delta was located. We have successfully kept Ten Delta's base a secret for months."

"I'm sorry about that. But Mr. Craver wanted a sightseeing tour before coming here."

"He's an asshole." James mumbled.

The tall captain was hard to evaluate, but James tried. Those dark blue eyes remained unfriendly until he got to know a person. His side arm worn in a shoulder holster remained unbuckle for quick handling. Captain Lindsay reminded James of those gunfighters back during the frontier days. As they walked around the chopper James quickly found the man easy to like. His three man crew after checking their aircraft headed for the cafeteria.

Lewis suddenly stopped and seriously looked at James. "Take some advice, lieutenant. Treat that man with kid gloves. Humor him. He can be a regular asshole if things don't go his way." Patting the fuselage the pilot continued. "He gets whatever fascinates him. It's that simple. Take this Chinook for instance. Attack squadrons along the Canadian frontier would give their balls to have this baby. But they'll never touch it. He told the manufacturing company what he wanted and they worked overtime to build the sweetheart. And this was done in a time when everything built goes straight to the battlefronts." He exhaled. The officer was listening, but he wasn't listening. The pilot knew right then that James Blackmore would have to learn the hard way how to work with Earl Craver.

"His type is what loses battles." James growled.

Lewis was offended. "This is the first time you two have met and already you formed an opinion. That's not really fair. I can't tell you how to deal with Mr. Craver, that's your problem and not mind. But I can tell you Earl Craver can be a friend if you need one. Or he can be your worse nightmare." After a short silence he thoughtfully looked about the hanger. "So what do you have in terms of airborne babies?"

"I have two Apaches and an old Chinook." As a last thought James said. "Ours is the CH-47D model 114 manufactured in 1979."

Rubbing his fuselage Lewis boasted. "This one has considerable advantages over yours. Powered by fifth generation T55-L-712 engines with an emergency rating of 6700 shp, my sweetheart can kick serious ass." He curiously watched the large iron door slowly rolling up. "She has improved avionics, bulletproof windshields, and greater service ceiling of 25,000 feet."

James exclaimed. "How the hell do you do that?"

"She was designed that way. But what really scares the shit out of unfriendly assholes is her firepower. I have three General Electric XM 214 automatic guns capable of firing 2500 rounds of 5.56mm short bursts with muzzle velocity of 990mm. There are ten Hellfire anti-tank missiles under her belly. My gunners can fire eighty-six 2.75 inch rockets from those special pods."

A marine ran up and excitedly reported. "Sergeant Tyler's patrol is entering the compound."

"Good," James anxiously replied. Excusing himself the lieutenant hurried toward the hanger door now opened. Lewis studied his emotions suspecting there was more to this relationship between this officer and Sergeant Tyler. After Lewis joined him he said. "Tyler's patrol was two hours overdue."

CHAPTER ELEVEN

The armored vehicles pulling into the hanger were Israeli Shoets. Lewis had seen them in action along the Canadian borders and they were nasty. When the cars stopped a husky black man stepped from the lead one and waited until his men were assembled in formation. Though Lewis couldn't hear what he was telling the marines it brought smiles to their weary faces. After that the tired marines hurried to the showers and hot chow. Tyler walked over and saluted. The captain suspected this formality was for his benefit.

"Rough patrol," James asked.

"Pretty much so, but we got pass El Capitan before running into another damned storm. We saw Russian armored vehicles but after the storm passed they were gone." Tyler said. "We were unable to pick up their tracks before your recall was received."

"What about the destroyer?"

"We didn't see it, but the bastard is out there." Tyler thoughtfully replied. "We saw a low flying Russian helicopter on our way back. But I don't think they saw us before we hid in a gully until they faded from sight."

"How about some coffee before you shower. I need to ask some questions." While walking to the mess hall they kept talking. "Anything else new out there?" James asked. Lewis quietly listened as Tyler reported the situation at the San Augustin memorial. This brought a deep frown to the lieutenant's face.

"Oh yeah, there was something else. I think Chatterbox has a hand on what's causing those bloated bodies."

"How so?"

"Chatterbox better explain it. I didn't follow his explanations."

Walking through the main corridor Lewis smelled baking pastries. Occasionally he softly whistled when recognizing old oil paintings on the walls. James explained they were removed from the ruins of expensive homes in Santa Barbara then abruptly dropped the subject. The captain later learned Ten Delta salvaged most of their requirements. Walking to the lieutenant's reserved table they sat after the cook eagerly brought over a platter of hot pastries and coffee.

"You run a tight organization out here," Lewis praised.

James grinned. "That's how we survive, captain." He drank coffee that was thick as motor oil and just about as tasty. After coming into the mess hall Chatterbox was motioned over to their table. "Grab a cup and sit." Looking at Lewis he said. "This is Chatterbox, our medical doctor." Turning back to the staff sergeant he asked. "So what's this about you linking the bacteria?"

"We may have big trouble if I'm right. First off, the bloated bodies are infected from exposure to radiation which isn't uncommon along this coast because of those nuclear explosions. I suspect this laid the foundation where our greenish slime festered. Then another agent filtered into their bodies." He stopped talking when Earl Craver walked over, thoughtfully regarded each man, and then sat.

"And you are?" Earl asked Chatterbox.

"Staff Sergeant Dennis Carter, United States Marines." Chatterbox was respectful, but immediately on the defensive because of Earl's curtness.

"Are you a doctor?"

"Third year med student before the war broke out."

There was a short silence before Earl said. "Very well, please continue." ·

Chatterbox looked at James who merely nodded. "On our way back we detoured to that campground above the Refugio State Beach. Do you remember talking with an old man named Barnes? He was pretty hostile about this war."

"Yeah, didn't he retire from Vandenberg some years ago?"

"That's the same man." The Negro leaned back in his chair feeling the exhaustion of their patrol creeping over his frame. The coffee tasted bad as usual, but his pastry was good. Of course the blueberries were from a can after fresh fruit became rare. "I remembered something he once mentioned. Barnes was an army colonel during the Vietnam War from middle 1966 through 1968. He flew specially converted Hueys assigned to Operation Ranch Hand. After leaving the Army he worked on the Vandenberg Air Base until his retirement."

"What's this got to do with your theory?" Earl suspiciously asked.

"Because Barnes recognized what I saw, but didn't know what to do with the information." Chatterbox angrily wondered who the hell this civilian was.

Earl frowned. "Let's cut the chase and get down to the bottom line. What's Ranch Hand got to do with your accusation?" When James started to interrupt he waved him into silence.

"We have either Agent Orange or Agent Blue on the loose."

"That's impossible." Earl sharply denied. "Agent Blue was rarely used and far as I know very little of it was left after the war." He gave the browned skinned marine a bitter look.

Chatterbox immediately founded a dislike for this man dressed in camouflages and shiny combat boots. Earl looked like a desk jockey but not a combat ready soldier. When looking James' way he saw the lieutenant was quietly listening to the discussion. "We have had radiation poisoning in this region since this war began."

He scowled. "But that comes with working a nuclear wasteland. We have areas along this coast that will be radioactively hot for the next 28,000 years." His voice became defensively hostile. "I didn't say 28 years, sir, but 28,000 years. Rather awesome to think, isn't it? We really did it this time. Today radiation poisoning is becoming as common as the common cold. And that's downright pathetic."

James interrupted Earl. "Why do you think Agent Blue is responsible?"

"The last five bodies we found gave me an opportunity to run some blood tests. There were high readings of arsenic and cacodylic acids. Agent Blue was made up of 54% arsenic acid with weaker compounds of cacodylic acid."

"That's hardly a reason to declare these agents are present." Earl defiantly argued.

"When all physical symptoms of Agent Blue contact are present that's evidence enough that it's out there."

James asked. "What is this Operation Ranch Hand?"

Chatterbox spoke before Earl could. "During the Vietnam War, it was a military unit that sprayed hostile territory with biological agents. Agents Orange and Blue were two of their most common used chemicals. Being very unpredictable these nasty agents later caused widespread suffering among our own troops exposed to them."

"Oh," James somberly mumbled. Turning to Earl he curtly asked. "Why are you arguing against their presence?" He paused then asked. "Is this why you're here?"

The presidential envoy suddenly became soberly defensive. "Actually, it has nothing to do with my presence. Please accept my sincere apology, Sergeant Carter, but I was startled to hear your explanation." He forced a weak smile that wasn't accepted by the angry marine.

"So is this stuff stored in California?"

"No. I vaguely remember a classified document about storages of biological chemicals on government facilities in Utah and Nevada. Nothing I remember referred to Californian storages. In fact, if I remember correctly there was Californian legislation outlawing such storages."

A duty orderly came into the dining area and informed James his presence was required in CIC on the double. While he was gone Chatterbox was questioned by Earl while Lewis quietly sat at the table. After Savannah joined them he remembered seeing her in the capital several times.

"How many bloated bodies have you found?" Earl asked.

"There's no way of telling. Our primary problem is this bacterium grows after radiation poisoning has infected the corpse for several days. That's why we have burned bloated bodies without seeing the green slime. Today was my first opportunity to see the infection in its initial stages. Knowing how long those bodies have been dead confirmed how rapidly this bacterium consumes flesh."

Earl looked at Savannah before suspiciously asking. "What do you think of Sergeant Carter's supposition?"

"The unanswered question remains . . . has our military used Agents Orange and Blue along this coast?"

"No, they haven't."

"What about the Soviets?"

"Not to my knowledge?"

"If they used it on their own people," Chatterbox argued. "Why wouldn't they use on us?"

Earl thought over the question. "Biological warfare is something you can't hide. If it was used we would have known about it. It's that simple. If the sergeant's suspicions are right there has to be another explanation why these people are being infected."

*　　*　　*

Minutes later James rejoined them at the table. His troubled expression warned Sergeant Tyler and Chatterbox another negative development had slammed Ten Delta. Timothy had left to check on the two Shoets from Tyler's patrol, but came back just before James returned. Savannah disturbed by Chatterbox's supposition privately concealed her fears another plague was maturing.

Thoughtfully looking at Timothy, James said. "After checking on Five Bravo, Thomas confirmed our suspicions. The radar site was burned and its personnel slaughtered."

"How about the other stations," the chief asked.

"The same thing happened to the other four sites. Radar equipment was smashed and its marines killed. According to the 365th the hostiles not bothering with prisoners knifed the survivors." James paused then bitterly continued. "At each site our American colors was thrown to the ground then pissed on. That was their final contemptuous regard for our stations."

Earl frowned. "That's interesting." After James glared at him he thoughtfully explained. "There's a KGB colonel named Mikhail Karsavin who always orders a defeated unit's colors urinated on. The knifing is done for two reasons. One is to show his contempt for their struggle. Second is shooting survivors uses valuable munitions. The last I heard that political commissar was with their armies along the frontier."

"You sound as if his presence is important?" Timothy dubiously asked.

Earl nodded. "It can be politically. Colonel Karsavin is very close to Premier Kossier. Our naval intelligence hasn't been unable to identify the ships or how many are in that task force. But if Karsavin is with them that means Kossier is sending his best reserves. This added strength with what they already have in the Gulf will tip the balances in their favor." The envoy was disturbingly quiet for a few moments. "That must not happen. Few people know how weak our naval forces are and even a slight change in power balances may hasten our defeat."

James frowned. "I would like to see one favorable thing happening in this region." he groaned.

"One problem may have been solved by Sergeant Carter's discovery. Now that we know what may be causing these infections we have something to work with.

I'll notify St. Louis and see if they can determine where these biological agents were illegally stored in California. Then maybe we can find those hidden storage sites and plug the leakages. What actions have you taken in regards to closing the gaps caused by those radar station losses?"

"I requested Thomas to station his men closer to Ten Delta. At the moment there's little we can do."

Earl somberly looked at each person at the table. "I know you're working with seriously limited resources. There's nothing I can do to rectify that. All the way across our military logistics board, we're short on everything from uniforms to munitions. We were hit hard during those first eight months of this war. Our industrial sector was seriously disrupted but the situation is improving. Changes are coming not only in the States but with our Allies. Countries are slowly staggering to their feet after devastating damages. However, all of this will be wasted if the Soviets destroy our Navy." He looked at their solemn expressions. "That's why we must give our military a breathing space even if only for several days. The sword is along this coast. Now you're the hope for our battered country. But unfortunately, St. Louis can not help you. Our resources are stretched thin everywhere. Somehow with the guidance of God you must interrupt that task force's progress."

"Ten Delta will try," James dubiously promised. "But we're small and unprepared."

Earl grinned. "That may be so. But the Bible boasts how David armed with a slingshot still killed the giant with a single stone."

James nervously chuckled. "I don't think Ten Delta has a stone large enough to do the job."

"Why are you here?" Timothy curiously asked.

The envoy shook his head. "I'm on another mission that's equally crucial for mankind's survival. Perhaps, it's time we discussed my mission. Do you have a room private enough to discuss a very sensitive operation?"

"We have a room used for conferences."

"That'll have to do. I prefer Major Davidson, Sergeant Carter, Chief Hickman, Sergeant Tyler, my aide Captain Lindsay, and you attend. Afterwards you can brief your men."

Another storm rumbled down the coast like a destructive hand trying to finish what Russian missiles and bombs failed to accomplish. Cushioned by Ten Delta's subterranean ceiling the loose crashing debris swirling around above wasn't heard. Gaviota was still not a place to be without protection. Further inland the wrath wasn't so bad. On this evening California wasn't a friendly State.

*   *   *

The war room as it was called was a large sparsely furnished chamber formerly used by Johnson and Johnson for oil storage. No matter what they did that faint odor of motor oil lingered. That was why the room was used only for conferences.

Maps of various Californian regions were mounted on the light blue walls. In the middle was a large world map. Red circled zones warned they were radioactive and inhabitable. Green specified that region was suitable for limited occupation. Blue circles stressed no prolonged occupation due to health dangers. Those nations with no lines were safe for unlimited residence, but they were few in number. Timothy and Tyler after reading some captured documents looked up. Their expressions were not encouraging. Earl sat at the table's end displeased with James' late entry. A silver coffee carafe sat on the table surrounded by China cups. Before sitting James casually poured a cup. Timothy knew this was the lieutenant's way of telling the envoy to stop his ordering.

"Very well," Earl sourly announced. "Now that everybody is accounted for I request armed guards be posted outside."

"No guards." James sternly argued.

"This is a classified meeting."

"So it is. But nobody will interrupt us. My staff knows if that door is closed a meeting is going on." James replied in an unfriendly manner. "So with that out of the way, what do you have for us?"

It was a moment before Earl spoke after a stern mood settled over him. "Very well. I would like to state this mission was hastily put together so there may be gaps. I'm relying on your individual expertise to correct those mistakes." Reaching into his pocket he ceremoniously withdrew a white envelope and handed it to James. The lieutenant slowly read it with a deepening frown. Earl waited a respectful time before continuing. "As the letter states, this mission is fully sanctioned by the President of the United States." He took the letter and returned it to his pocket. "First off, Lieutenant Blackmore, I need to know your personnel roster and their specialized fields."

It was a few moments before James slowly nodded. "We have fifty-six personnel attached to Ten Delta. Yesterday we lost one man due to an accident. Of that number only Chief Hickman and I are Navy." Staring Earl straight in the eyes he continued in a cold calm voice. "There are 5 fire teams of 4 men each, 2 fully qualified corpsmen, 4 combat intelligence specialists, 1 weapons squad of five men, 3 helicopter crews of 6 men, 4 communications/radio operators, 4 reconnaissance sergeants, 4 driver/mechanics, and 5 men specializing in demolition, artillery, and underwater related fields." He curiously studied Earl while speaking. "We're a highly specialized strike force detachment and that's how we survive."

Earl curtly asked. "Can you personally guarantee they'll follow orders without question?"

James didn't answer at first while debating whether to kick this pompous ass' butt or not. Ten Delta was a tight clannish group working a near deserted nuclear wasteland and he was questioning their loyalty. Timothy sighed softly and gave Tyler a quick glance. They both knew the envoy just made another mistake with the tally mentally kept by their hostile commanding officer. "Of course they're loyal." James growled.

The chief petty officer didn't comment about James' unusually harsh disposition. His interest was on this presumptuous envoy from St, Louis who came into their territory issuing orders as if he commanded the unit. There was another thing Timothy quietly observed about Earl. He didn't like Outer Perimeter Commands. This didn't surprise the executive officer. Ever since Outer Perimeter East Coast disgracefully shunned their obligations senior military commands considered the Outer Perimeter Commands as staffed with thugs and misfits.

"Chief, when you came to Ten Delta," Earl was losing patience with the sour mannered lieutenant and his bizarre group of marines. "What were the average temperatures?"

"Sixty degrees or so," Timothy said with a shrug of his shoulders.

"What about now?"

"Average day temps are in the low forties while night ranges may drop to 30 or so."

He thought of what it looked like outside. Prior to this meeting the chief went outside to check on their tower repairs. What he saw was disturbing. Their weather was going to be pretty bad after those storms passed. That is if they ever passed. Already the waves were crashing ashore and ramming their ruins' furthermost point near the shore. Churning whitish foam pounding across the rocks and debris was a mess. Some waves crested at ten feet and higher. Black clouds were everywhere. Not only were they dark and ugly, but there was something scary about these weather conditions. And that lightning, the chief pondered, was strange. It was more like a gigantic fireworks show high above the earth.

"Would you explain what's causing these drastic changes?" Earl asked.

Timothy thought about it for a moment. "Polluted cloud layers have seriously restricted sunlight from filtering through."

"That's close enough," Earl praised with a strained smile. Walking to the world map he then faced the others.

"Our globe is facing devastating violence caused by the ongoing warfare. But that isn't the worse challenge mankind is facing." He looked at those colored circles knowing what they represented. "Those colors have become our greatest challenge that we as an endangered species cannot afford to lose. Tons of floating debris and soot has deposited above the earth. There are millions of fires throughout the world that are raging out of control. This has continued for months and there's no end in a foreseeable future." He gave them a scant look before running his hand over the map's surface. "These conditions prompting prolonged hazy grayness are warning us Mother Nature is crashing down her heavy hand. There are regions normally having hot temps that are underway drastic changes. Radiation filtering into those layers are restricting vital communications needed during wartime." Returning to the table he sat. "While flying here I was startled at your widespread destruction. Ocean travel now limited to a few miles off the coast is suicidal further out."

"We don't get too much news down here." Tyler said. "So how far do these conditions spread out?"

Earl grinned. "That's a very good question, sergeant. Actually the worse place on earth is the North Atlantic. Traditionally that sector is usually bad. Strangely enough those conditions haven't yet reached the Gulf of Mexico. As for South America we don't know what exists there. Communications with that continent has been non existence since the war started. We do know Europe is fighting terrible conditions brought on by both the war and climate." His face was dark and worried.

"What's this got to do with your mission?" James asked.

"That is my mission, lieutenant. What do you think is earth's most urgent need?"

"Rain."

"And that's right. Even our strongest critics agree rain is desperately needed. It will wash clean the air and return much needed sunlight. Yes, gentlemen, rainfall is urgently required within a short order. But we can't afford to wait until the skies cleanse themselves. That may be too late for mankind. So it's up to us to introduce rain." Earl paused and smiled. "My mission is to jump start nature by causing it to rain."

"And how do you plan to do that?"

"We'll going to attempt a high tech version of the old seeding procedure to make rain. Basically, instead of using aircraft to spray the clouds we'll use rockets to explode the chemicals high above earth. That's where the largest concentration of polluted layers is found."

"I don't understand your reasoning," James stubbornly argued. "How will one rocket achieve this seeding?"

Earl found time to smile. "There won't be one seeding, lieutenant, but several well coordinated explosions. Hopefully, they'll start a global chain reaction causing rain."

"Providing you can achieve this," Tyler skeptically asked. "Where will you find the rockets? Obviously, you're talking about long range missiles, but weren't they used up during the first months of war."

"The French, British, Israelis, and Germans have such rockets. As for my part in this plan, we suspect one such rocket is located on the Vandenberg Air Force Base."

"That base was torn to shreds by Soviet missiles." James curtly informed.

"The rocket I'm looking is located deep underground."

"Do you know where it is?"

"No, but your friend does. He worked on specialized rocket guidance systems." After James and Timothy exchanged puzzled looks Earl calmly replied. "His name is Daniel Barnes."

Tyler muttered. "I never knew what he did, but never thought he was a scientist."

Earl smiled. "People can surprise you." After a brief pause he turned to James. "I would appreciate it if you brought Mr. Barnes to Ten Delta for safe keeping. He's become an important cog in a crucial mission."

"Anything else you need?" the lieutenant skeptically asked.

"Yes, before firing there are several issues requiring solutions." Even before he continued James knew his requests wouldn't be well accepted. "Of course, if the Russians discovered our plans they would try and stop us. A rocket like that in their hands would be used to further their war. While we're using it for atmospheric seeding, the communists would attach a nuclear warhead and probably fire it at St. Louis. Because of that possibility it's urgent we cripple the Russian presence in this part of the globe."

"And how do you expect to do that?"

Earl grinned. "That's a very good question. As you know the nearest communist stronghold is off British Columbia. That base is particularly important to the Russian ships because of their oil storage tanks. That's our first consideration, Lieutenant Blackmore. If we eliminated their source of fuel it would have to be shipped by tanker from Cordova, Alaska. Weather conditions make that a long dangerous sea route. With only one tanker available it would take weeks to restore the necessary fuel. It would be weeks before their task force could assume operations in the Gulf. Anything we can do to hinder those ships is a blessing for our battered Navy in the Gulf."

"You're asking the impossible." James bluntly declared. But Savannah caught the faint hint James wanted a crack at the job, impossible or not.

"Our troops along the frontier are fighting a war thought to be impossible, but they're holding on." Earl sternly said. "So what we need to do on this coast is pull off an impossible objective. This would give them a breather and at the same time give the nation's deflated morale a much needed boost."

"What support can we rely on?"

"Not much physically. Central Intelligence has a loose network of agents scattered throughout that region. For these last few months Canadian and British commandoes have fought a harassing front against the communists. Though few in numbers they will provide hard core intelligence, but little physical assistance."

The lieutenant's arrogance was gone. "So what are the other issues?"

"We need to cripple the KONSTANTANTINOVICH's participation in their plans."

"That's a mighty big order."

The envoy smiled. "I'm counting on you to come up with some clever plan. After all you have surprise on your side."

James uneasily chuckled. "It better be lots of surprise." With that said both Lewis and Earl knew the lieutenant was drawn into their plans.

"All right, let's get cracking on this plot of yours." James looked at Tyler. "Go and bring in Barnes. We need intelligence on that ship so I'll send Roscoe out." Looking back at Earl he asked. "What information do you have on the Russian base?"

"Lewis will provide that data."

"What can I do?" Savannah asked.

James was thoughtful for a moment. "What about tracking down storage sites for those biological agents? If the stuff was stored around here then we need to know where. Blocking that source may stop the green slime's spread." He shrugged. "Am I right?"

"It should."

James thoughtfully sat back in the chair. "What timeframe are we looking at?"

"According to our best estimates that base must be out of commission within the next 48 hours." When James gave Earl a nasty surprise look he merely shrugged his shoulders.

CHAPTER TWELVE

After dawn's approach activity erupted aboard the KONSTANTANTINOVICH as she crept from her Isla Vista anchorage. The waters were choppy though nothing like that last storm's fury. Weary of staying on the bridge Mikhail went to his cabin and after locking the door snatched his vodka bottle and flopped on the bunk. Though wading through questionable waters with the arrogant Captain Voronov, Mikhail's opinion of the ship as a whole stunk. This was going to be another long cold day. There was much work to be done. When the admiral arrived he must have his charges in order. The commissar knowing some of those shipboard damages were his fault would shift the blame. Because the eskadrenny minonosets' skipper skirted the Party's doctrines demanding total obedience, he was a prime candidate for blaming. Finishing two glasses of vodka the political officer stumbled from his bunk. He didn't realized how much time he had spent in the stateroom. The destroyer was already cruising up the coast.

On the bridge Mikhail found it difficult to stand. His intoxication was noted by everybody except him. Foul weather was the order for that day. Hostility was the best description. It was like his feelings for Captain Voronov. Once entering the nerve center all talking ceased as they glared at him with silent accusations. After scowling at them the seamen quickly went back to their duties. The captain sat in his chair contemptuously regarding the drunkard. As political officer Mikhail was supposed to be a shining example of the Party's ideals. But that wasn't so with this colonel. The ship's company snickered behind his back because of his vodka addiction. Mikhail Karsavin was everything the crew enthusiastically hated.

"What's the progress of your repairs?" Mikhail asked Karl.

The skipper unconsciously moved his head back when the man's foul breathing slapped his senses. "They're about 30% completion."

Feeling dizzy the colonel harshly demanded. "Why is this?"

"My engineers can only repair certain tasks while we're underway."

Mikhail suppressed his fury while stumbling out on the open bridge wing. He stared at the coastline one mile off her starboard side. Why didn't these people admit defeat? They were repeatedly routed on their battlefields and little was left of their once proud fleets of ultra-modern warships. Their massive air force was nearly eradicated. Her armies formerly the demon in Moscow's eyes was on the verge of annihilation. Although her cities lay in ruins the stupid people refused to strike their colors.

When the captain joined him on the wing Mikhail chose to look away. "The only way KONSTANTANTINOVICH's repairs can be properly completed, Comrade Colonel, is to stay at anchorage for another day. With these rough motions delicate welding and soldering can not be made."

"The ships are on their way." he stubbornly argued.

"Yes, so you have said. But if our repairs aren't completed this ship won't be seaworthy for the Gulf insertion." The cold winds slapped his face like a natural massage and it felt good. "My men are loyal to the Motherland, Comrade Colonel, but you have to give them a fighting chance. With their ship crippled they won't have an opportunity to fight in the upcoming battles."

Mikhail silently watched the ship plowing through those tossing waves like a cork. He briefly looked at Palo Alto Hill majestically rising 1394 feet above sea level. Its scorched slopes overlooked many arroyos emptying into a frenzy ocean. It was very depressing knowing that sight was duplicated many times in Russia. Mikhail felt his ruffled emotions calming down. What was frightening was how those mountain fires were destroying everything in their blazing paths.

"Captain, send the helicopter up for reconnaissance. Perhaps, they'll achieve what we have failed to." Mikhail curtly ordered.

*   *   *

When James walked into the hanger he found Timothy and Tyler rushing about like brooding mothers. The Shoets was idling while marines clothed in heavy winter clothing climbed through the rear door. Standing nearby Lewis and his crew quietly watched this activity. The armored car manufactured in Tel Aviv was heavily armed with extra weapons. Two 12.7mm machine guns were mounted atop the enclosed cab. Corporal Thorton was leaning over the carrier's cab adjusting their tripods. Sensing James was approaching he gave a snappy salute then went back fixing his guns the way he wanted. On each side were 7.62mm guns pointing to their flanks. The squad leader Sergeant Roscoe climbed down after bolting down another grenade launcher.

Peeking into the rear door Roscoe asked. "How many smoke grenades are in those racks?" There was a muffled reply from inside. "Sixteen should be sufficient." Turning to James he smiled. "We're ready to depart."

"Are you certain five men are enough?"

The black sergeant grinned. "Yeah, they'll do. Anyhow I need extra room for munitions." He adjusted his ammo belt. "Tyler wants us to stop by the San Augustin War Memorial and pick up a toy the Russians left behind."

"What toy?"

"We were going to surprise you later, but Tyler found a Sparrow HAWK launcher with fifteen missiles there. Those bastards were sitting up an artillery base when scared off." He paused then added. "Fifteen HE blast fragmentation loads can cause some sore butts."

"What makes you think they haven't returned?"

Roscoe grinned. "If they're there we'll send them packing to their communist heaven."

After James turned to Tyler, the Shoets passed through the iron door. "I have a funny feeling about that patrol."

"Me too."

Walking to CIC James and Tyler were joined by Earl and his pilot. Once inside James studied the plastic plot board showing Roscoe's Zulu Patrol departure route. The Presidential envoy was quietly impressed how smoothly Ten Delta operated. He watched the second Shoets depart carrying the chief and Savannah. Because the campgrounds where Barnes resided were only a short distance away, the major asked to ride along. After issued weapons she hurriedly climbed aboard. James wanted Tyler in CIC because he knew what was going on beyond Gaviota better than anybody else. Needing electronic eyes their short ranged radar was activated. Over in the corner with an unfolded map Lewis and Chatterbox plotted their raid on the Soviet naval base.

*   *   *

Sergeant Roscoe made a straight line for the San Augustin Memorial where they hooked up the mobile rocket launcher. The Russians hadn't returned because the American flag still wildly flapped in the strong winds. After that his patrol cautiously made their way over the winding Highway 101. When it became too difficult for traveling because of abandoned cars they used the Southern Pacific surface road. The ugly weather conditions hadn't improved. Several times when the carrier stopped Roscoe climbed out to study the rolling terrain.

The sergeant momentarily was swept back into a time when this beach area was the place to watch sea gulls flying about. It was a beautiful place to spend carefree weekends away from the marines. He looked around when Ebenezer walked up.

"Thanks," the sergeant said when his buddy handed over a canteen filled with Dr. Pepper. Supplies of his favorite soda drink were awfully low. It was time for another salvaging trip. "How's the men after that damned bumpy ride? I think Smith deliberately found every hole in the road to hit."

"They're all right, I guess."

Ebenezer looked at the huge black sergeant at his side scanning the coast line with binoculars. He was a mean street fighter with small eyes resembling black marbles. Though they served together he really didn't know the man who kept his private life a secret.

Ebenezer glanced about. Everything around here was vaporized. Like venomous serpents gradually creeping down the mountains fires cast gloomy shadows refusing to be sequestered by man. Finding no threat on the coast, Roscoe cautiously walked the road made damp from salty mists drifting in from the crashing waves. Once he stopped and knelt. Seeing this Ebenezer walked over.

"Find something?" he asked.

"Treads made by Russian armored cars no more than a few hours old. They're heading down the coast."

"Maybe they're meeting that ship?"

"A strong maybe," Roscoe agreed. Looking toward the idling Shoets he yelled. "Is our short range scanner on?"

A voice from with the carrier shouted it was running hot and heavy.

"We're sitting ducks out here. Load up and let's get the hell out of here." Roscoe anxiously said.

Everybody cursed when the carrier rumbled over potholes and turned into ditches to get around rubble scattered about the road. Several angry marines told their driver to watch for the holes. He gave them the finger while crashing through another small crater. Once on smoother stretches of highway the Shoets made better time. Roscoe stood in the open back scanning for threats. He had an annoying gut feeling the Russians were out watching and waiting.

"Sergeant," yelled the radar operator. "We have an airborne contact bearing southeast at seven o'clock."

The small radar set had a range of five miles and was manufactured for the French armies in Africa. Rated unreliable by Yuma they were issued to Ten Delta. After tinkering with the electronics Roscoe extended their range by two miles. Roscoe yelled at the driver to stop and he quickly climbed down and scanned the skies for their contact. About that time the operator shouted the contact was heading their way. The sergeant anxiously looking about saw a gully running into the highway. Shouting at the driver to back the Shoets into it, Roscoe after climbing a small knoll flopped down on his stomach. From there he could see the highway and the contact when it appeared.

Only for a moment did Roscoe let his thoughts drop on the pain he carried. He truly loved his wife Christine. But right from the beginning her parents tried everything to stop their wedding. Christine was stubbornly determined to marry the man she loved and ignored their pleading. After being transferred to Cherry Point Marine Corps Facility, Roscoe worked hard at smoothing out his rough edges. His whole world involved the Corps and Christine. That Sunday while holding morning mustering his whole world came crashing down. One Soviet low yield nuclear missile targeted the Marine base. Base dependent housing was among those sectors totally devastated. After snapping his attention back on the road, he watched two Russian vehicles rapidly closing the one mile distance.

"Ebenezer," he shouted. "Bring your Stinger up here!"

After scrambling up the slope and dropping on his stomach, he looked in the direction Roscoe pointed.

"We have two BTR armored vehicles inbound." the sergeant reported. "Here's my plan. Those machines have added armored plating up front. So forget about that. Their weak points are the tires. Aim at the rear machine's front ones and the Stinger's impact should knock out the tires and hopefully flip her over. She's armed with a conical turret 14.5mm machine gun and another coaxial 7.62mm machine gun. We'll take care of their troop compartment's six marines when they escape. We have perhaps ten minutes before they're in range. Shoot straight and don't miss. It's important you first take out the rear machine." Roscoe then looked over his shoulder and yelled for another marine to scoot his ass up the hill. While waiting for his arrival Roscoe told Ebenezer. "That machine is fully amphibious so they're probably the ones coming ashore."

"Sergeant," a short brown skinned marine anxiously mumbled.

"See those machines down the road. Here's what I want you to do. Ebenezer will take out the rear machine. The first one will be close to the gully when this happens. Take your Stinger and disable the damned thing. While that is happening Smith will pull the Shoets onto the road and begin immediately firing. From here we'll provide gunfire when the Soviets abandon their machines." He studied the marine's anxious expression. "Got that? Fire straight and true then get out of the way as the Shoets leaves that gully. All of this has to be on the button. Got that?" After the man hurried back down the sergeant turned his attention on the approaching vehicles.

"Know anything about those damned things" he curiously asked his partner.

"Not really."

Roscoe studied the boat-shaped front with sloped sides for a moment. "They're from the eighties and nineties. Their low profile makes them a difficult target. From here I would say both machines needs overhauls because those gasoline engines are laying down too much smoke. But when driven by a skilled operator they become a damned mean mother in battle. That's why you got to take out that rear one real quick."

Ebenezer raised his shoulder fired missile and took careful aim while waiting for Roscoe's command to fire. He was getting nervous as the Russians came nearer. Then the sergeant yelled to fire. The passive IR homing guidance sent a solid-propellant shaft hurling through the air. Originally designed to take down low altitude, high speed aircraft, the Stinger also proved deadly on ground bound machinery. Its infra-red seeking missile tore into the Russian vehicle's side. There was a thunderous explosion that halted the machine then slowly flipped it over. Both men ducked as its front machine began firing at the knoll.

"Hit the dirt!" Roscoe screamed. "The bastards have radar!" The ground around him was kicking up as bullets whizzed into the knoll. Roscoe heard one marine yelled in pain when taking a shoulder wound.

As Roscoe had hoped the lead BTR rushed toward the knoll savagely firing its machines guns. At a given signal the marine down below armed with another

Stinger quickly rushed out and fired. Without waiting the black man spun around and ran like hell for the gully. In a near impossible shot the missile tore through a top mounted firing port. There was a secondary pause then another explosion rumbled along that shore. The blast tearing off the exit doors sent flames quickly engulfing the doomed machine letting no marines flee that machine. The second armored car though flipped over was fighting for its survival. Its frontal machine guns continued firing until munitions were depleted. Some Russian marines tried running from the rear door but was taken out by Roscoe's gunners on the knoll. It had become a killing field with no enemy survivors. Then there was silence save for the burning machines. The battle lasted fewer than five minutes.

Scrambling down the slope Sergeant Roscoe stopped for a moment to check on his wounded marine's condition. After the corpsman said it was minor the sergeant ran to the first BTR stopping long enough to confirm nobody had escaped. The smell of burning flesh was powerfully strong on that road. At the second overturned vehicle he cautiously looked at the Russians sprawled around it. Ebenezer still carrying his Stinger was rifling a dead Russian's pockets before finding a folded map.

"Roscoe, over here!" he yelled. "Look what I found on this dead sergeant."

He slowly unfolded the Russian printed map. "Got some places circled in red grease pencil." Leaning the assault rifle against his leg Roscoe finished unfolding the thick paper. "I know this is Gaviota and here should be San Augustin." He curiously looked at Ebenezer. "Maybe that was their artillery post we found?"

They both heard the sound and anxiously looked at the skies.

"Get your Stinger loaded," Roscoe sharply ordered. Jerking his binoculars from their pouch he quickly scanned the skies. "Those damned smoke funnels probably alerted that chopper. It's definitely not an Apache."

"Do you see it?" Ebenezer nervously asked after reloading his air assault weapon.

"No, it's flying low but coming closer."

*　　*　　*

Ever since KONSTANTANTINOVICH left its anchorage Captain Voronov felt as if his head would explode. The political commissar never quit bitching about one thing or other. It was also obvious the tensions developing inside this iron maiden was dangerously close to mutiny. The captain knew this because of Colonel Karsavin's reckless behavior. Sensing the crew's contemptuous attitude the colonel started wearing a pistol. He didn't leave the bridge afraid if he did the helmsman would change course. Standing at the windshield Mikhail momentarily watched seamen lining the main deck with binoculars searching the shore for enemy troops. Because of those rough waters many sailors strapped their bodies to the lifelines to keep from being thrown overboard.

Purposely built for surface battle the destroyer was well suited for her tasks. With only one working steering shaft she struggled to maintain the knots needed to move through those opposing waters. From where Mikhail stood he saw the empty missiles tubes and wished there were reloads. He gave the men on bridge duty occasional dirty glances that redirected their accusing attention. Mikhail looked upon Russian seamen as lazy, unreliable, and treacherous. He frowned bitterly. The commissar knew when this war was over the Party was downsizing the naval force. It was the Red Army the senior commanders praised and gave the best equipment.

"Man overboard!" screamed somebody on the open bridge wing.

When Karl yelled to stop engines Mikhail angrily warned. "Stop this ship and I'll put a bullet through your brain!" When the captain hesitated he whipped out his revolver. "Don't press me, captain!"

"But I have a man overboard," Karl pleaded.

"I don't give a damn! Continue on our course or die!"

With angry obedience Captain Voronov instructed the helmsman to maintain course and speed. He then stomped over to the windshield where he saw his bewildered men returning to their shore searching. Though not seeing their disbelief Karl knew it was there. This was unheard of. No ship left their overboard men behind when it was so easy to pick him up.

Hearing Karl asking a repair technician if their MF hull-mounted sonar was back on station, Mikhail walked over with a disgusted expression. "Why are you so worried about sonar? Everybody knows the Americans lost their submarines in battle."

"Sonar can also warn us about sunken wrecks along this coast." The captain arrogantly snapped.

Before further discussion continued their attention was turned upon a bridge phone talker. "Comrade Senior Captain, Charlie One reports smoke columns." That was the code name for their shipboard helicopter. "Charlie One is investigating."

Angry at the pilot's vague information Mikhail sharply ordered. "Tell the stupid fool to give us coordinates and bearings!"

*   *   *

"There it is!" shouted a marine pointing up the beach. The small profiled helicopter was flying fifty feet above the waters just off shore.

"I doubt if it was called. We hit the armored cars too fast for that. It's that damned black smoke." Whirling about he shouted. "Back the Shoet into the gully. Hopefully, they don't know about it. Those with the Stingers get ready to take it out when in range." He thoughtfully watched the approaching aircraft through his binoculars. "Damn, that jockey has his balls up his ass. They're heading this way without evasive actions."

About the time Ebenezer fired his missile the second launcher sent another hurling. The daydreaming pilot tried jerking his machine out of harms' way, but it was too late. Both infra-red shafts struck the banking chopper. There were two unified explosions then seconds later burning debris fell onto the beach.

"Let's get the hell out of here," Roscoe shouted at his men.

"Just a minute," Ebenezer yelled. Standing on the road's edge looking down on the winding shore line, he pointed at four 55 gallon drums washed ashore. "What the hell are those?"

Without hesitation Roscoe speculated. "Could have been what those armored cars were looking for?" Ordering four marines down the twenty foot sloping sides to investigate, he watched as they grabbed one barrel and after some effort opened its top.

*   *   *

Mikhail angrily stood before the windshield after the phone talker reported communications was lost with the helicopter. While the bridge watch standers contemptuously watched the commissar leave the bridge, Captain Voronov ordered the destroyer slowed down. Just ahead of them he saw the long fingers of smoke twisting about before being blown away.

Coming on deck Commander Bogdanov thoughtfully looked at the captain watching his ship draw nearer to the smoke. "We may have suffered casualties, Karl, but at least we narrowed down the search grid. Ten Delta is within a short distance of those smoke tunnels." he solemnly said.

"Perhaps," he bitterly replied. "This Lieutenant Blackmore is like our winter winds back home. You can feel their chill but you never can grasp the wind in your palms."

CHAPTER THIRTEEN

Roscoe's patrol was returning to Ten Delta when their radar signaled another contact. At fast speeds it was rough towing the wheeled rocket launcher. Heeding Ebenezer's warning they pulled into the nearest ravine offering concealment. Even before the armored carrier braked Roscoe and his marines were piling out to establish firing lines. Roscoe hurried to the ravine's crest with his binoculars. It was five long anxious minutes before their contact became visible. Roscoe's emotions turned cold. Cruising off shore was a Russian destroyer.

"Oh shit," moaned Ebenezer. "We got to get out of here real quick."

After a quick scan of the immediate area Roscoe mumbled. "No can do. There's only open space for a mile or so. They would illuminate us before Smith shifted into third." He uneasily looked about. "We're trapped."

The corporal studied the ship's superstructure for a few moments. "Maybe not. Take a peek at their main mast its radar disk isn't rotating."

Roscoe did this then chuckled. "Well I be damned." He then heavily exhaled.

"But we still have major problems up the ass. I bet sure as hell fire controls for those damned 130mm twin turrets are working." He gave their crisis a short study. "We can't stay here. Do you see those sailors on main deck scanning the shore line? They'll going to see us when passing."

Ebenezer groaned. "Well, we sure as hell can't stay here. They'll blow us to hell either way."

After a few minutes Roscoe looked at his buddy. "There may be one chance in hell to get out of this alive. But it's only one chance and if we failed we'll buy our six feet." After telling Ebenezer to stay on the knoll and call down distances, Roscoe slipped and tumbled down the slope. "Hey, you marines, we got another crisis so everybody listen up. How many rockets do we have for that launcher?"

"Fifteen," somebody answered.

"Then do a full load." he sharply ordered. "Anybody know how to fire that damned thing?"

A marine named Benny held up his hand as if in class. "I do."

"Then do your stuff." Whirling about he saw Smith standing alongside his carrier. "When I give the word, tear ass out onto the road facing north then stop. We'll going to use the Russian rocket launcher on that destroyer." Though the marines didn't comment he knew what they were thinking. And they were right. His plan was crazy with only a small margin for success. If this failed then they were all dead. "Benny will stand ready to fire on my command." The sergeant was sweating from the stress of this crisis. "After we fire our loads everybody climb in and we'll tear ass for home."

Ebenezer yelled down. "Steady approaching. They'll be able to see us in another ten minutes."

"Roger that!"

With his binoculars Ebenezer studied the warship. "Sergeant, their main deck is loaded with 55 gallon drums."

"Roger." Roscoe thought about that for a moment. "Benny, can that launcher fire rockets at different targets?" When informed the firing system was electronic he curtly instructed. "Take out those damned turrets then concentrate on the drums."

When the destroyer came within firing range it was 156 feet of mean fighting machine even with a damaged superstructure and main mast. Roscoe was relieved when seeing its ten missile tubes were empty with one badly damaged. The warship was barely making ten knots through the crashing waves. Another plan came whirling into his busy mind.

"How much time do we have?" he yelled.

"Maybe five minutes. Do you see how she's moving closer to shore?" Ebenezer yelled back. "I think the bastard is having trouble steering."

Roscoe looked at the uneasy marines. "How many shoulder fired missiles do we have?"

"Four Stingers with three reloads each."

"Quick give me the ranges?"

"Two thousand feet is fairly accurate accounting for the strong winds."

"Good, that should do it. Climb up there with Ebenezer. After she's in range I want you to fire into those gasoline drums on its main deck. After expending your canisters get your ass back down here."

He watched the two marines hurriedly climb the loose dirt to join Ebenezer. None of them believed what they were about to do. The destroyer continued its sluggish approach without surface radar. Cruising electronically blind so close to shore was suicidal.

*   *   *

Ten Delta's radio operator stared at his equipment only for a moment before turning around and yelling. "Sergeant Tyler." When the master sergeant came over he anxiously reported. "Roscoe's patrol has sighted the Russian destroyer."

"Where?"

Everybody directed their total interest on the radioman as an anxious silence fell over CIC. "Roscoe reports enemy ship one half mile off the coast at Arroyo El Butio. Roscoe reports ship running without radar and her superstructure is seriously damaged." He held his hand against the earphones. "Roscoe reports they're trapped and can't make a run for it." The marine paused while listening then his expression changed to disbelief. "Sergeant Roscoe plans to attack the ship."

"He what?" exclaimed Earl.

James calmly accepted the report. "They have a mobile rocket launcher with them." He looked at the grinning master sergeant. "Tell me about this Russian weapon your patrol found abandoned." James glanced about to see Earl and Savannah moving closer for better hearing. Timothy having heard about the report rushed in to stand by James.

Uncomfortable with the attention on him Tyler solemnly replied. "At first we thought it employed Sparrow missiles, but we later learned they were AT-6 Spiral Anti-tank guided missiles. The Soviets designed a two wheeled carriage hosting fifteen glass-reinforced plastic tubes to mobilize their system. Each missile can be fired independently on individual targets. The heat seeking missile has an accurate range of 2 miles with a conventional shaped charge capable of defeating 600mm of armor."

"But can that damage a destroyer's protective hull?" Savannah skeptically asked.

"I don't think Roscoe will fire at the hull," James thoughtfully speculated. "He'll fire at the weaker skins above main deck." The lieutenant deeply sighed. "If he has time the sergeant could cripple that ship. But his main problem is firing before their twin turrets open fire."

"But you said their radar is blind." Earl interrupted.

"Roscoe reported their surface radar wasn't working," James corrected with a frown. "That doesn't necessarily mean their fire control system is malfunctioning. It's independent of the surface radar."

*   *   *

After satisfied everybody was ready, Roscoe rapidly climbed the sliding loose dirt to flop down alongside Ebenezer. The destroyer was rapidly coming into range. The sergeant still couldn't believe he was actually opposing a warship with anti-tank missiles and Stingers. For some reason he questioningly looked at the skies for a moment. The clouds were dark from soot and debris. Not a good day to die, he softly muttered.

"Now!" Roscoe shouted. "Commence Firing!"

After hearing that Smith slammed down on his gas pedal sending the Shoets roaring out of the ravine. With a spin of the steering wheel he jerked the machine into a northern direction then slammed on his brakes. The Americans were ready to confront the warship in a deadly lopsided battle. About that time seamen aboard the ship spotted the shore threat.

Benny calmly punched in coordinates sending the first long slender canister hurling from its tube. A Shturm missile roared the short distance then the ship's forward twin turrets exploded in a flash of flames as its 600mm armor plating was compromised. Damage control crews fighting those roaring fires were killed when a second Stinger missile took out the main mast that came crashing down. Benny quickly programmed another missile that sped towards the telescopic helicopter hanger. A Stinger canister tearing a gaping hole in the bridge's starboard bulkhead vaporized three phone talkers. Another anti-armor warhead crashing into a 30mm Gatling sent flames and debris spinning into the powerful winds. Alarms thunderously sounded as the warship began emergency turning away from the devastating shore barrages.

Captain Voronov, bloodied from the bridge explosion, leaned against the partially smashed chair shouting orders to his helmsman and phone talkers. Unable to return gunfire after an explosive charge crippled the fire control systems, Karl saw no reason to remain. Commissar Karsavin was in his cabin when the attack came. Thrown to the decking he suffered minor cuts that trickled blood down his face. When he finally made it to the bridge medical personnel was attending the wounded. Demanding what Karl was doing he found the word 'retreating' distasteful. But when informed their guns were destroyed and the Gatlings silent because of smashed fire control systems, he angrily accepted their withdrawal.

Six Shturm missiles committed serious damages when impacting, but it was the seventh explosive charge that violently shook the destroyer. Black smoke and reddish flames wildly spun into the air. A mass of men were killed while others were thrown overboard when those secured 55 gallon drums took a direct hit. Blinding flames fiercely rushed through the KONSTANTANTINOVICH limping to her anchorage at Isla Vista.

Back on the road Roscoe and his marines wildly cheered after the shock wore off they had actually crippled a large warship.

"All right, marines," Roscoe shouted when they calmed down. "We did it, but don't let your arrogances override your common sense. We don't know how many Russians are ashore. If there are more I promise they'll come tearing after our assholes. So let's get the lead out and head back to base. Ebenezer, how many Stingers charges do we have left?"

There was a short pause while an inventory was taken. "We have three left."

"Benny, how many missiles do you have left?"

"Seven."

Roscoe quietly appraised his men standing about feeling cocky. "We brought them down because their surface radar wasn't working. So they had no prior warning we were waiting in ambush. After Benny's Spirals smashed their fire control systems they couldn't fire back. Because of the storm's fury their captain was forced to cruise dangerously close to shore. This seriously limited his maneuvering options. And to mention their last problem, I noticed the ship was acting sluggish meaning their steering was screwed up. All in all, gentlemen, the Soviet captain was running with a stacked deck of cards." He frowned at their vanishing grins. "Still, you jarheads accomplished one of the most startling battles in the pages of warfare. With a handful of Stinger charges and a stolen Russian anti-tank gun you seriously crippled a damned Russian destroyer. So be proud of what you did, but on the other hand don't get too cocky. The damned communists aren't through with us yet. Remember they still have that task force coming down the coast. I promise they won't be this easy to fight back."

*   *   *

The radioman was excited when relaying Roscoe's message. "The burning enemy ship has limped from the engagement. No casualties among our men. Sergeant Roscoe reports they're on the way back." After the applauding died down he continued his report. "Prior to their battle the Roscoe ambushed and destroyed two enemy armored carriers with troops and downed one chopper."

Earl was shaking his head. "I don't believe all of this," he mumbled totally taken aback by their accomplishments. "Wait until St. Louis hears about this. They'll go wild."

After a few minutes James soberly warned. "The sergeant's men are to be praised for their successes. But the enemy won't take this defeat without savagely avenging the losses. The next time they come their fury will definitely be felt. From now on I wouldn't anticipate any mercy from those bastards. Any element of surprise we planned on has to be tossed aside. Soon as Roscoe returns we better activate our strike plans on that naval base." James then looked questioningly at Savannah. "Do you have anything to add?"

"No."

The lieutenant replied. "Since you're from Yuma Headquarters and obviously encountering the Russians before this, what do you suggest we do to dull their sharpness?" For the first time he voiced his suspicions she was from intelligence and not a minor staff posting.

Savannah avoided his questions while looking at the world map. "If I was directing this campaign our first strategy would be swiftly striking hard before they recover from this black eye. First we must eliminate their naval base as a threat and don't give them a chance to recover. Ten Delta must strike again and again. Throwing confusion into their ranks is something the Soviets don't effectively deal with. Cripple their task force's striking ability before they arrive along this coast. That can be done by destroying their oil supplies." She stopped talking and thoughtfully appraised the men. "The enemy wasn't expecting Sergeant Roscoe's astonishing victory. This will create confusion and doubt among their ranks. There's one thing you must remember about this whole naval engagement. The Soviet High Command can not afford and I repeat the High Command can not afford to lose their surface warships. They do not have replacements. From now on they'll respect Ten Delta and act more cautiously. Never forget one thing, lieutenant. Traditionally the Russians are an unpredictable and ruthless people. They do not lightly accept military or political reverses. To bring them down you have to act just as unpredictable. This screws up their thinking. With matters as they are today I believe that will be your only advantage." After speaking she shrugged her shoulders and thoughtfully regarded their quiet reactions to her advice.

*   *   *

After KONSTANTANTINOVICH made rapid headway from that hostile encounter, Captain Voronov angrily paced his bloodied bridge. He had seen enough that shame flowed through his body. There was a Shoets on that shore towing a Russian missile launcher. He briefly caught sight of their enemy on a small hill overlooking the beach. After that everything happened so swiftly it was impossible to evaluate in the heat of battle.

When Commander Bogdanov came on deck the captain was wiping splattered blood from the windshield. His vision was further restricted by broken glass. The frowning engineering officer silently appraised their damages. Nine men died on the bridge with vital instruments damaged or wasted altogether. With a defeatist sigh he stepped over to the captain.

"Are you all right?"

Turning away from his housekeeping Karl unsuccessfully tried smiling. "Best as can be expected. What about our damages?"

"Both 130mm mounts were damaged beyond repair and their gun crews killed. We have extensive damages on the superstructure. Number Two shaft housing has failed completely. Casualties numbered thirty killed with another twenty-six wounded. The gunnery department doubts if the Gatlings can be repaired outside of a shipyard." The commander turning around surveyed the damages then skeptically added. "We can patch the bulkheads, but I'm not certain if we have spare instruments onboard." The commissar coming on deck saw Bogdanov and left. "I ran into that bastard down below. He was chewing out a wounded seaman for not doing his duties."

"What did you tell him?" Karl asked after giving the dirty rag to an enlisted sailor sent up by the deck officer.

"I told him to grab his bloody balls and get the hell to his cabin."

Later when the ship was anchored at Isla Vista, the engineering officer came back to find the bridge's damages frantically being cleaned by crewmen. Even the captain's chair was welded to the decking. Karl stayed out of their way while munching on a tomato sandwich. This time the political officer didn't flee when Bogdanov came on deck, but stayed out of his way. Holding a clipboard the commander walked about scribbling down needed repairs.

Later Mikhail studied the two men conversing on the open wing. Whatever was discussed didn't make Karl very happy. Mikhail Karsavin was the exact opposite of Karl Voronov. Whereas the commanding officer was short and slightly overweight, the colonel was muscular built. The commissar moved with the lightness of a cat on the prowl. Karl knew the colonel arrogantly believed Russia's Navy was antiquated. Kossier believed it would be his armies that swept away their enemies. In his warped vision it was the KGB who stood as guardian of the Communist Party. The enlisted sailor assigned as Colonel Karsavin's orderly whispered the man slept with pistol under his pillow and it was cocked for instant usage. When KONSTANTANTINOVICH left British Columbia there were four bottles of vodka in his cabin. Now there was only half a bottle. While stepping away from a glaring welder's torch working on the damaged bulkhead his face was ribbed with shadows.

After the colonel finally left the bridge's offensive acid scents and thin swirls of smoke, the engineering officer walked over. "The ship has taken a bad beating." he solemnly advised the captain.

"When can she go into battle?"

"I really don't know. There are numerous damages my men can't repair. We don't have the tools, parts or even the needed skills to get this grand lady back in service."

"This won't do," Karl moaned after a short silence. "The Naval High Command's plans include KONSTANTANTINOVICH."

"Then they'll have to reevaluate their plans. This warship isn't going into the Gulf anytime soon." he paused then uneasily added. "I'm not even certain she will make it back to port." Worried about Karl's shocked reaction he continued in a somber tone. "I know how you feel, but there's nothing I can do to change this situation. Our radar was down so there was no way we could have known the Americans were waiting in ambush. Because we were cruising with one shaft, instead of two, the ship didn't respond fast enough to your emergency bells."

Karl replied after shaking his head. "Today's events are not favoring us, my friend."

*   *   *

The Shoets noisily drove over the winding surface road for thirty minutes without either Roscoe or Ebenezer speaking. What they had achieved still hadn't fully sunk in. The sergeant was uncomfortable in the front seat where there was limited space to stretch his long legs. Whenever the machine crashed over a pothole, and there were many of them, Roscoe's legs were painfully slammed against the dashboard. Then their radar operator shouted he had another contact. The Israeli military vehicle spun to an abrupt halt. After hearing this the marines loudly groaned their disappointment. They were impatient to get back to base. While the operator fine tuned the target's position Roscoe jumped from the carrier. Exceptionally high levels of electromagnetic disturbance were causing transmission problems. Hearing their grumbling Roscoe pounded on the carrier's side and this stopped their chattering.

Ebenezer climbed from the rear exit door carrying his automatic rifle. "They sure are persistent bastards."

"I image by now they're pissed as hell."

The corporal nodded with a dry grin. "Yeah, I guess I would be too."

Leaning against the carrier's engine hood the General Motors engine warmed Roscoe's large black body. He remembered with a frown how one bad winter on the farm, he volunteered to drive the family tractor because its engine kept him warm. Normally the carrier gave Roscoe a sense of comfortable security, but not today. The Shoets was armed with twin 12.7mm machine guns, a single 7.62mm on the rear, and a 52mm light mortar pad. Roscoe uneasily looked at the late afternoon hours heavily plagued with a menacing grayness. The sun tried breaking through the sooty overcast without much success.

"Sergeant, the contact is gone." the operator reported after sticking his head from the Shoets.

"What do you mean it disappeared?" Roscoe growled. "How the hell do you lose a contact that close?"

The corporal shrugged. "That's pretty easy around here. There are too many ravines and arroyos they can swing into."

"Maybe they drove out of range?" Roscoe anxiously asked while scanning the road's winding path with binoculars.

"Not a chance. When the scanner loses a target due to range differences a tiny yellow light blinks. It didn't this time. There's only a green one signaling we lost the contact."

Satisfied there was no Russian tailing them the sergeant ordered the carrier back to their base. This produced a soft clapping of hands. All the way back their radar tracked without targeting an enemy presence.

*   *   *

It was dark when Roscoe's Shoets slipped into Ten Delta's underground chambers. After all the applauding and praises faded, Roscoe walked to the cafeteria for food and debriefing with James. His perfectly cooked steak and mushrooms were delicious. It didn't matter if both came from cans. Along this wasteland there was no fresh produce or recently butchered meat. The men at Ten Delta had come to expect this.

"While checking Canada del Agua Caliente arroyo," Roscoe informed between sips of coffee and mushrooms. "We found tire tracks from heavy vehicles."

"Any idea as to who they belonged to."

"I don't think they were from Russian vehicles. But I could be wrong on that. We were recently in that sector and tangled with smart ass Mexicans. Whether they belonged to that weird ass political group claiming California for Mexico, I don't know."

James nodded. "That's one political problem we'll have to take care of, but not right now. Our plate is too heavy as it is. What kind of damages do you think the KONSTANTANTINOVICH took?" He paused for a moment. "Damn I'm glad our Navy doesn't pick such long names."

Roscoe pushed aside his empty plate and chuckled. "Maybe it's a long name, but she's mean as hell. The fact she was downloaded because of malfunctioning systems has no bearing on her fighting ability."

"How bad was she was damaged?"

"I don't think she'll be a problem for awhile."

Timothy and Tyler came into the mess hall arguing about something. Grabbing some food they headed for James' table. After sitting the chief petty officer smeared blueberry jam over his bread before saying sarcastically. "That report of drums lashed on their main deck was pretty interesting."

Earl and Savannah after collecting their trays of food joined the crowd at James' table.

Before touching her food Savannah looked at Roscoe and said. "Recent naval intelligence reported 55-gallon drums lashed on their ship decks. Though we suspected what their purposes were there was no confirmation as to why. You revealed how devastating that practice can be. But your encounter also revealed a serious flaw in Kossier's Navy. They are running short on fuels and having to haul extra fuel in drums. And as you displayed today it certainly makes the subject ship open to devastating damages."

"But a ship requires too much fuel to carry in drums." Roscoe quickly pointed out between bites of the steak.

"That's true. However, those drums provide fuel for their helicopters and ground vehicles."

Glancing Tyler's way Earl solemnly replied. "We also partially solved one of your problems. Army quartermasters unsealed highly classified documents stored in St. Louis back in 1986. You were right. Agents Orange and Blue shipments were stored without Californian State officials knowing about it." A worried look crossed his face. "According to classified manifests more than six thousand gallons of those chemicals are stored in concrete pits on the Vandenberg Air Force Base."

"Damned," Tyler angrily mumbled. "No wonder the victims are largely in our surrounding sectors. Vandenberg is only a few miles from here."

"If the drums were stored in lead-lined concrete pits," Savannah said. "There should be no reason they would have leaked."

James drank some coffee then soberly asked. "You aren't from around here, are you?"

"No."

"Then you don't know this part of the state is honeycombed with dangerous fault lines that frequently cause earthquakes. The vaults were probably cracked by our frequent earth disturbances."

Earl coughed to gain everybody's attention. "Perhaps, now is a good time finish my briefing that was earlier interrupted?" After everybody nodded agreement, he suggested. "Why don't we do it here in the mess hall?"

James dubiously interrupted. "I thought you wanted the conference behind locked doors?"

"With Sergeant Roscoe's brilliant victory today all of that has changed. Anyhow this area smells much better than that oily room."

"It's O.K with me." Turning to the chief, James said. "Find Tyler, he went to get that briefcase taken from the Russian carrier." While waiting for the Timothy to come back the lieutenant asked Lewis. "What's this about your modified Chinook? That aircraft is nothing short of a damned gunship."

Lewis grinned. "Who knows maybe my baby will come in handy." He shrugged. "You can never tell."

After everybody was gathered around the table, Earl began his briefing in a slow thoughtful manner. "Our primary objective is neutralizing that Russian naval port. Surprisingly enough Sergeant Roscoe may have stumbled upon the Russians' weakness. If they are experiencing critical gasoline shortages for their helicopters and ground vehicles, then it's crucial that base be eliminated." He grinned at their solemn expressions. "But Sergeant Roscoe found another weakness today. A weakness that our naval commanders in the Gulf have been advised to use against them. When their ships are carrying drums of gasoline secured on deck they're floating time bombs."

"How long have you suspected this?" James asked offended such information was kept from him. He gave Savannah a nasty look.

"She didn't know," Earl explained with a frown.

"And why didn't she?"

"Because her agency didn't have a need-to-know," the envoy casually said.

James stared at the presidential envoy for a few moments. "Obviously you people don't know your warfare history? During Bush's Middle Eastern wars the White House and Department of Defense didn't always share their intelligence. Because of that we got a damned good ass kicking."

"I believe St. Louis knows what they're doing."

"Well, I'm not that sure. Because the government downsized our military when the Russians did attack we were caught off guard. Just like on December 7th of 1941. And now we're paying dearly for their short sightedness." James growled. After deeply exhaling his frustration the lieutenant asked. "Just how are we going to neutralize a damned naval base?"

Earl looked around the table. "Actually your primary target is their gasoline storage tanks. Destroy those and we cripple the Soviet Navy."

"What kind of defenses are we looking at?" Timothy asked.

"That naval port isn't well guarded because the Soviets are experiencing manpower shortages."

"What kind of airborne threats are we looking at?"

"The Soviets' fuel shortages have limited their aircraft's activity."

"What kind of support can we expect?" Savannah asked while studying an unfolded map of that region.

"The British and Canadians have small bands of commandoes in that region. Other than infrequent hit-and-run raids the naval base is largely left alone. Those men will provide updated intelligence on your way there. They'll also launch some decoy raids elsewhere that hopefully will draw base security away from the main complex. Other than that, gentlemen, you'll be on your own."

"What can we do with only 57 men?" Timothy sarcastically asked.

"St. Louis wants the raiding party to involve only 20 men. The smaller your party the better chances you'll have destroying those fuel tanks."

"This sounds like a suicide raid," Savannah critically denounced.

Earl shook his head. "That's exactly what St. Louis doesn't want to happen. The President wants you to get inside that base and destroy the fuel tanks. Lieutenant Blackmore, you are to experience the lowest loss of men possible. Is that clear to all of you?" None of them acknowledged the order. "St. Louis expects you to successfully carry out your objectives, but this isn't the time for heroes. Our military is bleeding enough in battle."

James took the map from Savannah and thoughtfully studied the Washington coast line. "What other plans did St. Louis come up with?"

Earl slowly said much to their annoyance. "There are no real plans. That's your job, lieutenant."

"That's nice of them," James cynically replied. Touching the immediate region off British Columbia he shook his head. "The Zasulich Naval Base is roughly 1500 miles from here. I wager their outer perimeter defenses extents outward at least 200 miles in a surrounding circle. What about radar, airborne flights, and ground outposts?"

"I can obtain that info for you."

"When?"

"Half way there you're scheduled to land for refueling. I promise all the base info you'll need will be waiting there."

Timothy interrupted while running his finger over the map. "What about the KONSTANTANTINOVICH?" He looked at those around the table. "We still don't have reliable intelligence what she's doing?"

Tyler reached into his pocket. "One of our coast watchers was here a few minutes ago." He unfolded a torn piece of paper. "The ship has anchored off Isla Vista. He drew an outline of the ship's damages." After handing the paper to James the master sergeant kept talking. "Her superstructure is definitely damaged, gun turrets are out of commission, at least one steering shaft must be damaged, and their radar is smashed. Juan reported considerable work being done, but he doubts if that will restore the ship's fighting capacity."

"Do you trust this informer?"

Tyler was quick to curtly say. "First thing, Carver, the so called informer is a retired master chief petty officer with thirty years of sea duty. I think he knows what a Soviet warship looks like. These coastal watchers are doing a great service with a high risk for them and their families. Several watchers were already murdered by Soviet sympathizers."

Earl solemnly said. "That I didn't know. Your activities are fairly unknown in St. Louis."

"There's no reason they should be. We make weekly reports to General Paulson detailing everything happening down here."

"I have read his reports and there's no mention of disturbances or material shortages."

"Then he's lying." James bitterly replied.

"That's a mighty risky charge against the regional commander." Earl sternly warned. "The General is a popular man in St. Louis. Some say he may even run for president after the war is won."

James shook his head. "Then God help us." Before Earl could counter argue the lieutenant changed the subject. "As I see it there are two battles going on in this war. One is against the communists and the other is challenging nature." He paused and looked at the map. "Scientists always warned about the Greenhouse Effect Theory, but everybody scoffed at them. But now that it's coming down the chute nobody can get together to fight it."

The envoy quietly sat for a few moments before solemnly saying. "First we have to slow the Russians from bringing their task force down this way. After you get back the full plans will be unveiled. It's a very complicated agenda requiring precise timing." He warningly held up his hand. "But I can tell you right now that if your raid isn't successful we won't be able to execute our second phase." His expression reflected the troubled thoughts of their future. "It's really that serious." He looked at those seated around the table. "It is estimated one hundred million tons of smoke and debris has formed a thick encircling cloud above the earth. If those increases aren't stopped in the near future our sunlight will be reduced by 95%."

Tyler sourly asked. "How much time do we have before this doomsday cloud strikes?"

"Within three weeks." Studying their shocked expressions he said. "Only a handful of people outside the President's circle know this. It wouldn't serve any purpose informing the general populace. It would only cause panic and that we do not need."

Timothy finally shook his head. "You would think mankind would have learned their lessons by now?"

"Maybe mankind will never learn," Savannah sourly forecasted. "Maybe this isn't the first time such a crisis has ravished this planet?" Having their full attention the marine major continued. "Our literature down through time wrote about fires destroying ancient civilizations. Those vanished empires left little for us to analyze much less predict. Even the French prophet Nostradamus forecasted a great war occurring about this same time. And he wasn't the first to do so. In Mexican ancient myths we're told the earth nearly expired three times. Only with the help of their gods did those empires escape extinction. The Aztecs called our time frame the Fire Sun that would cause terrible conflagrations. This nuclear war certainly meets those expectations." After pausing she sipped some coffee while reflecting over what she had seen during a recent tour. "Fires are raging everywhere in what used to be our Eastern states. Death ranges into the millions. Even the Bible speaks of fire towards our end."

"So what's the answer?" James asked.

Savannah frowned. "There's only one answer and that's trust among men."

James shook his head. "Well, that's not going to happen."

CHAPTER FOURTEEN

Their meeting continued another thirty minutes before each went their own way. While leaving James abruptly stopped and faced Savannah. She blushed when told her supposition was some heavy stuff. Then with a heavy expression the lieutenant went to his own quarters. He had ordered the raid's participants to bunk early. Savannah finding her heart fluttering like a school girl's went to her room.

But Earl found coping with their problems mentally disturbing. Shutting the door to his quarters he flopped down in a chair. He couldn't find a comfortable position so after showering the envoy went to bed.

Southern California formerly was a land blessed with sunlight and delightful memories. That was before the Soviets' sneak attack. It wasn't sunny now. Earl's slumbering reflections were tattered and angry. Skies above this lush land were harsh and black allowing little sunlight through the debris and other pollutions thrown up by man's savage nature. The envoy tossed and turned on his bunk angrily demanding why something so beautiful could become so ugly and demeaning?

Finally, Earl throwing his blankets aside stood in the darkened room orienting his twisted emotions. Glancing at his watch he read the time as 2145. He had restlessly tossed for one hour and a half. After yawning Earl sat on the bunk. No matter what he tried those memories of touring the ruins with Chatterbox wouldn't depart. Gloom and death was in the air. Only jagged rubble greeted his silent plea for all of this to stop. When stumbling across two bloated corpses he nearly puked. The marines taking it in strive explained the only way to avoid going crazy was ignoring death.

Later when walking down the corridor to the hanger he heard rock and roll music drifting from one compartment. While next door Mozart's beautiful music toyed with his memories. He found his chopper crew lingering about the Chinook. It was easy to note their restlessness. His gunner handed the captain a warm bottle of beer.

"Sure as hell a lot of activity going on," he muttered.

"These crazy bastards are taking on the Soviet naval base." he casually replied.

The gunner didn't comment at first. "There are some crazy people here."

Another crewman looked up and smiled. "They're only marines dealing with the impossible."

"What about that storm front moving down the coast tonight? Won't that affect their mission?"

"The raiding party will be flying further inland and should miss its fury. If anything it should shield their approach."

*   *   *

Mikhail restlessly paced the near deserted bridge. Once darkness fell there was little to see beyond the ship's anchorage. The working parties ashore after extinguished all lighting sought the murky curtain's protection. Captain Voronov wanting to do the same on his ship was denied the request. The Russians did the only thing they could do by securing everything and batting down the hatches. The night promised to be long. Although preferring to wait out the storm in his cabin Mikhail followed the worried captain about the tossing ship.

"Why do you baby these Russian seamen?" the political officer complained while leaving the gunnery department.

"Treat a man like you would want to be treated and he'll do marvelous things."

After inspecting the devastated fire control compartment, the commissar slowly turned about with a frown on his face. "Can they accomplish the impossible? This space was totally smashed by that rocket attack." he bitterly demanded. "With no fire control your ship is helpless if those American destroyers leave Mexican waters."

The captain wasn't offended by his abrupt charges. "Even if we had fire control, Comrade Colonel Karsavin, we have no guns."

After his family was vaporized by missiles the ship's crew became his sole reason struggling for through this hellish nightmare. Each man knowing this responded in the same way. Few men aboard this ship welcomed the return of communism. During those few years the Motherland didn't have the noose of evil corruption around their necks it was a promising era. Though the new Russia tried accepting the Western World's freedoms, it didn't come easy. The average citizen searching for bread and gainful employment wasn't waiting while the democratic process sluggishly grabbed hold. Their brief moment in time slipped passed and the country sunk once more into communism's evil clutches. Returning to the bridge Karl had a damaged ship to nurse.

Commander Bogdanov found his captain on the bridge staring at a coastal map. "Don't you ever sleep?" he asked.

Karl tried smiling. "It's hard when your world is falling." For a few moments he stared into the darkness surrounding the ship. "So what's the word on our damages? Can they be repaired here?"

"Some can be while others require a dry dock. But I'm afraid that missile attack did us in as a fighting ship. I could promise you everything is all right, but it isn't."

"That's what I told the admiral but that went over like a lead balloon."

"Yeah, I imagine it would." The engineering officer was moody for a short while. "I think we must reevaluate our estimations of the enemy. They aren't as stupid as Colonel Karsavin would like for us to believe. What they did was unbelievable." He shrugged his broad shoulders. "Of course, sailing so close to shore set us up for that attack. This Blackmore fellow is a cunning fox and should be regarded as such. What about Major Darkanbayev's patrol? Have they called in?"

"No word on them."

"Then it's possible they're dead?"

Walking to the windshield Karl thoughtfully studied the powerful winds whipping along the coast. Without a moon it was impossible to see too far pass the glass. "Do you think it wise to stop working on the ship during night hours?"

"I strongly disagreed when the colonel proposed it. Ten Delta is in this region and whether we work through the night or not they still know about our condition. For now we're sitting ducks. But weather or not we must repair what can be done and regain our mobility."

The uneasy captain briefly paced the bridge before looking at his trusted friend. "I agree with you. Let's get our working parties back on the job. If our parties stay within the ship their labors may be slow, but at least we're doing something."

"If you'll going to disobey my orders," Mikhail harshly condemned the men, "then go all the way and commence all repairs!" The furious commissar stepped into the reddish glow from the night lights. "Well, don't stand there like fools do what I ordered."

"It's too dangerous to work outside, Comrade Colonel," Karl argued. "The winds are too strong."

"If the men can work inside then they damned well can work outside. Do what I say. Order the lights back on and get your working parties outside. There's much to do before this crippled ship can become an effective fighting machine again."

Minutes later external lighting flooded the darkness like a creeping wolf on the hunt. Within a short order pounding hammers and flashing welding machines was heard amidst the howling winds. Grumbling Russian sailors fought nature's fury while repairing their crippled ship.

*   *   *

Seeing Chatterbox crossing the hanger with a box under arm, Earl intercepted him at Ten Delta's old Chinook. "Did you talk with Barnes about biological agents stored on Vandenberg?"

The black man nodded. "Yeah, but he doesn't know anything about it."

"He told me the same thing, but I didn't believe him."

"Barnes complained there were too many secrets on the base. He swore staying abreast with his own project was hard enough."

"You seem pretty well informed about biological agents in Vietnam?" Earl suspiciously asked. "Why is that?"

"During one of my medical classes in college we studied the agents. They're pretty nasty stuff." After pushing his box inside the helicopter he turned to Earl and harshly said. "The way those were those defoliations were delivered people and plants never had a chance."

"And what were their delivery methods?"

"They used helicopter mounted gravity-fed sprayers to lay down one and half gallons over each acre. People caught in this spraying died from Cryptococcus." He wondered how this man could be so indifferent when friendly troops caught in the spray painfully died from the stuff.

"That's history, sergeant. We're dealing with today and not years ago. If we're to stop this plague from spreading those burial sites must be found."

Chatterbox abruptly became defensive. "You tell us where the damned stuff is and Ten Delta will dispose of it. But as I see it, right now our primary task is wasting a damned communism naval port."

"Do you think your people can destroy those fuel storage tanks?" Earl cynically asked.

"If we can't the squad will die trying." His voice became harsh. "I believe that's all our country can ask of us." Exhaling deeply he then said. "If you'll excuse me there are a lot of things to do before we leave."

After Chatterbox left Earl turned about and found himself staring at a hostile Major Davidson. "What do you want?" he snapped. It annoyed him her purpose being here wasn't totally explained.

"Why don't you leave these people alone and let them do their job?" she demanded. "Ever since arriving all you have done is downgraded these people. You're asking the impossible of them so step back and keep your damned remarks to yourself."

"Why do you care what happens to them?"

Savannah bitterly asked. "When are you going to get your head out of your ass? These people are all you have standing between getting the job done or defeat. Treat them with respect or get out of their way. And another thing . . . are you going on this raid?"

"Are you kidding?" Earl exclaimed. "That isn't my job." After questioningly looking at her camouflages he asked. "Why are you in those clothes?"

"You don't expect me to go on a raid in dress uniform, do you?"

"But it isn't your job."

"Winning this war is everybody's job, Craver. It's just some of us elect to contribute more than others." Savannah sternly denounced before walking away.

Visiting the mess hall Savannah found Timothy and Tyler studying a map spread on their table. They motioned her to join them.

"Are you sure you want to go along?" Tyler asked. "It's risky."

"I'm sure." There was a short pause. "Tell me something, sergeant. Have you heard of the Battle of Running Creek?"

"Yeah and probably every marine has."

"What do you know about it?"

"Last year a regiment of marines was ambushed along Running Creek not far inside Canada. There was no way reinforcements could be sent so they were on their own for four days. After fighting overwhelming odds only one hundred and twenty marines survived the battle. I know about that battle because two cousins and one brother died in that battle."

Savannah frowned. "I'm sorry about your losses. Though the odds for survival was nearly zero the regiment fought like wild animals to drive off the invaders. The battle was won because every marine did his best. It was hell in the highest order."

"Is that what the reports wrote?" Timothy asked.

"No, that is how I observed the battle." After another pause she said. "I commanded the northern flank. From Charlie Company only two of us survived that battle. Yes, I want to go along because it's my duty as a marine officer." She looked at both men and bitterly said. "I think I earned that right to fight again."

"Yes, madam, I know that you have." Tyler slowly said with a wide smile. "I'll follow you anywhere."

The chief petty officer slowly nodded with a thin smile. "You are just full of surprises. But tell me something, what do you think about this envoy?" Timothy asked.

"He's a damned prick. Fortunately your commanding officer isn't obligated to accept his warped suggestions. But Earl Craver does have an urgent project to conclude after our raid."

"Since you're with intelligence," Tyler asked. "What can you tell us about the Soviet Navy? Do we still have to worry about them?"

She drank some coffee then nodded. "Though there's a lot of confusion and misinformation about the Soviet Navy, they have serious problems just like us. Fuel obviously is a major worry for them. But they gave other pressing problems. Central Intelligence has learned their Naval High Command in the badly damaged city of Ashkabad, Turkmenistan is fighting French troops storming across the war torn republic."

"Then we have a chance to win this war?" Timothy cautiously asked.

"We have always had a chance to win the war. Maybe right now things looks pretty bad, but we aren't defeated. Commands like Ten Deltas is giving the country a fighting chance, gentlemen. Central Intelligence is particularly interested in the KONSTANTANINOVICH. They have aboard a political commissar named Mikhail Karsavin. The Allies want this man to stand trial for his war crimes. If we can capture him alive that would give Ten Delta another feather in their cap."

"What did he do?" Tyler asked while looking toward the entry where marines were coming in for early breakfast.

"He's one of their nasty dogs without a leash. In the war's early days it looked as if we may win and this caused panic among the Russian High Commands. Colonel Karsavin convinced Kossier to authorize the use of biological weapons. There was supposedly an out cry from their senior field commanders. It was Karsavin who sent selected teams of KGB goons to assassinate those opposing the policy. Hours later those biological armed missiles caused devastating numbers of deaths among our European Allies. Then nature turned upon Kossier. Clouds of deadly gases were soon drifting through Eastern Europe killing his own troops and civilians. Needless to say the commissar isn't a popular man among his own people. The only thing keeping him from being assassinated is his friendship with Kossier."

The anticipated storm hit the Californian coast approximately two-thirty in the morning. Even those in Ten Delta felt the earth's trembling. From San Francisco to San Diego there was nobody to prepare for the newest on assault and the destruction was enormous. Thousands of people needlessly died during those terrifying hours. Protected by high mounds of debris facing the ocean, Ten Delta escaped the crashing waves pounding the shore. Beneath the rubble, unconcerned marines prepared for their upcoming raid with emotions that were contagious.

*　　*　　*

At the moment Captain Voronov's only interest was a driving obsession to save his crippled ship. With his wife and family dead the KONSTANTANTINOVICH was his child. The current storm created a consortium of violence battering the anchored ship harshly rocking and tossing in those crashing waves driving up the shore. When food was brought he politely refused. He did keep a cup of hot tea in hand as everything became a thunderous hell hole. Nobody would sleep that night. His cursing working parties struggled to keep the numerous repairs on schedule. From time to time during the long night the warship's lighting would go out. Emergency lights would come on until overworked electricians isolated the problems.

Sulking in his cabin Mikhail finished off what remained of the bottle and began nervously pacing the rocking decking. Mikhail was convinced the Americans were hiding between the sprawling ruins at Vandenberg and Monterey in their camouflaged radar station. The commissar knew the old captain was upset how California's alluring beauty was eradicated during Russia's calamitous nuclear attacks. He didn't believe in such bleeding heart emotions. Damages during war were to be expected. He knew the captain's emotions were twisted after his oldest son's regiment was sacrificed at Running Creek in Canada. When a large cresting wave smashed against the ship the colonel was thrown to the deck. Clumsily getting to his feet the colonel cursed the Americans.

Wiping blood from a small forehead cut the colonel was angry. There was much about this mission that made him mad. The steady tossing was physically too much for this drunkard officer. Climbing back into his bunk blankets was pulled tightly against his neck. It didn't matter the ship's crew had been on station for fifteen hours without food and their stomachs were growling. He had forgotten why he ordered the punishment. Mikhail cursed aloud when he was nearly thrown from his bunk when the storm's fury became stronger.

While the KGB official moaned and groaned his disgust with the tossing ship, its master thoughtfully paced the bridge that he refused to leave. Two husky ratings stood nearby with the sole purpose of protecting the captain. Occasionally Karl would hear another rumbling stomach. When he looked about the guilty man sheepishly grinned. Staggering to the windshield Karl tried looking passed the water drenched glass. The storm was getting pretty bad. Though loudly objected to the rough weather the grand old lady steadfast held together.

When the engineering officer came on deck Karl looked his way. "How are the men holding up?"

"They are a tough lot, Karl. But it's bad outside and we already lost one seaman when he was washed overboard and I have three engineering ratings injured."

After a brief silence Karl exhaled and said. "Bring the men inside. This is crazy. There's no reason they should die out in that damned storm."

"The commissar will raise hell."

"To hell with the KGB, let's see them do the repairs." Picking up the telephone the captain dialed their gallery. "I want sandwiches distributed to the men at their stations."

*   *   *

For the last few minutes James pensively stared at the video monitor in his room. Connected to their main communications electronic bank he could, with a flip of switches, survey any direction from Ten Delta. The color pictures were hazy because of those driving shields of icy waters thrown into the air by the angry Pacific. This didn't matter because his thoughts were a thousand miles away. Though wanting a stronger drink coffee would have to do.

There was a light knock on the door. When he opened it Savannah stood there. "Would you like company?" she asked.

"Sure. What do you have in mind?"

His curt suggestion angered her. "Well, obviously not what you have in mind." She was turning to leave when James lightly grabbed her arm. "I'm sorry, but that wasn't not what I had in mind." He returned to his chair giving her plenty of room to make a decision. "I can offer you a drink before our trip." He gestured at the door. "Leave that open if it makes you feel better."

Savannah stood for a few moments debating whether to go back to the mess hall. In a few seconds she had her answer. Leaving the door open she entered and sat. She watched as James poured some Scotch in glasses. When passing Roscoe gave them a thin smile and hurried on. Savannah suddenly blushed.

"When are we leaving?" she asked.

"Soon as the storm lets up and that shouldn't be long now."

Savannah curiously looked about the Spartan furnished room. Her glance fell on a glass-framed picture. "Is that your wife?"

James nodded with a weak smile. "Yes. I was wounded in the last Gulf War and when gaining consciousness she was standing there. Dorothy was a Navy nurse."

"She's very pretty."

"Dorothy's bouncy personality made it hard to dislike her."

She was finding the chair uncomfortable. Sipping the warm smooth Scotch, she remembered her very strict Roman Catholic home where the evils of alcohol were taught. Those memories seemed so long ago. After graduation she attended medical school then joined the Marines. Though the lieutenant was staring it wasn't like those men in St. Louis. Savannah realized this man was very lonely who really wanted a woman to talk with.

"Where are you from?"

"South Bend, Indiana."

"Did you attend Notre Dame?"

"No, my father taught there. I was never impressed with the school and instead attended St. Mary's. What university did you attend?"

"USC."

"That was a good school. But why did you sign up with the Outer Perimeter Commands? They're not exactly the choice of duties."

"The Corps was short of qualified combat officers so I agreed to command Ten Delta. The duty along the wastelands has its ups and downs. Some of our problems should never come about while others we have no control over. Because our superior officer refuses to visit the coast, we experience everything from shortages of rations to spare parts. It requires a strong emotional man to garrison these stations. Up and down the coast from Oregon to Mexico there are thousands of forest fires raging out of control. Our major cities were wasted by missile attacks while their survivors are relocated to mid Western states. But not everybody wanted to leave their homes and it's these people who look to us for protection and assistance." He sipped Scotch and watched the monitor showing the storm letting up. "Militarily, we're here to provide early warning when Soviet spies appear in these wastelands. Though our bases are undermanned and badly equipped we do have determined men and that counts. Here at Ten Delta I have a bunch of good men."

"I was told you were aboard the aircraft carrier CLINTON when she sunk off the Philippines."

James nodded after a few moments. "That day I was on patrol when Russian torpedoes took her down. When I came back there was only debris and burning oil on the surface with a few survivors in the water."

"According to naval reports you never made it to land."

"That's right. My chopper wasn't designed to fly long distances with a full load. After ditching the wounded crowded into a rubber raft, paddled away, and never were seen again. A badly wounded marine sergeant and I climbed into a small rubber raft before the chopper sunk. Eight days later we were picked up by a French warship."

Savannah thoughtfully sloshed her Scotch. "Was that Sergeant Tyler?"

"Yes, how did you know?"

"I don't know. I sensed a special bondage between you two."

Sergeant Roscoe poked his head into the room and announced. "The storm is letting up."

James nodded and stood. The time for casual chatting was gone. "Good, have the raiding party mount up."

CHAPTER FIFTEEN

Mikhail was awakened by the strong aromas of cooking foods. For a moment he laid on his uncomfortable bunk's jumbled mess sorting out his drowsy mind. It was a few more minutes before the inebriated colonel angrily rolled from his bunk. That was a painful mistake. Excruciating flashes of pain shot through his body like burning rods. Flopping back onto the bunk the colonel moaned while rubbing his forehead. He waited a short time then slowly stepped from the bunk careful not to make any sudden moves. Mikhail carefully measured each step. There was pain but like before. He groaned this had to be the worst hangover he had ever experienced.

Mikhail stood on the cold metal decking for a short time before realizing the ship wasn't tossing so bad. Disrobing he disgustedly threw the vomit splattered tunic and white shirt into a pile. The colonel didn't remember stripping off his trousers and underwear during the night. When his hand touched dried smears on his thighs Mikhail groaned loudly. That explained why there was no clothing below his waist. This was getting stupid. Cursing himself the colonel stood under the tiny shower's icy waters without feeling the chill.

When a knock sounded on his door Mikhail slowly opened it with revolver in hand. On the other side was an enlisted man wearing a dirty white apron. He nervously looked at the handgun before thrusting the food tray at him. Before Mikhail commented the man was hot footing it down the passageway. Mikhail thoughtfully looked at the tray realizing how hungry he was. With his foot he slammed the door then placed the tray on his desk. The reddish borshch tasted the same as in Russia. He quickly finished off the beet-based soup then turned his hunger upon the cutlets of meat fried in egg and breadcrumbs. The twisted brownish sausage had hints of Ukrainian cooking. There were over allowances of garlic, pepper, and vinegar. While eating thoughts of more carefree days passed. There was a special restaurant in Kiev he frequently patronized. For eight roubles he was served a delicious zakuski followed by two hot dishes. That was washed down with a half liter of good vodka. Mikhail smiled. Sometimes he would join in old fashioned Russian dancing much to the patrons' delight. Those days were gone forever. Two German nuclear missiles vaporized the city that never had a chance. But Kiev was avenged when Soviet nukes devastated German cities of equal importance. Finishing his meal the commissar dressed. The past was the past. It served no purpose thinking of the past.

As the colonel walked onto the bridge he noticed the storm's fury had passed. The shore was within hailing distance and he was shocked at the damages laid across those hills. He saw the captain talking with two shipboard officers. When they saw him the weapons officer finished his discussion and hurriedly left. Hearing a faint commotion behind him, Mikhail turned to see two husky ratings enter carrying AKA-47s in hand. He scowled at their arrival, but this time the stern-faced men didn't nervously back away. He became cautious while thoughtfully analyzing the bridge personnel. In the corner an enlisted man with a manual on electronics was trying to understand the damaged multi-colored wiring. Judging from his perplexed expression he wasn't doing that good.

"How are the repairs progressing?"

"With these frequent interruptions we're marginally getting there." Karl replied without committing himself.

"Any contact with Major Darkanbayev?"

"Not a word." There was a shot pause. "The fleet admiral sent a message another ship was on the way to assist us."

"Did he say which one?"

"No." The captain walking closer to the windshield watched his engineering ratings repairing damages from impoverished scaffolding attached to the superstructure. Dressed in heavy weather gear the sailors looked like overweighed polar bears holding onto wobbly structures of steel and wood.

"When are they scheduled to reach us?"

"Late tomorrow afternoon."

*   *   *

When James joined the strike team leaders, Timothy was nursing his fourth cup of coffee. A few minutes later Earl came to the table with a Washington map. Since Tyler wasn't going he wasn't at the table. Getting a glass of orange juice the base CO sat at the crowded table with a grunt. Earl was silently disturbed all marines at Ten Delta were black.

"O.K., Craver," James asked. "What do you have for us?"

Handing over two decoded messages Earl patiently waited until James read them. Scratching his chin a couple of times the lieutenant laid down the message. "Not too encouraging are they?"

"Not really, but did you think this would be a walk in the park."

Motioning over his fifteen volunteers James waited until they pulled up chairs and somberly waited for the briefing. They silently studied his worried expression and smiled faintly when he greeted them with a loose hand salute. "All right, marines, it's time to get down to business. I hear rumors you want to play John Wayne." This brought a sprinkle of chuckles. "I can promise this objective will be damned tough and we're anticipating heavy losses." None of the marines said anything. Their faces were molded into cautious expressions with nobody speaking aloud their worried emotions. "Our target as you already know is the Soviet naval base at Zasulich. Our field intelligence remains sketchy at the moment but will change at our refueling stop. We know the port is protected by heavy guns on a ridge. The harbor is a natural one on the island's inland side. There are twenty-five wooden structures on the base with their communications complex on the northwestern sector." Studying their expressions he found no fears. "The base is guarded by Soviet marines who are as good as we are." For a moment his voice was like the sharpness of a butcher knife. "Our primary objective is destroying an oil tanker anchored in the harbor's middle. We suspect the Soviet Navy is short on fuel and wasting their storage tanks would put a mean crimp in their invasion plans."

While James spoke Earl thoughtfully studied the strike team. While Earl studied the men Timothy was analyzing this envoy. When in that gray suit he resembled a nerd from some hidden computer center. But when putting on those camouflages he looked mean just like those CIA types he had came across during his time in the service.

After completing his briefing James looked about for questions and several hands shot up.

"What about radar?"

Earl interrupted. "They have advanced over-the-horizon system with ranges that normally would illuminate your chopper long before you came in contact. But by the time you arrive they should be out of commission. After British Columbia fell a small core from the 101st Airborne stayed behind to harass the enemy. They were later joined by Canadian and British commandoes. These men are providing data for your mission." Earl paused to look about their silent ranks. "You will have three hours to complete your mission once those commandoes cripple the antennas. But here is your soft spot. The Russian engineers will have the system back on line in three hours."

"What about airborne threats?"

"They have four Kamov helicopters armed with Soviet air-to-surface missiles."

"What about surface-to-air missiles?"

"Soviets are experiencing shortages of such weapons so there are none on that base."

"What about support?"

"There will be no support, gentlemen. It'll be the fifteen of us." James thoughtfully looked at his men's solemn expressions. "But the way I look at it, jarheads, there's only one objective ahead of us and aren't we the best?" There was a thunderous agreement and loud stomping of boots. Savannah taken aback by their response smiled. "We depart in one hour."

*   *   *

At the last minute it was decided to take Lewis' chopper. After waving at their friends, the strike team loaded onto the helicopter that was pulled outside by an old tractor. Once away from the base Lewis quickly gained altitude and headed north. It was six o'clock with strong winds and dropping temperatures. While Lewis piloted the machine his co-pilot carefully monitored their radar monitor. Chief Hickman sitting alongside a small porthole looked down on what remained of Eureka. The ride was rough from its beginning. Their problems originated from those many fires raging through the Klamath Mountains. Thick black smoky clouds deposited tons of debris into an overburdened atmosphere. The lonely helicopter rushing through a reddish glow was roughly tossed about.

Chief Hickman looked at his watch. They had been airborne for two hours. It was another two hours before their scheduled refueling. James left the cockpit where he had stayed since departing Californian air space. He thoughtfully looked about the interior. Some marines were taking this opportunity to sleep. Over in the corner a marine was deeply absorbed in reading another Tom Clancy novel. Timothy chose not to think about the mission, but when he did its impossibility became clearer. His thoughts were interrupted when hearing James' voice. The lieutenant was slowly moving down the aisle chattering with his tensed marines.

"Chief," James greeted with a cordial smile. "How's everything going?"

"So far everything is all right. What about Lewis?"

"His whole crew is eager beavers, especially that Gunner's Mate Armstrong." The lieutenant sat on the hard benches and sighed. It was his verbal gesture of impatience. With head resting against the fuselage James asked. "Where did we go wrong, chief?"

Again the large Chinook became a bone jolting ride through resisting winds forced upward by huge fires. They were pounded around like a leaf in stormy conditions. More than once he heard angry curses when marines were slammed against the fuselage.

"I'm not sure we did," the chief solemnly theorized. "After the Cold War ended the world sighed a long relief. Russia was forgotten while they worked on individual nationalistic problems. After all what was there to fear now? The big bad bear was no more. Nobody heard the brown bear crying for help."

"Can you blame them? Hell, for nearly eighty years there hung over the world a sinister red dawning of violence. I can remember in school we were taught the evils of Russia. Anytime there was a political intrigue movie it concerned the Soviet Union. In the Russian schools they were taught America was the evil monster." James groaned softly when the chopper went through another heavy wind pocket. "With this taught on both sides there was little hope for a peaceful solution. Sooner or later one side was going to accidentally start a war. And once this came about there was no turning around."

"Whether that Russian sub accidentally fired their missile or not may never be known. But nobody took the time to verify what happened. Missiles filled the skies like swarms of locusts. While from airfields world over came the bombers. Everybody responded defensively and then later offensively." The chief's voice became harsh. "Bush and Clinton had downsized our military so much that when the dreaded Red Dawn did materialize America was unprepared. We were short on everything. There was no time to bring ships out of mothballs. No time to reopen closed airfields and naval bases. Before our army divisions were reactivated our major cities lay in ruins with flames consuming millions of bodies. It was a projected nightmare come true."

James stared without really seeing. His tormented thoughts were reflecting on that secret report he had read before coming to Ten Delta. NATO countries were swift to launch their toys and soon the Soviet Union was in flames. Though the nuclear exchange lasted only twenty hours its destruction was incredible. Loss of life was unbelievable. Europe was reduced to ruins. Accurate losses would never be known. Nations simply ceased to exist. France fell into chaos. Defeated on her battlefields, Great Britain continued their fight in Canada. With her nuclear weapons expended, American armies being annihilated on scattered battlefields, her navy power obliterated, and most of the states uninhabitable because of dangerous radiation levels America still continued her struggle for freedom. Though he was silent Timothy knew James was rehashing those facts from that alarming report. Most Americans didn't know how extensive this war crushed peoples and countries. Actually he wondered if they wanted to know. The general populace was scared enough with what they knew.

The Chinook shuddered through increasing wind pressure pockets. Her twin Lycoming engines roared defiance. Fifty thousand pounds of metal and flesh continued over the devastated landscape while few conversations were heard. After the lieutenant left Timothy silently nursed his own memories. Resting his head against the fuselage the chief sadly remembered his wife and kids. In those days it was easy to laugh and find happiness. His wife was a small woman who loved life and worked in the base library to help support the family. He smiled when remembering she never complained about life's ups and downs. She was in San Diego when enemy bombers came with their death and destruction. Hearing a marine discussing his plans to kick Russian butt the chief looked his way. The strike team wearing rim-flared helmets and camouflage clothing looked mean with those ammo belts strapped to their waists and frag grenades clipped to chest belts. The facial brown and green paints made the marines look like something from the Rambo movies.

James came back. "All right, marines, weapon checks. We land for refueling in ten minutes. Snap to it. Buddy check packs." Walking over to Timothy he said. "Double check the men."

Turning around James briefly watched the marines checking equipment and chattering with their buddies. All strike members wore night goggles strapped to the rim helmets. It was easy to feel the machine slipping lower to escape enemy radar. It was still fairly dark outside. To their inland side distant reddish glows plotted the raging forest fires. Flying at one hundred feet high Lewis was covering a dangerous course. At this height the Chinook's latest state-of-the-art radar was their best friend. He returned to the cockpit.

Standing behind Lewis, James studied the darkened terrain ahead of their swiftly moving helicopter.

"So far so good," Lewis muttered.

James watched the heavy machine roar over wasted terrain at five hundred feet. If they developed trouble there would be no time to respond before crashing. The Boeing Chinook was a very large box fuselage weighing more than 22,000 pounds with a length of 99 feet. Originally appearing on the military scene in the fifties it underwent many variants since then. During the Vietnam era Chinook played a major role in transporting troops and supplies. James had confidence in the airship or maybe it was because Lewis handled her so well. Designed to carry a payload of 44 troops and a crew of 3, their special modifications reduced the load to 21 men. Above him the thumping of 60 foot fiberglass rotary blades was harmonious with their gentle slipping through air space. Their computer system integrated radar warning system remained silent. James was surprised the Russians hadn't illuminated them.

*　*　*

After the helicopter landed marines quickly established security perimeters. James warned Lewis not to cut his engines until they were satisfied the landing was secured. To their rear raged a thunderous forest fire through the Olympic National Park. Where they landed was once a private airport. A gasoline tanker sat near a wooden hut. One marine rushed over and yelled its keys were inside. Marines quickly manhandled a heavy refueling hose to the Chinook's tanks. Soon the strong scent of gasoline was drifting in the winds.

"What do you think?" Lewis asked James.

"They're waiting to see if we're on the up and up?" James thoughtfully answered. It was easy to see nobody had occupied this landing strip for sometime. Powerful winds whipping through the area created small whirlwinds that scattered loose debris and sooty tiny particles.

"Ever been here?"

"Not me." James again consulted the regional map. "According to this we're close to Clearwater. If it wasn't for those damned fires we could save precious time and miles." The distant reddish horizon glowed from the dancing fires. Olympic Mountains reaching more than 7000 feet into the murky skies twinkled like a giant candle. "We continue on our designated course to this point and turn inland to cross Washington's tip to the Strait of Juan de Fuca." Gesturing if Lewis needed the map the captain shook his head. James then slipped it into his tunic.

One sergeant caught Lewis' eye. "Doesn't that man ever sleep?"

James smiled. "Roscoe sleeps when there's not a mission."

Lewis shook his head. "What's he trying to do grab every medal we have?"

James watched the sergeant walk their perimeter with assault rifle arrogantly braced on his hip. "He already has every medal we got, including the Medal of Honor." The lieutenant was glad that black man finally got his act together. "Roscoe is a big man walking around with a big hatred for the communists. Every man I have is physically stretched beyond their normal endurance. But we still fight to protect this region." He sinisterly grinned. "I guess if you took away our obsession for killing every one of us would need serious psychotherapy. But that's how Ten Delta works as a team."

"You guys are remarkable." Lewis praised.

James satisfied with their security wondered where the commandoes were. Sergeant Roscoe uneasily walked the perimeter watching the forest line one thousand feet away. Fast pumping the fuel their marines wanted to get away from this ghastly place. It smelled of death and these men knew that scent only too well. For a few moments Lewis watched Roscoe's cautious stroll about the chopper. Looking behind him Lewis saw his gunner's mate stand in the door for a few moments before jumping down. Inside the craft his co-pilot stared at their radar monitor. A fierce wind rushing through the area like unleashed demons spread the awful smell of burning wood.

"Why don't those commandoes show themselves?" Lewis complained.

"Oh, they're around here. I can feel them." James walked a few steps and stopped. "The fuel was here as promised. After we finish pumping they'll show up." The lieutenant gave the captain a smile. "That reduces their exposure." Looking about James saw many places where a man could hide. "While you're out here adapting survival codes lets you live longer."

"So what do you think of Earl Craver now?" Lewis asked.

James shrugged an I-don't-give-a-damn gesture. "Craver is a damned asshole."

Lewis chuckled. "Craver is very complex to understand."

James didn't agree. "More like a damned walking disaster."

"You should hear the adjectives he uses to describe you." Shaking his head in a teasing manner he added amusingly. "It would make a whore blush, lieutenant."

"I don't care what you say . . . the man is a damned asshole."

James thought over the issue while they slowly walked slowly about the immediate area. Their boots crunched noisily on dead leaves and debris. Even with the howling wind they easily heard that thunderous roar from nearby forest fires. With hands clasped behind his back James thoughtfully walked the perimeter. His camouflaged garments were neatly pressed with a dull finish applied to his combat boots. The trousers were bloused at the bottom. An extra ammo belt crossed his chest with frag grenades clipped to the canvas material. His face was paint smeared with jagged brown and green lines.

*   *   *

Sergeant Roscoe divided his attention between the refueling and their woody surroundings. He was worried about the missing partisans. Staying too long in the clearing was dangerous. The heavy rifle was part of his hand. Looking towards the pumping he saw they were wrapping up the operation.

Walking over to Corporal Thorton he asked. "See anything?"

"Naw, sarge, there ain't nothin' out there."

"Well, stay alert." Roscoe advised then walked away knowing the man was probably thinking about his girl friend back in Ohio. Then Roscoe stiffen when sensing somebody out there. But were they the expected partisans or enemy patrols? His hand tightened about his rifle. Turning quickly he caught James' attention and hand signaled trouble was in the making.

Before either man reacted, four men dressed in dirty camouflages stepped from the woods with rifles cradled in their arms. The first soldier pausing near the refueling operation thoughtfully looked about. When one marine atop the gasoline truck suspiciously regarded him the commando cordially waved then walked on. Sergeant Roscoe cautiously stepped forward to meet the intruders. The intruders were Americans carrying Russian AKA-47s. Their leader was tall with a bearded face. While two partisans remained near the trees, another stopped before Roscoe and James. Ten Delta's strike team strategically positioned about the clearing watched this intrusion with weapons ready for usage. Timothy when hearing the confrontation stepped from the Chinook with rifle held in firing position.

There was a scraggly appearance to this one as he held out his gloved hand. "Lieutenant Blackmore," he greeted in a gruff voice. "Charles Lanning."

James didn't hesitate to say. "It's not unusual when strangers appear among wolves."

Charles confidently replied. "A lamb can intermingle if needing to." His hardened facial expression softened after that. Looking at the ugly blackness drifting lower from distant burning trees he shook his head. "Looks like another damned storm is coming our way," he warned after a moment. Leaning his rifle against a leg the man withdrew a crumbled pack of cigarettes. "I should quit smoking the damned things before they kill me." He smiled at his dry humor.

With their code and counter code exchanged both men relaxed. James watched the old fuel truck pulled away from their helicopter. "Any trouble out there we should know?"

"Not now there isn't." Between puffing on his cigarette Charles talked. "We ambushed a mechanized patrol back some miles. We killed those suckers before they radioed in." He sneeringly drew a finger across his neck. "They joined their fellow demons wherever that may be." For a moment he looked about with sharp disapproval. "I don't want to tell you how to run Ten Delta, lieutenant. But we could have wasted you several times. You have lousy perimeter security." He showed sharp disapproval as winds whipped his long hair about the neck.

James stood there with a thin smile before snapping his fingers. The partisans cautiously turned as several marines quietly stepped from the woods with assault rifles pointing at the four partisans. "We're not careless, Charles old boy. If you had made a foolish move they would had blown your balls into the next county." James enjoyed his approving nod. "So what do you have for me?"

The partisan withdrew a folded map from inside his heavy coat. After spreading it on the ground the men knelt as Charles talked. The wind tried jerking it from his gloved hand. "Twenty-eight minutes ago the three Russian communications towers were blown up. Your clock is now ticking," He thoughtfully looked at each of those brown and green smeared faces staring at him. Winds over the last few days had gotten colder while in the mountains ice was freezing the smaller creeks. "That means, marines, you have exactly two hours and thirty-eight minutes as of now to reach your objective, execute your orders, and then get the hell out of there." He glanced at James. "Don't drag your ass because those damned communist bastards aren't dumb."

"How can you be so certain how long they'll be down?" Roscoe asked.

Charles smiled. "Because we have destroyed them three times before. Their engineering teams are eager beavers when they want to." His amusement departed. "Take my word for it the towers will be transmitting in three hours."

"What about airborne threats?" Timothy asked. "We were told there are Kamov choppers on the base?"

"There are four of the bastards, but they don't fly unless there are identified targets."

"Why?"

"They are so short on gasoline that Russian soldiers roam the coast siphoning what they can find."

"That explains those 55-gallon drums on that destroyer."

Charles nodded. "They have three mechanized patrols out at any given time. We blew one to kingdom come not long ago. The other two are being watched."

"What about ships in port?" James asked.

"Their destroyer KONSTANTANTINOVICH left a couple of days ago and hasn't returned."

James smiled. "She'll be out of commission for some time." While Charles listened half shocked James explained how she was ambushed.

"Good golly Molly, you mean your men damaged a warship that badly?" Charles could only shake his head in disbelief. "Well, that certainly cuts down your threats. There is an oil tanker anchored in the harbor. Except for some smaller craft that's the extent of their Navy in port. But of course you know about their task force coming down the coast? According to intercepted messages they're expecting the ships any day now." While rubbing his right eye the left hand kept the paper from blowing away. "This hand drawn map accurately lists every gun placement and known threat." The man groaned when standing. "Near the base's eastern flank are two anti-aircraft batteries that haven't changed places since the base was built. They have patrols riding around in jeeps. With their radar down they're electronically blind. Like I said before, don't even stop for a shit. If they go back on line while you're there . . . all I can say is you're in deep shit."

Their briefing went on for another five minutes. After the marines were loaded aboard, James looked over his shoulder to see the partisans saluting their mission. Then he closed the door while motioning Lewis to get the hell out of this nightmare.

CHAPTER SIXTEEN

Tyler found Earl sitting in the mess hall drinking coffee. Crossing the room he dropped a map on the table and sat. "We got big, big trouble," he cynically warned.

The envoy curtly asked. "Since when do you not have trouble?"

"I just finished interrogating one of our locals. Last night he heard heavy rumbling on Highway 101. But with that storm raging he didn't go outside. This morning he investigated and found heavy tracks . . . those that tanks would have."

"How reliable is your local?"

"Juan Lopez is very reliable. He was with the army's First Armor Division in our Middle Eastern War. So he should know what tank tracks look like."

"So where did Lopez find these tracks"

Tyler unfolded the regional map and pointed at a spot.

Earl became very disturbed. "That's Lompoc."

The master sergeant slowly nodded. "They're heading for Vandenberg Air Force Base."

For a few moments the envy rubbed his chin in deep concentration. "For my mission to be successful we can't have interferences from the Soviets."

"Then we need to stop them before their forces are entrenched." Tyler suggested. When Earl didn't respond the sergeant suspiciously asked. "Is there any reason the Soviets wants to stop your mission?"

"Possibly."

It was time for Tyler to be curt. "That's a rather vague answer."

"Lieutenant Blackmore isn't here to authorize insertions." Earl replied in an unfriendly manner.

Tyler scowled. "And neither is our executive officer. With that said, I'm the third in command. I don't understand what you're planning to do on the air base, but if the communists entrench those plans are cancelled. Remember we have only 56 men at Ten Delta." There was a short pause. "Anyhow, since this is your operation you can order reconnaissance flights to determine what's out there." The master sergeant frowned. "Of course, you can also choose to sit on your ass. By the time James returns your mission's objective will be in shambles."

Earl didn't like this curt-mannered black man telling him what to do. "Does Lopez know how many tanks are out there?"

"There's no way he would know without seeing them."

Earl was silent for a few minutes while Tyler impatiently waited. "Have Barnes come to the conference room."

After Barnes and Lopez were seated at the table Earl sat across from them. While the Mexican nervously regarded the Presidential envoy, Barnes decided Earl was like all other political career men-arrogant and self-centered. Tyler came in with warm bottles of beer and distributed them before sitting.

Juan Lopez was a short stout built Mexican/American who trusted Tyler, but found contempt and distrust for the envoy. When asked about the tanks the dark-skinned man carefully said. "Because it was stormy outside I never saw the armor. But I have heard them while stationed at our Baumholder garrison in Germany. They were Russian hand me downs to the German Army when East Germany folded." He looked at the sergeant. "They're the Russian medium battle tank."

"God," Tyler moaned. "Those aren't toys."

Earl shrugged uneasily. "I don't know that much about Soviet armor. So what are we looking at?"

"The T-55 medium tank is a fully tracked vehicle carrying a 100-mm rifled gun and one 7.62mm coaxial machine gun. It's that rifled gun we worry about."

"Can we stop the tank?" Earl cautiously wanted to know.

"The Stingers can take them out while our choppers are armed with Hellfire missiles. Our problem is getting close enough to do it. But the low-silhouetted hull with its dome shaped turret makes a difficult target." Tyler stopped talking. "But our main concern is how many of those bastards are out there."

"The Apaches can solve that mystery," Barnes recommended.

Tyler nodded. "They can. And while they're up maybe we can find who is dumping those tanks. A destroyer sure as hell can't." He glanced at the silent envoy. "What do you know about this task force?"

"Our intelligence has been unable to identify the ships."

Tyler frowned. "Well, they suck big time."

"We don't have the technology of past years. There are no satellites or ground sources to identify threats. With the world in chaos everything is second guessing and you hope it works. You should know that of all people." Earl paused then solemnly nodded. "But you're right, sergeant. An air reconnaissance may be in order and I want to go along." He looked at Barnes again. "Are you familiar with the Aristotle Project?"

Barnes studied the envoy with a dark expression. He was a medium height man with short brown hair and a stubby grey beard. "How did you know about Aristotle?" he suspiciously asked. "That was an extremely sensitive classified project."

"There are few classified matters these days, Mr. Barnes. But you haven't answered my question."

"I was an engineer on that project." After Earl demanded more information, the retired scientist settling back in his chair thoughtfully looked at those around the table. "Aristotle Project's mission was launching a special modified Minuteman rocket to study the chemistry of our upper troposphere and stratosphere."

"That was Vandenberg's official announcement." After Barnes scoffed the envoy continued. "Actually NASA was working on the insertion of another nuclear device into space. The program authorized by Defense in 2006 for a completion date of 2012 was running behind schedule because of the Middle Eastern Wars." He grinned at the engineer's stern silence. "Look I don't give a damn what you were reaching for. That's all history now. We were informed the program is inside an underground research facility within walking distance of Site number SLC-6."

"Vandenberg is in ruins." Tyler protested.

"What about it, Barnes? Did SLC-X escape the missile attacks?" When the man refused to answer Earl looked at the sergeant. "The air force base may be in ruins, but SLC-X was so strongly built it probably didn't suffer damages."

"What do you expect to find down there?" Tyler asked.

"One modified Minuteman rocket." Earl smiled at their surprises. "My mission is arming that rocket with a warhead filled with chemicals that hopefully will introduce rainfall. There are a total of nineteen sites throughout the world and all must be fired at the same time. We hope the rainfall will remove airborne debris and soot."

"Are you sure that's your intentions?" Barnes suspiciously demanded.

Earl indifferently shrugged. "And what would be my other intentions?"

"Supposedly all of our nuclear armed missiles were expended. Finding another missile would tip the scales."

"So that's why the Russians are sending tanks to those ruins?" Tyler cynically charged.

"It probably is. I really don't know. But far as we know there are no other nukes nor can they be manufactured. I'm not after the rocket to launch a nuke. But I do desperately need that rocket inside SLC-X within hours. We have a window to fire into and losing it even for another three days would be lousy."

Barnes asked after a short pause. "So what do you want me to do?"

"I'm told the rocket can be fired manually."

Barnes didn't commit himself. "It was designed to be launched either electronically or manually. But firing it manually requires extensive preparation."

"I'm told you're qualified to do this?"

"I'll tell you that after seeing the rocket."

*　　*　　*

Following the short refueling layover James walked among his silent marines. He knew none of their thoughts were on this war. Near the Chinook's middle he paused and smiled at Savannah quietly waiting for their entry into hostile air space. Outside the helicopter the cold wind was strong causing it to frequently shake and rattle when pushing through resisting currents. Below them numerous fires raged through forests and across mountains. The marines having witnessed these conflagrations too many times before didn't bother looking.

"All right, marines, listen up." James barked like a drill instructor. Jerked from their reflections the team obediently looked up. "Some of you will be issued new fire power so listen to Petty Officer Armstrong's instructions."

He looked over his shoulder to see a short gruff-mannered sailor stepping from the cockpit. Like other team members from Lewis' chopper, he didn't fraternize with the marines. But Ten Delta marines ignored their aloofness. The second class petty officer was dressed in sand colored camouflages. His dark green eyes slowly glared at each strike team member. There was a smirk firmly planted on his long narrow face. Armstrong wore a web belt with canvas holstered revolver, two strange looking grenades, and extra ammo for the handgun. Thinning brown hair was combed back.

His voice when speaking was loud and clear. "My name is John Armstrong, Gunner's Mate Second Class, United States Navy." He slowly looked at the attentive marines with those unfriendly eyes. "My friends call me Gunner, but you jarheads will call me Petty Officer Armstrong." Ten Delta marines stared with their own cold emotional scowling. "I'm here to show you a few new things in warfare. Your commanding officer boasted you're the best damned marines around these parts." He paused before frowning. "But during my long years in the Fleet, I have never met a marine worth a shit." When the helicopter hit another rough air pocket he grabbed a ceiling hand rail. "I can't even get up a fart to show my contempt for you worthless bags of shit."

James glared at the sailor before harshly suggesting. "Gunner, you're here to instruct my marines, not insult them. I highly recommend you do just that and forget about your smart ass remarks." He stopped talking for a moment. "Do I make myself clear, Gunner?" When the petty officer didn't respond James' voice became demanding. "I didn't hear you, Gunner!" After a moment Armstrong nodded. "Very well, now continue with your training."

Armstrong sucked in his breath then loudly said. "Listen up, jarheads! This is a HJT-32-AT grenade. It's a new fragmentation blast/concussion type that's not on the military inventory." Holding up the object he kept talking while avoiding James' unfriendly glare. "This ugly baby is plastic matrix holding 6300 tiny sharp cutting blades. Pull this bouchon pin and throw. Don't stand there picking your nose but throw and dive for cover. Fuse time is ten seconds. Within sixty feet these mothers will rip the guts out of any standing human. They will slice the hell out of a tree." He handed the grenade to a marine. "Look at it. Examine it like your girl friends' tits. The HJT-32-AT is an Austrian invention which hit the markets in 2009." Arrogantly bracing hands on his hips he scowled at the marines. "Remember the drill . . . pull pin . . . throw like hell . . . hit the deck."

Armstrong was the son of poor dirt farmers in Arkansas. Between school hours which his mother forced him to attend, John plowed bad soil that rarely produced decent crops. He quickly created a dream world that wasn't crowded with reality. All he wanted was three square meals and pay to send home to his aging parents. He somehow graduated from school. After enlisting in the Navy he found a home aboard ships. Sucking in his breath he looked about the cramped interior. When the helicopter went through another bad patch of air he indifferently grabbed that railing above his head. His piercing eyes never left the marines examining the black object. When it was returned he clipped the device to his canvas belt.

"Very impressive toy," James praised.

"Yes, sir, and there are very short supplies of them. Only very sensitive operations are issued this type." After that he squatted and opened a metal olive green box bolted to the decking. Those marines near it saw dark green foam cradling five rifles. Lovingly picking up one he held it high while talking. "Now for the second half of your class, jarheads, this is a P38-M-20 rifle. This British killer machine's issuing is restricted to highly classified black operations. The Soviets don't know about its existence." He suddenly glanced at a private and bellowed. "Looks innocent, doesn't it?" His voice again adopted that harsh cynical tone. "But, jarheads, this ain't an M-16!" He patted a marine's head and invited. "Look at it. It ain't loaded so you won't get hurt." Ignoring the black man's hostile reaction he straightened up and continued. "The British were still experimenting with it when this little war popped."

The helicopter passed over a thunderous forest fire sending invisible dancing heat through its cramped interior. This wasn't ordinary heat and John quickly longed for that fresh air found at sea.

"This laser-directed rifle has advancements even those damned science fiction movies would love. This is the latest in laser technology. Loosely resembling an M-16 from our Vietnam days, this baby has a solid plastic butt stock, perforated plastic hand guard, and modified front sight protector. The butt stock is retractable for easier transport. There are five selections for fire control . . . three burst and the others automatic. Its weight is 5 pounds unloaded. Accuracy range is 563 feet." James watched him sarcastically pace the aisle. "Now for a word of warning. The British discovered this rifle overheats when fired too long on fully automatic." Reaching up he unscrewed its dull black barrel. "This is removable. Inserting new barrel requires sixty seconds." He occasionally glanced at the lieutenant after discovering he was interested in the laser rifle.

"Now we get to the nitty-gritty of this ass ripping rifle." Holding up the rifle he declared. "If Iraq had this weapon when we invaded our forces would have been chewed to pieces." He smiled. "But they didn't and we only have a few to pass around." Laying down the rifle for a moment, he took a black square pack from the box. After buckling the pack on his back he picked up the rifle. While holding the weapon in his left hand, Armstrong unsnapped the back pack with his right hand. "Remove one of these mothers." He took the curved banana magazine clip and pushed it into a top slot. "This, jarheads, is its power source." He sneered at them. "If you were listening then you heard the words power source and not ammo clip. This clip contains compressed energy which is what lasers are all about. Here close to this trigger guard are two tiny lights. Right now the yellow one indicates a new power charge has been inserted. When yellow changes to green you're ready to lock and load." He proudly smiled. "When the green goes out . . . you're ready to fire. When the light flickers red . . . you have exactly one hundred and fifty bursts left."

A marine spoke up. "How many shots does that thing carry?"

John furiously looked at the marine's light brown skin and bellowed. "This, boy, ain't a damned thing! It's a P38-M-20, the best damned killing machine on market and you better damned not forget that!"

Before the marine jumped up James stepped forward. "Petty Officer Armstrong, I suggest you keep to the subject." He was nearly touching the man's face. "The next time you insult my men I'm going to smash your balls! Am I understood?"

For a moment the gunner's mate stood firm while the marines stared with their own hatred worn like badges. Then after unbuckling the back pack he continued as if nothing had happened. "This is known as a ZP-11-LPP. It's the power source for your P38-M-20. It may sound complicated, but it isn't. This pack carries six power changes. That's enough for one thousand firings." He grinned at their astonishment. "Yeah, that's right. This allows you to kick ass much longer." He returned the power pack to the case. Turning around he thoughtfully studied the silent marines. "If you aim at a man . . . intend to kill him. A laser rifle doesn't wound." Pointing at the box he said. "A warrior can easily tote two packs since they weigh only five pounds each. If you had noticed when I had the weapon out there was a slender scope. That's a FVE. The Full Vision Enhancer allows total visual command through darkness, fog, or any other bad condition."

ᛁᛁ   ᛁᛁ   ᛁᛁ

KONSTANTATINOVICH's captain quietly stood on his repaired bridge contemptuously watching the drunkard KGB colonel arrogantly stumbling about. Karl was certain the Americans would eventually seek them out now that his ship was crippled. Morale aboard the warship was at its lowest since the war began. Only because of his influence over the crew were their mutinous emotions controlled, but for how long. He watched his working parties hurrying about their assignments. Many damages were temporarily repaired while their sensitive electronics was down. The gun turrets could only be repaired in a shipyard. His gunnery department patrolled the decks with shoulder fired missile launchers, a weak defense, but better than nothing.

"We finished repairing the forward generators," Commander Bogdanov informed. "There's nothing my people can do about the steering shaft's housing. It was badly scored." With a deep sigh he drank some coffee and studied the shore line. "When do you think they'll come after us?"

"When we least expect them. Lieutenant Blackmore is a cunning fox. Knowing we're down for the count he'll play with us at his leisure." Karl contemptuously watched the commissar stagger from the bridge. After tightly clasping hands behind his back the captain was silent for several moments. "At one time we had an opportunity to win this damned war. The Americans were caught with their pants down. However, the window for victory was narrow and short lived. But men like that cursed fool doomed our people. They think through their asshole and not their brain. Even if by some miracle we were to win what is there to conquer? Her cities are in ruins and the awesome American industrial might smashed."

"Does anybody ever win a war?" the engineering officer softly complained. After handed the daily summary the commander slowly read it aloud. "Kasulich forecasted another unstable weather front moving down from Canada. We can expect the current temperatures of 38 degrees to drop even further. Wind speeds currently 28 miles per hour will increase. Our present visibility of five miles will sharply decrease." He was silently disturbed with the report. "Radiation count is 4% above normal and steadily rising." After a few moments the engineering officer looked at his captain. "What about our reconnaissance patrol? Have we heard from them since yesterday?"

"No. I have entered in the ship's log that Major Darkanbayev is missing in action and may be dead." Karl thoughtfully replied. "I recommended no further patrols until the task force reached us. But of course permission was denied. Last night two armored patrols supported by mechanized infantrymen were landed off Point Arguelio. By now they have established positions on the Vandenberg Air Force Base."

The commander nodded his approval. "Then they're two days ahead of schedule. So where is the ALEKSANDR?"

"The amphibious vessel will return tomorrow sometime. Last night after dropping off the strike forces she made her way to San Diego. There another armored strike force was landed. They will link up with Mexican forces and return up the coast."

"Surely our government isn't shaking hands with those Mexicans?" he suspiciously asked. "They're nothing but street thugs."

"Maybe, but their objectives are different. The Mexican cause is annexing California in the name of Mexico," Karl indifferently explained. "Their battle cry is California illegally taken from Mexico will be returned. Their activities will remove attention from us and that is good."

"But Mexico lost the territory in their 1800s war with the States." After Karl shrugged the commander sarcastically added. "Maybe they should give Mexico back to the Indians from whom they stole it?" He sinisterly chuckled. "Of course, you know that isn't about to happen." There was a short pause. "This war is all about corrupted politics. With the Americans' spine broken those Mexicans think they can just strut in and claim the land. But I think the Americans will never let that happen."

"Dirty politics is what this damned war is all about, my friend." Karl walked out into the icy winds to study their defenses ashore. "They'll come at night when we're most defenseless."

Joining his commanding officer the commander said. "We have outposts along the shore east and west for one mile in each direction. We have two motorized patrols randomly driving the stretch. But without radar we're basically relying on visual contact."

*   *   *

Because he wasn't pilot trained on the attack helicopter, Tyler flew the clumsy old Chinook. From Gaviota the master sergeant flew low along the coast to Point Conception then swung inland. After crossing over the air base's outer boundaries Earl was startled at the extensive damages from those Russian air attacks. High pressured fires from the National Forest and Santa Ynez Mountains pushed smoky clouds toward the aircraft. Barnes and Earl viewed the destruction as Lewis' Chinook flew its low altitude reconnaissance toward the test and development site SLC-6-X. In the rear ten heavily armed marines sat stern-faced and ready for fighting if that fell their way.

"I never knew the base was this big," Earl mumbled.

"Vandenberg is awesome." Barnes agreed. "It really was impressive to see from the air before those communists came. She was extensively used for the launching of unmanned government and commercial satellites into polar orbit. Another sector was responsible for intercontinental ballistic missile test launches to the Kwajalein Atoll. It wasn't until 1955 that the Air Force recognized a need for secured test sites."

"But why here? It's flanked by heavily populated areas."

"When the government brought the 86,000 acres in 1941 it wasn't crowded. In fact, early pictures show this area as very remote and secured. During the forties Vandenberg was named Camp Cooke where the Army trained their armored divisions. It was deactivated in 1946 and reactivated in 1950 for the Korean War. Mothballed again in 1953, the base was about to fade into history when the Air Force chose the remote site for testing their missiles."

When flying over those areas close to the ocean Earl groaned his disappointment. "The launching tower at SLC-6 has been destroyed."

Tyler glancing at the envoy anxiously asked. "Does this mean the project is cancelled?"

Barnes skeptically interrupted. "It may not be. SLC-6-X was developed in a complex deep beneath the ground. The Air Force factored everything in including earthquakes. I'm willing to bet those chambers are still intact."

Suddenly Tyler yelled. "We got an incoming!" Sharply banking the chopper the master sergeant went even lower while leapfrogging over twisted ruins of former launching towers. Behind them the hostile missile tore into the devastation and exploded. "We got company down there!" Speaking into his helmet's communicator he hurriedly reported. "Mother Hen, Mother Hen this is Black Hawk, we're under attack over the air base." Looking at Barnes only for a second he shouted. "Quick where the hell are we?"

After Ten Delta got their coordinates the sergeant yelled to hold when seeing another incoming missile on direct impact. Tyler fought the controls to swing out of the rocket's path. He may have missed the flaming rocket if there was another minute of desperate maneuvering. That short range rocket clipped the fuselage sending the machine in a twisting rush towards the ground.

Since they were flying so low the large clumsy machine skidded across the uneven ground and abruptly stopped several feet from some ruins. Quickly unbuckling his seat belt Tyler stumbled back where his marines were recovering from the crash.

"Anybody hurt?" he shouted. The strike team all shouted they were all right. "Let's get the hell away from the chopper!" Glancing at Earl he asked. "Did you get through the call we're down?"

"They acknowledged we're down."

Tyler stood in the drifting smoke from the crashed helicopter for a few moments. "It'll soon be dark and the enemy holds the advantage then." The sergeant walked over to Barnes who was leaning against some twisted beams. "Are you all right?" When the engineer nodded he asked. "You know this terrain better than any of us. We need shelter until daylight. But it has to let us keep an eye on things around here." Gesturing at the crashed machine he added cynically. "That confirms the enemy is around here."

"Why don't we go back to the base?" Earl asked.

"It's over twenty miles to Gaviota and if we tried running the Russians would chop us to pieces. And with the strike team away Ten Delta can't afford to rescue us. We'll wait until daylight. When they come back the lieutenant will fly air support for the other Chinook and pick us up."

Earl uneasily looked about. "You do know the enemy may attack tonight?"

"It's a good possibility. I would if I were their commander. So where do we hide that offers good shelter and defensive command of the terrain?"

It was a few minutes before Barnes anxiously escorted them to a partial underground bunker offering a good visual sweep of the surrounding land. The few men hurried through the near darkness. The old fashioned bunker built in 2005 permitted close up viewing of launching rockets. Not that far away in the shadows was SLC-6-X's secret complex.

"All right, marines, find a place where you have a clear view of our situation. I promise we'll have visitors sneaking around before morning." Minutes later the Chinook burst into flames then exploded. "Well, if they didn't know where we were they do now."

CHAPTER SEVENTEEN

When nearing the enemy installation Gunner opened the olive box. After James pointed out his best sharpshooters the gunner's mate handed each a new rifle. The lieutenant went back to where Savannah sat nursing her troubled thoughts. Gunner shook his head while hearing the men boast how good they were. They were like youngsters getting their first BB gun for Christmas. The major briefly glancing at James wondered why she felt so light-headed when he was around. Because the flight was brutally opposed by powerful winds their crucial timetable was off. In a couple of hours darkness would again fall across the wasted land.

Savannah disapprovingly watched the gunner's mate arrogantly moving among the men. "In another time that man would have been discharged for his racist attitude," she softly denounced.

James nodded. "He probably would have." Observing the sailor talking to his selected sharpshooters the lieutenant said. "But beside his cultural faults Gunner knows his profession. And in a war such as this we need his kind."

Lewis yelled back. "Drop zone within twenty minutes."

After crossing into enemy air space with no opposition James was encouraged. The partisans apparently had committed their part in this strike. James looked at his watch for the last time and shouted equipment check. Truman silently cursed the white-ass lieutenant because they had just finished a weapons check one hour previously. But this officer you didn't argue with. After James nodded Truman's weapon was in fine condition he moved on.

Passing his weapons' check Truman flopped down on the hard bench and thought about his girl friend back in Ohio. This native of North Carolina thanked God the war's savageness hadn't touched that state. It seemed long ago when he last kissed her then left for the Outer Perimeter assignment. Seated across from the marine Timothy watched the marine's mouth widen from the smile.

"Hey, Truman," the chief jokingly called. "If you don't stop thinking about that gal, a Russian will put a bullet up your ass."

Truman laughed. "That ain't going to happen to this boy. I'm lucky." he boasted.

Over Astoria, Washington Lewis changed course and swept inland for forty miles before turning toward British Columbia. Their present course took them to Victoria. Twenty miles from this city, the Air Force captain corrected his headings to fly over the ocean. This would bring them in on the island's seaward side. Still no enemy interceptors challenged their illegal intrusion. After James was summoned up front, his men curiously watched the furious Pacific Ocean pounding the seaward shores of Vancouver Island.

"What about radar?" James asked.

"Clear channels after those towers were brought down. Hopefully, this will give us a smooth entry." He quickly studied his fuel gauges with a frown. "The constant battling those headwinds has seriously used our gasoline."

"Will we have enough until the refueling point?" James asked with some concern.

"Oh, we'll make it back." There was a short worried pause. "Have you noticed the island's forests aren't burning?"

"Yeah, I noticed."

Their helicopter was hopping over tree tops like a toy plane in the hands of a child. At this low altitude no radar could illuminate them even if the towers were operating. "I guess we should be thankful the Russians are thinly stretched along this coast. Their best troops are on the Canadian battlefields." James frowned. "Then again we're coming in from the seaward side and obviously they never factored this on their defenses."

When they were twenty miles away from the naval facility, Lewis dropped even lower. Charlie stood behind his door mounted machine gun. Within minutes the helicopter touched ground without opposition. Afterwards the strike team quickly moved out with Truman on point. Once they were out of sight, Lewis and crew made their preparations for a swift departure when the marines returned.

*   *   *

As the handful of men cautiously set up their security perimeters around the bunker, it was hard to perceive this massive destruction was once America's gem of missile research on the West Coast. Russian long range IBM missiles had within minutes reduced the sprawling complex into rubble. Huge buildings once housing space research were flattened like thin paper. For weeks the air base had burned. Now debris and soot from nearby forest fires coated the terrain. Tyler and one of his marines found a pile of rubble affording an excellent view of the immediate area. Barnes soon joined them when not wanting to stay inside the bunker. Night goggles permitted them to see through the developing darkness as another day ended.

While Stan scanned the darkness with special night binoculars, Tyler and Barnes laid on their stomachs staring at what existed beyond their little plot of ground. The wind was icy and at times reaching 20 miles per hour. Visibility was limited.

All in all it was a bad night to be out roaming around. Barnes hoped the Russians also thought so.

"So you worked here?" Tyler asked in a low whisper.

"For fifteen years following my retirement from the Air Force." He was quiet for a short time. "There was a lot of history on these grounds. At one time more than 18,000 military, dependents, and civilian contractors were part of the Vandenberg family. We were a city in itself." he proudly said. "You wouldn't believe the enormous pools of talent on this base. We were committed to about 7000 range operations a year. No matter where you look, there is history plastered on every mile of this air base."

"What were you working on?"

"I reckon it's all right to discuss our project since it'll never lift off the ground. We were modifying a unarmed Minuteman III intercontinental ballistic missile. Its final objective was launching a payload of highly sensitive instruments that would analyze our planet's chemistry. Sometimes I suspected the Air Force had another purpose for it. But whether they did or not our budget was in the hundreds of millions. Three other missiles were successfully fired at the Ronald Reagan Test Site on the Kwajalein Atoll. After finally solving the launch problems we turned our efforts on solving the payload issues."

"Were you on base during the attacks?" Tyler shivered in the cold night air even though wearing heavy insulated camouflages.

"Yeah."

"How did you survive the blasts?"

"SLC-6-X's underground chambers were built like a vault. At first we thought it was another earthquake. But we quickly learned hell was breaking loose on the surface."

"Do you think the launching system is still intact? There's incredible destruction out there."

"It was intact when I abandoned the chambers months ago. But I'm more worried about those bad earthquakes ripping through this region following those explosions. A lot of those damages out there were caused by shakers."

Corporal Stan Davis was a short marine topping only five feet two inches. His dull eyes were deceptive because he saw all and forgot nothing. This Alabama native was the last marine reporting to Ten Delta. After six years in the Corps he possessed no ambitions to advance. The light-skinned Negro was never in trouble though he did have a terrible temper. Corporal Davis knew when to express his fury and when not to. His specialized rating was electronics and aviation mechanics. Stan generally got along with his peers, but he refused to torch the bodies they found. Since the others never objected James left the matter along. Before the war came Stan wasn't religious though his father and grandfather had been Baptist ministers. After months of bloody fighting Stan changed his attitude and read the Bible constantly. He prayed to who many claimed was a cruel uncaring god. Unlike Chatterbox he never preached his religious beliefs. Laying on his stomach the corporal cautiously scanned the darkness with his night binoculars.

"Do you see anything?" Tyler asked.

"This place is dead as a doorknob." Stan uneasily muttered. Unconsciously his gloved hand reached out touching his AKA-47 lying at his side. He was the only marine at Ten Delta choosing the Russian assault rifle named after Avtomat Kalashnikov. In his hand the short, stubby submachine gun with thirty round Banana-style magazine was deadly. His newly found religious beliefs didn't embrace forgiving the cursed Soviets.

"Well, they are out there," Tyler whispered. "I can feel it in my gut."

Stan kept cautiously scanning his designated grid with the night penetrating glasses. The scent of death around them was terrible. That foul odor of decomposing bodies trapped in the rubble was enough to gag a person. Cold winds whipped in from the ocean thunderously howled over the terrain. He patted his coat's side pocket and smiled. Stan was never without his small Bible. Then his body stiffened after sensing movement in the darkness.

"Sergeant," he anxiously whispered.

"Yeah, I see them. Stay low for now. Let's see how many more of their buddies are out there."

*　　*　　*

After Truman eagle-eyed something ahead the team hit the ground. In a hunched over posture James silently made his way to the point. The black marine gestured ahead of them. In a clearing huddled around a small campfire were three Russian soldiers. Judging from their lack of security they didn't anticipate trouble. Their guns were lying on the ground while warming their hands over the fire. After listening to their chatter James learned they were an isolated patrol. The men were buried after Ten Delta killed them without a struggle. Darkness had already settled over the well worn path they hurriedly followed.

The Ten Delta strike team reached their objective without further incident. The area around the damaged communication towers was brightly illuminated with search lights. From their woody positions overlooking that naval base James thoughtfully surveyed the situation. Strong winds off the ocean sprayed the forest with a cold dripping mantle. Standing in the shadows of a large tree James thoughtfully appraised the small compacted naval port. He couldn't understand why with the partisan activity this facility wasn't on high alert? Roscoe suspiciously swept the base with his infra-red binoculars.

"Cocky little bastards aren't they?" the sergeant asked after a few moments. "I count three armored vehicles and ten Russians guarding the towers' repairs. From what I can see from up here the base is going about normal business." He suspiciously shook his head. "They are either cocky as hell or stupid beyond belief."

"The partisans mentioned the base is extremely understaffed," James mumbled. After turning his attention towards the base's far end, he momentarily observed the engineers frantically repairing the fifty-foot towers. Their radar would soon be back on line.

"Any idea how we're going to take down this base?" the sergeant asked before glancing over his shoulder when Timothy joined them.

"Not at the moment." The lieutenant watched Truman scattering their men in defensive positions. Each man carried anti-personnel sensors that would warn of approaching warm-bodied threats. Nobody could surprise them, but still James felt uneasy about the whole mission. Numerous tall trees surrounding around them were heavy with moisture that dropped tiny pellets on their faces. After turning his binoculars toward the waterfront he curiously said. "To the port side of that water tower is a warehouse where trucks are loading crates then stacking them on the dock."

"That means the task force will be here anytime?" Timothy speculated.

Roscoe adjusted his night enhancer then studied the structures along a waterfront with only one pier. "This place was built in a hurry." Wiping dampness from his face Roscoe again studied the base. "This place may be compact but it's garrisoned by a large number of sailors and marines. Getting close to those fuel storage tanks is near impossible with those mechanized and foot patrols. They would spot us before we reached the chain linked fences." What little moonlight was passing through the heavy overcast was to their advantage.

"The base's major firepower is those twin batteries of anti-aircraft guns on that knoll over there and a small gun on the oil tanker." Timothy thoughtfully speculated. "But because that tanker is unloading fuel they won't use their gun."

Vancouver Island, the largest island off West North America, was separated from Southwest British Columbia by a series of narrow waterways. Encompassing over 12,000 square miles the land mass is dominated by the Vancouver Island Ranges. That was an extension of the Coast Ranges running along Oregon and Washington coasts. Its highest peak Golden Hind was over 7000 feet high. After Russia overran Canada they built their only naval base in North America at Kasulich.

For ten minutes James studied the base trying to formulate a plan. Repairs on those damaged towers were nearing completion. With a weak grin he looked at Timothy. "What did Earl warn us about that tower on the pier?"

"He said it was filled with gasoline."

"That's what I thought he said." James glanced at Roscoe. "What would happen if we lobbed an incendiary shell into its guts?"

Timothy answered. "It would blow wide apart. But we don't have an incendiary shell," he pointed out.

James grinned. "That's a secondary problem." For a few minutes he fine tuned his plans. "That tanker anchored in the harbor is unloading fuel through a large hose dipping into the water and coming out near those two fuel storage tanks? I would guess there's more than two hundred thousand gallons of gasoline stored there, maybe more." The lieutenant lowered his binoculars. "It would be a terrible shame if an attack came while they were transferring fuel."

"It might work if we had heavier guns, which we don't," Timothy gruffly replied.

"No, we don't but they do." The lieutenant pointed out the anti-aircraft batteries across the base. "We may have to borrow them." Looking at the grinning sergeant James asked. "What do you think about that?"

"It sounds good to me."

"We know the Russian Navy is desperate for fuel and those storage tanks hold their largest reserve on this coast. If we destroy that fuel the Soviets may become reckless which our Navy could capitalize on."

*   *   *

The air force crew stayed in the small clearing surrounded by tall woods while waiting for James' return. Cold winds blowing in from the ocean denied them any warmth outside of the helicopter. To these tensed men it was as if hours had sluggishly passed since the strike team disappeared into the woods. Lewis sat in his pilot's seat thinking about the Navy lieutenant. He certainly was a cool-headed man and that was what Ten Delta needed. The captain finally left the chopper to stand outside studying the ugly clouds of soot spreading over the globe.

Vancouver Island hadn't reached that stage of defloration as California had, but the grim process was starting. Several times Lewis plucked a blade of grass or snapped a leaf from the trees. Everything was getting crunchy. Lewis again looked at the darkened skies wondering when it would rain again. The infamous Greenhouse Theory was rapidly maturing. Lewis thoughtfully looked about the clearing. The Indian was standing in the opened door close to his machine guns. Gunner was inside curled up alongside their portable heater reading a weapons' manual. Joshua nervously wandered about the machine keeping his thoughts private, but Lewis figured they were about his dead wife.

Charlie grumbled after jumping from the helicopter. "Damn, this place can get on your nerves."

"It should be over before long then we're out of here." His dubious feelings were rather obvious.

"That bunch sure is a cocky group."

Lewis agreed with a weak smile. "I guess that's how you survive in this wasteland. I know that I sure in hell couldn't do it." When Charlie walked away the captain gruffly asked. "Where the hell are you going?"

"I'm going to take a crap."

The captain didn't say anything and let the cold wind roughly massage his face. Walking aimlessly about the small clearing suddenly Lewis stopped. About the same time James' strike team crept onto the knoll, Lewis heard loud Russian voices beyond their clearing. Lewis quickly raised his hand demanding silence. Gunner came out of the chopper with his assault rifle held for firing. The belching Indian returning from the woods saw Lewis hand signaling hostiles were in the area. Joshua had stopped wandering the moment Lewis motioned there was trouble in their area.

*   *   *

The taking of their objective was executed within minutes after the first marine hit the knoll. Its defenders were dispatched without opposition. The radio operator seated at a small campaign desk was slumped over while his blood soaked a novel he was reading. Dashing into a small tent James startled their junior officer sitting in his underwear writing some reports. The Russian never had a chance to draw his revolver. When James left the flapping tent his men were silently securing the knoll.

Careful to remain out of sight James walked over to the knoll's crest. The hill overlooked the base and from its four hundred feet he was given a good view. His binoculars only confirmed what was suspected. These Russians were very reckless with their base security and were no wiser the batteries were in their control. Strait of Juan de Fuca's waters weren't as rough as along the open coast line. Where there was no light, the monocular night vision enhancer broke through the darkness presenting an acceptable hazy greenish view.

Timothy and Roscoe joined their lieutenant. "See those helicopters?" he asked. "They're our first priority."

"Agreed," Roscoe said. "I have been watching them. Their crews are in that trailer close to the runway. If they get airborne we don't have a chance."

Timothy scanned the fenced perimeter while they talked. "And another threat are those motorized patrols riding herd on the fences carrying mounted 50mm machine guns and they have shoulder-fired missile launchers."

"Right on," James agreed after a few moments. "What do you know about those guns?"

"They're Swiss made and easy to fire. Truman is figuring out their adjustments right now."

Roscoe lowered his binoculars. "How much time does Truman need?" After the chief mentioned maybe twenty minutes the sergeant shook his head. "Not good enough. Truman better be ready to fire in another ten minutes at the max. Those engineers will have the towers illuminating in another few minutes." When the chief dubiously looked his way the sergeant explained. "If they can transmit the base will call for help. We still don't where that landing ship is or if they have attack choppers aboard."

"That sounds good to me. After grounding those choppers fire at the towers and decommission them once for all. Then Truman will neutralize those motorized patrols. With those out of the way concentrate firing on that oil tanker." He looked at the twin anti-aircraft batteries for a moment. "Truman is operating one, but what about the other?"

"I'm firing it." Timothy confidently announced.

*   *   *

Lewis' cautious search quickly produced the source of laughter. A heavy duty truck was parked on the single lane road with a flat tire. One soldier was jacking up the wheel while another stood with an automatic rifle. Supposedly he was standing guard though his main interest was the changing of that tire. At one time their Ford truck belonged to a Canadian freight company whose logo was painted over with a crude red star. Another man standing in the shadows with rifle cradled in his arm was too busy smoking a cigarette to see threats before they struck. Occasionally the man chuckled at the dry-humored jokes the other Russian was telling.

Joshua attached a silencer to his rifle and was about to bring down the soldier when Lewis shook his head. He gestured to let the man finish changing the tire. The marine sergeant smiled approval and waited with rifle aimed at the lazy soldiers. Minutes later when the job was finished they were easily shot. While the Indian stood security the others hurriedly checked the truck's cargo.

"This is a supply truck," Lewis explained. "Wonder where the hell it came from?"

After ripping off a box top Gunner exclaimed. "Holy shit, these are Grails." When Lewis came over the marine angrily said. "They're shoulder-fired Russian missiles." He pointed at five foot shiny rockets tightly packed in a gray box. "That SA-7 rocket throws a damned mean punch. There must be twenty of the mothers."

"Hey, you guys, come here a minute." Joshua summoned in a low voice. His husky voice expressed no emotion either way. The war had long ago wasted his desire to laugh or even cry. By the time they rounded the truck he was holding a round disk about the size of a large pancake. "Look at what I found . . . damned magnetic mines."

Lewis touched a dark blue bag around the mine. "What are those?" he asked.

"Floatation rings. When the Soviets throw these into the water they sink just below the surface. When a ship comes along its hull attracts the mine and they chalk up another ship."

"Where have you seen them before?" Lewis curiously asked.

"Toward the end of 2006, terrorists were throwing them in the channels our patrol boats used. I lost a few good friends to the bastards." Joshua said.

"Damn, Lewis," Gunner anxiously said. "We ran across a treasure cache."

"Let's get them back to the chopper. They may be of use later on."

After the weapons were secured inside the Chinook, Gunner found another treasure. Five metal containers were found behind the front seat. Lewis was against loading the deadly explosive aboard, but in the end he agreed. The items were tightly secured then covered with a green tarp. Until the strike team returned Lewis decided to remain away from the chopper. Those napalm canisters worried him. In fact, they scared the hell out of him.

CHAPTER EIGHTEEN

What Tyler and Stan thought were enemy intruders was only a mess of steel beams and rubble reflecting brief flashes. The winds gently rocking the twisted metal caused it to appear as if tanks were on the move. Both men breathed deep relief before hot footing it back to the bunker. Earl was sitting inside the observance bunker nursing some minor bruises and cuts from the crash.

Barnes got up when Tyler entered. "Trouble?" he uneasily asked.

"It was a false alarm. Just some twisted beams and rubble that looked like tanks in the darkness."

Earl grumbled. "I shouldn't have let you talk me into coming. Now we're trapped."

The master sergeant cynically glanced the envoy's way for several moments before gruffly speaking. "It wouldn't have mattered night or tomorrow . . . it's the same. We know the Russians know we're interested in Vandenberg. Night gives us the advantage. And anyhow Delta knows where we are so I wouldn't worry too much about it."

Stan had been outside for two hours and his body hurt like hell from the constant icy winds. Ever once in a while those terrible scents of decaying bodies drifted his way and he puked his guts out. During the night Tyler checked his post three times and left. Stan was on this outpost because of his remarkable night vision. Back home he hunted coons and never failed to brag one. But that was a game and this was for real. The marine looked cautiously about his responsible grid. Man was in violent discord with nature and it was slashing back. Walking against the strong winds he occasionally glanced at those darkened skies and didn't need to be told how bad things were becoming. Even the appearance of a single bird on the wing would have comforted him. But this hadn't happened since December when Russia's symphony of destruction played its terrible tune. Stan grunted and continued his cautious slow walk. The AKA-47 felt heavy in his gloved hand.

Stan suddenly stopped walking and anxiously looked about the ravaged landscape. "Tyler," he softly spoke into his radio. "We got trouble one hundred feet at three o'clock."

*   *   *

Within minutes Timothy was familiar with the Oerlikon air defense batteries. Climbing down from his elevated chair, the chief petty officer walked over to where Truman was seated in his gunnery chair studying the controls. He had pulled off the Russian stenciled tape revealing English and German instructions. The chief asked if he was ready and Truman gave the thumbs up. Satisfied everything was ready Timothy returned to his battery some forty feet away. When James came up he said they were ready then lowered his heavy ear protection.

Savannah walked among the battle ready marines studying the situation. Timothy was seated behind a bullet proof shield providing unlimited visual control. The older man was strapped on a metal suspension chair to keep from being thrown off. Mounted on a circular disk the twin 35mm guns could rotate 180 degrees either way. Directly before the gunner was a computerized system of blinking multi-colored lights. Each battery had two loaders to keep the guns supplied with munitions. She smiled at the chief before joining James now standing away from the guns and waiting to provide coordinates and target identifications.

James was voice connected to the two batteries by radio. After receiving the coordinates of those helicopters both batteries came to life. Timothy looking through the 3D electro-optical mini-sight felt the gun slowly rotating with a dull hum until locking on the unexpected targets. Squeezing the trigger his guns fired 35mm fragmentation shells. Armed with electronic impact fuses the explosives sped through the night like avenging demons. The first two Kamov machines immediately burst into flames. Their crews rushing from the trailer were consumed by the violence. The third chopper's powerful Isotov engines were furiously whirling the rotary blades. There was another enormous explosion as a single ball of flame sent mangled pieces of metal hurling through the air. The fourth machine grounded because of repairs was easily eliminated as a threat.

With the primary threats eliminated James turned to their secondary targets. The naval base required no time to realize they were under attack by their anti-aircraft batteries. Shell after shell explosively ripped across the base now glowing in a reddish harsh illumination. Thick black clouds of smoke accented by orange flames rose above the port. Twisted metal glowed from the numerous fires sweeping through the isolated naval base. In a matter of minutes Zasulich no longer existed as a working military facility.

"The tanker," Savannah shouted while looking through her binoculars. "It's going to battle stations!"

James turned his attention to this new threat. "Waste that tanker! It's at battle stations!"

When the first gunfire sounded the crew aboard that tanker ran for their battle stations. Their ship became a death trap under hostile fire. Highly flammable fuel filled her bunkers. Men courageously braved open decks to disconnect dangling

fuel hoses before fragmentation shells sent the ship into flames. Truman walked a
stream of shells across the ship's main deck blowing apart men and causing numerous
fires to break out. Then Truman hit the fuel hoses suspended from three shipboard
cranes. While seamen stared in frozen panic flames from gasoline filled hoses spun
giant flaming balls into the night. For a moment it seemed the 11,000 ton ship was
actually lifted from the waters then slammed down again. As the invading Americans
watched with cold indifference, the burning ship was twisted and shattered from
explosions that sounded like angry thunder from her bowels.

With binoculars Savannah coldly watched Timothy firing into the giant storage
tanks creating roaring fires that illuminated the entire area. When satisfied the oil
tanker was finished, Truman turned his twin guns on other targets of opportunity.
The tower close to the wharves exploded into savage flames. Burning gasoline
poured down on surrounding buildings like flood waters smashing over broken
embankments. Through her glasses the major observed the waterfront become a
raging calamity generated by engulfing fires. All about the base plagued by roaring
flames and swirling black smoke burning men ran about screaming for help that never
would come. Flowing fires was consuming everything on the base. Badly trained
soldiers unsuccessfully ran about seeking refuge from the deadly gunfire. But there
was no escape from the anti-aircraft batteries.

While scanning the burning hell with his binoculars James muttered. "I can't
believe we're doing this." He glanced at Savannah.

"They didn't think an invading force could hit this far up the coast."

Staring through his target finder Truman eliminated one target after another with
ease. During World War II these guns first appeared on the battlefields and were even
to this day a favorite with worldwide militaries. He had the Swedish manufactured
weapon on automatic fire of 550 rounds per minute. Its operation was smooth
to the touch. A high speed computer controlled the periscope and laser guidance
during tracking phases. At the moment of optimum hit probability, Truman received
an acoustic alarm instructing to fire. Through his periscope the marine tracked a
group of men running along the wharves fearfully fleeing the devastation. Sending
a stream of fragmented shells into their center he was astonished when small barges
tied alongside exploded. More columns of swirling smoke and dancing flames spun
into the night.

"Lieutenant," Truman yelled. "I'm out of shells!"

"So am I!" the chief exclaimed while climbing from the gunnery seat. He looked
at the loaders and smiled. "Hey, you guys did a great job."

James gave the burning base a last look then shouted. "Spike the gun barrels
and smash their controls."

After that James' strike team slipping into the darkness retreated to the nearby
Chinook. It was a steady trot with his men pumped with excitement from their
staggering victory. Truman ran ahead scouting the path for hostiles. They had
accomplished another major strike at the enemy's throat and that felt good. Behind

them a brilliant glow of burning fires illuminated the island's tip. Still stunned by their easy victory Savannah trotted alongside James with a wide smile. With all of the death she had witnessed over the last few months, this action bloated her emotions that finally they were slicing the Soviet monster's throat.

Truman was running point when suddenly the immediate area was shattered by gunfire. Ten Delta marines scattered into the ditches along the winding path. The thunder of battle stung those cold damp slopes of green. Here and there erupted explosions as grenades were wildly thrown into the darkness. Unable to see the enemy, James' men fired blindly hoping their bullets would find homes. Those men with the laser guns waited for targets. But the new grenades quickly blasted wide destructive gaps in the woods. Screams of wounded soldiers was heard among the exploding grenades. Overconfident of their numbers the Russians charged the trapped marines. Carefully choosing her targets Savannah picked off running Soviet soldiers. James glancing her way saw how cool the major worked under hostile conditions.

"Iron Eagle to Skyview," James shouted into his radio. "We are trapped and need extraction now!" Though the radio transmission was frequently interrupted with static his urgency was clear enough. After receiving acknowledgment the lieutenant returned his attention to the fighting. "They're on the way," he shouted to Savannah who nodded while tracking some charging soldiers then squeezed her trigger.

Truman watched short bursts of machine gun fire to his right frontal position. The gunner would fire then quickly drop to the ground for cover. There was a pattern to his insanity that Truman figured out. When the man again lifted his head there was swift response on Truman's part. After jumping to his feet the black marine angrily fired into the forest hearing a painful scream in return. But before dropping back into the ditch Truman felt a burning sensation when his perspiring body was slammed against the damp earth. It was if a giant hand had reached down and slapped his puny body. Truman found the night colder than usual while laying in that shallow ditch painfully gasping for breath. There was a rattling in his throat that was unfamiliar to Truman. Something was wrong he whispered as blood trickled from his mouth.

The marine could hear a thunderous thumping sound coming through the night air and then powerful winds raced across his face. He didn't look up because he couldn't. The wounded marine was finding it difficult to lift his hand much less his head. A warm substance coated his face as Truman warned his buddies to watch for machine guns out there. Tears flowed down his cheeks. This wasn't supposed to happen to him. He was going to survive this cursed war and go home. His girl friend was waiting. Now a pain was squeezing his chest. Truman coughed and spitted blood. The roaring sounds were louder now. The faint shouts of his buddies as they gently lifted his body seemed to be in the distance. As they hurried over the ground with him Truman heard the lieutenant encouraging him to hold on. They were going home. Gunfire from the forest was now scattered as surviving Russians fled.

The strike team spread out offering security while four others carried the limp marine over a winding path to the clearing where Lewis waited for them. The extraction would have to be quickly done. James doubted if the Russians would remain disoriented too long. When they came back it would be with revenge and no mercy expected from either side.

Trotting alongside Truman, James kept saying. "Hold on marine, we're going home."

Truman's mind was in turmoil. He wanted to tell them it was all right and they must get the hell away. He tried to, but words wouldn't pass his dry lips. That heavy weight on his chest was worse. When lifted aboard the chopper Truman experienced a weightless feeling passing through his icy body. He could barely see the lieutenant wrapping his wounds. Another marine was cradling his head in his lap as the helicopter lifted into the air. Icy winds poured through the open door where the Indian stood with his mounted machine gun. This wasn't supposed to be happening. His girl friend was waiting back home with plans to start a family.

Savannah looked at the bloodied body. "Will he make it?" she emotionally asked.

James shook his head.

Suddenly Truman wasn't feeling pain as a corridor of warm light bathed his spirit. He happily recognized his brother and sister waving at him. The war's ugliness was no longer his problem. With a grateful sigh Truman grasped his sister's hand and walked into the light. James gently closed Truman's eyes. The excitement of their amazing victory was washed aside as grief for their fallen comrade was expressed. After pulling the blanket over the dead marine's body Roscoe walked to the bench and sat with a groan. Maybe Truman was difficult to know at times, but he was a Ten Delta marine and to these men that was all that mattered.

*　　*　　*

It was late when KONSTANTANTINOVICH's captain was awakened in his sea cabin. He had retired early knowing tomorrow there would be much to do. For a moment he laid in the dim lighting reorienting his muddled mind. Then slowly swinging his short hairy legs over the bunk's side he stood up yawning. Seeing the enlisted radioman nervously standing in his opened door he took the single sheet.

"Comrade Captain, this is a top priority Bravo/Tango message."

The reference to Bravo/Tango meant trouble originating at Kasulich. He quickly read the message as a coldness flooded his body. "Was this confirmed?" Karl harshly asked.

"Yes, Comrade Captain."

"Very well, please inform the duty officer to immediately summon an officers' meeting on the bridge."

The news rushed through Karl's emotions like a dull chopping axe. That single loss spelled doom for KGB's bold ambitions in these parts. The lost of that isolated naval base was more than a crippling defeat. Russia didn't have the resources to rebuild such a complex. For a moment another realization struck his mind. The vicious Politburo would demand somebody in a responsible position be punished. Kossier excused his failures by arresting, hanging, and stripping those he blamed. Since this war began many fine Russian officers lost their lives because of that stupid policy. While quickly dressing the captain suspected his own career was hanging in the balance. Hurrying to the bridge Karl didn't hide his tears. What had happened to his beloved Mother Russia? When would Rodina's young men stop dying in this endless war?

The shipboard officers gathered on the bridge uneasily observed his facial expression. Colonel Karsavin came in shortly afterwards with a wretched expression that surprised Karl. The commissar normally was in control of his arrogant emotions. It was obvious the ship already knew about their crushing blow at Kasulich.

"By now you know what happened two hours ago." Karl awkwardly reported.

A junior deck officer nervously asked. "Was it a major American force?"

"No," the captain answered after a short pause. "Actually our naval base was crushed by a handful of marines from Ten Delta." He quietly observed their shocked reactions. "That is right a handful of marines under the command of Lieutenant Blackmore destroyed the installation and killed more than eighty percent of their base personnel. How did this happen? How could a handful of marines commit such massive damages? It was because our comrades became careless with their defenses." His voice became very harsh. "KONSTANTANTINOVICH was crippled by this bunch of marines so we know how clever these men are. They use available resources and act accordingly. You must stress this to your security teams. They can not relax or we all die. No further damages to our ship must be allowed." Clasping hands behind his back the captain paced about the gathered officers. "Henceforth, I want all security measures tripled." Karl abruptly halted and scowled at his men. "Until our task force arrives we're the vanguard of Russian hopes in this region. We must not let Mother Russia down again. The Americans after tasting blood for the second time will come after us. But this time we will be ready. They must pay for our defeat at Kasulich."

"When will the ALEKSANDR be back?"

"I don't know their timetable. But I'm certain by now they know about Kasulich and are sailing there to offer aid."

"What about the task force?"

Mikhail defiantly spoke. "The fleet's arrival is top secret."

After the officers were dismissed Karl walked onto the open bridge wing and thoughtfully studied the shore activity. It was another several hours before daylight and Karl anticipated trouble from the Americans. When Mikhail joined him he turned and frowned.

"That armored detachment the ALEKSANDR landed on Vandenberg," Karl somberly questioned. "Can they be recalled for security?"

"No," the commissar sternly denied. "Their commander has his own orders to carry out. KONSTANTANTINOVICH is your responsibility and not his."

Karl gave the political officer a cynical glance then looking over the railing saw their empty torpedo tubes. The last 533mm fish was expended months ago and there were no replacements available. Even his 8 missile launchers were empty. The warship used their final allotment of SS-N-22 missiles in a battle off Africa two months ago. A Japanese countermeasure unit shot the shafts out of the skies before reaching their objective. Karl bitterly sighed knowing his ship was reduced to a helpless hunk of metal.

*   *   *

Upon their return to Ten Delta James was informed of Tyler's situation on Vandenberg. Contact with the trapped marines revealed there were no casualties. It was decided a rescue would be delayed until morning when there was light. James stopped by the mess hall where his marines had gathered. There was no laughter among the men. Truman's death had dampened their excitement. He refused a meal but took a cup of coffee to his table. Savannah after changing clothes joined him.

"So what did Yuma say when informed of Kasulich's destruction?" she asked.

He forced a weak chuckle. "I'm not certain if they believed us or not." The lieutenant was silent for a few moments. "Actually, if I was distant from the scene and some lieutenant reported the devastation of a Russian naval port, I'm not certain if I would believe him or not."

She sipped the coffee for a moment. "It was a remarkable classic textbook miracle."

"This will be the last time something like that happens. The Soviets are really pissed now and they'll come after us like a damned hurricane." He played with the cup before saying. "The next time we meet them it'll be with force and not cunning."

"But you don't have a strong enough force to throw at them."

Gunner walked up but didn't interrupt until Savannah finished talking. "I just wanted to stop by and offer my praise for a job well done." He smiled. "It was beyond belief." James nodded his acceptance. "I also would like to apologize for my rudeness back on the helicopter. Those marines of yours are about the best hunks of flesh I have seen in the Corps."

"You should tell them that and not me."

"I have already done that, sir."

"And what did they say?"

"Not much."

James suggested grimly. "Give them time and they'll come around. My men having been through a lot these last few months aren't in the mood to forgive right now." The lieutenant coughed then drank some coffee. "Gunner, luck was riding with us tonight. Those Russians weren't first class troops and were just plain dumb.

So we gave them a bad black eye that tremendously damaged their invasion plans. When they come back it won't be with third class troops."

Gunner nodded. "You're probably right. So we need to cut down the odds."

James frowned. "Do you have a plan?"

"I might. On the way back my friends and I discussed this little problem. Having spent two tours with the SEALS I'm qualified in handling explosives, especially those of the underwater caliber." When James motioned him to sit he did with a grin. "Right now we have a major problem with these Soviet warships in our backyard."

"But the destroyer is badly damaged," Savannah pointed out.

"While she remains afloat that ship is a threat. If their task force rearms her tubes she wouldn't have to sail to be become our worst nightmare. From Isla Vista the ship can fire her missiles anywhere within a 70 mile sphere."

"You have a point there." James slowly sipped his coffee while studying the cocky gunner's mate. "I assume you have a plan in mind?"

"Well, first off I need to explain something. Five months ago naval intelligence studied two destroyers that were abandoned after devastating battles. There was one modification aboard them that interested our people. What makes this important is both ships were the same class as KONSTATANTINOVICH. With their supply lines seriously stretched, the Red Navy is storing munitions in spaces not normally used."

"Exactly are you talking about?"

"I'm interested in," Gunner replied, "three spaces close to the fantail."

After grabbing a tray of food Lewis came over and sat.

"Your Gunner was telling us about a plan to take out the destroyer."

"I have already heard about it." he said with a frown.

Savannah didn't hesitate to ask. "You don't sound too enthuse about it?"

"I'm strongly against it."

"And why is that?"

Lewis chewed his scrambled eggs for a moment then said. "Why don't you let him tell you?"

After that Armstrong gingerly approached his plans that sounded brilliant aboard the helicopter, but now he silently had doubts. "We know the warship is crippled and that's our sole advantage. There's no way she's going to sea. While you guys took on that naval base we ambushed a supply truck. Among its cargo were sea mines. My plans are to swim underwater and attach those mines on its screws. After attaching the explosives the swimmer returns to shore and is safely away before exploding them. With the munitions stored near the fantail KONSTANTANINOVICH will be removed from our threat list."

James frowned. "So that's what the whispering was all about?"

"It'll work," Gunner promised.

"It'll definitely kill the swimmer."

"He'll get away."

"Let's say you manage to get in without detection," James argued. "It'll be coming back that will probably get you caught. Maybe the Soviets were careless in the past, but not now." He looked at Lewis' cold silence. "What's your opinion of this plan?"

"It's nothing short of a suicidal run."

"Who will be doing this?"

"I wanted to, but Joshua won the toss."

"How do you intend to get there?" James asked. "I need the Apaches and Chinook tomorrow to extract Tyler's people."

"Airborne platforms would alert them we were coming. I thought about borrowing one of your Shoets. That should get us there without detection."

After a few minutes evaluating the operation's odds of success, James finally nodded. Gunner stood with a broad smile and left to tell the others.

Savannah thought about Gunner's plans for several minutes after he left. "Do you think that'll work?" she asked.

"More crazy things than that have worked around here." James dubiously replied.

"And what about you, captain? He's one of your men. Do you think they can do it?"

"Do I think it'll work, probably so. I don't think the Soviets will expect an attack from underwater. But will Joshua come back . . . no." Finishing his meal the Air Force veteran pushed away the plate. "And that's why I'm against it because it's suicide."

Timothy came into the mess hall and after sitting thoughtfully looked at their gloomy faces. "We just got word from Yuma. There were two large shipments of Agents Blue and Orange sent to Vandenberg in 1975. All paperwork on the storage locations was misfiled years ago."

Savannah groaned her disgust. "So we're back to square one."

The chief nodded. "It looks like that."

"Do you have any good news?" James sarcastically asked.

"I have some updates that aren't encouraging. Naval Intelligence identified another ship in that task force as the amphibious ship ALEKSANDR."

"What do we know about her?"

"Reliable intelligence estimates she's transporting 500 Special Marine Assault troops and 20 attack tanks." Timothy paused for a moment. "It was probably her that landed those troops in San Diego?"

"Have any of our locals reported enemy movement in that area?" James asked.

"No, but Mexican annexation troops pretty well control that region. If the locals did see suspicious movement they wouldn't tell us. We aren't welcomed down that way."

CHAPTER NINETEEN

Lewis was dead set against his crew embarking on their suicide strike, but he didn't stand in their way. Once the Shoets was away from Ten Delta Gunner drove east on Highway 101 along the coast. Though it was a high profile route the team needed to make good time. But still progress was at times slow because of numerous car wrecks and other rubble caused by the explosions. After some thirty miles they left the major highway for a slower route on Highway 217. Later parking the armored car they walked the remaining distance on foot. Anticipating outer perimeter patrols they were surprised when none were encountered. Isla Vista was reached by maneuvering through massive destruction caused by war and earthquakes. They found a spot affording a good view of the ship's anchorage though the ocean winds was icy cold.

With night binoculars Joshua studied the anchored destroyer. "Damned, I wonder how that warship keeps from running aground. They're that close to the beach."

Laying on his stomach the gunner's mate thoughtfully appraised the vessel. "Holy shit, Ten Delta did cripple the hell out of that ship. I can see massive damages to the bridge which they are rapidly repairing. But both gun turrets are badly twisted and won't be a worry. Their lifeboats are gone." There was a short pause before Gunner remarked. "I can tell you those boys back at Ten Delta are nobody to screw around with."

Joshua nodded. "Then why don't you give them some slack. Quit calling them boys for one thing."

"They're black boys."

"So what does that matter? They bleed just like you and me. They kill just as you and I. So I don't understand your problem?" When the prejudiced man looked at him with a dumbfounded expression, the marine shook his head and turned back to studying the ship. "Their radar is off the line. Take a look at that radar dish and mast. They aren't working. Then take a close gander at those missile tubes. There's nothing wrong with them. All they need is rearming and Ten Delta is history."

The Indian was leaning against a mess of fallen rubble with his binoculars. "Hey, man, look at those damned waters. That's pretty damned rough to be swimming in." With fifteen years in the Marine Corps, Horace considered the service his only home. His body was tall and muscular built with dark brown skin from his Sioux heritage. The dark brown eyes were unfriendly and trust was an emotion he rarely expressed. The men aboard Lewis' helicopter were among the few he called blood brothers. "Do you think it's feasible to try swimming right now?"

Joshua slowly shook his head. "It's not going to change, Bro. What you see is what we got today, tomorrow, and later. But I have swum in rougher conditions." There was a short worried silence. "Anyhow take a look at that activity down there. Those communist bastards are all over that ship. That means that task force is on the way here. If they get here and rearm her we have big do do on our hands." Turning he looked at his two buddies. "There's another problem maturing down there. Their security activity on shore isn't that bad right now, but it'll get tighter. No, it's tonight or never."

Gunner finishing his appraisal knew Joshua was right. "Are you certain you want to do this? Nobody will think any different if you change your mind. That's a rough half mile swim underwater through choppy waters."

"I'm in all the way." he said in a manner warning this was his last discussion.

The marine sergeant Joshua was of medium height with a lean compact body possessing little fat. His gray eyes were much like Lewis' in that they were cold and distrusting. This war had a way of harshly changing people. Pain was noted in Joshua's eyes and expressions. After his last command was blown to bits the explosive expert acted as Lewis' co-pilot. His facial features were pinched with a short snub nose. After sixteen covert operations behind fierce battle lines he was sick of the war's never ending killing. The marine never stopped missing his wife who died in New York City. Joshua felt the cold winding blowing against his face. For a few moments he thought of those times they walked along the beaches at night holding hands.

With a deep exhaling the marine sergeant muttered. "No use delaying this strike."

Horace helped him dress in the black scuba gear. Because there was no powder to make the rubber suit easier to slip on it was dumped in some nearby waters. Soon as the cold suit touched his bare skin Jos groaned softly. The wind was increasing its strength meaning another storm was rolling down the coast.

Gunner was again scanning the warship. "The water is too rough so you got to swim all the way underwater. There are lookouts on deck, but they seemed more interested in this shore line than the waters. Stay under even at the ship. Those working parties are everywhere with portable lights that makes the water look like daylight."

Joshua nodded. "Yeah, I already saw that."

After his air tanks were strapped on, Joshua looked at each of his buddies. "If something happens out there, remember I love you crazy fools." There was a sadness in his eyes that neither failed to notice.

"Nothing will happen," the Indian argued. "You're my blood brother. We Sioux don't let slimy Soviet pukes disturb our lifeline. Just go and do your thing then get back here on the double. Then we'll have a beer." There was a dull chuckle that failed to relay his amusement.

Joshua crept closer to the water then with a wave pulled down his face mask and slipped into the choppy waters splashing ashore. Staying in the shadows his buddies watched the waters knowing beneath their turmoil Joshua was swimming against strong undercurrents. Finding a safe place to stay out of sight the men faded into the darkness.

* * *

Colonel Karsavin spent more time on the bridge than anywhere else aboard the ship. He frequently debated his decision of staying aboard and not going ashore with the troops. At least there he would be away from that scheming Voronov and his rebellious crew of incompetent fools. But that was changing after the ALEKSANDR arrived at Isla Vista. He planned to transfer his things aboard. This warship was a political failure and by leaving he wouldn't attract Kossier's attention. During Russia's troubles times it was wise to strengthen ties with those in power.

He was standing in the cold when Karl came out with night binoculars. He acknowledged the commissar's presence then raised the glasses. "What do you expect to see out there?" he asked.

"I don't know," the captain admitted after lowering the night enhancer. For a few moments he studied the political officer's aloofness. "I find it difficult suppressing my fears more trouble is on the way."

"ALEKSANDR soon will be tying alongside us then matters will improve. The admiral approved your request for missiles. That should erase this thorn in our side."

Karl frowned. "But first we must find Ten Delta; otherwise, the missiles are of little use. These men are like the wild winds from a North Seas' storm."

Mikhail grasped the life railing while thoughtfully staring at the darkened shore. Earlier that evening he reluctantly agreed all working parties on shore should be brought aboard. "Some years ago while traveling this coast as a tourist I was a lieutenant in military intelligence. Though finding Monterey a delightful city I saw something else. There was a sinful consuming illness most people didn't see or want to see. The city was crowded with rich capitalists greedily feeding on the overworked cadavers of their working class."

"How did you arrive at that conclusion?"

"I talked with many women and men in the lounges and bars among the city. They burned my ears with their contemptuous complaints." Mikhail denounced. He waited until the ship tossed and rocked as more choppy waves came rolling in from the ocean. "It was then I recognized one ugly undeniable fact—America was set on a collision course to enslave Rodina."

"I won't argue about America's corruption. That we have known about for many years." Karl finally said. "But Ten Delta is like many American military units. Though isolated and alone on this devastated coastline they'll fight to the last man. And because of that single fact we must be totally alert or they will kill us." He briefly looked at Mikhail's contemptuous expression before again studying the shore. "Never forget we're on their soil. That makes a man savagely fight even when it appears impossible to achieve victory."

*   *   *

Swimming through the churning black waters Joshua kept close tabs on the small florescent dial strapped to his wrist. While underwater the electronic directional finder was his only link in finding that destroyer. It was dreadfully cold beneath the crashing waters. This chill quickly penetrated his rubber suit numbing his limbs. Struggling through the powerful currents of swirling whitish wash his body began tiring. It was proving to be much harder than anticipated.

These cold waters didn't permit his dwelling on any subject for very long. Soon he saw his dead wife in her favorite yellow dress. Joshua smiled to himself. No matter how difficult this swim became he was determined to finish. And he would because his wife was at his side all the way. Soon the marine felt his body giving in to the tremendous strains those crushing waters above were forcing upon his will power. The staff sergeant kept his objective in mind. Drawing on his body's reserves the man stubbornly continued the painful swim. This was another impossible task he must finish. By now he was breathing hard and each gasp was painful.

His chest felt as if a powerful balloon was drawing on its final reserves. His stomach became knotted and tight. Shoulder muscles ached fiercely with each move. Some thoughts were pleasant while other reflections developed into confusing mazes. Struggling through increased debris and churning waters blinding his path the sergeant pushed ahead. His arms ached like they never had before. Each stroke was a thousand demons pounding his flesh. With a faint grin Jos remembered what his drill instructors said in recruit training. When in trouble, they preached, keep the mind free of negative thoughts. Softly hum the Marine Corps hymn if need be. This he did and from within his troubled thoughts came that cutting edge.

*   *   *

Mikhail stayed on the wing for a few minutes then reentered the bridge for its warmth. The captain soon came in and both men were handed cups. The hot tea felt good going down the throat. By now the commissar had tasted enough salty mist on his lips to last a lifetime. He longed to be back on land commanding tanks. The night was drawing late and yet he didn't want to be in his bunk. The colonel felt destiny was riding within his reach.

An enlisted radioman came on the bridge and looked about. Seeing the political officer he came over with a message. Unfolding the page Mikhail read the report with a faint smile. Maybe things were beginning to turn their way. "Those troops disembarked on Vandenberg have stirred curiosity." Having the captain's attention he continued in a boastful manner. "Their patrols reported Ten Delta marines on the base."

"Have they engaged?"

"No, they're waiting until morning."

"Was it a large body?"

Mikhail shook his head. "No, it's a small reconnaissance patrol."

Karl shook his head. "That isn't good. There are too many sightings of Ten Delta and each time they bring trouble."

"That shall shortly change." the political officer curtly predicted before walking away.

*   *   *

Then suddenly out of the swirling chaos beneath those dark waters, Jos saw the shadowy hull protruding into this murky forbidden kingdom. The infra-red mask provided visual contact while he pondered his next move. In his distorted view the monstrous twin screws were large as automobiles. In the following few minutes he struggled against the powerful resisting forces keeping him from the pitching hull. Finally gaining footage he clung to the crusty metal. Time was running against him. Attaching one mine he laboriously repeated the procedure six times. Several times when roughly pushed away he regained his place at the screws. In order to achieve their hopeful results all fifteen mines must be attached. This job required enormous will power with all the churning waters trying to interfere.

*   *   *

Commander Bogdanov appeared on the fantail with three divers in black rubber gear. While Gunner and Horace anxiously watched through their glasses another officer joined them. The wind was blowing their scarves in the coldness while Karl vigorously rubbed his gloved hands. Three armed sentries backed away while engineers prepared to go into the waters.

The commander was facing his captain while talking. "My damage control teams reports an occasional thumping below the hull. I need to know what's loose before we bring those missiles aboard."

"Very well, have the divers do a quick survey then get back aboard." Karl advised before returning to his bridge.

While the commander stood at the railing there was that dull thumping that sounded through the lower decks. It was like a groaning frame protesting the abusing rough seas. With face masks on and their air tanks secured, the four Russian engineers dropped into the choppy waters on a routine inspection.

*   *   *

It was becoming hard to remember the words to that soul stirring Corps hymn. This made Jos angry. He quickly chastised himself for being weak. When the sharp thumping sounded he nearly jumped out of his skin. Then it was gone. The marine fearfully looked about wondering what the hell that sound could be. Then after a few moments Jos attached the last three mines. In his mind reflections of those cursed mushroom clouds over New York City kept popping back like a horrible nightmare. Whenever his thoughts weakened Joshua thought of that red banner with its golden hammer and sickle flapping in the winds. That was enough to strengthen his resolve to finish this task. Their Navy was counting on him. The surface waters above him were getting rougher. Churning debris sometimes blinded his view of the job at hand.

The staff sergeant was about to swim away when spotting a loose mine. After grabbing hold of the propeller's edge he awkwardly pulled his way over. Jos spent the next three minutes readjusting the device. That was when a deep rumbling sound shook the shafts. Before he could react the shaft rotated only a few inches. But his hand was caught. Desperately trying to jerk it loose he saw something swimming towards him.

There was a moment of suspended surprise between the Russian divers and Jos. When the Russian swimmers raced toward him, Jos muttered a prayer for forgiveness and pushed the remote device on his wrist.

*   *   *

Mikhail staggered down the passageway as the ship tossed in the choppy waters. When meeting seamen he frowned as they ignored him in passing. This only made him angry. But soon the Party would have their revenge on the rebellious Navy. After this war was won the surface fleet would be disbanded. They had long ago outlived their place in Russian history. Mikhail looked at his expensive gold watch seeing it was nearing dawn. After a seaman scrambled down the ladder he started up.

That was when a loud explosion shook the ship. Almost immediately collision alarms echoed then another thunderous eruption shook the entire ship. Half way up the ladder the brooding colonel was brutally thrown to the decking. For a moment he tried getting to his feet, but this was short lived and unsuccessful when another deeper explosion sent flames racing through the lower decks. That was all the political officer remembered after thrown against the bulkhead.

*   *   *

"Holy shits," Gunner muttered as flames leaped upwards. "The ship's guts were ripped out."

"Jos didn't make it," Horace cried.

"Did you really think he would?" the gunner's mate asked. "But we got to get out of here now. If there are patrols around here those fires will flush them out like flies."

As the two fled to their hidden Shoets it was too dark to see their emotions. They were thankful no interferences were met during their hurried retreat. Once the Shoets was on Highway 101 heading back Gunner called the base. Even on the highway it was possible to look back and see the flames reaching high above Isla Vista.

*   *   *

When the summons came James ran down the corridor to communications. Sensing its urgency Savannah quickly followed. It seemed every time she had a moment alone with the lieutenant something came up. Even before the report was voiced James knew the data was important. Timothy was standing behind the radioman scribbling down notes. After he was through the chief grabbed the sheet and read it before looking at James with a wide grin.

"It's from Gunner. KONSTANTANTINOVICH is burning and totally disabled."

Taking the message James hurriedly scanned its contents. "It's listing to the port." When Lewis came in with a troubled expression and expecting the worse James said. "Your people put the warship out of commission. With her fantail practically blown off and listing to port she won't last very long. Gunner estimated high casualties among the crew."

"What about my crew?" Lewis anxiously asked.

"Gunner and Horace are on their way back."

There was a tensed silence before the captain asked. "What about Joshua?"

James didn't answer at first, but his wretched expression told Lewis enough. "I'm sorry, but Sergeant Voss didn't make it."

The captain stood for a moment feeling his emotions churning with hatred for the Soviets. Then without a word he left the chamber. When Savannah started to follow James grabbed her arm and shook his head. It was best to leave Lewis alone until his crewmen returned. Though not agreeing she obeyed. The people inside communications recognized the fortunes of war were riding their chariot while extracting high costs.

Ten Delta's radioman after receiving the message anxiously scanned the frequencies hoping to intercept new Soviet transmissions. It was only a few minutes later that he looked up with a start. Standing nearby studying the regional map James' arm was nudged by Savannah. She pointed at the radioman anxiously copying down an interception.

"Lieutenant, KONSTANTANTINOVICH broadcasted urgent pleas for assistance. ALEKANDR is cruising at flank speed and should reach Isla Vista later this afternoon."

James felt as if his blood had drained to the feet. "Now we really got trouble." he mumbled. For a moment the officer couldn't think straight as the implications of that message sunk in. Swallowing hard he walked the few steps to that regional map. "Chief, where's that NATO identification manual on Soviet ships?"

"Got it here," Timothy replied while pulling the blue manual from a shelf. When asked for the ship's specifications it was a few moments before he found the listing. "She's a powerhouse with two SA-N-4 twin launchers and a quad of SA-N-5 missiles." He nervously looked at James. "She carries two twin 76mm missiles launchers, four 30mm Gatlings, one 122mm rocket launcher and twenty-one naval 2X20 barreled guns. She's a damned floating death trap for anybody coming close."

"What about surveillance abilities? None of this sounds good."

"Well according to this, that amphibious monster has the latest generation of Head Net surface radar and six helicopters of the new Kamov attack class. Last year she was commanded by Senior Naval Captain Ian Bethinski, a hardnosed veteran from many of the battles we lost pretty badly. There isn't any reason think that he isn't aboard now."

After a long silence James finally said. "It'll be dawn before long. Our first task is rescuing Tyler's group from their little mess. But first we need to determine the size of that Soviet armored group on the base." he bitterly exhaled. "This is all coming together far too fast for us to respond."

Savannah sensing his helplessness softly encouraged. "Ten Delta accomplished the impossible before. So why can't Ten Delta do it again?"

"It's different this time," James said. "The first time that warship foolishly stored filled fuel drums on deck. Because they weren't expecting an underwater strike Joshua destroyed the warship with underwater mines." Looking at the map again he slowly warned. "But this ship coming isn't second rate nor reckless. They have a captain who is notoriously known for his brutal shrewdness." He looked at the woman and cynically admitted. "We have limited weapons while that beast carries enough firepower to take out twenty radar stations."

"So what are your orders?" the chief asked.

James took time arriving at a decision. "All right, this is what we're going to do. There are three hours before dawn so let's use them to the fullest. I want both choppers armed with armor piercing missiles. We'll wait until Gunner returns to hear what he has to say. Notify Tyler we're coming at dawn and lay purple smoke to mark his position. Anything beyond his smoke will be considered unfriendly and blown to hell. Send a coded message to Yuma advising them of our situation."

When James walked from the room confident his orders would be obeyed, Savannah asked. "Where's he going?"

Roscoe grinned. "Going to shower, shave, and dress in a clean flight suit. The lieutenant has this thing about going into battle clean." He shrugged at her surprise. "I guess everybody has their little quirks."

CHAPTER TWENTY

Thirty minutes later James came into the mess hall refreshed and ready to take on the Soviets in battle. The dining tables were crowded with chattering marines dressed in battle gear. Ten Delta was at Defense Posture Able meaning the site was geared for offensive operations that morning. Sergeants mingled with their squads while discussing their grids of responsibility. There were strong combinations of tension and eagerness to fight. Few marines greeted their CO when he walked through the chow line though he didn't expect them to. They had their own assignments to learn in a very short time.

At his table Savannah, Roscoe, Timothy, and Lewis sat eating and talking about Earl's mission at Vandenberg. Making room for him Savannah smiled after he was seated. James slowly chewed his bread with blackberry jam while studying their various expressions. That one emotion lacking in the mess hall was laughter.

"Did Gunner get back?" James asked.

"Yeah," Timothy solemnly said. "In their debriefing it was confirmed the explosions ripped the ship a new asshole. Gunner doubts if she can last more than a couple of days. They said fires were everywhere when they got the hell out of there."

"Fires can be extinguished." James said while eating some eggs.

"It's not the fires that's her doom, but a gaping hole where the fantail used to be. And she was badly listing to port. Even if her missile launchers were rearmed, the ship isn't in any physical condition to be a firing platform."

James swallowed his food then drank coffee before soberly saying. "Sergeant Voss did his country a great service this day. I'm very sorry he died, but before this day is over I'm afraid many of us will join him. Ten Delta is now alone on this coastal wasteland that Mexico and Russia wants to conquer. But California is part of the United States even if she's mostly uninhabitable. Today we fight to ensure our Stars and Stripes continue fluttering above this land." He thoughtfully looked at their silent faces. "Who is staying here?"

"I agreed to stay with ten men as security." Savannah replied. Pushing away her plate the marine major suddenly found food distasteful. "The chief already explained your lock down procedures."

"I have been thinking," Roscoe thoughtfully said. "We'll need more men to make it through today. With what we're looking at there are bound to be heavy casualties. So why can't Yuma release the 365th to your authority?"

"But they're relocation troops with few trained in boot camp." the chief argued. "The pathetic way some of them handles a rifle I rather be in another state if we go into battle." There was a pause. "Anyhow, we have already tried getting them released, but General Paulson denied the request."

"It's strange," James thoughtfully mentioned. "But frequently I forget they're even around." There was a serious frown on his face for a few moments. "But the 365th does have 375 men in uniform. Right now it doesn't matter if they're battle trained or not. We'll all have to fight for our lives before this is all over. Why don't you try again, chief? Stress the fact we're facing annihilation if more men aren't sent down this way. Who knows? Maybe the General will be having a generous day and offer us help, though I doubt if that's going to happen."

Savannah angrily replied. "But he has to help."

James frowned. "That man does only what he wants to. Not once has he inspected this territory. All the General does is sit on his ass and complain about how bad things are."

An enlisted radioman rushed into the mess hall and found James. "Sir, Tyler is sending frantic messages. The enemy is on the move."

"Damn," the lieutenant snapped. "The Russians are moving earlier than we anticipated." After ordering the alert sounded he hurried to communications to find activity in there as frantic as on the battlefield. "Hurry up and give me the facts."

The radioman explained while James studied the updated regional map. "The static in our transmissions may be natural or electronically introduced." When James silently asked for his opinion the enlisted man firmly said. "We're being electronically jammed."

It was Stan's voice transmitting from Vandenberg. "Blackbird to Blue Jay, we have enemy movement." James heard Tyler's voice as he took the radio. "Stan, give me the map coordinates now! E-4 . . . F-9 . . . 4HH." The sergeant's unsteady caused James some concern. He was always calm in battle. "I have approximately one hour contact window. Ground troops numbering over three hundred are supported by armored vehicles and at least 20 heavy attack tanks." The lieutenant could hear the distant clanking of tracked vehicles. "This is a full frontal assault and we need Eagle assistance now."

"Tell him we're on Condition Red and lay down purple smoke in ten minutes." James ordered before rushing from the room. In the hallway he met Savannah on her way to communications. "You now have Ten Delta's defense in your hands. We'll get back as soon as we can. After we leave put Ten Delta on lock down and stay that way."

After Condition Red sounded frantic activity erupted inside Ten Delta. Heavily armed marines quickly loaded into Lewis' Chinook that was already pulled outside.

The two Apache helicopters also were outside waiting to depart. Impatience ruled inside the compound. Assuring that all conditions were met Chief Hickman was everywhere shouting orders and rechecking weapon loads. Communications Specialist Sergeant Richards impatiently walked in front of the regional map while another marine waited with grease pencil to trace troop movements on the plastic plotting board. Savannah now commanding the facility's defenses stood quietly observing the smooth operation. Television monitors provided an immediate visual control of the surrounding area. She had ten men with which to operate communications and defend the facility.

"Hanger doors closed and locked." a marine reported while watching the monitoring screens.

"Very well," Savannah said. "Inform security personnel Ten Delta is on lock down status."

*　*　*

During their short flight to Vandenberg Air Force Base, James had time to ponder their unfavorable crisis that was rapidly developing. The helicopter's co-pilot sat behind and just below him. His duties as electronics and gunnery specialist required full attention. The Apache attack helicopter was sleek lined with nose mounted sight sensors assisting the crew while in flight. Pods on both sides of the cockpit housed the deadly warship's avionic and electronic systems. Two 15349 shp engines provided the complex machine's swift power. It was still an hour until dawn, but murky conditions created by an overburden debris cluttered atmosphere would make it semi-darkness.

James spoke in his radio mouthpiece. "Glassford, how are you feeling?"

"I have seen better days," his co-pilot replied.

"Yeah, I know how you feel. But today I guess we earn our pay."

Suddenly an alarm warned them of an airborne threat. Glassford calmly announced they were being pursued by an unidentified source. To their rear in the distance James saw black columns of smoke bellowing from the burning warship. Wakefield flipped opened a cover over a set of red switches. He then advised James their 16 Hellfire anti-armor missiles beneath the Apache was activated.

"Do you have an identity?" James asked.

"It's now identified as an American Cobra AH-1."

"We don't have any Cobras in this region."

"It probably was captured by the enemy."

James nodded then pressed his radio button. "American Cobra, you're flying in unauthorized air space. Please identity yourself." He broadcasted four times without a response. "It's enemy flown." Contacting the second Apache flying below him James instructed. "Apache Two, do you have a Cobra on your screen?"

"Roger that."

"It doesn't respond to my calls so take her out." James ordered. "Rejoin me after your strike."

Their machine's Honeywell integrated target search and detection data identified the terrain challenging Tyler's position as heavy with hostile contacts.

*   *   *

Shuffling his body on the pile of rubble Stan calmly watched those enemy forces slowly moving towards them. His fears disappeared once Tyler said there was no way of escaping. Their salvation depended on those Apaches arriving in time.

"It's strange how your body reacts to negative conditions," the marine mumbled.

While observing shifting enemy movements through his glasses Tyler indifferently asked. "And how's that?"

"One moment you feel you'll shit in your pants from the fears pounding your body. Then the next thing you know everything is calm and cool. Crazy, isn't it?" Stan studied the Russian vehicles moving in a flanking pattern.

"That's because you're doing what the Corps trained you to do. Kill stinking Russians." A frown touched his face when Tyler pressed his radio transmit button. "Blackbird to Blue Jay, do you copy? Enemy armor identified as Second Regiment of the Russian Thirty-Second Armor." After his message was acknowledged, the master sergeant looked at Stan. "We're really in deep shit, buddy. Last I heard the Thirty-Second was fighting along the Churchill."

Stan forced a thin grin. "You just can't trust those Russians, can you?" Rolling back on this stomach the sergeant thoughtfully observed the spreading tanks. "So what have you heard about that armor group?"

"They're a bunch of ruthless bastards not knowing the word 'mercy."

Stan nervously chuckled. "That's nice to know." For a few minutes he studied a nearby ravine carved out by exploding missiles then yelled. "We got intruders." He was pointing at a clump of dead weeds screening the sloping terrain into an unnatural ravine.

Tyler quickly turned his glasses in that direction. It was a few moments before he saw camouflaged soldiers moving crouched over toward their outpost. About that time dirt geysers was thrown up around them as armored vehicles began firing on their scattered positions. Tapping his machine gunner on the shoulder Tyler waited while the man swung around his tripod weapon.

Soon a steady stream of 5.65mm bullets sped through the early morning air. The ground ahead of them was stitched like a quilted cloth. Several screams rose from the gulley then there was silence from that spot. About that time a tank drove through the smoky screen. One of his marines armed with a Russian made AKS-74 mounted with BG-15 grenade launcher fired three times at the tank's underbelly. The explosions brought it groaning to a halt as fires broke out. The abandoning crew was brought down by a hail of bullets. Russian infantrymen running around the burning tank charged Tyler's weak defenses with blazing guns.

The smell of gunfire and explosions stung the immediate area. Smoke clinging to the ground drifted around in small patches. While firing his assault rifle Tyler kept evaluating the situation that wasn't good for them. His eyes were watering from thick camouflaging smoke pouring from generators atop a tank. Several feet down from him Ebenezer leaned against some rubble wrapping his wounded right arm. More than once he dived for cover as bullets cut through the trash.

Stan's radio began declaring. "Blackbird, Blackbird lay down your smoke."

"Hey, Tyler, the lieutenant wants us to lay smoke."

Tyler shouted all right and jerking a smoke grenade from the web belt threw it into the middle of their positions. A dark spot in the skies was drawing near. Then another larger dot appeared not far behind the attack helicopter. The wind was strong so just to be sure Tyler threw another signaling grenade. The pyrotechnic mixture belched before igniting the drifting purple smoke. The positioning signal only lasted eight seconds, but that was long enough to pinpoint where his men were trapped. The battle rapidly spread around the Americans with the fierceness of a terrible winter storm. It didn't matter where the handful of marines fired their gunfire brought down Russians.

With no time to cheer James' arrival, Tyler stood against a ravine wall firing his assault weapon and observing what the enemy was doing. Though there was no confusion among the charging enemy the sergeant knew there was a hesitation in doing so. The monstrous 44 ton tanks halted while sputtering and coughing whitish smoke from their exhausts. For some reason the charge petered out while infantrymen knelt around their metal shields waiting for orders.

*   *   *

After noting the spreading purple smoke James started his attack approach. Seeing a Russian tank furiously firing at his trapped marines, James increased his approach speed while enemy tanks wildly fired at his chopper. The Apache's primary objective was destruction of enemy armor. Thus he carried into battle an impressive deadly array of armaments. For suppressive gunfire there was seventy-five 2.72 inch folding fin aerial rockets (FFAR) inside the pods. James also had at his command the tank killer Hellfire laser-guided missile system.

"O.K. you bastards," James shouted into his radio. "You want to play?"

Their target acquisition and Designation Sight System was activated. Through his Forward Looking Infra-red/Integrated helmet and Display Sighting system, Glassford saw everything he needed. After pressing the red button locked-after-launch (LOAL) rockets shot from the wing pylons in a blazing birth of destruction. Reaching speeds of Mach 1.7 four Hellfires plowed into the enemy armor charge. The iron coffins quickly became burning shells for their trapped crews. The few managing to escape were shot down by Tyler's marines. The enemy's confident ranks reduced to panic-stricken soldiers were on the wrong end of a turkey shoot. With General Electric engines purring the Apache roared over the scattering enemy infantrymen. With 30mm chain machine guns laying down a terrible ground suppressive gunfire James' Apache became an angel of death. Firing 50 round bursts at six second intervals the bullets created bloody paths of death. The hydraulically driven gun turret traversed 110 degrees back and forth while sowing a noisy bloody path.

Russian infantrymen tried escaping the Apache's murderous gunfire and barrages of bullets from Tyler's entrenched men. But those tanks still in the fight created a living hell in the skies. James evasively flew through bursting anti-aircraft flak while suffering some damages. Speeding over the tanks his chopper sharply banked and dashed over the ocean's choppy waters before abruptly turning for another strafing charge. Glassford was totally engrossed in his electronics and radar. Black ugly puffs of explosives filled the skies while shaking the Apache when it passed over.

*   *   *

Finding temporary relief from the Russians' armor gunfire, Tyler calmly took in the situation while his men kept firing at the retreating enemy. During all of this the Chinook passed through the bursting shells and black puffs of smoke and landed near the bunker where Earl and Barnes were. There was still plenty to worry about even if the armor hardware was cautiously withdrawing. A Russian marine was probably the best warrior Russia put into battle. He was well trained and packed with enforced belief his country could do no wrong. Courage was something the Russian marine had no shortage of. He repeatedly charged into furious gunfire until either achieving his objective or death. Tyler finding his hatred so strong for the Soviet Union there was no lack of courage. When the first Soviet soldier charged Tyler fell to the ground while firing at the camouflaged figure. Bullets ripping into the man sent bits and pieces of flesh splashing down on the prone sergeant. With a disgusted grunt the sergeant jumped up while throwing off the bloody pieces.

Along the jagged knoll there were too many Russians breaking through their weak lines like a curved sharp sword. All around him explosions repeatedly tore into the ground. Screaming soldiers with the red star on their sleeves charged these trapped Americans who were standing fast. Tyler heard two of his men defending the left flank scream then there were no sounds from that sector. A squad of soldiers armed with automatics charged his position shouting communist slogans and wildly firing. Tyler dived to the ground to avoid those bullets charging through the icy air. Then leaping up he sprayed the frontal attack before diving into another position. The enemy though suffering heavy casualties kept coming. The tanks shifted their approaches toward the weaker left flank while armored cars drove straight toward them. The Apache darting about the general area randomly fired into those scattering infantrymen ranks. Then while sweeping over the fourth time Glassford let loose with another Hellfire barrage into the armor units.

Though the enemy was slowly withdrawing because of fierce gunfire from James's Apache their positions were still threatened. Grabbing his radio mike Tyler anxiously reported. "Blackbird to Eagles One and Two, we have Condition Broken Arrow. I repeat Broken Arrow. Withdrawing to sector H-10 and firing red smoke." He hoped James heard the message as numerous explosions were thunderously rocking the general area. Retreating enemy tanks kept fiercely firing their anti-aircraft resistance. Only for a few moments did the sergeant see James' Apache flying through thick exploding black puffs then he was again fighting. "Damned it must be murder up there." Tyler muttered while scrambling from the trench.

"Withdraw! Withdraw!" he screamed to his men. "Sector H-10! Sector H-10!" He was shocked to see only a few marines staggering through the drifting red smoke. At one point Tyler dropping to his knee fired steady bursts at charging enemy soldiers. "Move it! Sector H-10 now!"

*   *   *

Thundering back toward the tanks surviving their initial attacks Glassford activated his FFAR system. After computers received launch data it automatically released the rockets in a fiery spread. Six fingers of flames hurled toward the helpless locked on armor. Those 2.75 inch rockets tore through armor plating as if it was paper. With 2500 one ounce steel flechettes exploding the impact zones became bloody massacres. Another two rockets streaked angrily into the horrified ranks of soldiers still advancing on Tyler's crumbling defenses. After dawn broke on the land, sunlight feebly illuminated the nightmare sparing neither side. Burning tanks cloaked in black swirling smoke were scattered about the terrain while bloodied bodies laid everywhere. Fires burned where minutes ago explosions ripped apart the already scarred ground. Lifting above the cries of the wounded were those moans of the dying. Making one last pass assuring the armor threat was crippled James was about to check out their landed Chinook.

Suddenly Glassford calmly advised his pilot. "We're illuminated." A blinking red light signaled their Aircraft Survivability Equipment (ASE) had activated radar jamming countermeasures. The Chaff/flare dispenser was blinking yellow indicating active status. James' electronics officer noted video printed warnings of an inbound surface-to-air missile. "We're locked on."

"ASE activated and dispensing," James responded. The flashing yellow light on his display was replaced with a red blinking. Chaff now unloading into the air would hopefully confuse that inbound missile.

"Threat identity," James asked after a few seconds.

"Threat identified as a Russian Grail."

The Russian SA-7 (NATO codenamed Grail) was a non nuclear missile over four feet long with a fairly good infra-red guidance system. Its rocket launcher truck was quickly identified on the burning battlefield. James' sharp banking caused the first rocket to crash into a burning tank. Ignoring its explosion's smoke and flames James flew through the violence.

"Two rockets launching," the weapons officer advised James. This time his voice was slightly uneasy.

Both men saw the flames erupting as two slender frames came to life and shot into the skies. James quickly went into evasive tactics to confuse the new launchings. Warning lights on his display stated their AN-ALQ-144IR was activated. Located behind the rotor mast was a device generating pulsed IR energy that confused the missile's projected objective. The canopy's optically flat windshields, roof panels, and curved side panels offered them excellent visual contact with the missiles. James' responsibility was flying the aircraft while his co-pilot managed the weapons. Both men were busy in battle.

"Chaff released," Glassford advised. He didn't expect a reply from James.

As the rocket's radar tracked James' helicopter their dispenser hurled thin hot confusing strips behind them. The AS-7 wasn't a smart missile so it couldn't distinguish the differences between countermeasures and its actual target. Fooled by the chaff the rocket crashed into the earth.

"Second rocket is still locked on," the co-pilot calmly said.

"Roger that," James said before jerking the helicopter into a sharp roll.

The Apache's winning trait in battle was its full aerobatic ability in performing loops, splits, and hammerhead stalls. As James sent the chopper through these rapid evasive tactics the fuselage never once groaned protests. All of his turning and wild looping confused the missile and it crashed in the ocean.

With the last threat out of their way James headed back to eliminate that rocket truck. The noisy pinging of bullets against the helicopter was something James never got use to. Designers incorporated light weight Kevlar armor plating that was unfriendly to small arms gunfire and shell splints from calibers up to 23mm. It took one Hellfire to tear apart the rocket launcher. Time after time James flew low over the battlefield strafing those fleeing troops with his chain machine gun. The few armored cars still fighting were destroyed. Explosions and curling black smoke choking the general area concealed Russia's attack that faltered then crumbled altogether.

On their last flyover James darted to the ocean then committed a sharp roll and headed toward the few tanks still viciously in the battle. Locking in his Target Acquisition and Designation System, Glassford selected his Hellfire option. Hellfire was a military acronym meaning HELicopter Launched FIRE and forget. Now rapidly approaching the clustered surviving armor James grinned. When the Apache went into its low level approach the ground troops wildly scattered. Reaching up Glassford flipped down the one inch cathode ray tubing over his left eye.

There was a slight whoosh and the helicopter lurched as four missiles rushed ahead of them. The rockets explosively plowing into the tanks caused a blinding flash of flames. Those explosions hurled hot metal and chunks of human flesh over the general area. Sergeant Tyler was ducking when a leather helmet with its bloody head sailed passed his shoulder. Minutes later James made another security pass over the battlefield. His marines were hurriedly loading into the Chinook. He saw Tyler half dragging a prisoner across the burning terrain to Lewis' chopper. When the Russian stumbled Tyler angrily kicked him back into mobility. Only when the large helicopter was airborne did James relax.

CHAPTER TWENTY-ONE

After James' helicopter was pulled into the hanger he was informed his presence was required in the conference room. This time there was a definite sadness hanging over Ten Delta. Men were lost during that battle. James briefly stopped in the sick bay to check on their wounded. Chatterbox was busy closing wounds or giving the less serious cases medications. After receiving the status of their losses the lieutenant walked to the conference room. Inside he found a Russian tied to a chair while Tyler and Timothy angrily stood in front of him. Savannah was softly discussing something with Earl when he entered. Their conversation halted.

"What do we have?" James asked while removing his gloves.

Tyler bitterly said. "His name is Vicktor Biryuzov, age 32, heavy weapons specialist." He handed over some documents taken from the man's wallet. "According to his military ID card, Lieutenant Biryuzov's unit is the Thirty-Second Armor."

"And this you dispute?" James studied the ID card, two travel permits, and one photo of a young Russian beauty.

"Yes, I do."

"Any reason to?"

"The Thirty-Second is fighting on the Churchill River. I know this armor group's reputation and what happened out there this morning wasn't the Thirty-Second. Back along the Churchill I personally saw them in action. Those bastards don't recognize the word retreat." Roughly grabbing the man's arm he snorted. "This man is wearing the red arm patch with gold hammer and sickle."

James dubiously looked at Tyler. "I thought they all wore that patch?"

"Not the Thirty-Second. They have had special privileges since World War II. That armor group has more decorations and citations than any other Russian unit. There was something else I noticed out there. Those tanks aren't what the unit uses. I don't know who they are, but most certainly they aren't the Thirty-Second."

After a few moments studying the Russian James wasn't that impressed. He was tall with a husky built. His skin was dark with very flashing black eyes that stared straight ahead. He noticed the cheaply manufactured brown camouflaged garments.

According to Tyler the Thirty-Second was a very elite division. If that was true then this captured soldier didn't look very elite.

"Continue interrogating him. Find out all you can." he sternly instructed Tyler. "I want Earl, Barnes, Savannah, and the chief in the cafeteria for a conference." At the door he stopped and turned around. "If he refuses to cooperate I don't care what it takes, but find out what these bastards are planning."

In the hallway James stopped and looked at Earl. "Did you have a chance to check out that rocket?"

"We never got close to its entry."

James sarcastically replied. "Well, you may never get another opportunity."

"That rocket has to fire on time." Earl sharply insisted. "Mankind's existence depends on firing those rockets at the same time." He shook his head. "I don't think you understand the gravity of this situation, lieutenant. We have to introduce rain before the Greenhouse Theory takes total hold."

"Are you certain the theory hasn't already locked its jaws around the earth? Look around us. Have you seen the dying grass, trees, flowers, and vegetation? And what about those fires still burning out of control? My men have burned thousands of corpses while only God knows how many more are decaying in the rubble of our cities. People are dying all around us because of the deceasing sunlight. Hey, even the oceans are protesting the planet's devastation." James paused to catch his breath then continued. "I fully understand your problem's gravity, but I also have my own problems. If Russia grabs hold of this coast we won't recapture it without serious bloodshed. That's what I have to erase before jumping into another frying pan."

"But—"

"We'll get to your problem in time, but right now I have to reevaluate our grim situation. More than half of my men are either dead or wounded with no reinforcements coming the way. But I sure as hell have a hostile naval force coming my way."

When Earl started to argue James didn't see Savannah quietly shake her head.

James looked at Timothy. "Have we received a reply about transferring the 365th to this immediate region?"

"General Paulson hasn't responded either way."

Going into the mess hall they went through the chow line selectively dumping food on their trays. Gathered around the table they ate in silence. Only when the meal was nearly finished did Savannah finally break their fasting of words.

"What Ten Delta achieved in the last two days is simply incredible. It's beyond anything thought possible. Your destroying that naval base will seriously affect Soviet movements in this region. Then on the tail of this the Russian destroyer was put out of commission. Today a handful of your men drove back the Soviets with staggering losses among their ranks." She paused and smiled faintly. "Maybe now we're seeing that promised light at the tunnel's end. Only a few more pushes and the enemy will be crippled."

"My men are doing their job, but there's only so much they can do. Our ranks are reduced while supplies are critically low. I would say right now Ten Delta is seriously hurt."

Earl studied the lieutenant for a few moments. "What do you need the most?"

"Manpower," James quickly declared.

"Our troops are committed along the Church in a death struggle."

"We don't have to draw troops from there. There are reinforcements in our region that General Paulson refuses to release."

Earl was silent while studying this brash-mannered officer. "I assume you're referring to the 365th Regiment?"

"Yes."

"But they aren't combat trained troops."

"Hand them a rifle and they'll fight because there's no other option. Either they fight alongside us or they'll die after we fall in battle."

Earl stood after draining his cup. "The 365th will be transferred to your command. Forget about General Paulson. He's one of those generals who sits in the backwater of wars and wonders why history forgot him. I'll call St. Louis with your request. Now if you will excuse me I must rest. That rocket will fly tomorrow even if Barnes and I have to drag it into a firing position." Forcing a weak smile he left the hall.

Timothy watched him leave. "General Paulson is a very powerful man who doesn't like his authority bypassed."

Savannah smiled. "Oh, he'll have the transfer completed within hours. General Paulson doesn't know what power is until he tangles with Earl Craver."

"I hope so. We don't have that much time left. We kicked their butts today, but this isn't the end. Tyler believes those troops aren't the Thirty-Second. The puzzling question is why were they posing as the Thirty-Second? And who were they really?" James glanced at Timothy. "And what's even more unnerving is how many more units have they inserted?"

"Maybe that explains the increased activity from those Mexicans crying for California's annexation by their government. The Soviets are obviously inserting military advisors to help them organize."

James thoughtfully rubbed his chin. "That makes sense." Slowly exhaling the lieutenant examined the problem. "The Mexicans will have to wait until we take care of the Russians." There was a short pause. "Or until they take care of us. So, here's what I want you to do, chief. Draw up battle plans for challenging the Russian insertions. Assuming we'll have Thomas' people by tomorrow then include them in your plans." After the chief nodded he asked Savannah. "Want to take a walk?"

*　　*　　*

After entering the hanger where there was an explosion of activity James said. "Up to now the Russians played with us in isolated incidents. I'm certain tomorrow will be a very different situation. I expect them to throw everything they have at us to settle this matter once for all."

"Until coming here I never heard of Gaviota." Savannah replied while walking around the helicopters being prepared for tomorrow's battles. "Now it may be the turning point of this damned war."

"People living along the coast know this area very well. Actually the name is used a lot. The city of Gaviota is 150 feet above sea level. We have the Gaviota State Park, the Gaviota Pass, and the Gaviota Peak 2468 feet above sea level." James paused to look about. "Maybe after tomorrow another name will be added . . . the Gaviota Battlefield."

Savannah studied his worried face. "I know you have much on your mind, but tomorrow the enemy must be smashed. There's a precarious balance of sea power in the Gulf that must be shifted our way. Right now the Red Navy numbers sixty-four destroyers while our Navy's similar numbers are blockaded in their ports. Military considerations rapidly changing along the Churchill River are mostly against us. Our regiments are driven back with staggering losses. Armor losses are crippling and we have no way replacing those tanks. America's future along the river is presently very gloomy." She stopped walking to thoughtfully look at the lieutenant. "The bottom line is if those ships reach the Gulf the critical balance of sea power will be tipped and America loses the war. It's that simple."

James frowned. "I believe that warning has been preached often enough."

"Yes, I know. But I just wanted to remind you how important tomorrow may be. I'm in a position to know things even Earl doesn't know. I'm sorry to rest this burden on your shoulders, James, but everything is riding on tomorrow. If we lose . . . America will cease to exist. We simply do not have the manpower to fight another front against the communists."

James chose not to reply. Walking over to his helicopter James watched his mechanic unloading the 30mm chain gun for its daily check. With atmospheric conditions as they were helicopter weapon systems were verified daily. The shiny 1200 rounds of M789 HEDP lay on the concrete in its belt. James personally preferred the high explosive dual purpose rounds over high explosive incendiary munitions. He stood there for a few moments before the sandy haired mechanic knew he was there. Having worked with James aboard the aircraft carrier, he enlisted in the Outer Perimeter Forces to stay with him.

"I forgot to ask," Savannah asked while gesturing toward a group of marines practicing loading and unloading the new P38 laser rifle. "How did those rifles work on the battlefield?"

"According to Roscoe's team they performed great and scared the shit out of the Russians. I guess they had never seen them." James said with a grin. "But those rifles take some getting use to so Stan is drilling them."

Walking over to Lewis's Chinook they stood watching Gunner welding a bracket to its side. The captain came over and greeted them with a suspicious frown.

"What's he doing?" James asked.

"He has a plan for tomorrow. They are brackets for some canisters of napalm we found at Kasulich. There could be an opportunity to play around with them tomorrow?"

"How's your crew holding up?"

"I guess as best as can be expected. The Chief was Joshua's blood brother so he wants revenge while Gunner generally hates the communists. My chopper is a mean machine and now the guys want to make her even more monstrous." Lewis explained.

"Tomorrow we can use all the help you can provide."

"You can count on us." the captain promised. After seeing there was nothing else to say he walked back to his machine and curiously watched Gunner's work.

As they wandered about the hanger Savannah said. "They don't talk much, do they?"

"All the time they have been here rarely have they talked with my men. They're loners bearing a hatred for the Russians and waiting to spit their venom. But judging from what Joshua accomplished they aren't afraid of dying. And tomorrow that may be a big plus factor for all of us."

She glanced at the triangle arm patch all Ten Delta personnel wore. Inside the green was a dove with crossed swords beneath. The words 'Victory or Nothing' was in black lettering. It was a harsh statement that may soon be proven. She knew Outer Perimeter Commands were hastily organized, but it was shocking how they were haphazardly supported. To correct these serious shortcomings the President would have to intervene. But first they would have to defeat an overwhelming superior naval force.

Outside temperatures had dropped another ten degrees since their battle that morning. But inside Ten Delta everything was cozy. Before leaving the hanger Savannah looked around. Those marines training with their new rifle was all business. James' mechanic having finished his belt inspection was reloading the chain gun's ammo. He softly hummed a country tune while working. These men busy preparing for tomorrow's battle weren't panic stricken. Ten Delta's atmosphere was like the night before a general's formal inspection. Walking into the mess hall both grabbed cups of coffee and sat. Anxious marines discussed tomorrow's tactics with their squad leaders. Savannah noticed there was a wide cultural range among Ten Delta's marines.

A marine came and reported. "Tyler requests your presence."

"Did he learn anything?" James asked after quickly draining his cup.

"He may have learned where those armored groups are coming ashore."

"Very good," Standing James looked at Savannah and politely said. "If you'll excuse me, major, I need to look into this?" They then hurriedly left the mess hall.

*   *   *

When James entered the conference room he stopped short. The prisoner was slumped over in his chair. His mouth was closed with a strip of tape. The face was badly beaten while his eyes were puffed closed. James took in what he saw with a frown before looking at Tyler.

"Sorry, sir, but the bastard wouldn't cooperate," Tyler sheepishly explained.

James nodded. "That doesn't surprise me." Walking over to the prisoner he contemptuously looked at him. "What did you learn?"

"Well, for starters his name isn't Vicktor Biryuzov. Real name is Peter Fedin, a lieutenant Colonel with the Soviet Marines' Forty-Fourth Regiment. That regiment is probably the closest thing to Satan himself. Kossier uses them to remove political problems inside Russia."

"So why are they here?"

Tyler brutally jerked the unconscious man's head up. "Now that took some convincing before he told me everything. The Forty-Fourth is here to purge all unfriendly sources to Russian domination along this coast."

"Shit." James moaned.

When the door softly closed both men turned to see Savannah thoughtfully staring at the prisoner. "What else did you learn, sergeant?" she curtly demanded.

"There will be fourteenth interrogation centers. Colonel Fedin is here to evaluate the political climate."

"You don't seem too surprised?" James curiously asked.

"That's because I'm not. We have suspected this was their plans after a minor official defected several months ago."

For a moment James stared at this woman. "And who is we?"

"Military Central Intelligence."

"I thought you were with a military commission?"

"That was my cover."

"Then you knew who was attacking us today?" Tyler asked.

"At first I didn't. But when Tyler insisted that wasn't the Thirty-Second out there, then I knew who was compromising this coast." She motioned for the sergeant to hand over the prisoner's wallet. While they silently watched she studied the cards and picture removed from the leather case. "We suspected Kossier was up to something when Colonel Fedin abruptly disappeared some weeks ago. Then Intelligence started intercepting rumors. Key personnel from his elite regiment faded from sight." She gave the documents back to Tyler. "Army intelligence along the Churchill reported certain armor units were pulled back. Four weeks ago three companies of trained killers, or what Kossier fondly calls his Soviet Realignment Units, dropped from sight. We had most of the missing pieces for our puzzle." She looked at Tyler and forced a weak grin. "You just gave me the final missing piece, sergeant. Now we know what Kossier is doing."

James was puzzled and at the same time suspicious. "So what is Kossier doing?"

Savannah looked at the men before saying. "Kossier is invading California."

There was a short silence before James sarcastically asked. "When were you planning to tell us this?"

"Initially, you didn't have a need to know." she replied with a sheepish shrug.

"When the CIA was abolished I thought back room secrets were over." Tyler charged. "I guess that only a hopeful dream. Nothing changes, does it?"

"Not when it comes to military intelligence gathering. We had one chance and it had better be right. Great effort went into making the Russians believe we were putting all of our hopes in the Gulf and Kossier fell for it."

"Now what do we do?" James growled. "Hell, we have a naval task force coming down from God knows where. And all I have to challenge them are two Apaches, thirty-three marines, and maybe some relocation troops." James shook his head. "Not much to throw at the enemy."

Savannah grinned. "It may not be as dark as you believe. For starters, Major Thomas doesn't command a raw bunch of recruits doing relocation labors. The 365th is really a covert commando unit from the 10th Strategic Division. Fearing California may be Kossier's secondary target they were sent here months ago."

James cautiously asked. "What about Earl?"

"He doesn't know what's going on. He was our high profile decoy and the Russians are still confused why he's in California."

"So he isn't firing a rocket from Vandenberg?" Tyler asked.

Savannah shook her head. "No, he really is going to fire that rocket if its launching pad is intact and workable. The earth needs rain."

James was reacting cynically. "Boy, you people sure are throwing around lots of bullshit. So what about our two destroyers off Mexico? Are they really short on fuel or is that another lie?"

"The warships are fueled, armed, and ready to do battle once their captains receive the proper code." Savannah looked at the unconscious Russian colonel then made a-oh-well expression. "Sergeant, it would be a serious mistake if this man escaped. Everything we have worked for would go down the drain."

Tyler looked at her for a moment. "What do you suggest, madam?" he suspiciously asked.

"Kill him and bury his body deep." she said without remorse. "Nobody else is to know what I have told you. But be prepared for a major offensive. They're not sure what is going on but they know Ten Delta will challenge their arrival. I have already notified Major Thomas to haul ass to Gaviota."

CHAPTER TWENTY-TWO

James came into the communications room and looked about. Two large plastic plotting boards outlining the coastal region were being rolled out. One marine monitored their surveillance cameras surrounding the complex. Another radioman silently listened for radio communication between enemy forces. So far the air waves were quiet. He glanced at Savannah standing before the wall map thoughtfully studying it. The major was one surprise after another. The lump nervously settling in his stomach wouldn't leave. Tomorrow would be the deciding factor whether California stayed American or not. There was no use denying they were the underdogs in tomorrow's activities.

Walking over to the radioman he asked. "Do we have enemy activity?"

"Everything is quiet."

After nodding he joined Savannah. "I don't understand why they haven't sent out reconnaissance patrols."

"They have we just haven't detected them."

"Roscoe goes out in ten minutes with a patrol. I need to know what's going on beyond Gaviota. It's too quiet out there."

"What about the chief's battle plans?"

"He's just about finished."

The radioman announced. "I have a voice message coming over."

"What is it?" Savannah asked quickly moving over to his table.

The marine nodded. "Somebody named ZuZu One is confirming the Russian warship FEDYUNINSKY ten miles off San Francisco bearing on a southern course."

She grinned. "Now they're bringing out their toys." After the name was marked on the plotting board she said. "FEDYUNINSKY is a destroyer we thought was lost off Africa two years ago."

"What about the other ships?" James asked not feeling good about this new development.

"There's the amphibious ship ALEKSANDR and two troop transports we know about for sure." she admitted. "If anything else appears it's another surprise."

James frowned. "It seems Military Central Intelligence has many surprises."

After tiny red lights on the monitors scanning their exterior began blinking the operator declared. "We have intruders on east grid four, sector one-four-nine." He magnified his cameras one and four. While the cameras went fuzzy as their imagines enlarged he continued his report. "Six males spread out in V battle formations. Weapons carried are Heckler & Kock assault rifles, Steyr SSG sniper rifle mounted with Kahles telescopic sight, and 5.56mm LMG machine guns with top load clips." He watched the figures for a moment before confirming. "They are Soviet Marines."

"Very well," James said. "Magnify camera six."

"That's identified as a PSZH-IV armored vehicle." After the camera zoomed in James observed two heavily armed marines standing alongside watching their comrades spread out their searching.

Gunner and Lewis came into the operations to join the gathering. The gunner's mate came over and thoughtfully stared at the monitors showing the enemy patrol. "I could use that vehicle," he solemnly said. When James questioningly looked at him he explained. "If I had that armored car, traveling to Point Conception would be no problem."

"And why are you traveling to Point Conception?"

Gunner looked at the monitor for a moment before walking to the plotting board. "The captain and I have discussed this and it may work." He touched a spot on the board. "Here at Point Conception the land sticks out. Enemy ships because of the tumultuous waters further out will hug the coast. Right here is the wreckage of our destroyer JOHN CANE. Her captain drove the burning ship aground after a surface battle nine months ago. If positioned aboard the wreckage a man would have a close shot when that enemy warship cruised by."

"But that's suicidal," Savannah dubiously charged.

Gunner glanced at her with a challenging grin. "The way I look at it, madam, tomorrow will see many suicidal efforts."

James wasn't convinced. "How do you plan to accomplish this?"

"By using a Russian Grail missile and I'm counting on that warship carrying fuel drums on deck." He shrugged. "I probably won't sink her though the damages would hopefully be serious enough to cripple her."

Savannah studied the map while talking. "Point Conception is off the Vandenberg Air Base."

Gunner nodded. "That's why with that BTR I might get pass Russian patrols. At least it's a try. And as I see it any reduction in enemy forces is a plus factor for us tomorrow."

James pondered the request for a few moments then slowly nodded. "Tyler," he said. "Take a few men and take out those men. We have a man who needs their transportation."

After Gunner and Tyler left the room Savannah looked at James. "Your men sure like to dive into near hopeless endeavors."

James grinned. "Out here, major, every day is a near hopeless endeavor." While talking the lieutenant watched the armored vehicle's mounted cannon slowly menacingly rotating. Russian soldiers armed with shoulder-fired Javelin missile launchers were defensively scattering.

*   *   *

Tyler's team had wasted no time departing Ten Delta and blending in with the ruins. Local weather outside the underground complex was again nasty. Winds coming in from the Pacific were icy and strong. Loose debris whipped about like toilet paper in a storm. More than once they dived to the sooty ground as solids hurled through the air. Two point marines carrying laser rifles moved with the alertness of cats on the prowl. Their cautious trek through the ruins and up into Gaviota was without incident. Within minutes Tyler was studying the Russian vehicle sitting not that far away. The Russians returning from their quick reconnoiter were huddled around the protective vehicle. Above the howling winds Tyler heard more cursing when another soldier was struck by flying debris.

Goggles protected his eyes from the stinging sandy grains peppering his flesh. "I only count five." he grunted.

"There were six soldiers." Gunner argued. "I counted them on the monitor."

"Then where is that sixth man?" Tyler skeptically asked while quickly studying the surrounding area. His view was seriously hampered by rubble piles.

Before he could speak again a grenade denoted close by showering them with crashing debris. The marines immediately ducked for cover while firing at the enemy now scattering away from their armored vehicle. Two Soviets were instantly taken down by laser beams. Tyler quickly scrambled over the rough surfaces to another point offering better visual contact. It took only a minute to pin point where a soldier hid in ambush. A grenade saw the end of him. With this threat erased the master sergeant crawled to another position while ducking enemy gunfire all the way. Then within seconds their threats were eliminated. He lay silent for a moment wondering why its cannon hadn't fired. This was solved a few moments later when Tyler discovered the driver and gunner were dead.

"What happened to them?" Gunner asked after the bodies were dragged from the vehicle.

Tyler quickly checked the bodies then stripped their jackets off. Moments later he stood with a worried frown. Using his radio he called Ten Delta. "We have two men inside the transport who died from that green bacterium." He glanced over his shoulder when hearing the engine roar. Before he could intervene Gunner drove away. "Damn fool." he mumbled.

*   *   *

Hurrying into communications after returning, Tyler found the lieutenant and Savannah waiting for him. "What the hell happened out there?" James asked.

"We eliminated the Russians after a short firefight. But the soldiers inside the BTR had minor showing of that green slime. While I was examining their bodies Gunner got into the machine and drove away." He looked at the major. "Chatterbox never determined if that stuff was contagious."

"We aren't certain how it's transferred."

"Then what you're saying is once a person contacts the bacteria it spreads fast."

"Gunner," she soberly warned, "may contact the fungus from inside that vehicle"

Lewis somberly spoke up. "I doubt if he really cares one way or other. He knows the enemy will become suspicious if their BTR doesn't make contact within a given time. Gunner is using that time to reach the wreckage before this happens. And with some luck he may." When the Indian came into the center the captain informed. "Gunner left in a captured BTR for the CANE." Horace stood staring at the map then with a grunt left the room. After a few moments of cold silence he sighed deeply and said. "If you'll excuse me, the Chief and I still have some modifications to complete on my helicopter."

"Now what will you do?" Savannah asked after they departed. She could hear the Indian's furious discussion with his captain out in the hallway.

"Nothing until I hear from Roscoe."

*   *   *

Roscoe didn't have to travel north to know trouble existed among Vandenberg's sprawling grounds so he pointed his patrol south. The Shoets was passing what was left of the El Capitan State Beach when Roscoe called for a halt. Getting from the armored vehicle he thoughtfully studied the outlying devastation with a suspicious eye for detail. Though not seeing anything out of the ordinary his finely tuned mind told him otherwise.

There was trouble in big capital letters brewing out here. Hearing Ebenezer coming up from behind Roscoe looked over his shoulder and nodded.

"See anything?" the corporal asked.

Pointing at the ground he said. "There has recently been plenty of activity around here. The Russians are using Coast Highway as their primary transport route."

Roscoe noticed the corporal had left his AKA-47 rifle in the car and was now humping a Vietnam era M-60 machine gun. Wrapped around his barrel chest were 450 rounds of 7.62 linked ammo. Four grenades were clipped to his belt. An ugly K-knife was slipped behind his belt. Having seen him practicing with that jagged blade knife, Roscoe shuddered every time he hit a tiny spot with alarming accuracy. Over his right chest were four smoke grenades. None of his men wore rim helmets choosing instead campaign hats. Ebenezer wore an Austrian cap with a dark brown cloth tied around his forehead. Roscoe definitely wouldn't care to challenge him in battle.

"What do you want to do? Isla Vista is only a short distance ahead of us."

Roscoe looked around. "Let's park the Shoets in those trees over there. Get our men strategically positioned in those rocks on both sides of the road. This is a good position so we can see both directions." He briefly looked around before furthering his instructions. "Have a marine climb on that pile of ruins. He'll be able to see to our inland flank. Now get to it."

There was a shuffling of activity lasting ten minutes before Roscoe looked about and grinned. A passerby couldn't even see there was an ambush established along this section of highway. After hiding with two marines in the rocks the sergeant settled down for an impatient wait. Ebenezer joining him several minutes later flattened his body against the cold damp stones. Before the war there was obviously some type of construction project requiring large rocks. But they made a good defensive position.

Roscoe chuckled.

Ebenezer frowned. "What's the matter with you?"

"You look like Rambo with all that gear strapped on."

The corporal shrugged. "Well, who the devil are you supposed to be? Chuck Norris?"

Roscoe looked at his own gear and grinned. Outfitted in standard jungle fighting camouflages he carried an M-16/grenade launcher combo. Twenty high-explosive 40mm grenade rounds and 360 rounds of M-16 thirty-round magazines were attached to his specially made vest. Three grenades were clipped to his web belt. Light brown and lighter green paint was smeared over his hands and face. "What's wrong with this? It's standard going out to kill Soviet bastards gear." After that his amusement faded. "I'm sure this is where the Soviets are running their patrols and convoys."

"What are we looking for?"

"Mostly raw intelligence. Hopefully, one of their vehicles will have a map showing their intentions." As night approached the winds' icy biting sting was more noticeable. Their heavy thermo underwear kept the bodies warm, but failed to soothe their uneasiness. "With a major battle shaping up tomorrow the Russians will send patrols out. We'll have to wait until one comes along. How's your arm?"

Ebenezer shrugged. "It's been better that's for sure." He then tapped the shoulders of a man squatting in the rocks scanning the road. "See anything?" After the marine shook his head he looked back at the sergeant. "Have you ever wondered what the Russian soldier thinks about before a battle?"

"Nope, that it would be humanizing him and I'm not about to do that."

"But he's human no matter what his political thoughts are."

"The Soviets are stupid fools little better than a dirty dog. Look around and what do you see? Our land is wasted with millions of people dead because they started their damned war." He angrily shook his head. "I won't give those bastards the decency of dying like humans because they aren't. God wept after seeing what happened to his creations."

It was a short time before Ebenezer remarked in a very solemn mood. "Well, in my heart I have to believe they're humans."

Roscoe grumbled. "Whatever."

Two hours later a marine across the road signaled the enemy was sighted. Jumping from his position Roscoe ran to the Shoets where a marine was hunched over their French radar tracking unit. "What have you got?" he anxiously asked.

"I picked up a contact east two miles down the road a minute ago. Then my contact vanished."

"Explain."

"The contact was moving before pulling off the road."

"Keep your eyes peeled on that screen." Roscoe ordered while scrambling from the Shoets. After cautiously venturing onto the road with binoculars he studied the highway. But it was too dark to see that far. The French manufactured radar only had a range of five miles. When Ebenezer joined him the sergeant mumbled. "Radar illuminated a contact two miles down the road. Then we lost him."

"Maybe he's out of range?"

"No, Stevie said the contact was lost."

"Then he probably pulled off the road and cut his engine."

"That's my thinking. The question is did they illuminate us and are waiting to ambush us?" After seeing nothing visible on the road he lowered the Weiss binoculars. "Or maybe our friends are setting up artillery distance points for tomorrow?"

Ebenezer softly mumbled. "Now let me see . . . if our radar lost the contact two miles east that would put them around Canada de las Panochas arroyo." He nodded though Roscoe didn't see him. "The arroyo could easily hide a vehicle."

The sergeant agreed with the corporal's reasoning. Along this coast there were many crooked ravines branching down from the mountains and spilling into the raging ocean. Their evasive contact remained black. After a few moments Roscoe looked at Ebenezer.

"Make sure the guys' night goggles are working. Have the driver and machine gunner stay with the Shoets. The carrier will slowly approach the arroyo with lights off. Everybody else will follow me and trot to that arroyo while staying off the road. I know everybody knows this area so that shouldn't be a problem. Now let's see what the sly little bastards are up to."

*   *   *

Gunner reached his destination without interference from the enemy. Though that afternoon their attack force was devastated they weren't yet broken. After reaching the CANE's wreckage he quickly camouflaged the captured Russian armored vehicle. Boarding the beached destroyer was a dangerous slow task that took several attempts and a bruised arm. From the captain's twisted bridge chair he was able to see both directions. These freezing hours were easily compared to his time on a naval Antarctica research team some years ago. Though the heavy clothing provided warmth there were margins for improvement. A fire would have been great though common sense won and he shivered. As time slowly passed a chill penetrated his thick clothing as if it was flimsy paper. Soon his body was trembling as if somebody had dropped an ice cube down his pants. Vapor trails repeatedly drifted from his mouth when breathing.

Gunner counted the hours that were slowly passing. Again he was bitterly alone. But it had been like that since Russian missiles pounded San Diego into ashes. Nothing would ever ease the immense pain of losing his family and everything he held dear. He was able to see dark stains on the bulkhead and needed no confirmation it was dried blood. He was superstitious about such things. That's why he never visited the Pearl Harbor Memorial. These were the private worlds of their dead. Crashing waves pounded the wreckage sending many disillusions drifting through his fearful mind.

Gunner heard it long before the huge ship came into view. A quick analysis told him it was impossible to do damages to the amphibious vessel passing within spitting distance. Gunner hugged the bulkhead so not to be detected by those search lights probing the darkness. The sailor helplessly watched the 158 foot long ship fade into the murkiness and soon its noises wasn't heard.

He had to make a quick decision. Ten Delta must be warned the big ship was heading their way. None of the ships were expected until day break. But if he radioed the information Russian frequency scanners would pin point his position. Then his chance to cripple the other destroyer supposedly on the way would be lost.

*   *   *

James was in the hanger inspecting his Apache when word came his presence was needed in communications on the double. Running down the corridor he rushed into the operations center to see Tyler and Savannah at the large plotting boards. Their wretched expressions told him trouble was arising.

"Gunner just warned us the ALEKSANDR is heading our way." Savannah informed.

"How long ago did he call?"

"Five minutes ago. Do you think they're launching their invasion tonight?"

The lieutenant shook his head. "I seriously doubt it. It's too dangerous with this weather and devastated conditions along the coast." He stood in front of the board with a frown.

"Then what about that ship?"

"Their admiral is probably positioning his ships for tomorrow's battles."

"What do we do?"

James looked at Savannah and soberly replied. "We wait."

*   *   *

Their fast walk through the darkness was rough, but Roscoe wouldn't slow the pace. They needed raw data that contact may provide. Before long Ebenezer pulling a red cloth from his pocket tied it around his head covering the nose and mouth. This reduced airborne sooty debris from getting into his mouth. Some of the others followed his example. Nobody complained of the wearisome trot. More than once Roscoe softly cursed the soot covering the ground. Dust generously coated their perspiring bodies. This blackish soot spotting their painted faces gave them monstrous appearances. After reaching their objective, Ten Delta marines cautiously scooted into positions overlooking the arroyo.

Sure enough parked backed into the arroyo was a Soviet PSZH. Roscoe quickly appraised the situation. A Russian marine stood behind his 7.62m machine gun. Two more soldiers were huddled against the sides with weapons pointing at the road. Roscoe gestured Ebenezer to take up position some twenty feet from him. His killing field would contain the armored vehicle. The man crawling away was soon in place. Unclipping four frags Ebenezer laid them on the dusty crest. After signaling he was ready, the corporal directed total interest on the enemy. The sergeant observing his cocky counterpart near the PSZH wondered what their objective was. Roscoe regarded this as a poorly selected ambush site because the Russians were easily blocked in.

Raising his M-16 Roscoe aimed at the sergeant and pulled the trigger. The high explosive 40mm grenade impacted its target before their enemy reacted. The resulting blast scattered bloody tissue and blood and the bloody contest was on. The AKA-47 rattled off several clips before Stan hurled grenades as fast as he could. The leaping geysers of soil and twisted human parts made him smile in appreciation. When the firing began the Russian gunner tried swinging his gun around. But he was at a disadvantage and was blown to bits by the grenades dropping onto the vehicle.

The marines charging down the loose arroyo sides found no resistance. The enemy laid about the sooty ground as their blood seeped out. While checking out the Hungarian armored carrier Roscoe found a leather briefcase. Stan and Ebenezer were checking for surviving enemy soldiers when the Shoets pulled up. Stevie yelled there were no contacts registering on his radar. Roscoe weakly waved his acknowledgement without taking his interest from a map.

After joining his sergeant Ebenezer asked. "Find anything worthwhile?"

"Maybe," Roscoe asked after showing him the leather map. "What do you make of these symbols?"

The corporal studied the map for a few moments then looked up to nervously say. "Shit, Bro, this is a military grid of our immediate zones. The red dots are tanks and there are five just around here. The green dots are armored cars and there are nine ashore. Counting the three we already wiped out that still leaves six. This blue zone is probably where the invasion will land."

"And the purple zone at Isla Vista would be KONSTANTANTINOVICH'S anchorage." Roscoe thought about the data then snapped. "Get the men loaded up and let's hot tail it back to Ten Delta. The Lieutenant needs this data."

"What about that vehicle?"

"Let's take it back. We may be able to use it."

CHAPTER TWENTY-THREE

When the Shoets and captured carrier drove into the hanger there was a crowd waiting for them. After dismissing his men Roscoe and Ebenezer walked with James to communications. There were the usual rounds of 'glad to have you back safe' then the marines returned to their assignments. Roscoe noticed Savannah was grease penciling in symbols on a map board. Observing a marine marking a course along the ocean, the sergeant walked to the board. Talking inside the room was kept at near whispers as information flowed back and forth.

"What's happening?" he asked James.

"Gunner reported ALEKSANDR passed Vandenberg thirty-five minutes ago. Her captain was traveling dangerously close to shore."

"They should have passed here by now."

"They should have," James solemnly agreed, "but our lookouts haven't seen hair or hide of that ship." Roscoe shook his head. "Why would her captain intentionally sail close to Vandenberg then go further out when passing here?"

Savannah looked over at the sergeant. "Our visibility is restricted to one mile and even that may be debated at times. But you're right ALEKSANDR probably cruised further out at sea."

After a moment the sergeant frowned. "She's positioning herself for tomorrow's battles."

"You're familiar with this coast so where do you think she'll land her troops and equipment?"

He didn't hesitate in replying. "There's only one good beach for such landings. And that's between the Refugio and El Capitan State Beaches." He pointed at the map taken from that enemy armored carrier. "On their map is a straight red line between the beaches. I figure that's their landing site. Also we took out a reconnaissance carrier in that area."

"Why not further down the coast?" she curiously asked.

"Too many populated areas along the coast which means heavy devastation. Further down toward San Diego you run into massive radioactive ruins." He folded his arms and grinned sheepishly at James. "It's between those beaches. Mark my words. I have been studying this possibility for the last few months."

"What about that Mexican annexation movement you keep talking about?"

"That's a double-sided sword." the sergeant thoughtfully speculated while looking at her penciling. "I believe there are political motivated militant groups out there who'll fight alongside the Russians. But I also strongly believe most Mexicans will see the Soviets for what they are—politically unreliable."

"What about the Mexicans living in California?"

Roscoe shook his head. "The average Mexican believes America is a much better life than in Mexico. Though insisting on having their own culture they won't join the Russians in this fight. Hell, some of my best informers and coast watchers are Mexicans."

After Savannah grunted and turned back to her board Roscoe looked at James. "What about Gunner?"

"No word since his last transmission."

Roscoe wasn't that happy. "If he transmitted then the Russians by now knows his coordinates?" The lieutenant sadly agreed. "Then why the hell didn't he get out of there?"

"We don't know. Our best guess Gunner is waiting for the destroyer MOSCOW to pass and he'll take a shot at her." James paused then solemnly added. "Look, we all know why Gunner went there. It was a suicide mission from the start. And even if I ordered an extracted it would be too late." The CO again paused. "Gunner's Mate Armstrong is a true hero, Roscoe, and most heroes die alone. He's buying us time by reducing the odds. We're not going to waste those luxuries he's purchasing with his life. Now let's get our thoughts on how to save lives at Ten Delta. But first tell me about that reconnaissance patrol you wasted?"

"They were Soviet marines from their 27th Amphibious Corp. That's the second fighting force we have identified so far. Kossier is dead serious about taking California. But there was something new we found on them. Each had an English/Russian translation manual." He frowned. "That's how cocky sure they are of this invasion. In the carrier was a box of Russian flags they intended to raise after we're defeated."

Savannah walked over and joined them. "What about their weapons?"

"The weapons and armored carrier were recently manufactured. This is unlike those soldiers on the air base disguised as the Thirty-Second Division." The sergeant folded his arms. "It looks as if history is repeating itself. During World War II on the Eastern Front, Moscow frequently sent second rate troops to initially fight the Germans. Then while the Nazis caught their second wind Soviet elite troops stormed in. That's what they're doing to us. They tested our strengths and now we're about to get kicked in the ass."

After a radioman handed James the short message it was read with a deep frown. "I guess Earl Craver did what he promised. St. Louis has authorized the 10th Strategic companies attached to Ten Delta with Major Thomas retaining battlefield command."

"What the hell is the 10th Strategic?"

James forced a thin grin. "History is repeating itself on both sides. It seems that Major Thomas wasn't commanding a relocation team out here. But the 365th is actually part of the 10th which is a battle hardened special forces group." He shrugged his shoulders. "This is just like a movie where in the end everybody is somebody they weren't supposed to be." There was little humor in his last words.

Roscoe bitterly replied. "Nothing changed even when our cities were blasted into radioactive ruins." Shaking his head at the thought he asked. "Has the chief finished his battle plans?"

"Yeah, they're done. You squad leaders will be given assignments later on tonight. The chief is in the mess hall chowing down if you wanted to talk to him."

No, not right now, but I am going to catch some sleep. This running around has drained me. When is our briefing?"

"I'll send somebody to wake you up in plenty of time."

*   *   *

Time seemed suspended to Gunner's shivering body. Retaliatory winds howled through the CANE's wreckage while icy breaths swirled through ripped bulkheads and down darkened empty passageways. Thunderous protests were belching from the destroyer's bowels as dangling pieces of equipment noisily banged against metal bulkheads. Unsecured equipment crashed back and forth inside battered compartments. Gunner's wild imagination identified these as infuriated spirits of those dying during the ship's last battle. Huddling under blankets found in a locker he soon discovered their dampness provided little warmth. Gunner's muddled thoughts made it exceptionally hard to concentrate as waves crashed over the listing main deck. The black curtain was shattered by frequent streaks of lightning shooting across the indifferent heavens.

Each time his weary mind, already numbed by the coldness, drifted into a near sleep something deep inside warned him. Slapping his face to regain orientation the gunner's mate impatiently waited for the MOSCOW. He reasoned if that amphibious vessel had passed its destroyer screen would be right behind. He thought about Joshua giving his life to cripple the other destroyer. That took courage Gunner was unsure if he had. Lewis and the guys were good men. There were times he objected to their reckless behavior, but he soon learned that was how they handled this nightmarish world. The war was still undecided and its outcome could go either way. Once again the wreckage moaned and rattled as another crashing wave tore against her hull.

Right after that another wave shook the ship and caught him off guard. Losing his weak hold on the metal coffee cup holding coffee it rolled wildly about until finding its niche in a bloodied dark corner. His thoughts were confused but in the end decided to drink the coffee from its thermos. It was then the gunner's mate saw a brief flash on shore that sent an emotional chill through his body. After throwing the thermos in the chair he rushed to the bridge's broken windows and cautiously looked out. It took the sailor a few moments to adjust his night vision but what he feared was true. Russian soldiers after finding the camouflaged carrier were showing interest in the wreckage. He counted ten soldiers milling about and knew there was more.

Even with the howling winds drowning all noises Gunner heard the unmistakable roar of a large naval ship. He whirled about. That could only be the MOSCOW. After seeing what the soldiers were doing ashore, he figured it would be several minutes before they investigated. That may allow him to complete his objective. Dashing over to the corner where he had secured three Grail missile launchers he quickly loaded them. Firing at the MOSCOW would have to be done rapidly without a second chance. Now to make matters worse he had nosy marines on shore to contend with.

Then suddenly like a monster storming from its cloak of darkness the MOSCOW was briefly visible. What he saw sent shivers up Gunner's spine. The ship displacing 7800 tons of raw energy and a violent character came nearer. The captain was cruising dangerously close to shore with 19 knots churning from her steam turbines. Gunner momentarily thought either that was a damned wise captain or he was just plain crazy. A quick rush to the battered bridge bulkhead revealed those soldiers were wading through shallow waters to the dangling gangplank. Gunner knew he had just enough time to fire one missile at the ship. Then he would have to rush back to the quarterdeck and fire at the invading soldiers.

Grabbing a Grail launcher he positioned himself close to the bridge's port side. With his night enhancer Gunner was able to see the warship fairly clear. She would be in range soon. The ship carried a full array of gun mounts, A/S weapons, and torpedo tubes. But her missile capability he feared the most. Focusing his glasses on the twin SA-N-4 pods, Gunner counted 40 shafts of death. He knew missile control would be fully manned because the ship was at battle stations. Her Head Net C class radar would be busy probing the darkness for dangers.

The frigate moved closer to CANE's half submerged wreckage.

With firm determination Gunner talked with his dead wife promising to join her in a few minutes. But first he had something to do. It was three minutes before firing time and Gunner knew there was no escape, but who wanted to run. Gunner's Mate First Class John Armstrong momentarily thought about all those men entombed aboard this fighting ship. They met their deaths fighting for America and now were waiting for him. After a short prayer Gunner activated his portable missile launcher.

Then it was time.

*   *   *

Pacing about the MOSCOW's spacious bridge Colonel Karsavin nervously studied the developing events with concern. Injured when KONSTANTANTINOVICH was attacked the second time an ALEKSANDR helicopter had airlifted him to the MOSCOW. According to the admiral Kossier would tolerate no further failures. Now it was vital they find Ten Delta today and quash that pest once for all.

The political officer uneasily walked to the windshield wondering where Lieutenant Blackmore was hiding. He was a serious threat. Already one destroyer was crippled and their mini invasion of Vandenberg Air Force Base reduced to shattered companies. And each time Ten Delta fought them off with inferior numbers. He sighed. Tomorrow would be different when their invasion forces stormed ashore. Ten Delta would be unable to drive them off this time. He heard the ship's commanding officer coming on deck. He was still worried about tomorrow. Lieutenant Blackmore had an uncanny habit of jerking smashing victories from defeats.

"Comrade Captain," Mikhail sternly asked. "Does radar register clear?"

"Our only contact is the ALEKSANDR ahead of us."

Mikhail found this commander officer more to his liking. He was totally unlike Captain Voronov. The senior captain with more than twenty-five years in the service was with stout body packed with hard muscles. His dark eyes and narrow sharp features were inherited from distant family Chinese linkages. He walked the ship like a thunderous storm about to explode. His men feared him while the officers contemptuously tolerated his brutal heavy hand. The dark blue uniform was without a single wrinkle.

"Was the helicopter outfitted with that napalm canister?"

"The task was done as ordered." The captain walked to the windshield and thought about that explosive jell aboard his ship. With those secured gasoline drums on deck the napalm was more than dangerous. When combined with the exploding fuel drums that jell could sink the ship as if a powerful bomb had dropped down her throat.

The captain yelled at his helmsman to keep their course trimmed or he would find himself thrown into the brig. His nervous helmsman acknowledged the order while disguising his hatred. The petty officer silently cursed his captain for recklessly hugging the coast. There were wreckages scattered along this coast with some partly submerged and others fully visible. But tearing along at 20 knots in a dangerous region and at night combined to make a quartermaster's nightmare. He heard a lookout reporting ship wreckage grounded on Point Conception. Impatiently waiting for orders to change course headings that would safely take them around the wreckage, the helmsman never got the correction.

The captain's phone talker on the bridge suddenly shouted. "We have an airborne threat off mid ships! Time of impact: two minutes!"

After hearing that warning Mikhail raced onto the wing bridge to look for their threat. Already anxious commands were being shouted about the bridge. Gunnery control computers directed the forward 30mm Gatling guns toward the coast. It was too late to outmaneuver the approaching missile. For a few moments the KGB colonel recognized his recklessness of having napalm loaded onto the chopper. He couldn't see the helicopter desperately rising from its pad for a quick escape.

Mikhail fearfully saw waves splashing against the low flying missile. Shipboard guns were laying down a vicious screen of opposition that made the night seem like daylight. "It's going to break through!" the colonel screamed.

There was no time to run from the bridge as impact would be within seconds. The missile rushing through icy winds crashed into the lower decks below the bridge. There was a sharp rumbling explosion as the Grail exploded. But what happened afterwards proved even worse. Flames reaching out from the initial explosion ignited those secured gasoline drums. Because he wasn't holding onto anything Mikhail was thrown against the open wing's armor plating. But this saved the man's life as flames raced over his head with its life sucking hunger. He felt a throbbing pain in his chest as breath was jerked away. After his initial shock the political officer awkwardly got to his feet. Holding his forehead to stop a deep puncture's bleeding above his right eye, Mikhail was horrified at what he saw. Most bridge personnel were dead and the command center was in shambles. Several smaller fires illuminated the wreckage. Only for a moment did he pause before rushing to the bulkhead's phone and dialing engineering.

"This is Colonel Karsavin. The bridge is destroyed and your captain dead. Transfer steering to secondary stations. Assume 12 knots, maintain current coordinates . . ."

Mikhail first heard that thunderous whoosh then a near blinding explosion that spun a reddish glow across the ship's aft sections. Somewhere within the violence a terrified voice screamed the helicopter sucked into the violence was now coming apart. Remembering the napalm Mikhail was horrified. The shock waves that blast created were enormous as MOSCOW trembled within the impact's crushing circle. A senior glavnyy starshini grabbing the new commanding officer threw him to the decking just as a sheet of flames rolled across the ship. He felt something slimy and hard strike his back. When stumbling to his feet seconds later he saw the signalman's twisted body was sliced in half. Mikhail's tailored uniform was torn and bloodied. His face was bleeding from flying glass and the left arm hung limp. But he had survived another death shaking incident and that was all which mattered to the colonel.

"Bridge, forward steering now has control."

"Damage control teams," Mikhail shouted. "I need damage reports. Secure all damaged compartments! Increase speed to 20 knots." He noticed those few ratings staggering on deck calmly established communications with the damaged compartments in a short order. "Radio, notify ALEKSANDR we have received major damages and burning. Aft sections are nearly blown away with mid ships flooding. We have suffered heavy casualties. MOSCOW maintaining steady course and will join you."

*   *   *

As the radio message was received all James could do was stand and fight back his tears. After Gunner signed off they heard rapid gunfire in the background then silence. Turning around the lieutenant observed the others' tearful response to the gunner's mate last transmission. In these nightmarish days it was all right to be emotional over your losses.

"All right, marines, we have a job to finish tomorrow, but when you're fighting those damned bastards remember Gunner and the others who have died here. We're not about to let their passing go without revenge." Seeing the others nodding he turned back to the plotting board. "Gunner reported his missile caused enormous explosions aboard the MOSCOW."

"Lieutenant," a marine radioman excitedly said. "Our lookouts said you have to see what's passing."

James and several others ran outside to climb on some ruins. They didn't need night enhancers to watch MOSCOW pass not far from shore. The warship was engulfed in a brilliant glow as fires destructively roared through the fantail and superstructure. Wreckage of the helicopter landing pad hung dangerously down the side. Though fiercely burning the warship struggled through those crashing waves. There was no cheering on shore. Just a solemn acceptance another warship wouldn't participate in tomorrow's battles.

"What the hell did Gunner shoot at?" Tyler asked amazed by the extensive damages.

"I don't know, but he sure as hell eliminated her from the battles tomorrow."

Crossing the hanger James saw Lewis and the Indian working on their helicopter. Walking over he stood for a few minutes while they ignored his presence.

"I'm sorry about Gunner," he finally said.

"Gunner was a good sailor." Lewis mumbled.

"Did you see the ship?"

"No, but your marines told us." Lewis rubbed his nose then said. "Now maybe he'll find that peace he was seeking."

James nodded after realizing he wasn't invited into their grievous world. After a deep sigh he somberly said. "Be in the conference room at four-thirty for a briefing." He received no reply from the air force captain.

"They're taking his death pretty hard." Savannah remarked when joining his walk to the mess hall.

"Yeah, they are. But this war left men with smaller circles of friends and usually no loved ones so each death is suffered with deep pain." Entering the dining area where marines with heavy expressions sat talking in whispers, he curiously asked. "You haven't lost anybody, have you?" Grabbing cups of coffee they sat at his corner table.

"Is it that obvious?" After he nodded she said. "Ohio hasn't been hit by the war's devastations."

"What about brothers and sisters?"

"I'm the only child. I have cousins and several uncles who are involved in the state's defenses."

"If you haven't lost somebody dear to you it's hard to feel that deep terrible pain." He gestured towards the door. "See that blond marine talking to his squad sergeant. His family was in San Diego now he has nobody. His brother died in our naval battles off the Hawaiian Islands. Roscoe lost his wife when Cherry Point was taken out by a long range missile. Even our cook lost everybody when Dallas was bombed. He creates crazy meals just to keep his mind occupied. Tomorrow he'll pick up his weapon and go out to fight. I really hate to be the Russians whom he meets. His hatred is like a simmering obsession to brutally kill anything associated with Kossier's bunch."

"And what about you?" she carefully asked.

James silently nursed his coffee for several moments. "My wife was a nurse in Germany when this war started. She was scheduled for rotation back to the States in two weeks. When the bombs stated falling she helped evacuate our dependents at her army garrison."

"What happened?"

"The battle viciously raged for four days until finally their munitions ran out. I'm told all surviving soldiers and nurses were lined up then a tank ran them over." James coldly stared at his coffee cup. "So everybody here has a grudge with the Soviets. That's why no mercy is shown to the bastards." After a few moments he deeply inhaled and replied. "If you don't mind let's change topics."

"I'm sorry," Savannah gently said while laying a hand on his.

"You can't change what has happened. You approach each day with hopes the future shall be better." He toyed with the cup before asking. "I read those battle reports you brought from St. Louis. Are our butts really getting kicked or is that another deception our government is feeding the public?"

"I can't tell you what's actually unraveling. But I can say that political and military issues aren't as bad as they may appear."

James wasn't comforted by her vague words. "What about the weather?"

Savannah frowned. "Now that is bad news. If we don't soon introduce rain mankind will simply fade away. Something like the dinosaurs did millions of years ago. There's no way to candy coat our global situation."

"And can Craver reverse the doomsday threat?"

"His colleagues and he have worked on their little plan for months. There's great hope it will change the climatic trend."

James waited a few moments before asking. "And if it doesn't?"

Savannah frowned. "Then millions of years into our future one day an archaeologist finding evidence of this lost generation will ponder what had happened."

CHAPTER TWENTY-FOUR

Timothy hurried into the mess hall. "Major Thomas radioed the Russians aren't waiting to attack tomorrow. A large convoy of troops and armored vehicles are on Highway 101 just west of the Emma Wood State Beach and heading this way."

"A night attack in this weather," James exclaimed. "They're crazy." He had by this time entered communications and was consulting the regional map.

Tyler looked away from his listening to intercepted Russian radio traffic. "The Russians are well known for doing crazy things."

"Where the hell did this armor group come from? It's for sure that amphibious ship hasn't landed troops this fast." James was tracing his finger along the coast.

"She probably landed that group days ago. That would explain who wasted our radar stations down south. It also explains why we haven't received intelligence from the locals toward San Diego. The Soviets were isolating that region and we didn't even know about it."

"Get hold of Major Thomas, I need to talk with him."

"If we transmit the Russians will pin point our location." Tyler warned.

James frowned. "At this stage of the game I seriously doubt if that really matters. Go ahead and call Thomas. We need updated information on that armor group."

While waiting for his connect the lieutenant uneasily paced in front of the plotting board. "Chief, have you ever served aboard an amphibious ship?"

"I was aboard the USS BOXER (LHD 4) in 1995."

"What about this Russian ship," James dubiously asked, "is it comparable to ours?"

"Probably though ours were of a superior design."

"What about weaknesses?"

"We shared the same weaknesses."

"When are these ships disadvantaged?"

"When they are unloading or loading."

"In your opinion can ALEKSANDR safely unload during this weather?"

"Not safely. No amphibious captain would endanger his ship that way. When the well deck is flooded rough waters crashing inside would damage their equipment."

He stopped talking to think over something. "The one thing we could do and they can't was unloading equipment by helicopter. But even that is risky with the ship tossing about. No, the captain will have to wait until morning when the ocean is calmer. Even reckless as the communists are they won't risk disembarking equipment in these rough seas."

James thoughtfully agreed. "So if we isolated their forces by attacking that armored column there would be no reinforcements until morning." He forced a grin. "By striking our blow now we can destroy one force and take on ALEKSANDR tomorrow morning."

When his connection was made James took the telephone and spoke at some length with Major Thomas. After disconnecting he walked back to the plotting board with a worried expression. "The Russians are shrewder than we thought. The amphibious ship didn't stop at Isla Vista as anticipated, but is laying off the coast at Point Dume this side of Los Angeles. They'll land their troops and equipment in the Point Dume State Beach area."

Savannah stood at the map for a few moments with chin cupped in a fist. "It makes sense if you're evaluating their movement on a broader scale. This armor column closes on Vandenberg where they hook up with their forces there. Then we can expect a sweeping move toward the Dume Beach landing." She ran her hand across the board. "It will be a classic reaper movement crushing everything in their path. Once additional forces land they will push up the coast. We'll be forced into a crushing circle probably somewhere along here in the Santa Barbara area. We'll have to fight three independent forces . . . those from Vandenberg . . . the survivors from those two destroyers . . . and the Point Dume landing forces." She turned around with a sarcastic glare. "With our limited resources there's no way we're able to challenge three separate advances."

The lieutenant briefly studied the map. "Then we'll have to cut and dice." James recommended. "First on the chopping board is stopping this armored column from reaching Vandenberg."

Lewis silently studied the board. "We'll take care of the ALEKSANDR so you take care of that armored column." When they looked at him he shrugged his shoulders and sheepishly grinned. "As you said, lieutenant, cut and dice."

"What are you planning on doing?" James asked.

"I rather keep that a surprise. Fewer people knowing our intentions better off the Indian and I are." Then with a loose salute the captain left the conference.

Savannah asked. "I wonder what they're up to."

"If they plan attacking an amphibious vessel it's another suicide mission." Tyler sadly groaned.

Savannah looked at the master sergeant and cynically asked. "Why are you taking this so calmly?"

Without looking at the woman he said. "Because in Outer Perimeter suicide runs aren't uncommon. This is a nuclear wasteland, madam. We don't have the luxury of calling in the cavalry every time things get rough." Glancing at James he calmly asked. "Where are we going to hit them?"

"Thomas is too far away to help us in this pinch, so I'll use the Apaches to trim down their numbers. Earl will have to wait until this mess is over before looking for that rocket."

"I don't have time to wait, lieutenant." the presidential envoy protested. "Mother Nature waits for nobody. That rocket has to fire on time. I'm afraid there's no room for argument."

The lieutenant angrily whirled about. "Mr. Craver, if you want to stomp around on Vandenberg then go for it! But you'll go alone. I need every man for this upcoming battle. But I'll tell you right now, if you're stupid enough to go there'll be a welcoming committee waiting for you. We may have clipped the Russians' wings, but not by a long shot did we crush them altogether. After taking care of the invading troops we'll help, but not until then."

"You seem certain the Russians will be defeated."

"Are you certain the rocket is there?"

"I hope so."

James frowned. "You aren't certain, but you're going to look. Well, I'm not certain if we can stop the bastards, but we're going the same. That's the way battles are fought." For a few moments he watched the envoy storm from the chamber. "Nasty little bastard, isn't he?" he commented with a dry grin. After exhaling his frustration James sourly remarked. "He doesn't realize if we lose today there won't be a firing."

After folding her arms and staring at the plotting board Savannah groaned. "Oh, I think he knows."

James made an 'oh-give-me-a-break expression. "Well, out here in devil's paradise that's known as reality."

"So what are you going to do?"

He turned to Roscoe. "Go tell the mechanics to rearm our Apaches with armor piercing shells. We got some serious ass kicking to do. Hopefully they won't expect helicopters from the darkness." Looking at the radioman he said. "Get a fix on the columns' latest whereabouts from Thomas." Turning about he looked at Timothy. "Keep your channels open between my birds and here. If we're shot down execute those plans you made." James somberly looked at Savannah. "My plans are attacking the armored column and wasting as many as possible. That'll at least slow their advance. Lewis said he had a plan for messing with the ALEKSANDR, so I'll count on that threat being removed. Once the column is neutralized we turn our attention on those destroyers at Isla Vista. After that we can deal with those Russians at Vandenberg." He confidently studied the plotting board. "There is no way we could attack them as a whole. That would be suicide. So we'll cut and dice each threat." He smiled at her silence. "Do you understand my plans?"

The woman looked at his cocky attitude for a few moments then grinned. "Just for the record," she asked. "What if things don't go your way and the Russians kick your ass? What are your orders for us who are left behind?"

"If we all fail in the field, my dear," he soberly advised. "Ten Delta has secondary defenses in the Inez Mountains. Head for those hills because after our defeats there's nothing you can do to stop their invasion. Eventually you'll have to make your way to Yuma." There was a short pause during which he faintly grinned. "But Ten Delta doesn't plan on failing, my dear."

*   *   *

Helicopters had evolved into deadly weapons since the Germans introduced their Focke-Achgelis Fa 223 during World War II. Originally designed for a search-and-rescue role, the Korean War witnessed its emergence as an offensive platform with guns and rockets. From that time onward the rotary wing aircraft gained a more aggressive role in warfare. Of course, on this dismal day Lieutenant Blackmore wasn't interested that Hitler's Luftwaffe invented the chopper. His troubled thoughts were elsewhere once the two Apaches roared into the night's howling winds. Sharp lightning ripped across the skies. He quietly mumbled this was not a good day to die. His co-pilot/electronics officer nursed his own uneasiness about this flight into the jaws of death. After reaching six hundred feet the two black birds turned east for their clash with the evils from Russia.

The Apache's fuselage's length of 49 feet and height of 15 feet made it an ugly machine of war when in the air. But pilots all the way back to the Vietnam War swore ever lasting blessings on her wicked performance. Like vicious birds of prey, from their nose profiles revolved TAD/PNUS turrets resembling something from the Twilight Zone. James was seated behind his instrument panel crowded with analog and digital controls. The wide video display (VDU) prominently in the center displayed altitude, speed, secondary weapons control, and vital status information. James' right hand confidently gripped the joy stick between his legs. Icy cold eyes confidently read dials and readouts confirming their 21,000 pounds of metal and wiring were doing everything it was designed for. Seated directly below him separated by a clear bullet proof screen, Glassford quietly studied his own panel that was the heart of their weapons systems.

Occasionally glancing to their right he saw the second Apache flown by Staff Sergeant Larry Hastings. A ten year Marine veteran having flown civilian helicopters before enlisting, he replaced the other pilot after he died from a fall. The man waved. James rated him as a cold blooded man behind the controls.

"Column in sight," Glassford announced fifteen minutes after departing Ten Delta. "There are maybe forty vehicles running with their headlights on."

"Activate radar jammers." James ordered. He saw the long column five hundred feet below rapidly approaching like a winding twinkling necklace.

"Roger that."

Glassford's primary duties were electronic interferences and target acquisitions. It was James' job to pilot the craft. A radar jamming antenna mounted on the TADS sent out signals confusing enemy radar and fire control tracking systems. Suddenly a red blinking panel light warned of enemy fire control activity. He calmly reported. "We have hostile tracking." While he talked target information fed into their fire control system. The sergeant selected their proper weapons system. Glassford watching the scattering headlights advised. "We're receiving hostile fire."

"Roger that. I'm going in," James barked. "First take out those hostiles then we'll handle the ground troops." The Highway 101 was dotted with numerous gun fire flashes as the chopper roared down for a strafing pass. After leveling out at four hundred feet James was astonished at the number of exploding shells around the warplane. Assuring they didn't collide with anything belligerent James was using his AN/AAQ-11 PNVS system. Through the Integrated Helmet and Display Sight (HADSS) he saw real time imagery of their approaching situation. The monocle lowered over his right eye gave him high resolution abilities. "This is going to be rough, old buddy, so watch out. You have the firing controls. Good luck." There was a pause. "All right, baby, show daddy what you can do."

"Roger that," Glassford responded. His panel's multi-colored lights twinkled like a Christmas tree on his plastic face shield. "Now activating FFAR."

The Apache swiftly swept toward Hungarian-built armored personnel carriers now abruptly halting while their gunners fired at the approaching threat. Tracer bullets spaced every tenth slot streaked across the darkness. James felt their pinging as they harmlessly struck the thick bullet proof glass. Knowing the Apaches' fury those PSZHs savagely fought back.

James' voice was worried. "I see no tanks. I repeat there are no tanks down there." That remark was primarily for Ten Delta's benefit.

After the panel lights blinked advising their M-261 launcher was hot, Glassford squeezed the trigger. The 70mm rockets rushing from their launchers quickly locked on designated targets. Their M-255 warheads contained 2500 one ounce steel flechettes (darts) that abruptly produced bloody results. Two soft-skinned vehicles quickly burst into flames while screaming Russian soldiers were mowed down like wheat in a field. The whispering Apaches passed over then suddenly darted upwards to begin another murderous charge through this demoralized Russian column. Some armored cars strongly resisted while several crews abandoned their vehicles before the helicopters came back. This section of Highway 101 was no longer cloaked in darkness, but red glowing balls illuminated the ghastly scene of death and chaos. James observed two eight wheeled armored cars quickly turning around to contest their second run. Armed with a 14.5 machine gun and 7.62 guns they were hardly a threat to the helicopters. But their crews stubbornly fired at the approaching choppers. Glassford after firing two 70mm rockets saw their folding fins automatically straightened once in flight. Each impacted shattering the machines and killing their men trapped inside.

"Eagle One to Eagle Two," James radioed. "Do you see the tanks anywhere?"

There was a short pause before the second helicopter answered. "Negative on that, Eagle One."

Though Glassford heard James softly cursing his concentration was on the weapons' panel. Coming in for another murderous sweep over the combat zone another two rockets armed spun through the night air. One after another armor piercing rocket was fired until the nineteen missile load was expended. But there was no need to continue firing. Not one Russian vehicle was left untouched as flames swept through the column. Several explosions noisily erupted among the fires as munitions were cooked. Where forty sets of headlamps once stretched out along the highway, now forty fires burned furiously in the howling winds.

"The Russians have left the building," Glassford nervously chuckled.

"Yeah, but where did those tanks disappear to?" James said as the Apaches departed that battle zone. "Eagle One and Eagle Two have stopped the armored column with total destruction, but no sight of those tanks." The radio transmission to Ten Delta was without acknowledgement. "Apache One and Apache Two now entering phase two."

Both choppers swinging away from the burning destruction flew inland while keeping the ocean in view. Hostile winds pounding the helicopters caused spotty difficulties in controlling. At times the platforms shook and tossed like children's toys. Lightning was now more frequent with boisterous deep-throated rumbles of thunder. In such pandemonium it was impossible to hear their relatively quiet General Electric engines purring above their heads. By now the warplanes were flying low over Arroyo San Agustin's high point. They slightly banked toward the ocean before leveling out for another low run along the ragged coastline.

"How are we doing?" James asked his co-pilot. The winds pounding the chopper were causing some difficulty in handling.

"The enemy hasn't painted us yet." Glassford skeptically replied. "But I haven't picked up any illuminations and tanks of their size just don't fade into the woodwork. They must have shut down all systems."

"They could be waiting in ambush for Thomas' columns?"

*   *   *

When MOSCOW finally made it to Isla Vista her fate was fairly certain. She was listing fifteen feet to port and rapidly losing power with flames spreading through the ship. After dropping anchor safely away from KONSTANTANTINOVICH's still smoldering wreckage, Colonel Karsavin ordered their wounded transferred ashore. While this was taking place he refused medical attention for his injuries. The political officer stood quietly in her bridge's blackened remains angrily staring at those crashing waves running ashore. Their few lifeboats were struggling to stay afloat while transferring the wounded. Mikhail knew his troubles were definitely traced to Lieutenant Blackmore's puny command at Ten Delta. No matter what they did to find the radar station, their efforts were always thrown back with crippling losses. The cursed weather wasn't helping their struggle to dominate this part of the world.

The bandaged communications officer found Mikhail standing in the bridge's twisted wreckage. "Comrade Colonel, we received word from our forces at Vandenberg. They were seriously mauled in a battle with Ten Delta." He nervously swallowed when the colonel scowled at him. After the political officer gestured he continued the lieutenant said. "Six armored vehicles in flames, eighty-six men killed, thirty-two wounded. Our defenses are stable, but expecting further attacks during the day."

A few tensed moments passed before Mikhail nodded and cynically ordered. "Inform their officers the column must stand fast until help arrives."

He stepped over smoking debris to breath fresh outside air. A glance over at the crippled KONSTANTANTINOVICH's low profile in the choppy waters confirmed their growing bad luck. There were few promises events would get better. When it was reported another lifeboat had collapsed with all men lost, their desperate situation became worse. He reluctantly ordered the deck officer to suspend transferring until morning. At least he had another ace in hand. A large armored column disembarked from the ALEKSANDR several days ago in San Diego was moving up the coast to reinforce their scattered forces. Not for several hours had Mikhail drank vodka and his body craved it. When the ship's short pudgy engineering officer came on deck, he wondered what bad news he had.

"Comrade Colonel," the commander sharply greeted after loosely saluting.

With a deep displeased sigh Mikhail turned to accept his report.

"Forward and aft gun turrets are out of commission. We have flooding in lower compartments and engine room reports two boilers badly damaged. The helicopter deck is being chopped away. Aft steering is disabled with most electronic systems down." He stopped reporting for a few moments while Mikhail's attention was drawn to the shore. "We also have a large hole on starboard aft that was isolated and patched."

"What about causalities?"

"Forty-one percent of crew either killed or injured."

Mikhail ignored the commander's silent accusation he was responsible for this disaster. If the political officer hadn't ordered their helicopter loaded with napalm canisters, the attack at Vandenberg would have produced only minor damages. The dark-skinned engineering officer from Siberia was no stranger to battle. After his family perished from American long range missiles his hatred for Americans was deeply fueled. But this war cruise experienced disasters that never should have happened. It didn't mattered they were caused by conditions beyond their control. Their objectives had been seriously compromised and this caused concern among the crewmen. After their captain and executive officer were killed the political officer assumed command. This transfer of command was silently disputed by the crew.

"What about KONSTANTANTINOVICH?"

"Within two days she will sink. Captain Voronov after transferring his surviving crewmen to shore set up tents for shelter. But if the Americans attack they will be hard pressed to fight them back." Gesturing at the unruly waters he added. "Weather conditions prohibiting shore runs aren't expected to change until late afternoon." He disgustingly sighed. "Unfortunately, Comrade Colonel, those same conditions are preventing ALEKSANDR from transferring her troops."

"What about the MOSCOW? When will she be seaworthy?"

The commander stared at the political officer with a bewildered expression. "Comrade Colonel, this ship will never engage the enemy until she goes into a shipyard for major repairs."

Mikhail became hostile. "That's impossible. Therefore, commander, your engineering department will have to make the necessary repairs. This ship must be ready for battle. The Americans have two destroyers off Mexico and if they come this way our ship can match their guns. Nobody else can."

"I'm sorry, sir, but my department doesn't have the capability of doing major repairing. We need either a destroyer tender or shipyard to do this."

The colonel angrily threatened. "If you don't make the repairs, commander, I'll have every tenth man shot for disobedience! Is that understood?"

Neither officer noticed the disruption of activity as enlisted men stood in opposition.

"Comrade Colonel," the commander cynically challenged. "You can shoot every man aboard this ship and the repairs still won't be done. It's impossible, sir. Those repairs in question require cranes and skilled personnel. We have neither. Between napalm canisters and secured fuel drums on deck the fires' devastation was total." His voice dropped to a loose respectful tone. "I'm sorry, but we can not do the jobs required."

Further discussion was interrupted when an excited runner from radar charged into the bridge. "Sir, radar reports airborne target inbound at fifty feet above surface. Bearing northeast . . ."

CHAPTER TWENTY-FIVE

Worried about the tanks' disappearance, James instructed Sergeant Hastings to continue searching the coast and take out any targets of opportunity. Then the lieutenant banked to his right and went prowling for those missing tanks. The night was dark and only with the night goggles pulled over his eyes was Hastings able to continue his flight. All of this reminded the staff sergeant of those science fiction movies he had seen as a kid. His co-pilot Billy Edwards was from Bakersfield, a distinction he boasted of many times at Ten Delta. There was nobody to see after the war and this rested heavily on their minds over the last few months. Now it seemed of little importance.

"See anything?" Hastings asked. All he could see below them were ruins and more ruins scattered along the coast. Following the bombings and missiles attacks the surviving population went crazy. Looting and torching of buildings became so widespread the National Guard and dwindling police departments couldn't control the civil disturbances. That was when law and order simply collapsed. Ten Delta spent more time harshly dealing with this ugly problem than anything else.

"Radar is clean."

"Why don't we fly over Isla Vista?"

"Why do that?" Billy's husky voice asked. "There are two destroyers hanging out there."

"Yeah, I know that's what Thomas said. Maybe we can update their conditions."

Billy shrugged knowing there was nothing he could do to change that redneck's mind. So he went back to monitoring his instruments. The Apache was a multi-mission attack helicopter designed for aerial weapons-delivery platform. Its two seats made the machine ineffective as a rescue vehicle. Billy always felt secure seated in the lower front seat listening to the engine's soft whirling.

"Hey, up there," he spoke into the radio mike. "Keep an eye on our fuel. This baby has been sucking up fuel the last few weeks. Probably needs its gas filters changed, but we don't have any."

"Roger that." Hastings said. "We'll worry about that later on. But right now take a gander over that hill where I see fires burning. That's probably those communists' warships. We're going to take a peek. Get your weapons hot and heavy?"

When suddenly appearing over the slight hilly area they saw anchored in Isla Vista's harbor two enemy destroyers under attack by onboard fires. Hastings swore softly when seeing them helplessly lying in the choppy waters. KONSTANTANTINOVICH was no threat and soon would slip under the ocean. Though badly damaged the MOSCOW wasn't finished with her fighting. Banking sharply to the port Hastings saw machine gun fire ripping the night air with its tracers and bullets. They were of a caliber that ineffectively snipped at the chopper's sides. But as they made another sweep heavier calibers began firing from the warship. Hastings knew those puffs could send them spinning into the ocean's depth. When several cracks appeared in their cockpit glass he didn't tell Billy.

"How are you doing?" he hurriedly asked.

Hastings didn't know Billy's face was bleeding from shattered glass when bullets broke the windshield. Wiping sticky blood from his eyes he lowered his head. "Still hanging in there." he painfully mumbled. "Are we going in again?"

"Do we have a choice?"

"Nope, do you want one?" There was silence from his co-pilot so Hastings said. "Send the message and let's get this over with." Reaching over he over patted the small American flag taped to his panel. "Hang in there." Those were his last words before banking his machine at fifty feet and starting their final charge.

When gunfire became so intense he was unable to get through, Hastings pulled back on his stick and sent the Apache climbing into the skies while gunfire and larger explosions erupted all around him. After a barrel row he charged back down like an angry bull. Billy having to bypass their damaged fire control systems sent down a solid screen of gunfire. The Apache finally straightened out ten feet above the choppy waters. Still carrying forty folding fin rockets Billy started firing as they swiftly neared the burning ships. While this was going on he sprayed MOSCOW's decks with their 30mm chain machine gun. Gunners on that ship were hurled from their positions by the bullets. Rockets smashed into the listing ship's hull with devastating results. More flames spun into the illuminated skies. New holes near her waterline sent waters thunderously plunging inside. The Apache's high explosive incendiary shells were dooming the warship. While this was happening, Mikhail was transferred ashore cursing this seemingly unstoppable helicopter wasting his command.

Hastings felt the chopper's terrible shaking as she roared through the damaging gunfire screens. In the co-pilot/gunner's cockpit was a multi-purpose optical tube with handgrips hosting smaller circular switches. It was through this system Billy operated his weapons. Now its torn optical tube dangled between the seriously wounded marine's legs. Blood was splattered about his little domain. A transparent blast shield between the two men usually protected each man from shell fragments. That last hit cracked that glass in several places. Blood ran down the glass in several small streams.

"You got the controls," Billy painfully moaned while shifting command of his weapons to the pilot's panel. Everywhere around them whizzed passed bullets. Tracers made colored streaks through the cold night air. MOSCOW's heavier shells were now striking the machine with greater regularity. Another fragment tore through the cockpit hitting Billy's shoulder. He screamed in pain while blood gushed out.

"Hang in there, buddy," Hastings nearly shouted.

"Take out those damned bastards for me . . ." Those words passed his tore lips before the man from Bakersfield slumped over. His war was over.

"You son-of-bitches!" Hastings screamed while dropping even lower where the ship's guns couldn't hit him.

The Gatlings maintained its heated gunfire through which Hastings' badly damaged helicopter was tearing. Hastings knew there was no way he was surviving this charge. He could feel his stick's increasing sluggish control. But all Hastings saw was that narrow explosive tunnel he was passing through to get at that fighting warship. He punched the button sending his last Hellfire charging toward the hull. After expending his missiles Hastings knew the chain machine gun was about to run out of munitions. Somehow the burning Apache flew through those crushing impacts. By now his instrument panel was a shambles with thick choking smoke adding further confusion inside that bloody cockpit. The staff sergeant cried out after small metal fragments ripping through the glass lodged in his chest. Amidst all of that smoke and flames Hastings saw the frigate badly listing. Hellfires repeatedly impacting with deafening explosions were so powerful that fragments spinning ashore caused the Russians to run for cover.

Hastings was having a hard time seeing with blood streaming down his face from a head wound. Another injury to his disconnected arm was spurting blood like a revolving fountain. Fortunately the Digital Automatic Stabilization Equipment (DASE) was still operating. That electronic system automatically took control after Hastings' hand slipped from the joy stick. More pieces fell off as more shells exploded around the doomed helicopter. Hastings knew he was dying, but intended the enemy would pay a dear price for his death. There were still four rockets left in one pod. He reached the firing switch and in his hazy thinking created by a lost of blood waited for that last moment.

From a distance a soldier from Thomas' covert group quietly watched the Apache tearing through a living hell of exploding shells and bullets accented by colored tracers. Before crashing into the defiant MOSCOW, Hastings fired his rockets then with a laugh watched a world of darkness snatched his soul. The explosions aboard that ship tore a large hole in the main deck that sent ripping punctures down to the water line. The waters rushing inside couldn't be stopped and the political officer knew that warship was dying.

*   *   *

Those in Ten Delta's operations silently listened to that static with tearful knowledge another of their number had sacrificed his life. It was Timothy who broke the stunned tension. While marines returned to their work the chief wiped away his tears. Hastings and the petty officer had been friends since this war began. Cursing the Russians he walked over to their plotting board. With a red grease pencil he circled KONSTANTANTINOVICH and MOSCOW as removed threats. Earl sat in a chair near the radioman quietly watching this staff function under a heavy grievous mantle. The envoy tried conversing with Savannah and didn't understand why she coldly rejected his attempts.

"Now what?" she nervously asked the chief petty officer.

"The Apaches destroyed the armored column, but not the tanks. James has to find them before they out flank our defenses."

"How long can James stay up?"

"Those choppers have three-hour combat flight endurances." he answered with a worried expression.

One speaker above the plotting boards allowed real time communications with the airborne and ground troops. When James' voice came over everybody turned their attention toward that box. "Apache One to Eagle Nest, requesting a 1040 and 1170." Then the box went silent.

Timothy grabbing the interior radio mike loudly announced. "Now hear this, we have incoming Apache for 1040 and 1170. Now get the lead out!" After that he returned to his study of the plotting board.

"What's a 1040 and 1170?" Savannah asked.

"James was asking for refueling and rearming. Then he's probably going out again. His Apache is the only one we now have. Any air reconnaissance we have now depends on him." His attention was on the board.

"But he's the commanding officer," she objected. "Why can't somebody else go out?"

Without looking at her the chief said. "Because there's nobody else who can fly the helicopter." Glancing at Earl for a moment he coldly asked. "Do you know what Lewis is up to?"

The envoy shook his head. "No, I don't. You know as much as I do. They aren't talking that much not even to me. All I know is Horace welded a pod for those napalm canisters to the machine's sides."

The chief shook his head in admiration. "That son-of-a-bitch is going to ram the amphibious ship." He noticed the envoy didn't comment either way while suspiciously glancing at Savannah. After the phone rang an enlisted man told Timothy the Apache was inside the hanger. "C'mon, Savannah, let's see what James is up to."

They arrived in time to see James and Glassford climbing from the machine. Savannah saw the bullet holes without commenting. Taking off his flying helmet the lieutenant gave it to a mechanic who carefully wiped the shield clean. Nobody spoke while the CO gave instructions for refueling and rearming his helicopter. The co-pilot hurriedly scooted around the aircraft.

"I guess you know about Hastings?" Timothy asked.

"Yeah, we listened. Before coming back we flew over Isla Vista and yeah those two ships are done for. The Russians that were ashore gave us light gunfire, but nothing we worried about." He nodded his thanks when a sandwich and coffee was handed over by the anxious cook. "What about Thomas? Have you heard from him?"

"Off and on, but he's pretty busy. One of his columns is in a major fight in the Port Hueneme vicinity."

"Did he say what they had?"

"Lightly armed ground troops for the most part with a sprinkling of old armored vehicles. Thomas did say the Russian soldiers were reinforced with Mexicans from the Annexation Movement. His last report indicated enemy resistance was crumbling in some inland regions. Increasing numbers of locals opposing the annexation are providing valuable intelligence."

"What about Lewis?"

"He flew out minutes before you landed. We don't know what he's planning or where they flew to."

James smiled between bites of his canned Ham sandwich. "Maybe we can win this damned struggle." He watched as his mechanic carefully fed a belt of 1200 rounds into the 30mm machine gun's cavity. Another marine team was fitting 16 Hellfire laser missiles into their pods. "We can't find those damned tanks and that worries me. Since we don't have tanks their disappearance could later prove to be a nightmare."

"They were last seen near the Emma Wood State Beach." Tyler theorized after walking up. "I have studied our coastal maps and there aren't that many places they can fade into. There are only ruins and some ravines up the coast. So I don't understand why your radar hasn't detected their movements."

"What about Thomas' patrols?"

"They also lost track of them."

"So they're camouflaged and waiting." James coldly predicted.

"What about those Russians at Vandenberg?"

"They aren't maneuvering. Thomas' perimeter patrols reports they appear to be waiting for reinforcements."

James nodded. Finishing his sandwich he ordered Glassford to grab a bite before they departed. Draining his coffee he handed the cup to Savannah and smiled. "So what we have are two burning warships, isolated pockets of enemy troops at Vandenberg, and one armored column wasted. But we have a handful of attack tanks on the loose." He asked for a regional map that was quickly fetched. Unfolding the AAA auto map he stared at it for a few minutes. "Helicopters are easily heard coming so the tanks are remaining undercover."

"So we need to flush them out."

Tyler solemnly asked. "Do you think they'll still in the Emma Wood area?"

"No," James said with a shake of his head. "I'm predicting those bastards are leap frogging during the night. That could mean they're much closer than when last seen."

"But wouldn't Thomas' people have seen them?" Savannah challenged.

"Maybe. Has Thomas lost patrols in the last few hours?"

"A couple are missing."

"Where at?"

Tyler took the map and after a short study said. "One was last heard from here in this Carpinteria sector. A few minutes ago Thomas radioed he had another ground patrol missing here at Santa Barbara. I still say those armor groups are on the move."

"But wouldn't you have detected them while coming back?" Savannah challenged James.

"Not if they heard my Apache coming and shut down their systems. In the darkness they would physically blend in with the ruins." He was silent for a moment. "You're forgetting those T-90 main battle tanks can move fast. We have no defenses against their 125mm main gun. So it's up to my Apache to destroy their butts." The naval officer frowned. "But first I have to locate the bastards."

"Where do you think they are?" Tyler asked.

"Probably somewhere passed Goleta by now. Those damned T-90s can scoot ass, people. Their plans are probably to reinforce their broken units on the air base. So let's narrow down our search grids to that route. This is my plans, Tyler. After leaving here I'll fly to an elevated point overlooking the 101. There we'll land and wait until the tanks are positively spotted then engage them. I want you to take what men we can spare and set up a road block somewhere along the Refugo State Beach. I'm betting they will pass by there."

"But how can you be so sure they'll take the 101?" Timothy asked.

"Because they need speed and that leaves only the 101. They have to reach the air base before Thomas brings up his main force. Remember, chief, we shot up their supporting troops. Traveling without infantry support isn't good for armor." He paused and thought over the speculation. "There's no doubt they're heading toward the air base with utmost speed. We got to stop them from connecting. Tyler will harass them along the road." After turning to the chief he instructed. "In my office is a manual. It has the codes Thomas' radiomen uses. Radio the major our plans and ask for assistance." Walking to his Apache he accepted the helmet from his mechanic. While putting it on James continued talking. "Chief, we got to move fast. There's no time for reckless blunders or doubting our plans. The enemy may be running wild, but they still have the strength to kick our ass. They were hit hard this evening and it's our task to keep slugging it out. We can't give the bastards a chance to regroup. We can't afford that. Hit hard and keep hitting hard. Make them pay for every mile they roll over American soil." After climbing into the chopper he waved for it to be pulled outside.

Minutes later James' Apache faded into the cold evening on his crucial mission. Activities at Ten Delta didn't tarry after that. After assembling his motorized team Tyler hurried through the night to the Refugo beach area some miles away. Inside operations Timothy briefly studied the map before making another decision. He sent Roscoe to establish ambush positions at the El Capitan State Beach area. From there they would blast the tanks when they roared pass. After inflicting damages on the armored column Roscoe was to join Tyler's group. Their orders were simple—repeatedly hit and run. Without infantry support the Russian tanks wouldn't give chase.

"Do you think this will work?" Savannah skeptically asked. "If Tyler and Roscoe are wiped out there's nobody to stop them until Thomas arrives." She stopped for a moment. "And that would be too late."

Timothy stared at the plotting board for a few moments before mumbling. "Then they must not fail."

CHAPTER TWENTY-SIX

After Stan drove onto the 101 he gunned the BTR they had captured. Hell was expected to break loose once the sun tried coming up. Though the evening hours had been a blessing to Ten Delta, Roscoe knew there was much fighting left before peace drifted over this wasted land. With no interference the squad reached El Capitan State Beach in a short time. There was no shortage of hiding places among the ruins while establishing their reconnaissance positions. In this area the attack had come while panic stricken people were fleeing the violence. Burned cars were overturned everywhere the eye looked. But they had a fairly good view both directions on the highway and this suited Roscoe.

Positioned atop an overturned big rig's trailer Stan laid on his stomach with a pair of night vision binoculars. The icy winds sweeping in from the ocean was a biting annoyance. Roscoe joined him after assuring their postings were adequate for a swift getaway when the time came. The other ten marines were scattered in various points along the road. One man stayed in the enclosed armored carrier ready for their swift retreat. Standing behind the twin 23mm cannon a marine waited.

"Ten Delta kicked ass tonight," Stan uneasily boasted. "And it's about time." Even with winter camouflages the night was cold and he often softly cursed.

"Why don't you quit bitching about the weather," Roscoe grumbled. "How long have you been here? Eight months? That's time enough to be get use to the coldness."

"I'll never get use to this damned coldness, sergeant." There was a short pause. "I still can't believe a handful of men put two destroyers out of commission. That's awesome, Bro." While talking he never stopped watching for the enemy.

"We did it because the Soviets were stupid enough to put fuel drums on deck." The sergeant was solemnly quiet for a few moments. "And we had plenty of help from above."

"Damn, Bro, you're beginning to sound like Chatterbox."

"Well, truthfully I was never that religious. Christine had all the religion in our house. But I'm beginning to understand what she always talked about."

"What was her religion?"

"Baptist and I guess I'm going along those lines. But don't expect me to be a Bible thumper like Chatterbox."

Stan chuckled. "Chatterbox can really get on your nerves with all that stuff about Heaven and Hell. But it helps him and I guess that's all that matters."

Roscoe nodded while scanning the darkness with his glasses. Memories of his wife briefly flooded his thoughts. Because Christine was very religious her parents tried blocking their marriage. They denounced him as too rough for their daughter. But Christine rebelliously resisted and won in the end. She later learned to her horror though Roscoe loved her tremendously the Corps she couldn't compete with. This became the focal point of their arguments. Though he tried soothing the differences, his devotion to the Marine Corps was too powerful. When a chill ran through his body Roscoe's thoughts were snapped back to reality. When Cherry Point Marine Corps Station was vaporized he wasn't there and she died alone on that base.

"Do you think they'll come this way?" Stan asked.

"It's the fastest way to Vandenberg."

Time crept passed those men on that highway while waiting for a Russian tank column. The skies were black while frequent streaks of lightning burst across. The thundering was louder than usual. As usual those ocean winds were icy cold while temperatures gradually dropped. The threat of a Greenhouse effect was grim reality through most of the world, but the dazed populace was too busy surviving to notice. Behind them reddish glowing consumed the forests at an alarming rate. Ten Delta knew they had to be extinguished, but without rain that was impossible.

"Sergeant," Stan excitedly said. "We're going to have company for dinner."

Roscoe quickly swung his attention down the highway. The hairs on his neck seemed to stand up. Noisily moving over the cluttered highway was a long line of tanks. Driving fast the drivers used their headlights that created a long winding necklace of small lights to appear.

"Damn," Stan cursed. "Those mothers are big."

"They're heavily plated so we fire at their track sockets. Disabling the damned things is our hope. It'll be up to the Apache to finish them off." He glanced at the marine and said. "Our job here is to observe and report. The lieutenant will do our housekeeping, got that?" He paused then added. "Tonight I don't want any damned heroes." Reaching for his radio mike he crisply reported. "Night Dog to Eagle's Nest. Confirm heavy tracks on coordinates 3 . . . 2 . . . 6 moving approximately 30 miles per hour. Estimate at least 60 tracks."

"Eagles Nest to Night Dog," the radio crackled. "You're instructed to withdraw to the base. Do you acknowledge?"

"Night Dog to Eagles Nest, I roger that." Roscoe said then hurriedly looked at Stan. "You heard that. Let's get the hell out of here before our guests open fire. I'm sure they heard my transmissions."

While running across the road yelling for his marines to reload, the BTR was quickly driven from its hiding. About that time Roscoe heard the screaming of an incoming 125mm shell. The Russian vehicle spun around and headed for home as the explosion impacted a nearby wreckage. Scattering debris and soil showered the fleeing armored car. Several more explosions blasted the highway as computerized fire control systems tracked Roscoe's retreating squad until they rounded a curve and gunned the engine for home.

"Damned that was close," Stan mumbled.

"Those tanks have laser tracking," the sergeant predicted. "Eagles Nest from Night Dog, inform Eagle One those tracks are armed with laser tracking." After Ten Delta acknowledged he sighed a long deep relief. "Let's hook up with Tyler."

They had only driven ten miles from El Capitan when small arms gunfire sprayed the wheeled armored vehicle. Roscoe shouted at the driver to dash into some nearby ruins. After that was done Roscoe's squad quickly exited the stopped car and prepared to counterattack their unseen opposition. Judging from the gunfire they had driven into an ambush. Ten Delta marines scattered like frightened mice to establish their defenses.

"Machine gunner over in the rubble," Stan shouted.

"Use your Stinger to take it out." Roscoe shouted when seeing one of his men topple when bullets sprayed his position.

Stan inserted a battery coolant unit into his gripstock. Carefully looking through the plainly designed sight, he adjusted the ring to first of three notches. Stan observed heavy gunfire from a well protected site while gently running a rough palm across his sweating forehead. Stan's warhead was a high explosive/fragmentation with hit-to-kill proximity fuse. After looking over the Stinger's guidance control panel, Stan pressed the trigger. When clearing its shoulder-fired launcher a solid-fuel dual thrust rocket motor fired a low burn. This sent a narrow rocket hurling toward the unsuspecting machine gunner and seconds later plunged into the rubble. A swirling reddish flame shot upwards. After the explosion there was no gunfire from that spot.

Then another surprise burst upon these Ten Delta marines as a rumbling BTR crashed through the rubble it was hiding behind. Its twin machine guns blazed a devilish nightmare as two more marines were chopped to pieces without warning. A marine jumping from his hiding threw two grenades under the vehicle. Following the dual explosions it rolled to a halt. But the disabled BTR's twin guns continued spraying deadly bursts about its immediate area. Stan quickly reloaded the Stinger and fired. There was a thunderous eruption aboard the carrier as the guns exploded followed by stored munitions. Afterwards Roscoe gave little attention to the burning vehicle. He had other problems. Russian infantrymen were storming from the ruins rapidly firing their heavier caliber weaponry.

Stan and another marine private named David were caught in deadly cross fires and unable to escape. Grabbing his automatic weapon the corporal kept firing at charging infantrymen until his clip was expended. Jerking the empty one out he was reloading when David shouted grenade and dived to the ground. Stan didn't have time to react and the explosion tore him apart. Screaming curses on the Russians

David jumped up while rapidly firing his assault rifle. But there were too many and when his weapon clicked on empty he used the rifle as a club. David was able to slam a couple of Russians before they shot him several times. With an astonished look the marine's lifeless body tumbled to the ground.

Roscoe saw his squad being chopped to pieces. Grabbing his radio he called Ten Delta. "Eagle Nest from Night Dog, we're overrun by BTRs and infantrymen."

When a bullet crippled his hand he dropped the radio mike. Clumsily holding his heavy rifle the wounded sergeant joined three other surviving marines. They backed against piles of rubble after finding escape impossible. High above them were the sounds of lonely Apache coming nearer, but they knew it would be too late. Their captured BTR was burning with two dead marines aboard. When shouting Russian infantrymen charged their weak stand the final roar of gunfire rose above the harsh evening winds.

*   *   *

Timothy sadly circled the position outside El Capitan. "A good marine sergeant died with his squad this day." he moaned.

Savannah studied the map for a few moments. "They are chopping us to pieces, chief."

"Yeah they are, but not without heavy losses." He thoughtfully looked at the map. "Companies from Thomas' command are fighting large numbers of Russians in the Cleveland National Forest outside of San Diego. Here where Camp Pendleton Marine Base used to be, large numbers of enemy infantrymen are tied down in heavy fighting. A column of motorized Russian infantrymen coming down from Oregon was chopped to pieces by Canadian and British troops. And in this region we have badly mauled enemy forces on Vandenberg, smashed their armored column on the 101, and destroyed two warships. We have accomplished that much and about to attack another large tank column." He nodded. "All in all, I would say we're bleeding them real bad. Those are losses Kossier can not militarily afford."

Savannah was silent for a short time before skeptically predicting. "If Lewis neutralizes that amphibious ship Kossier's naval presence along this coast will be seriously threatened."

*   *   *

Leaving their safe zone Lewis flew low over the water to escape ALEKSANDR's surface radar. Horace was sitting in the co-pilot's seat quietly watching the choppy waters beneath their helicopter. His friends' deaths affected him and this Lewis noticed without comment. This cruel demanding war was stripping everybody of their loves ones back home. After maturing friendships the war stormed in and tore those loose. Lewis wondered if that anger was causing him to attack the amphibious ship off Point Dume.

Observing how the lightning was splitting the dark heavens with rapid brilliant flashes, Lewis finally commented. "Have you noticed the weather is getting worse?"

"No sun." the Indian grumbled. "World today a bad place to live. Gods are angry with people and punishing them."

"Whether God is angry or not isn't a topic for discussion. But if mankind hopes to live much longer Craver had better do his thing real quick."

While talking the Air Force captain divided his sharp eye on the green illuminated instrument panel and their negative weather. Tuned to Ten Delta he heard about Roscoe's death. Ten Delta was being cut to pieces by superiorly numbered enemy formations. Though performing near impossible miracles over the last few hours, only so much could be done by a handful of men.

His Chinook was upgraded with a new digital advanced flight control system allowing the pilot to fly the helicopter and operate its electronic weaponry system. With Joshua dead operation of this giant bird was solely in his hands. He frequently glanced at the missile approach warning system's dials that warned of any threats. The forward looking infra-red weapons' complex system was installed prior to his leaving St. Louis. With this far reaching radar handling up to eighty different threats his chopper was a real threat to the enemy. Unlike the Apache's whispering engine, the Chinook's two noisy turbo shaft power plants were heard from some distance.

Horace was watching the digital map display when he somberly replied. "Point Dume is two minutes ahead." Unbuckling his seat belt the Indian said. "I'm going to the machine guns in case our electronic goes out." After exchanging a firm Indian handshake the man went back into the cavity. In his tormented mind this was pay back time. The enemy killed two of his friends and revenge must be extracted before meeting the Great White Spirit.

The Chinook was flying so low its propellers' wash sent icy sprays against Horace's face. While buckling the waist harness the Indian thought about those good times in the Marine Corps. Pulling on his helmet he plugged in its intercommunications cord. "I'm ready for some serious ass kicking. Disconnect the electronic weaponry system for my door machine guns. But leave the port side gun on its tracking system. If I'm going to die, I want to actively take some of those white-faced bastards with me."

"Roger that." Lewis said after seeing the red light identifying starboard guns go black. "You're on your own, Chief, and may the gods have mercy on us." One minute later Lewis warned. "They have us painted. Get ready for some intense gunfire . . . there she is. She's a damned mean looking monster."

ALEKSANDR was lying anchored off the shore in rough waters that prevented her bow ramp doors and stern ramps from opening. Almost immediately after the helicopter came into view her twin 76mm and 30mm Gatlings began rapidly firing. Their electronic fire control systems tracked the enemy aircraft. Fortunately for his

Chinook the twin mounts couldn't lower enough after Lewis started his approach. All around the heavy helicopter water sprouts were mushrooming and black puffs filled the skies. Though weighing more than two Apaches those airborne explosions were still rocking the metal monster. Aboard the amphibious vessel crewmen were frantically rushing to battle stations. Lewis activating his port machine gun sent explosive shells that killed many running seamen caught in the open. Several vehicles parked on her upper decking burst into flames.

Charlie was so intense firing his 7.62mm gun he didn't notice smoke swirling about his feet. His bullets were splattering death across the ship's main deck. A Hellfire missile sped from its pod and destructively rammed into the aft gun turret. After passing over the ship Lewis made a sharp right turn and headed for another pass. Heavy caliber bullets filled the air between the chopper and ship. Gunfire tore into the helicopter's main frame as pieces of metal fell into the choppy waters. Lewis fought his sluggish controls praying they would reach the ship before crashing.

The staff sergeant laughed as his weapons achieved frightening tolls on the fighting ship. Then crying out in pain the Indian grabbed his stomach as blood gushed out. Swallowing hard the veteran struggling to his feet clutched his machine gun and commenced firing again. Steams of bullets continued hitting the aircraft as they charged the bolshoy desantny korabl. Larges stores of gasoline stored in 55 gallon drums numbering over four hundred took a direct barrage of 50 caliber bullets. The flaming results shook the ship as an uproarious explosion hurled fireballs high above the anchorage. Through passageways rushed masses of consuming flames. Men caught down below were vaporized. Oil lines burst under pressure adding crashing forces to those already devastating the warship.

The Chinook was caught in an unforgiving screen of gunfire that ripped apart the helicopter. Somehow Lewis kept the helicopter heading toward its target. The captain paid little mind its main frame was falling apart. When Lewis was close the ship's portable weaponry was causing serious damage to the American helicopter. Lewis fought his resisting controls after receiving several smashing hits. Then the moment of truth was on them. Smashing into the waterline with devastating results the napalm canisters individually exploded. A huge waterline hole appeared where the helicopter drove into the ship crashing everything in its flaming path. Lewis had struck the ship's weak point. After gaping holes ripped open its decks flames spun down passageways like screaming demons. The ship's water tight integrity didn't hold fast against the thundering vibrations and explosions. Lower deck hatches were torn off their hinges as rushing waters swept screaming sailors into another swirling nightmare. This amphibious ship known in the Soviet Navy as a bolshoy desantny korabl was badly built in too many places. She was doomed once the tons of explosives sent spinning balls of fire into the night. Maybe if the waters were calmer, damage control parties would have had a fighting chance controlling the listing ship. But not with that night's roaring wrath. The deafening tearing of those loaded vehicles bursting into flames added another notch in her protesting this dying.

*   *   *

Timothy turned away from the map when informed the ALEKSANDR had exploded at Point Dume and was sinking. "Do we have confirmation as to what happened?" he slowly asked though knowing the answer.

The radioman nodded. "Thomas' patrols in that area saw Lewis' helicopter ram the ship."

James' excited voice sounded on the speaker. "You won't believe what's happening along the 101." There was a pause during which they heard thunderous explosions in the background. "Our two destroyers from Mexico are blowing the hell out of that column of tanks. Damn it's going to be a massacre down there. The Russians trying to turn around are bumping into one another. There's not enough room for them. The warship's guns are blasting them to hell one by one and there's nothing the Russians can do about it." They could hear Glassford shouting his approval in the background. "They don't need us around here so we're coming home. Tell Earl we'll do what he wanted at dawn."

While wild cheering erupted inside Ten Delta's facility, Timothy hurried to the hanger to wait for James' arrival. His step was brisk for the first time since the war broke out. This was like those movies when everything was going wrong then at the moment of defeat the cavalry arrived. After the Apache was pulled inside and its crew happily climbed out the chief rushed over. Laughing Savannah rushed up to hug the lieutenant. Marines not on duty ran into the hanger cheering knowing that evasive light was finally appearing in the tunnel.

"The Russians' stranglehold has been broken." Savannah happily cried.

"We got word a few minutes ago Thomas' columns are driving back the enemy in several sectors. I guess the Mexican Annexation Movement seeing what was happening quietly melted into the woodwork." Timothy briefed James. "For the time being we can forget about them as a political threat. But I'm sure they will come back later."

"What about Tyler's patrol you sent out?"

"Tyler radioed they're on the way home and put the beer out."

James lost his wide smile. "But we paid a dear price for this moment." he sadly reminded the gathering marines. "And we must not forget our friends who died these last few hours." For a few moments he studied the smiling faces staring at him. "Victory isn't in our hands yet, but that crack is eroding the enemy's willingness to die for his cause of evil. There's lots of work left to do. With the coming of daylight we have another job to do and the enemy soldiers on the air base will oppose our efforts." He laughed and looked about. "I don't know about you guys, but I'm hungry as hell."

*   *   *

As they walked to the mess hall James looked at Savannah. "After this war is over I know a good restaurant in town that's very romantic." He shrugged. "Maybe it's in shambles, but we'll take a bottle of wine and pretend everything is like it was before hell broke loose."

"I'll like that, lieutenant." she agreed with a sweet smile.

There was already food on the serving line and a happy cook standing behind the counter. Timothy realized this was the first time he had seen this man truly smile. James piled his tray high with scrambled eggs and sliced ham. Toast with jam was put on his tray by the grinning cook. The mess hall was different without the usual tensions while men laughed and joked around. For a few minutes they tried forgetting about their losses. Everybody knew there were battles ahead of them and more men would die. But Russia was losing major battles and that was a reason to celebrate. After a battle James was always starving. This time he was hungry as a horse and happy as a Nun on Sunday morning. The whole facility was swept into this joy as if it was a contagious virus.

Between bites James talked. "Do we have updated intelligence regarding enemy presences on the air base?" After the chief shook his head the lieutenant chewed some food. "We need to know what's going on out there. This morning we go seeking Craver's rocket and I don't want any surprises." He looked at the fork of eggs before thoughtfully saying. "You know these eggs taste just like the ones I had when growing up on the farm. Damn they're good." Smiling the officer then cheerfully looked around. "Chief, look at our men. When was the last time you seen them like that?"

"Yeah, they're happy. But soon we go on that base and some more will die."

Nodding the base commander said. "But dying is different when you can touch victory. When fighting a hopeless war you often times ask if sacrificing is worth it." He looked around the table. "How about you, Mr. Craver, have you ever felt like that?"

"Sometime."

"Every time I give an order knowing my men might die a part of me withered away. Ten Delta became my personal hell. But what made it so bad was Kossier's winning this damned war. Every time our troops walked into battle they got their butts kicked. It was as if America wasn't supposed to win this one."

"Then why keep on fighting?" Earl asked.

"The same reason Gunner died and the same reason Joshua gave his life so others could live. Roscoe went out tonight knowing he was going against tremendous odds. But each man walked out. Thorton died fighting even after life had given him such a rotten deal from childhood. Those men died so we may keep the flames of freedom burning."

"Very inspiring words, lieutenant," Earl praised.

"Sometime inspiring words decides the outcome of battles."

CHAPTER TWENTY-SEVEN

The early morning hours passed very quickly for those at Ten Delta. When the sun rose over the horizon Californian skies were a heavy gloomy gray. Those standing watch either in operations or outside hidden in the ruins watching for intruders were relieved. When James came into the mess hall dressed in his flying suit his table was occupied by Savannah, Tyler, Timothy, and Earl. The cook motioned the lieutenant to his table then prepared his tray of food and brought it over. James had to have his cup of coffee to start the day. Everybody at his table were dressed in camouflages and armed for that day's activities.

"By the time you returned this morning," James said to Tyler, "I was fast asleep. Since nobody woke me up I guess that means your squad didn't see anything."

"Refugo Beach was quiet as a church mouse." He smeared strawberry jam on his toast. "But they sure as hell were out there and intercepting our radio messages."

"And in your opinion," the officer asked. "Where would that be?"

Tyler gave the matter some thought before saying. "The Russians aren't stupid even though they committed some pretty serious blunders these last few days. But they still have an excellent communications network. Their troops know by now the two warships were destroyed. Everybody up and down this coast will know the amphibious ship was blown up. After Thomas' soldiers battered their scattered columns, I'm sure they'll make for the nearest sector offering the best security."

"And that would be?"

"The air base." Tyler speculated. "Vandenberg has a coastal outlet and there are still troops on the base. If I were the enemy commanders, I would head for the air base and make a stand there until reinforcements arrived."

Earl was disturbed by his warnings. "You mean we have to fight our way onto the air base?"

"I highly recommend we deal with the Russian threat before looking for your rocket." James said after a short silence.

"I won't wait any longer," the envoy harshly declared. "Ever since I arrived there has been one excuse after another why I can't go after the rocket. There's no time left. I have to fire that rocket today." He roughly sat the cup down. "None of you really understand the serious gravity of this problem."

Tyler curtly replied. "Oh, I understand, Mr. Craver. I understand what the Greenhouse Effect will have on mankind. Maybe I'm not as smart you and don't fully understand its complexities, but I understand." His face turned red with anger. "Now you must understand our position. On Vandenberg we have undetermined numbers of Russian soldiers with more on the way. We could go there now and start searching for your rocket. The problem with that is the enemy will interfere and the launching shaft may be damaged or even destroyed. Now is that what you want? Or would you prefer waiting until we have eliminated this threat? Then we can work without dodging grenades and heavier gunfire." Indifferently shrugging his shoulders James leaned back in the chair.

After the envoy angrily departed the mess hall, James looked at Savannah with an amused expression. "I guess that means he'll wait?"

"Earl Craver can be very difficult to work with." she warned.

James frowned. "Well, that you don't have to convince me of."

Savannah sat quietly for a few moments toying with her coffee cup and studying the lieutenant. "So how are you going to eliminate the Russian wart?"

James grinned. "Very carefully." He then looked at Timothy. "We'll need some soldiers from Thomas' companies. See if you can arrange that. Our timetable has to start in two hours. Glassford and I'll go airborne and see what we can find out. Tyler will take as many of our men as possible and coordinate his efforts with Thomas' people. Ten Delta will be our control headquarters so Savannah will be in charge." He paused and thoughtfully rubbed his chin. "Was there anything I overlooked?"

"Nope," with that said the chief petty officer left.

"Does Ten Delta have any more magical packs up their sleeve?"

James laughed. "We don't have magical potions out here, my dear woman. Ten Delta simply capitalizes on the Russians' blunders." His light heartiness faded. "And I must admit there have been many opportunities." The lieutenant finished his buttered toast. "I'm afraid today it'll be old fashioned ass kicking on both sides."

*　　*　　*

James walked to the hanger where he found marines already standing in small formations waiting to load onto the carriers. For a few moments he studied their youthful faces. The Marine Corps' fierce loyalty still welded courage among these men from various walks of life. Once he walked over their chattering stopped.

"In a short time you'll race to stop the communists' push along this coast. And they'll be expecting you. Reconnaissance patrols have already reported six BTR-152s armed with twin 23mm cannons. But we have met these bitches and know they can be smashed. There will be scattered PSZH-IVs. No matter how tough they may be we know how to crack their balls. Here's some more bad news. You can anticipate

Grail shoulder-fired missile launchers among these Russian ranks. So watch out and duck like you never have ducked before." James started pacing in front of the solemn-faced men.

By now word spread the CO was addressing his first detachment about to go out. Marines hurriedly flowed into the hanger to listen though their ranks were much smaller than a few days before. Men quietly stood about listening as if James Blackmore was Moses speaking to his people. Those few in operations watched on their monitors. Savannah and Timothy stood in the hallway watching with wide smiles. Even Earl and Barnes stood at the entrance solemnly listening.

James' facial expression was one of great pride. His eyes flashed contemptuously when speaking of the enemy. "What we're about to do today is why we're here in the first place. Do not forget these men killed, tortured, raped, and looted what we Americans stand for. This day much blood will flow, but it'll be the blood of those Russian bastards. It will be on Vandenberg Air Force Base that history shall this day be written. Because it'll be there Ten Delta and her allies stopped the sadistic communist conquest of this coast." There rose a thunderous approval for his words. James raised a hand above his head. "For it shall be written that on this day a handful of United States Marines and Army infantrymen courageously fought back the murdering savage enemy who dared to stain our soil!" Again the loud applause drowned out his words. "Today there will be no mercy shown this cursed enemy. When the battles end only our colors will flutter. Only our marines and soldiers will be standing. There will no prisoners taken today."

Savannah proudly looked at the chief. "Damned after those words, I'm ready to pick up a rifle and march into glory."

Timothy chuckled. "You'll have your hands full right here."

*   *   *

After James walked to his helicopter a strange silence lingered for a few seconds. Then the hanger seemed to vibrate from the wild cheering among that handful of marines. At his chopper James finished dressing in his flight gear. There wasn't enough time to conduct his final inspection so the mechanic did it. While the machine was pulled outside James sat in the cockpit observing Sergeant Tyler's men loading into the two armored cars.

Once the Apache was airborne they went into combat readiness. The helicopter was armed with three different weapon systems. For suppressive fire, the chopper carried a 30mm chain gun with 1200 rounds of high explosive shells. These incendiary bullets easily took out soft-skinned vehicles and committed heavy hurt to harder-skinned armor. Neither man talked. Glassford activated their cannon using Target Acquisition and Designation (TADS). Their single cannon mounted in a hydraulically driven turret registered hot. This weapon was able to spurt 650 rounds per minute with a muzzle velocity of 2165 feet per second. Sharply banking after leaving Gaviota, James headed for the air base on a quick aerial reconnaissance. After that they were going to check on the 101 highway coming up from Santa Barbara.

Flying at one thousand feet James hoped to stay out of harm's way until evaluating the dispersing of enemy columns. Behind them and inland was the Los Padres National Forest's sprawling thunderous fire storm. After quickly studying the burning terrain resembling a Hollywood horror movie, James knew it was nowhere near burning itself out. Millions of acres along the coastal region were already blacken leaving twisted trunks reaching to the angry skies. The lieutenant felt a sickness heavily settling in his stomach's pit like a stone.

Glassford seated below him spoke into the mike. "We searched far as Goleta without sighting motorized activity and found nothing in the Santa Ynez valleys." His eyes remained on the radar monitor. "So where did they disappear to?"

"Oh, there's plenty places in the Santa Ynez Valley to hide. But they'll come out to play real soon. Don't be so impatient."

After flying over what was left of Solvang and Mission Santa Ines, James headed toward Vandenberg. When nearing Ynez River's winding course, Glassford calmly called out. "We have hostiles bearing grid nine-four-three running southwest." His eyes stayed on the recording imagery. "There are four . . . I repeat four armored cars accompanying one battle tank." There was a brief pause before he warned. "Also I count four trucks with troops." Moments later as the helicopter swung around to investigate this sighting, Glassford advised not too calmly this time. "They have painted us, lieutenant."

Knowing Ten Delta had the information James said. "Let's pay them a visit, shall we?"

Without further words James began his attack approach on the enemy column six hundred feet below and nearly two miles away. The Apache's weaponry limitation was firing missiles in pairs every three seconds. Surging the engines if this wasn't followed was a strong possibility though it had never happened to him. But his attention was driving the aircraft and this was a full time matter. Glassford monitored the onboard computers providing colored, real world, magnified images of their designated targets. Their lonely chopper sped toward the column snaking across the Inez River.

After the alarm warned of an oncoming missile countermeasures were automatically activated. His radar target acquisition system programmed the fire-and-forget Hellfire air-to-ground missiles. Other measures were rapidly activated. The dumb surface-fired missile followed the chaff dispensed from the Apache and harmlessly exploded.

"We have an armored car firing missiles." Glassford said.

"Roger that. Take it out."

James began evasive actions while swiftly approaching the scattered column now furiously firing at the airborne threat. Glassford fired two Hellfires that upon impact their targets went up in flames and smoke. Their automatic 30mm gun was kicking up chunks of dirt that spun into the air like showering rocks. The bullets were devastating the soldiers' ranks. After three furious passes the rolling stock was left in flames and infantrymen lying about like twisted dolls. Having roared over with missiles and machine gun bullets ravaging the column the enemy never had even a slim chance of winning. Three times they charged this enemy column before James was satisfied they had a successful strike and flew away. Behind them columns of back smoke rose high only to be scattered by the strong winds.

"Well, that was an easy strike." Glassford muttered.

"The Russians are losing their motivation to fight." James explained with a worried expression. "They should have put up a better fight than that."

"Let's hope they keep on losing that motivation." Glassford sourly replied.

"Eagle One to Mother Hen," James radioed Ten Delta. "One small motorized enemy column identified in the Santa Inez Valley east of Mission Santa Ines. Same destroyed." After they acknowledged his message, James changed course and headed for the air base. He had an annoying feeling their next strike might not be so easy.

*   *   *

One hour after leaving Ten Delta, Sergeant Tyler's squad connected with a motorized column from Major Thomas' regiments. The four trucks transporting thirty soldiers were escorted by two Humvees armed with mounted 50 caliber machine guns. A tall lanky black lieutenant stepping from the lead Humvee casually returned Tyler's salute. They were two miles inland from Government Point and the skies were with black rolling clouds and splitting streaks of lightning. Sharp cracks of thunder frequently sounded. All around them were signs of recent battling.

"Sergeant Tyler, sir." the master sergeant reported though not certain if he liked this cocky lieutenant or not.

"Lieutenant Madison. What do we have going on out here?" He watched two marines jump from their Shoets and cautiously trot up a slight embankment to look about.

"We have unidentified numbers of enemy soldiers on the air base."

"What about their support?"

"During our recent engagement with the enemy four light tanks and three armored vehicles were destroyed. At the moment we don't know how many armored vehicles are on the move."

"Have you reconnoitered?"

"No sir, we were fighting other hot spots and didn't have the men to spare for reconnaissance." Tyler remained silent after noting the young lieutenant's disapproving glance.

"Sergeant Bellows!" Lieutenant Madison yelled. After a short Spanish staff sergeant ran up he pointed towards the launching towers' wreckage. "Take a squad and check out that area."

"Sir," Tyler interrupted. "If I may suggest . . ."

The officer gave Tyler a cynical glance then motioned his sergeant to do as ordered. For a few moments the black lieutenant regarded the fifteen marines unloading from the carrier then with a disapproving grunt walked to his trucks.

"Chatterbox," Tyler yelled while crossing to the Shoets. "Take our men over to that knoll and establish positions."

He watched his marines hurry away under the cynical attention of Madison's soldiers who were unloading and milling about. Minutes later he joined the Ten Delta marines now completing their static defenses. After squatting in a shallow ditch created by a bomb explosion he carefully studied the outlying terrain with an enhancer aide. Coming over Chatterbox stepped into the ditch.

"What the hell is wrong with those damned soldiers?" the junior sergeant asked. "They act as if this is a Sunday picnic."

"They are a little cocky, aren't they?" Tyler replied with a dry grin. "But they'll learn real fast."

Chatterbox nodded. "Good thing we brought along that Hawk launcher. I have a sneaky feeling it may come in handy later on today."

Tyler nodded though his interest was on his men positioning the Sparrow/Hawk carriage launcher toward the nearby launcher towers. Defensively this wasn't an ideal position, but it would have to do. His marines hastily digging trenches were soon in the holes ready for fighting. Down the knoll Madison's soldiers still weren't preparing for battle. The master sergeant knew it was useless warning the officer his men were in harm's way by staying in the open. Grunting something about worthless officers, he watched the squad trotting across open terrain to a nearby launching tower heavily damaged earlier in the war. In those few minutes they were exposed there was no place to quickly seek cover. Chatterbox glanced at Tyler and shook his head.

"Which of those towers were we supposed to check out?" Chatterbox asked while watching Madison's soldiers foolishly exposing themselves. "Where the hell did those idiots go to boot camp?"

"Beats the hell out of me," Tyler was silent for a moment. "They sure aren't smart, are they?"

Minutes later Major Thomas arrived on the firing lines. Tyler already had his men positioned along an elevated stretch of land. It faced the enemy forces that had stopped a mile away. Seeing the tall army officer jumping from his Hummer Tyler walked over with a half grin.

"Hi, Thomas," he greeted with a sour grin. "And how goes the army's pride and joy?" There was no contempt in his words.

"We're just peachy as hell and what about you? I hear tell some pussy ass marine platoon needs their ass hauled out of a jam." He chuckled. "So they call the United States Army to do it." Thomas was dark-skinned with large black eyes. Faded green fatigues hung loosely on his straight frame like a flour sack. After they walked up the slight incline to thoughtfully look about, he shook his head. "I only count fifteen men in the foxholes. Where are your other men posted?"

"What do you see," Tyler said, "is what I got."

Major Thomas studied the marine sergeant for a moment then with binoculars looked at the Russian column across the devastated terrain. "How did you plan taking on a large enemy formation supported by armor with only fifteen marines. Hell, I know you marines think you're supermen, but this is suicidal."

Tyler shrugged. "Suicidal or not this is all we can spare. In the last few hours Ten Delta has been hit pretty hard."

"Well, for the moment the Russians aren't in a hurry about attacking. That may be to our advantage."

The army officer kept evaluating what lay in front of them one mile away. He wondered if they were waiting for another column. The major thoughtfully gauged the winds sweeping in from the Pacific that were cold as ice. Looking over his shoulder Thomas recognized Chatterbox squatting alongside the Shoets arranging medical supplies in a metal box. Another marine he didn't know was inside the armored car scanning the radio frequencies hoping to intercept enemy transmissions. For a while he watched his infantrymen now establishing positions on both sides of the marines.

Pushing the binoculars into their leather case hanging around his neck the major frowned. "It looks like we're in a damned strait jacket out here, sergeant. All I could bring was fifty men and some heavy weapons. The rest of my command is scattered up and down the coast engaging the enemy. I'm happy to boast the 10th Strategic is pulling off some startling victories just like you guys have done the last couple days."

"This war stinks like shit. It's a war of shortages and no reinforcements."

"Our campaigns on the Churchill are draining the manpower barrel. They're recruiting forty and fifty year olds and even that doesn't fill the gaps. All of us commanders are fighting with what we have for the time being."

"Yeah we all know how bad it is. But still it doesn't make the situation any better to work with." He pointed at the enemy armor vehicles barely visible in the murkiness that was daytime. "What do you think those assholes are doing?" Tyler asked.

"It's hard to say. The Russian mind is like a toilet. You never know when they will flush. How long have they been doing that?"

"Probably," the master sergeant skeptically replied, "for two or three hours."

"They're waiting for more troops."

"But by now they must know we're outnumbered."

"That doesn't matter. Your reputation has them stumped."

The two walked the defensive lines evaluating if any changes could be made. The infantrymen dug in their heavier weapons while Tyler's machines guns commanded a killing field zone. The major thoughtfully looked about satisfied with their defenses. Many Russians would die before over running these defenses.

"How's Truman doing these days?" Thomas asked. "I haven't talked with him for several weeks."

Tyler looked at the army major. "I didn't know you two knew each other."

"Yeah, we're from the same neighborhood."

Tyler stopped and thoughtfully looked around them. "Truman brought the farm during our naval base raid." After a short pause he walked over to the Shoets. "We got anything new about the Russians?"

"They're quiet as a church house mouse." Chatterbox stood with a grunt and stretched his arms. "That usually means the bastards are getting ready to attack."

"Roscoe told me you knew something about that damned launcher. We lost Benny."

"I know enough to fire the mother if that's what you mean." They walked over to the Russian mobile rocket launcher. "While I was in med school our class went to Fort Bragg and watched some medical demonstrations. While I was there the army was messing around with one of these captured in Eastern Europe. The Sparrow/Hawk can be a deadly bastard in the right hands. We have nine missiles loaded with another twenty in the racks." He looked at the sergeant. "I recommend we use those shells sparingly." Leaning over Chatterbox lovingly ran his hand over the sleek rocket. "The missile is a cruciform configuration with tailing edge controlled by rear ailerons. Its guidance system is a state-of-the-art design hosting an array seeker antenna."

"What's the firepower?" Major Thomas was impressed with his knowledge. "This is the first one I have seen."

"Its warhead is HE blast fragmentation possessing a high single-shot kill probability. A 2-stage single chamber propellant motor hurls that rocket at supersonic speeds. We call it a MIN-23B mobile surface-to-air weapons systems." He looked at them and grinned. "The Soviets nicknamed this system 'Stalin's Asshole Blaster'. As with any Russian system the damned things are touchy with their fair share of quirks. Some of them are pretty damned dangerous. I'll admit it's touchy, but in the right hands Stalin's Asshole Blaster lives up to its nickname. The damned thing will blow holes right through an attacking armor group."

"Hey, sergeant!" yelled Ebenezer from the mound. "We got a BTR and some soldiers moving our way."

Tyler and Thomas raced up the rubble pile then dropping to their knees observed the enemy advance.

"It's a patrol sent out to test our defenses." Thomas said after lowering his glasses. "We have seen this several times over the last few months. The Soviet Army recognizes three basic forms of defensive actions. Conduct a meeting engagement swiftly followed by breakthrough and finally climaxed by bloody assault pursuit." He waved his hand motioning his cocky lieutenant over. "They learned their doctrines by wading through knee-deep blood and guts when Nazi armies stormed across Russia in World War II."

"The Russians fight differently from anybody I saw in the past," Tyler muttered.

"And where was that?"

"I was with the marines in Iraq, Iran, Syria, and finally fighting the North Koreans. Each of those countries fought their wars differently." Tyler groaned after bringing the glasses against his eyes. "But I swear these Russians are too damned unpredictable."

In the following few minutes the master sergeant thoughtfully evaluated what he saw a mile away. The Soviets were cautiously initialing their first offensive stage as the armor moved about the field. For a few moments he glanced at the darkened skies. They expected the enemy would attack with the coming of dawn. Both the Army and Marines learned their enemy preferred fighting during the day. Lightning sent bluest shafts of illumination splitting across the skies.

Without lowering the glasses from his eyes, Tyler spoke. "That BTR has a man standing upright with binoculars scanning our positions. I don't think the bastards know exactly what we have up here."

"They probably don't. You have wasted their patrols and they're without air reconnaissance. No, they probably don't know what we have entrenched or how many men. But because of the nasty ass kicking they got from Ten Delta, the bastards aren't taking any chances."

"Then we need to waste the bastards before they get too close."

After a few moments of thoughtful study the major nodded. "I'm in total agreement. Why don't I send a team out there?" Without waiting for Tyler's reply, he looked over at his shoulder at the lieutenant standing quietly behind them. "Danny, choose a Stinger team and take out that BTR." There was a short pause. "What about that patrol you sent out? Is it still missing?" After the lieutenant reluctantly nodded he sternly replied. "Then they're dead, Danny. Chalk off that squad and the next time listen to a master sergeant. He didn't get his promotions standing around scratching his ass." He turned his back on the officer. "Don't play hero out there. They have a patrol sniffing about for our weak points. Make sure they don't find them. You lost Jose and he was our best experienced sergeant. Just remember what they taught you at the Academy about ambushing patrols and you should be all right."

After the infantrymen crept into the shadows and was soon out of sight, Tyler looked at Thomas. "We're losing our experienced top guns with no replacements stepping up front."

"That's happening in all the battles."

CHAPTER TWENTY-EIGHT

The rough terrain around the launching towers once was level, but that changed when Soviet missiles abruptly impacted that Sunday morning. The Russian submarine missiles were programmed to strike at the Air Force Base's critical sectors. Very quickly the missile launching pads were wasted and that was followed by another wave of missiles that removed all military response units. These explosions disturbed the many fault lines running through this part of the state. It wasn't long afterwards that a series of powerful earthquakes devastated the still burning region. Dawn hadn't broken when Lieutenant Madison and six infantrymen crept from their positions. Staying within the darkened shroud, they quietly moved across the wide wasted stretch of land that separated the Russians from those Americans entrenched along a two block area.

These soldiers from 10th Strategic Command stalked confidently through the early morning hours. Their black lieutenant from Boston cautiously waved his men to hit the ground. Then crawling to a low hill's crest line he scanned the darkness with his night enhanced glasses. The Russian patrol after changing their approach was creeping through the darkness. They were trying to sneak around American lines and come up from behind. Madison motioned his staff sergeant to join him. While waiting he turned his attention to the handful of Russian infantrymen flanking the BTR armored vehicle noisily nearing the American lines. They were the decoy in this encirclement tactic.

His staff sergeant regarded the vehicle for a few moments before cynically saying. "Noisy bunch of bastards, aren't they?"

Madison nodded while watching the BTR bounce over uneven ground. Its twin 23mm turret was moving around in a creeping motion. Their mounted 14.5 KPV heavy machine gun worried the lieutenant. "What do you know about that damned thing?" In the Academy not much time was spent studying old Soviet equipment. Now he wished they had.

"Like what?"

"I'm concerned about its firing capabilities."

234

Lying on the ground made damp from ocean spray blown across the land, the sergeant thought about the question for a few moments. "I remember that machine gun can traverse 360 degrees with an elevation of 80 degrees and depression of 5 degrees. That I remember from my first encounter with the damned thing." There was short pause. "I also remember its 14.5mm API projectiles will penetrate anything we have on the field."

"We have to take out the damned thing." Madison decided. With his glasses he swept the expansion of rolling devastation. "The land will give some cover while it's dark, but after daylight they'll mow us down."

With their objective fixed in mind the infantrymen quietly moved out. Why they were trying to be so silent didn't make sense because the howling wind concealed their running footsteps. Their plan was to cross a sandy area sheltered by dead trees and dig in. There they would wait until the BTR was so close it couldn't back away. Madison felt they had one good chance taking out the armored vehicle. It was easy digging foxholes in the loose dirt. Madison had his Stinger teams spread every one hundred feet. Not that far behind them army and marines quietly waited as icy winds swept in from the tumultuous Pacific. Above them the usual bunched black clouds of soot and debris hovered like a condemning cloak of death. Within running distance waves were crashing ashore and trying to claw their way up the sloping banks. Failing in this endeavor the white foamy waters retreated allowing another attempt to come rushing forward.

Madison found an ideal position just above his scattered Stinger teams. Among some fallen concrete slabs he was offered some protection from heavy caliber gunfire. The lieutenant intended to give coordinates to his firing teams. Also from there he could without being seen watch the BTR slowly approaching.

One of his firing teams was a young soldier named Tommy. He was new to the 10th and Madison hadn't got around to knowing him. The man was a loner and quiet mannered. The officer could see the soldier hunched down in his hastily dug hole. According to his staff sergeant Tommy was an excellent shot with the shoulder fired missile launcher. Checking his launcher for the tenth time since leaving the others, Tommy was dissatisfied with this whole war. If he had this choice the army wouldn't have seen his butt. He should have fled into the Arkansas' mountains and stayed there. In the first place he didn't like taking orders from that black lieutenant. Where he came from that was unacceptable.

*   *   *

For the last few minutes Savannah thoughtfully watched a large number of Mexican and Russian soldiers roaming a short distance from Ten Delta's underground facility. Earl and Barnes stood alongside her observing this new threat.

"I would say they have us cornered," Barnes nervously said after a few minutes of cold silence.

"What are we going to do?" Earl demanded.

Savannah gave the envoy a dirty glance before again watching the enemy wander about the street close to the facility. "We wait them out." she mumbled.

One of the corporals came into operations and studied the scene outside before frowning. "I checked out the compound, major, and found nothing threatening out there. And to be on the safe side I activated the explosives after coming back in."

Earl whirled about to glare at the marine. "What explosives?" he snapped.

"The hanger doors have explosives packs in case the enemy breaks through."

"Are you crazy?"

"No sir. But you don't want to be captured by the Mexicans. They have a nasty reputation when taking female prisoners."

The marine James selected as corporal-in-charge of the facility's defense was Ezekiel Butterworth. He was the second Apache's mechanic, but after his helicopter was shot down he was now a marine grunt. Born in Oakland, California to a white father and black mother, Ezekiel was light skinned with few features of his mother's race. The corporal was of medium height with black curly hair and brown eyes. It was these narrow eyes that momentarily scowled at the bitching presidential envoy.

Looking back at the major he solemnly recommended. "Madam, the way those intruders are moving around they know Ten Delta is down here. They're just trying to figure out how to get down here. We may have to abandon Ten Delta. There is no way we can defend the base against their numbers."

"And where the hell do we go?" Earl demanded. When Barnes gave him a warning glance the envoy really got mad. "What's wrong with you? I don't want a damned corporal telling me what to do!"

Ignoring the abrasive civilian the marine respectfully spoke to Savannah. "Ten Delta has an escape tunnel for events such as this."

"And does Ten Delta have an escape plan?"

"Yes, madam." The corporal stepping closer to the monitor studied the enemy troops now moving cautiously down the winding street which stopped at the facility's ruins. "We'll need transportation to get away. The enemy left four Mexican soldiers with that BTR. Just behind them is the camouflaged opening we'll come out of."

While closely observing what the corporal was pointing out Savannah suddenly cursed softly. "Well, I be damned." She frowned. "See that man leading the column down the street? That's KGB Colonel Karsavin, one of the war criminals our Allied Commands want to see hung." She shook her head. "That man has more than six cat lives."

"So what is our next move?" Barnes asked. "Those soldiers are beginning to search the ruins leading down here."

Corporal Butterworth said. "It won't take them long to find out this area is inhabited."

"How many hostiles do you think is out there?"

"At least eighty with automatic weapons plus shoulder-fired rocket launchers and two BTRs. We're outnumbered in every way."

"How much time do we have?"

"Thirty minutes, give or take." the corporal estimated with a helpless shrug.

"So what's the procedure for abandoning Ten Delta?" Savannah asked after a thoughtful pause. The corporal was right. There was no way they could defend the base.

"First we transmit the code 'Broken Lance'. That'll tell the lieutenant and Sergeant Tyler Ten Delta is about to be overrun and we're following abandonment procedures." While talking the corporal walked over to a cabinet and removed two remote devices. "We have always talked about this possibility so alternative plans were discussed. We will go into the Santa Ynez Mountains. With no interferences we should be there in about three hours."

"But they're burning," Earl protested.

"Not this section. The fires have already passed there. Several weeks ago we found a hunting lodge protected by rocky terrains in the forest. Everybody else will go there when they can." The corporal was saying as he told the radioman to send out the call. "We have supplies and everything else we need up there."

"This is Mother Hen, this is Mother Hen." the radioman was anxiously broadcasting. "Broken Lance. I say Broken Lance."

There was a short pause before they heard Tyler's voice. "Good luck."

Moments after Tyler acknowledgment James' strained voice was received. "Good luck, Mother Hen."

For a minute or two those in operations stood silently staring at the dead radio. Then Corporal Butterworth snapped. "All right, marines, it's time to rock and roll. Let's make tracks out of here before those bastards get in. Everybody grab weapons and a backpack from the supply room."

While everybody rushed from operations the corporal and Savannah watched the enemy moving down that winding street surrounded by rubble. "Confident little bastards, aren't they?"

"Probably think they have us cornered." Savannah reached up and touched the lead figure then angrily said. "Colonel Karsavin is directly responsible for many of our captured troops being butchered." She shook her head. "But every time we think we have him the son-of-a-bitch escapes."

"Well, he won't this time. There's only one way back to the street and in a few minutes that path will be a flaming hell." The marine thoughtfully looked about the room before saying. "It's time to go, major. There's nothing we can do here that'll help the war effort."

In the hallway eight marines stood around bundled in heavy winter clothing and wearing large backpacks. Each man carried an assault rifle with solemn expressions they were abandoning what had been their home for the last several months. One marine handed Savannah a heavy insulated coat and backpack. She slipped the garment on then pulled the hood over her head. While Corporal Butterworth buttoned up his coat then checked the weapon's munitions supply, Savannah studied this small band of men retreating with her. She wondered what their thoughts were. One marine had taken the Corps' colors and after folding it slipped the red flag into his back pack. After satisfied everybody was ready the corporal trotted down the corridor to a door. The last man had passed through the escape passage when a loud explosion sounded. The Russians had blown the hanger door.

While the marines crept from their concealment, the few Russians standing around the BTR and two trucks failed to notice them. The careless soldiers were easily killed.

"Everybody into the BTR," Butterworth ordered.

Walking a few feet away from the vehicles he removed a remote from his pocket. With a smirk Butterworth pushed the first button. There were deep rumbles as a series of high explosive packs inside the cavity exploded. Black smoke and flames shot high into the skies. Then while Savannah stood at his side he pushed another button that exploded additional explosive packs hidden along the street. The air was stung by thunderous explosions that shattered the path to Ten Delta. Then without comment the two walked to the Russian armored vehicle and climbed in.

*   *   *

The Czechoslovakian built armored carrier smelled badly of unwashed bodies, but it was warm inside. Seated alongside Savannah in the troop compartment, the corporal grinned when somebody passed around a thermos of hot coffee. He laughed nervously when a baby faced private said he grabbed the coffee because it was cold outside. Up front the driver knowing the way to that hunting lodge chattered with the shotgun armed cook. Another marine was seated on the roof manning their twin 14.5mm machine guns. Exposed to the chill he wore a ski mask over his face and accepted the coffee thermos with a smile At first glance it appeared they were on a training mission. But each knew they were alone in a hostile country where death could pop out unexpectedly at any time. The dark skies were unfriendly while a chilly wind blew in from the angry Pacific Ocean. Their future was up for grabs. Any passing thoughts of a peaceful time seemed foreign and distant.

Savannah looked over at the thoughtful corporal. "When you pushed that remote button what did you mean this was for Truman?"

"Truman and I were on Midway last year when the Russians attacked that island." he said after a short pause. "While stationed there I didn't know Truman who was with security. Being that I was a helicopter mechanic our paths didn't cross that much. I got to know him when we were among the last marines extracted by submarine off the island."

For a few moments Savannah stared at her gloved hands. "Then you know Colonel Karsavin commanded that invasion force?"

"Yeah, I know." There was pain in his brown eyes when glancing over at the major. "We held out for eighteen torturous days before the island finally fell. I had buddies in Midway's hospital. After coming ashore the murdering bastard walked among our wounded in the sick bay and shot them in cold blood. He had no reason except he wanted to."

Savannah solemnly promised. "Colonel Karsavin won't be killing any more marines. Nobody could have lived through those explosions back there."

*   *   *

When Chatterbox joined Tyler in the foxhole dawn was arriving in this wasteland. "I heard Ten Delta went Broken Lance." he sadly mumbled.

"Yeah."

"Have you heard from them since then?"

"Nope, but then I don't expect to. They're on their way to the lodge by now."

Borrowing Tyler's binoculars the man carefully swept the outlying terrain. "The bastards are still doing nothing out there." After laying the glasses down he asked. "Have you heard from the lieutenant?"

"No. The last I heard he landed as planned and was waiting."

"What about those destroyers? Where did they disappear to?"

"They headed for British Columbia to make certain no other Russian surfaces were up there. We're on our own until they return."

Chatterbox sighed. "I feel better today than I have in months." he finally said.

"Why is that?"

"I dunno. Maybe because we seriously kicked Russian ass and there's a better prospect the United States isn't going down as we thought."

Tyler smiled. "It is a good feeling, isn't it?"

"Yeah, for a while I thought our black ass was done for."

The master sergeant picking up his glasses thoughtfully studied the static Soviet armored column across the wide expansion of wasted terrain. "But our bad times aren't over yet, Chatterbox. We still got to stop that group out there and they outnumber us pretty badly." He then swung the binoculars toward the ocean side until sighting the lonely BTR now stopped close to the shore. Somewhere out there was that Army major and his Stinger teams. "I wonder what the damned communists are thinking right now. And more important what the hell are they doing?"

*   *   *

For the last hour James and Glassford quietly sat in their Apache parked on a woody knoll offering concealment. One hour ago they had received the message Ten Delta was going Broken Lance. The emptiness they shared was privately nursed. The old factory had been their home for months. Broken Lance meant the facility would be blown up. From where they sat it was possible to see the raging Pacific and outlying countryside. The strong icy winds blowing in from the ocean was felt when they shut down the engines. Fires aboard the doomed Russian warships still sent up columns of smoke that was quickly fanned out.

"Do you think everybody got out?" the co-pilot finally asked.

"I dunno, but let's hope so."

When their radio distorted by static began transmitting the code 'Black Thunder', James thoughtfully spoke into his helmet communicator. "That's the call for us to ride cavalry, buddy." The lieutenant flipped on switches bringing his two General Electric gas turbine engines back to life. The Apache quickly lifted into the windy skies with their engines whispering death to all she encountered.

*   *   *

"Hey, sarge," Chatterbox whispered into his hand radio. "Take a look at that pile of rubble to our northeast forty degrees." He waited until Tyler grunted so what. "I saw movement over there."

"How many?"

"Ten or fifteen . . . maybe more"

There was a short silence before Tyler said. "I don't see anything."

"There was movement out there."

"Don't get gruffy with me. I believe you, but I don't see anything. Who do you have down there?"

"Billy Woods and Eddie Sprindle."

"They're good men," Tyler replied.

While Tyler spoke he was sweeping the area with his glasses. The rugged terrain scarred from numerous missile attacks and earthquakes made it ideal landscape for small foot patrols to move about. Those armored formations across the wide expansion were motionless as tombstones in an isolated cemetery. Tyler turned his attention toward the lonely BTR down by the shore line. This situation wasn't as fluid as the communists wanted while waiting for orders. But they were sending out patrols seeking confirmation on Tyler's positions. What he wouldn't give to have couple of mortars to put down barrages in that suspected sector.

A few moments later the master sergeant became worried. "Chatterbox, I can't raise Billy and Eddie. You better check them out."

With two men accompanying him, the staff sergeant crept among the shadows to where those two marines had dug their foxholes. Though the sun had appeared it was so filtered by the sooty atmosphere little sunlight got pass. The three marines fell to their stomachs and crawled the last few feet over rubble and disrupted terrain. Already Chatterbox had a gut feeling something was wrong. Inching to Billy's foxhole he let out a soft curse. The marine was slumped down in his hole with throat slice opened and his lifeless eyes looking at Chatterbox. He heard another marine whispering Eddie was dead. After hearing soft movement to their left he yelled to hit the dirt. While diving into the two holes, flashes of gunfire abruptly exploded around them.

"We're compromised!" Chatterbox yelled into his radio before dropping it and firing wildly at the figures running through the shadows.

The whole area became a confusion of violent gunfire and exploding shells. With the brilliant flashing it was now possible to see what was confronting them. Chatterbox's blood ran cold when seeing hundreds of infantrymen running across the rugged terrain.

Tyler's position was among some launching tower ruins made worst from the earthquakes that plowed through this sector of the sprawling air base. He thoughtfully watched enemy platoons approaching through a narrow path winding through the ruins. Scattered along the defenses lines his marines were busy firing at the enemy. The master sergeant raised his Grail missile launcher lifted from a fallen Russian. The two BTRs accompanying the infantrymen were about to regret their approach that allowed no means of withdrawing. There was a dull snap as its missile departed with a flaming tail. This solid-fuel dual-thrust rocket impacted against the first BTR. It rolled to a sudden halt and burst into flames. There was another tremendous explosion when its munitions cooked and instantly torched the surrounding soldiers. Soon as that rocket impacted Tyler was shouting orders to his men. There was another column of Russians crawling from the southern flank.

Quickly reloading the tube with a fresh coolant unit Tyler waited until he could see the now charging Russians. The marines crouching in their foxholes waited until the Russians recklessly dashed up the knoll and then jumped up. Their deadly gunfire briefly stunned the advance and when they hesitated Tyler fired another Grail missile.

Chatterbox anxiously crawled like a serpent to Tyler's foxhole. There he shouted to be heard above the gunfire. "There are enemy formations swinging around our rear."

"That must be those ship survivors." Tyler evaluated their breached positions. "How much longer before they arrive?" He unconsciously ducked as soil blown into the air fell upon them.

"Thirty minutes or less, they're motorized and driving pretty hard."

Without hesitation he yelled at a nearby marine. "Inform Major Thomas to pull back every other man for a rear line defensive position. Chatterbox, get your team over at the Hawk and let's see about greeting those bastards." After the runner rushed away the master sergeant dived to the ground as an incoming shell exploded nearby. Afterwards he jumped up and grabbed his fallen assault weapon. "If we don't stop that column dead in its tracks they'll overwhelm us!"

CHAPTER TWENTY-NINE

"Lieutenant," one of Madison's corporals yelled. "We have an intrusion over by the shoreline . . . sixty degrees north."

When the army officer shifted his attention there he saw another BTR roaming the rugged shore. Before he could evaluate this development the first explosions fell among the American defenses. He ducked low in his hole as geysers of dirt came raining down. One of his Stinger teams targeted the first BTR and fired. Moments later the vehicle blew up. Its flanking infantrymen not killed in that explosion scattered only to be mowed down by automatic gunfire. The early morning hours became a living hell while gunfire devastated the area and armored vehicles laid down barrages of tearing explosions. Screaming rockets destructively tore into both sides. The rugged terrain already devastated by earlier bombs and missile impacts was further eroded by this new explosion of violence. Neither side expecting mercy knew only victory would be tolerated. In only a few minutes the landscape was crowded with burning vehicles and its soil stained with blood from fallen Americans and Russians.

While the battle raged Lieutenant Madison thoughtfully observed another BTR slowly driving about the shore. It didn't wander too far away from its original course. Madison knew that lonely vehicle was advising Russian commanders where the Americans were shifting their positions about during the fighting. Adding to those rapid exploding bursts of violent illuminations, the skies became alive with sharp lightning bolts. The army lieutenant's attention was again drawn to that radio/communications vehicle with its high antennas popping about in the furious winds driving from the ocean. For some reason Tyler's people weren't paying attention to that vehicle. He didn't know Tyler's marines were withdrawing sections of their resources to challenge another breach about to break through.

He yelled at his sergeant. "Bring a team and let's take out that BTR down by the water."

The sergeant finally saw the BTR partially shrouded by drifting smoke from the battlefield. Gesturing for two Stinger teams to follow, the man crawling from his hole jumped up and started running across open land. Behind him ran two men toting their Stingers. Lieutenant Madison was in the lead of their wild zigzag course toward the Russian vehicle. Almost immediately the protecting infantrymen opened fire. Even when the lieutenant felt a burning sensation in his shoulder he kept running. It was too late to fall back. The opposing gunfire was furious and heavy. Madison heard one of his soldiers scream then fall. From the smoke and flames of exploding shells another running soldier snatched the Stinger and continued running toward the BTR.

Madison was so intent upon reaching the BTR he failed to see the scattered small holes. The next thing he knew his body was tumbling and in the process lost his rifle. Still rolling the lieutenant clumsily regained his footing. There was no time to search for his fallen weapon. Jerking his side arm from its holster he kept running as if the Devil was chasing him. All around the charging soldiers explosions erupted as the BTR defended its position. Just to his right an infantryman screamed as a shell exploded in front of his sprint. Madison felt bloody flesh thrown against his face. Still there was no time to stop.

Lieutenant Madison was only thirty feet from the Russian armored vehicle when he experienced a stinging sensation in his chest. The officer never knew when he crashed to the ground.

*   *   *

The thunderous sounds of battle were to his rear while Sergeant Tyler lay atop a pile of twisted beams and broken stones. He was thoughtfully watching the enemy's motorized column slowly approaching. It was a mixture of civilian trucks and several school buses hauling troops. A cold chill darted through his already overstrained emotions. Scattered among the ruins were marines and soldiers from Thomas' 10th Strategic Forces waiting for another opportunity to kill Soviets.

Glancing down several feet where Chatterbox squatted with a Stinger launcher, Tyler said. "Pass the word. The lead BTR has a portable rocket launcher. There are two more armored vehicles near the middle with a third BTR at their rear." After giving the orders he turned his attention back to the winding column. Once again they were outnumbered.

Near the road hiding in a motel ruins Sergeant Richards clutched his shoulder fired rocket launcher. There was a hardened determination on his boyish facial features that wasn't there months ago. When this war came he was working as an auto loan officer in Omaha, Nebraska. Like the others that day crowded around television sets, he watched horrified as the Soviet attacks were detailed by panic stricken reporters. Back then all he thought of was racing his modified Mustang and tumbling with his girl friend. But finding himself in a nuclear wasteland fighting Soviet invaders never crossed his mind. Richards avoided the war until his girl friend joined the army. When she died fighting on the Churchill battlefronts, he enlisted in the marines. After that his carefree attitude vanished and in its place was a cold obsession to seek revenge for her death.

HERMAN LLOYD BRUEBAKER

The lead BTR came closer while marines in the rubble impatiently waited. From their positions Richards couldn't see the whole column. His attention was focused on that first BTR's twin machine gun turret slowly revolving. Sergeant Tyler mentioned he was to fire once then high tail it to another position. Skies above the Southern Californian coast were anything but friendly. Black rolling clouds charged across the heights. Sharp lightning bursts were more often than before. Those thunder claps had become ear deafening. After waking up that morning Richards decided this was a good day for killing. He waited until the last moment before firing. In his tunnel attention all he saw was that lead BTR. His mouth felt dry while the stomach churned violently. Even with all the killing he had done since this war began, Sergeant Richards didn't like killing. But when those bothersome feelings stirred, the Nebraskan farmer remembered his many friends who were buried in forgotten graves. Then his killing passion came back.

The Soviet driver had lowered a plated protector over his windshield. But Richards knew the machine's weak design points. There were two Javelin rockets and Richards intended to put his to good use. The marine sucked in his breath before squeezing the trigger. There was a loud whoosh as the Stinger missile sped to its target.

The enemy inside the BTR must have been warned as its rear door suddenly swung open. Horrified troopers poured out knocking one another down in their rapid departure. That shaft carrying its high explosive/fragmentation shell traveled incredibly fast. While enemy soldiers abandoning their disciplines scattered, Marines overlooking the scene opened fire. There were blinding flashes and explosions as swirling fingers of flame and smoke shot up. Soldiers torn apart by the blast were hurled in all directions.

Within seconds of the first explosion the Russian column fell into panic. Soldiers abandoning their transports were brought down by the marines' murderous gunfire. A bus exploded while its flames consumed the running infantrymen. By now the entire area was trembling from those impacting explosions. Tyler's few well positioned marines were drawing a bloody knife across their enemy's throat. It was clear by now Kossier's hopes for a Californian conquest was going up in flames.

Hugging his elevated spot Tyler skillfully worked the Austrian Steyr SSG 69 rifle. Taken from an earlier battlefield he found its accuracy a blessing. The marine repeatedly fired this manual bolt action rifle bringing down a man each time he squeezed the trigger. There was no remorse on his perspiring face. When the magazine was expended he calmly slipped in another. Thoughts of Roscoe dying on that battlefield increased his hatred for the Soviets. Finding their advance abruptly halted by those marines hidden among the rocks, the enemy's motivation began waning. Though their sergeant angrily shouted at the men this didn't stop the retreat. One of Tyler's men put a slug through the husky Russian and that ended his shouting.

When the second BTR made a dash through the savage gunfire their efforts to stop it was unsuccessful. That was when Richards made his grandstand play. Wanting to make certain he sent a missile straight through the slotted driver's window the sergeant rushed from his safe haven and immediately fired. A missile roaring from its tube trailed a flaming tail that shot through the narrow window. There was a moment before an enormous explosion shook the vehicle then flipped it over.

What happened then was like a slow motion movie scene. The machine gunner atop the machine kept firing even as his vehicle rolled over. Caught in the open with no chance to flee Sergeant Richards was tore apart by the bullets. As he fell to his knees there was a thin smile celebrating his score then the man tumbled over. Like so many men from Ten Delta that morning, the war was over for him.

*　　*　　*

The Apache roared onto the raging battlefield with its fire control radar (FCR) classifying then prioritizing stationary and moving targets. The two General Electric gas turbines pushed the machine at 145 miles per hour with a three hour air time limit. Seeing the battles down below James knew three hours wouldn't achieve their objectives. He heard Glassford say their weapons were hot and ready. Panel lights suddenly indicated their rockets were launching. The folding fin aerial rockets streaked toward selected light armored vehicles now trying to dodge the approaching shafts. As the Apache roared over the exploding machines Glassford activated their 30mm automatic machine gun. The bullets switching the ground cut humans to pieces and tore into soft skinned vehicles like angry locusts.

James was banking for another charge over the battling men when Glassford shouted they were locked on by radar. Though the dispersing chaff drifted away it didn't deter the swiftly approaching ground-to-air missile fired by one of the BTRs. Both men felt the abrupt violent jolt as the rocket tore pass the Apache while clipping its main propeller. The damage was serious enough that the rotary wing aircraft spun to the earth. There was a thunderous crash when the helicopter plowed into the ground. Neither man inside moved as smoke poured from the doomed machine.

*　　*　　*

After firing his last Hawk rocket Chatterbox lead a group of soldiers and marines back onto the hill to challenge an enemy whose motivation was gone. This made the staff sergeant confident the Russians would be defeated that day. Their once superior numbers were sharply reduced. Scattered armor units now noisily burning gave an unharmonious cry to the moaning wounded or painful dying screams. Though their ground resistance was slowing the Russian approaches, it wasn't until Blackmore arrived that the tide of battle turned. Squatting behind some stones Chatterbox watched the helicopter dart about the battlefield spreading death and destruction like a wrathful god. He groaned when seeing the rocket tear from a BTR knowing the chaff wouldn't fool it.

After the rocket ripped off part of the Apache's whirling propeller, Chatterbox knew the lieutenant was in trouble. The staff sergeant watched the chopper crash not far from where he stood. Yelling for a squad to follow he tore out across the uneven ground shooting along the way when Russians tried intercepting him. There was too much confusion on the field for the Russians to pay that much attention to a downed helicopter. When the Apache crashed its long propeller tore loose shaving off the lower front cockpit. When couple marines tried removing Glassford's bloody body it quickly proved impossible. The impact had driven part of the instrument panel into his strapped body. Chatterbox doubted if the man had suffered at all because the accident had happened so quickly.

"The lieutenant is alive." a marine yelled.

Chatterbox ran around the twisted metal in time to see the lieutenant being pulled from his seat. It appeared other than a few small cuts on his face the commanding officer was physically all right. About that time explosions started falling around them. The enemy had decided the downed aircraft must be important after all. After James sluggishly regained his bearings they all ran back towards the knoll. Bunches of Russians stopped their fleeing and challenged the Americans caught in the open. Thomas' soldiers were laying down a fierce covering gunfire that slowed the enemy's eagerness to stop the running Americans. When they leaped into the foxholes Chatterbox hadn't lost one man in the rescue.

"How do you feel?" Thomas asked after crawling over to the hole where James and three of his men huddled. The skies' thunderous objection of the battling humans spit long flashing fingers across the grayness.

"Sure felt better," James groaned while Chatterbox sewed his deepest forehead cut. "What about Glassford?"

"He didn't make it." Chatterbox solemnly said. "Hell you're lucky you even survived. That chopper took a nasty nose dive." Finishing his treatment the staff sergeant thoughtfully looked at the lieutenant. "But your arrival turned the tide. The Russians are broken for now. Their casualties were heavy while their armor is in flames. I would guess their fighting for today is through."

"What about our own losses?"

Chatterbox paused repacking his medical bag. "We didn't do that good. Roscoe, Stan, Eddie, Billy Bob to name a few."

James stretched his right arm after Chatterbox wrapped it in a tight ace bandage. His attention was on the battlefield's confusion of burning vehicles and the drifting cries of their enemy's wounded and dying. "So, Thomas, did we break them today?"

"Yeah, we did do that. But we would never have accomplished it if your men hadn't taken out those three warships. According to the prisoners my men captured the Russians were stunned their ships went down. I don't think their deflated emotions ever recovered from that." The army major thoughtfully looked at the battlefield. "And you know when thinking about it that was the most amazing battlefield achievement in the books."

James grinned. "We merely capitalized on the enemy's blunders." He paused. "My men's courage and sacrificing was the right combinations at the right time." For a few minutes the lieutenant stared at the confusion before him then looked at the major. "Now what happens? Ten Delta is gone with majority of my command wiped out."

Soldiers from the 10th were rounding up prisoners by the time arriving reinforcements mopped up resisting Russian squads. Standing in the glare of burning vehicles, Thomas and James quietly surveyed the destructions that were in great abundance no matter which direction the eye looked. It was a few minutes before Thomas answered James' question and this was after serious thought.

"It's almost certain Kossier's political ambitions in California are smashed. And more importantly the Red Navy doesn't have the resources to replace those lost ships. That alone was a major blow for the communists. Assembling another invasion force is out of the question because Russian campaigns in Canada are now running into snags."

"Political cracks are that serious?"

"They're worst than serious. Throughout the world opposition is rising from the ashes to violently challenge their presence. We have begun winning battles along the Churchill that Russia cannot afford. Countries having suffered through the nuclear explosions and bombings are slowly rebuilding." He paused and smiled. "And guess what, Chatterbox, among the first buildings to go up were their churches."

The staff sergeant frowned. "It took blowing up half of the world before mankind turned back to God."

Thomas replied. "Who ever said mankind was the smartest creature on earth?"

James had stared at the burning wreckages and dead bodies lying before them for a few minutes. "Do you need us around here?" he asked.

"No, we got it under control now."

"Chatterbox, get our men together."

"Where are you going?"

"After Ten Delta was abandoned my people headed into the mountains to a mutual gathering place. I want to check out their dispositions."

"Sure, take off. But make certain you maintain communications, James. There are still hostiles out there. Maybe the Russian are finished, but you still have the Mexicans on their little crusade." When James started to leave he said. "Lieutenant, this war will be over before long and a massive rebuilding will have to take place. That gal from St. Louis has the trots for you. She's a prize you shouldn't let slip away."

"You know Savannah?"

"Yeah, have for several years. We went to the same college. As I said before she is a prize not replaceable in these gloomy days." When he was about to object the major frowned. "I know that you loved your wife very much. But Dorothy is dead and there's nothing you can do to change that. I seriously doubt if she would have wanted you to mope around the rest of your life. Mankind is given another chance to live a better life. Don't let it slip pass. Get your ass up that mountain and take Savannah in your arms. You have a full life ahead of you. Be sure there's a gal at your side whom you trust and can be proud of. After we put our weapons aside and start rebuilding there's a long road ahead of us."

Thomas and James walked down the knoll to an armored car where Ten Delta's handful of survivors were climbing in. "How do you know she's has the trots for me?"

James asked. They stopped to watch a column of solemn-faced prisoners marched pass under the watchful eye of their army guards.

"Tyler told me."

"Oh, he did eh?"

"Your men looks out for you whether you know it or not."

Looking around James asked. "Speaking of my men . . . I don't see the Chief. Where is he at?"

"I got a message from him earlier. He's with a squad of marines and some of my men heading to your meeting place. They fought a battle not far from here and won."

Tyler came over. "We're ready to scoot out of here. I just got a message from the Chief. Watch out for roaming Mexican squads. They're on the warpath."

"Are they bandits or Annexation people?"

"He said they were Annexation squads."

Thomas looked at James and asked. "Does it make a difference?"

"Yeah, makes a lot of difference. The Annexation groups are far more discipline and military regimented. The bandits are just savages looking only for women and booty."

For a moment Thomas looked at the seven marines in the Shoets before asking. "Want to take some of my men with you. If you run into trouble along the way your men are pretty battle weary."

"We're all battle weary. No, you better keep your men in case the Russians try a feeble offensive. We'll be all right."

"O.K, have it your way but at least keep your radio on."

CHAPTER THIRTY

For the last hour the captured BTR noisily followed the winding road leading into the mountains. Timothy sat up front with the driver while uneasily watching the passing scenery that was blackened by previous fires. It was a gloomy depressing picture accented by black rolling clouds and occasional lightning streaks. Before departing the coastal theater of horrors, the chief looking over his shoulder saw those towering black smokes where the Russian warship wreckages rode anchor. At times he prayed this was a terrible nightmare that soon would go away, but it never did. So while the skies turned blacker and Ten Delta marines died in battle, the prospects of a happy ending seemed further away.

"Do you think our fighting is over?" Galvin Harper asked. Not only was Galvin their last surviving radioman, but he was Ten Delta's only private still alive.

Timothy looked at the driver. "I guess the major parts are over though we still have mopping up to do. Take that for instance." He was pointing at a burnt out pickup truck with a Mexican flag fluttering from its roof. "That problem will take some time to solve. It was festering for a mighty long time before this war came." For a few moments he watched the scarred terrain they were passing. "A lot of good men have died making sure those colors keep flying. We're not about to let them down, private."

"What are we going to do now that Ten Delta is no more?" For reasons Galvin couldn't explain, but without Ten Delta he felt dangerously naked.

"We'll probably build another one."

Further conversation was halted when their small radar unit began warning of unidentified threats. Timothy quickly looking around found no concealment. After yelling to stop he quickly jumped from the Shoets and rushed over to an elevated position. From there he had visual control of the region. Recent fires wasted trees and everything else standing in its path. Half a mile away he saw another road winding up the mountain. Chief Hickman directed his binoculars in that direction and a few moments later saw their primary threat.

"I see them now," Timothy said. "There's one LAV-25 driving in front of four Humvees coming up the rear and all has Marine Corps markings." There was a short pause. "Those men are probably Mexican bandits judging from their appearances. The column has stopped while its occupants are pissing on the road."

"How many bandits are there?" Galvin asked.

"I count maybe thirty. How many Stinger reloads do we have?"

"We have two or three."

"Then get them ready to fire." When Galvin didn't answer he looked over his shoulder at the marine. "What's keeping you?"

"Eh, chief, we're only six people. There are thirty bandits out there with heavy weapons."

"So?"

"Are you looking to get our assholes blown to Hell?"

There was a deep frown on Timothy's face when he spat. "I know I'm about to blow your asshole to Hell if you don't get the lead out of your damned boots. Now move it!" His anger passed after sighing. "Look, Galvin, I know there are thirty Mexicans coming this way. And I also know they have heavy weapons with them. But what are we to do? Turn tail and run like hell for Momma? Galvin, this is war and we're short in numbers. There's no Ten Delta we can run to. Our people got chopped to pieces everywhere we turned. I'm not even sure we'll reach the lodge before the Mexicans corners us. But what I do know for certain is there are thirty damned wetbacks coming this way using Marine Corps vehicles. That means they got the articles from our dead marines. Now that ain't right in my eyes. We have two or three Stinger reloads that can reduce those odds. So why don't we use this opportunity to wreck chaos on those bastards. Who knows . . . we may even win."

The radioman stared at the chief petty officer for a few moments then grinned. "Damn, Chief, you're crazy as a fruitcake." With that said the marine trotted off to carry out his orders.

The LAV 25 was a lightly armored amphibious vehicle designed primarily for the Corps during their Middle Eastern Wars. Timothy watched the 8-wheeled troop carrier sluggishly move over the road while two bandits sat on the top with assault rifles. Behind it noisily came two squat shaped Humvees. It was obvious these troops were ill trained for combat because of their reckless behavior and few security precautions. But with the enemy's superior numbers the Ten Delta marines were again at a disadvantage. Timothy looked about and saw his few marines in ambush positions. Above them sharp lightning flashes continued streaking across the skies while deep throated thunder claps sounded.

Hidden among some dead bushes skirting the rocks Galvin squatted with his Stinger launcher. He silently watched the winding column slowly approaching as if they were on a Sunday outing. Atop the 15-ton LAV those two Mexican bandits cradling their rifles attentively stared at the skies. They obviously didn't know the two Apaches were shot down. Once the LAV was within range Galvin stepped from his concealment and quickly aimed the launcher. With an angry defiance the Stinger missile roared through the icy winds once its infra-red seeking capabilities were activated. The two bandits having seen him jumped up and began firing. Their opposition was almost instantly eliminated by Timothy's machine gunners. Once that high explosive warhead tore into the LAV all hell broke loose on that lonely stretch of highway. Throwing down the now useless portable launcher, Galvin jerked the automatic rifle off his back and began firing at the bandits jumping from their Humvees. The ground around his boots became alive with bullets walking across the uneven terrain. Galvin dived into a shallow ditch and continued his fight from there.

One Humvee either hoping to escape or trying to outflank the enemy never got far before another Stinger missile ripped open its side. There was an enormous explosion then the twisted hunk burst into flames. But Galvin didn't see this since he was busy fighting off screaming Mexicans. When his rifle's magazine was empty there was no time to reload. Throwing down the rifle he jumped from his hole and charged the surprised bandits while wildly firing his revolver. Observing his predicament Timothy was rushing to his aid when seeing the private go down under a burst of machine gun bullets that riddled his body. Without stopping the petty officer kept firing his weapon while running through the bandits' ranks. The bandits' charge was stopped by his murderous gunfire. When reaching the grounded marine Timothy quickly knelt down checking Galvin's body. The private was dead. After that Chief Hickman angrily stumbled to his feet while awkwardly reloading his weapon.

After the enemy was rapidly reduced to a few challenging bandits they fled. Timothy turned about seeking other challenges, but there was only burning vehicles and scattered dead bodies. Standing among this carnage were two dazed marines having survived another murderous charge by their enemy. He walked over to them. The young marines not acknowledging his arrival kept staring at the dead bodies.

"O.K, marines." he softly ordered. "Let's load up."

"What about them? Aren't we taking our dead with us?"

Timothy thoughtfully stared at the scattered dead before saying. "We don't have time for that. Later we'll come back and collect our dead. Right now we have to reach the lodge and set up positions."

The short freckled-faced lad having survived his first bloody battle was shocked at the coldness he felt after killing his fellow man. "There are more? I thought we stopped the Russians."

"Those men aren't Russians, private, but Mexican bandits feasting on our people's misery. And yes, there are more coming. We may have broken the communists, but we haven't snapped these bastards' spines yet."

＊　＊　＊

After arriving at the Santa Inez Park lodge, the handful of Ten Delta survivors hurried about that rocky terrain surrounding the stone building preparing what few defenses they could. Though Earl joined in his contributions wasn't much help.

Barnes though somewhat restricted because of his poor health stacked rocks around a firing pit facing the single road. There two marines established a machine gun removed from the armored car. Then they climbed in to await the enemy everybody knew would eventually come searching for them.

Savannah found Corporal Butterworth standing on some rocks scanning the winding road with binoculars. "You sure they will come this way?" she asked. The wind was bitterly cold in the mountains and her heavy coat didn't help that much.

After handing his glasses to the major, the corporal pointed down the mountain road. "About a mile and half pass that dip in the road, do you see them?"

It took her a few moments before his target was spotted. "Yes. Who do you think they are?"

"Most likely they're bandits. The last few months we have had problems with their looting and murdering. But we never could corner the slime balls in a fight. The bastards are too chicken to mess with trained soldiers. They only molest helpless civilians or women out looking for food." The marine leaned against a tall rock and sighed. "They must have seen us coming this way or saw the BTR's tracks. Either way following the trail they'll eventually come this way."

She handed the glasses back to the sergeant. "They have halted down there."

"Yeah, the bastards are figuring the odds about coming this way. My best guess they will sneak upon us once night falls."

Currently they were too far away to be any danger. Looking about Savannah saw another marine among the rocks armed with binoculars monitoring the distant bandits. The private lodge was tucked among blacken tree trunks and rocky uneven ground. From where they were there was an excellent view of the narrow dirt road winding down three hundred feet before disappearing into burnt out forests. At one time this region must have been very beautiful and serene.

"Why was this place chosen for a getaway?" she asked. "There's only one road."

He grinned. "Five hundred feet above us hidden among those trees is a communications tower that was operated by the fire fighters. The fires left it undamaged. One of our people spiced into its system and ran wires down to the lodge. Before long Daniel will have contacted Yuma." The sergeant slowly turned around. "This place is really easy to defend. We did some work up here several months ago. Scattered around the perimeter are remote controlled landmines." He shrugged. "They're for the most part anti-personnel mines and won't stop armored vehicles. But with the exception of that road armor can't make it up here."

"Pretty clever."

"That was the lieutenant's idea. He has a thing about escape routes." When seeing the pain in her eyes the sergeant said. "I wouldn't worry about the lieutenant, madam. That man has more lives than a damned cat. His Apache went down on the battlefield so most likely our people rescued him. He'll be up here before night."

She mumbled. "I hope so. Let me have your glasses again." For a few minutes she silently observed those bandits down the road. Without the binoculars they wouldn't have been seen. "What's the difference between those bandits and Annexation fighters?"

"Lots. The bandits are no more than street hoods, but the Annexation Movement operates as a military unit. The Annex people fight to take California, Arizona, and New Mexico back. They claim the states were taken from them unfairly. It's all about politics. But with the bandits it's all about lust, loot, and murder."

"Are these bandits clever?"

"Not really."

When hearing grunting behind them, they turned to see Earl noisily climbing the small rocky knoll. Savannah wondered how this man ever made it in the Special Forces then later as a CIA agent. The corporal didn't bother suppressing his dislike for the envoy and walked a few steps away to study the bandits down the road. They were having an intense discussion that lasted a few minutes.

"Hey, corporal." the other marine softly summoned, as if afraid his voice would be heard down the road. "Did you see that?"

"Yeah sneaky little bastards, aren't they?" After turning to Savannah he crisply reported. "The bandits drove off . . . but some of them disappeared into the trees."

"We'll have visitors later this evening." the major mumbled. "Do you have plans for this situation?"

"Yes, madam."

She grinned at his eagerness. "Then put it into place and we'll welcome the bastards."

*   *   *

The captured BTR rumbled and rattled as if it would fall apart, but it ran and that was all Timothy cared about. He kept thinking about Galvin's final stand against the Mexicans. All the man wanted to do was finish out the war and go home. He never would forget how the tall skinny black man always smeared oily lotions on his skin much to his peers' amusement. The sooty air caused his sensitive skin to flake and this bothered him. When his driver drove over a bumpy spot in the dirt road he gave the man a dirty glance.

Another marine riding atop the armored car manning the twin machine guns let out with a curse when his head slammed against the turret. That was when he caught a brief glance of something metallic some ways off the road. At first he thought it was a car's wreckage and there were thousands of them scattered about the countryside, but he quickly changed his mind. It was now moving and this sent warnings up his spine.

"Chief," he yelled several times while banging on the roof top for attention.

Timothy opened the side door and poked his head out. "Yeah, what's up?"

"I think we got company over in those woods."

"What is it?" he shouted to be heard above the engine's roar.

"It looks like an armored vehicle of sorts." The gunner stared at the woody area that had somehow escaped the fires' ravages. Their BTR made so much noise he couldn't hear anything, especially something that far away. But his inner emotions warned this still unidentified object was unfriendly. Then his face paled. "Oh shit, chief," he anxiously shouted. "It's a damned Soviet tank!"

The chief was about to yell to his driver to put the metal to the floor when they all heard the screaming incoming shell. The marine went through a series of automatic motions as his foot slammed down the foot feed, whirled the steering to create an evasive target, and started yelling at the outside gunner to tell him where the damned thing was now.

"It's going through a ravine now," the marine yelled. "We got another two or three minutes before it emerges! Drive like hell or we all die!"

The tank's 125mm main gun's shell slammed into a rocky terrain showering the retreating BTR with debris and pulverized rocks. The marine outside ducked as debris fell on him. They were in a serious compromised position. There was no place to seek haven and if trying to flee would certainly find their vehicle in the tank's tracking sight. While Timothy leaned from the BTR noisily bumping over the uneven road he caught a brief glimpse of their intruder. He recognized the armor as a Ukrainian built T-80 battle tank. This sent chills rumbling through his already strained emotions. The low silhouette tank suddenly burst from the ravine. There was no way they could out run that machine's fire control system. The bottom line was they were about to die.

"See that rocky knoll ahead of us," Timothy shouted. "Head for it then at the last moment we're abandoning the BTR before a shell splatters our balls." Grabbing hold of the door he looked up at the roof and repeated his orders.

The Soviet tank rumbling over the ravine's edge straightened out then began tracking the fleeing BTR. Occasionally its coaxial machine guns let loose with short bursts. Bullets whizzed about the armored vehicle now bumping and rattling over rough terrain in a last ditch bid to escape certain death. When Timothy shouted to jump both the driver and outside gunner instantly obeyed. After hitting the ground the three men quickly leaped to their feet and ran for concealment among the rocks. They could hear the V-84 diesel engine roaring its defiance as the heavy tank rumbled over Californian soil. Its main gun fired twice more with one explosive projective taking out the still rolling BTR. Bursting into flames the Russian armored vehicle flipped over then rolled several times before coming to a halt. Minutes later the vehicle's stored munitions cooked. The second shell exploded near some rocks where they had dived for protection. Timothy cursed when some pulverized rocks gazed his forehead.

The driver peeked over the edge to see that tank stopping several hundred feet away. "Damn, chief, we're trapped." he complained.

"Shut up, at least we're alive." the chief angrily said.

The chief petty officer's attention was on a low, rounded turret centered on the hull. The commander's cupola was on the turret's right side. Timothy was certain the tank officer was pondering his next move. When the tank didn't challenge them, the chief knew the Russians were uncertain if they had died in the crash or not. The Chief asked several questions from the gunner who was leaning against some rocks watching the idling tank. When he didn't respond the chief crawled over to him. With a deep sigh he gently pulled the man's rifle from his hands. The marine gunner was staring into space with eyes that saw nothing.

"We're in deep shit, chief." the other marine mumbled.

"Yeah, I'm afraid that we are." There was a short pause before Timothy asked in a serious manner. "Did you remember to put on clean shorts this morning?"

"Eh?"

"Did you remember to put on clean underwear this morning? My mother always said if you were going to die it was best if you wore clean underwear."

First there was bewilderment on his face then this was slowly replaced by a grin. "Do you know something, Chief? You're crazy as a damned fruitcake."

"I rather die with a smile than a frown." Timothy groaned. Peeking from their hiding place he saw the Russian tank's cannon occasionally turning. "Their commander is unsure if we died in that explosion or we're hiding up here."

"What are we supposed to do now? Hell, our rifles are pea shooters against its armor plating. If we jumped up its radar will paint us." he bitterly glanced at the naval petty officer. "So what are we supposed to do? We can't sit around here all day!"

"I dunno." While talking he was looking about them. There was too much empty space to run across. The tank's radar would spot them before too many steps were taken.

"What do you mean you dunno!" the marine suddenly growled. "You are supposed to have answers for everything. You're a naval chief petty officer. You guys know everything. All I want to know is how the hell do we get out of this pickle?"

"Get a hold of yourself, marine!" Timothy abruptly snapped. "Whimpering like a damned pussy isn't going to help us. Now calm down and that's a damned order." Both men hugged the rocks when the machine guns again let loose. Then there was silence again. "They're not sure what's up here."

A few minutes later the T-80 battle tank lurched forward as its powerful engine moved it over the rocky uneven terrain. Timothy knowing there was little they could do against this metal hunk figured their time just about was up. That was when the first explosion fell on the tank. This was followed by another that destroyed the frontal tracks. Rumbling to a halt the cannon barrel slowly turned to the right side just as another explosion impacted the hull. There was a puff of black smoke curling from beneath the tank. In the next couple of minutes two events erupted. A marine running from the rocks rapidly climbed onto the hull and popped a grenade into the commander's hatch. This produced a thunderous explosion that hurled that marine from its top. But he quickly rolled to a stop and leaping up ran like hell for cover before the machine guns commenced firing. But there was only a grim silence from within the tank. Black smoke was spinning from under the stalled tank. Only after he was certain there were no survivors inside the tank did Timothy leave his hiding place.

"Thought you may need help," James happily replied after greeting the chief.

CHAPTER THIRTY-ONE

When the strong winds abruptly came across the region soot layers was disturbed causing difficulty in seeing more than a couple of hundred feet ahead. James cursed this came at a most inappropriate time for them. Knowing there were hostiles in the general region and unable to detect them was not good. For a few moments the lieutenant stood alongside the BTR sensing something was different with the weather conditions. There was a faint dampness in these winds that weren't blowing in from the ocean. When the master sergeant trotted up after checking the handful of men the officer glanced his way. By now the soldiers had lowered their night goggles for protection from the flying corruptions.

"How are the men?" James shouted to be heard above the howling winds.

"They're all right." Tyler said while uneasily glancing around. "What the hell is going on? I never have seen weather like this before."

"I don't know. Get the men inside the armored cars. At least there's some protection there."

After the sergeant hurried away, James bewilderedly turned around several times trying to get his coordinates right. Within minutes all normalcy seemed to drift away. The lightning streaks appeared more brilliant even when infiltrating the heavy overcast. Even the winds' dampness carried a strange feeling. Nothing seemed right. The swirling soot and other loose debris were too thick to see through. James struggled against the pounding winds to reach the BTR. After climbing in he cursed the damned sooty smell that was so strong it was choking. Eight marines were packed inside like sardines in a can. They looked to him for an understanding what was happening outside. But James didn't have answers.

Using a hand radio Tyler contacted the other two vehicles and learned everybody was safely inside. James quietly sat observing how the BTR awkwardly handled the rough weather. It was easily compared to being inside a shaking metal can with a handful of rocks. The rapid flashing lightning penetrated the driver's thick glass window bathing inside the BTR. Even not being outside James knew there were major climatic changes hurling down on the devastated Californian region.

Normally a calm person Timothy found it hard to suppress his uneasiness. "What do you think is happening out there?" he asked.

"I don't know. Whatever it is certainly suggests a major weather change." He grunted when the heavy vehicle violently shook. "The winds are getting nasty that much I know."

Benches along the sides provided seating for nine marines while more men sat on the flooring. This created a stuffy overcrowding that made it hard for Tyler to make his way to the front when his name was called. James only gave him a brief glance then went back to talking with the chief. When he was ignored the master sergeant pushed his way to the small radar set and sat.

It wasn't much later that Tyler called out James' name. After stumbling his way through the packed confinement, the lieutenant looked at the radar monitor's four blinking red lights. James uneasily glanced at Tyler.

"How long have they been there?" he asked.

"This weather is playing hell with electronics," the sergeant explained. "Though I detected them four minutes ago that doesn't give us a reliable timeline."

"Hostile?" James asked.

"According to this Friend or Foe Identifying device," Tyler replied, "the approaching land vehicles are friendly." There was a short pause. "But considering we're inside a Russian armored unit I would say those targets are unfriendly."

"A safe assumption," James stared at the screen for a few moments. "How far away are they?"

"They are now two miles by northeast with an irregular approach. That could mean the weather is opposing their travel or the vehicles are lost."

The lieutenant looked at his master sergeant and asked. "Do you know where we are at?"

"I only know the map coordinates."

"How fast are they going?"

"According to this radar they're moving very slow." Tyler kept staring at the screen. "They have stopped again."

"Doesn't that damned thing have a target identifying ability?"

"It isn't working." Tyler pointed at another digital screen below the radar.

James leaned over and slammed his fist against the box and it suddenly started working. "There. The best solution for a damned Russian made instrument." Moments later the screen scrolled the identifications of their approaching threats. "That's not good. One BTR-60PU . . . now that could be good for us. Two MT-LB amphibious armored tracks are to the rear. The middle vehicle is another BTR."

Tyler noted his solemn expression and asked. "Those mean something to you?"

"I would place high bets on that column," James said with a skeptical grin. "We may have stumbled across the invasion's command group. In the past the Soviets used the BTR-60PU as a forward command vehicle."

Timothy said. "That may explain those messages Thomas' people intercepted the last few days. His decoders were never able to decode those messages originating from different positions. The Soviets traditionally never uses static headquarters during land invasions. Instead, they prefer mobile units."

James grinned. "This may be our golden opportunity. With the Soviet invasion already in shambles if we captured those command vehicles we would know their detailed plans." His voice dropped to a near whisper as hope shined in his eyes.

Tyler nodded a skeptical expression. "We only have a handful of men and no heavy weapons. Not to mention our munitions are low. How do you plan to take them out?"

"Beats the hell out of me," James mumbled while directing his attention on the stalled column. "It appears they are making camp." For the next few minutes the lieutenant thoughtfully watched the Russians. "What the hell are they doing now?"

The chief petty officer studied the situation through his binoculars for a few moments. "That's interesting. That antenna they're raising is for long distance transmissions."

"Maybe they're calling their naval base in Canada?" Tyler suggested. Laying between the two men he slowly scanned the Soviet camp with his binoculars.

"No, I don't think so." James disagreed. "In the first place we wasted that base. And what was missed I'm certain our destroyers finished the job. No, that antenna would be used for much longer distances." He glanced over at the chief. "What about the rest of that task force? What happened to them?"

"I haven't heard. They probably hot tailed it back to Russian waters."

"And left behind a high ranking general? That doesn't sound too smart. Look to the left of that antenna truck. See the short fat man dressed in the brown uniform? That must be their invasion commander. And for what I can see from here the man is damned pissed about something."

"We don't have third class soldiers down there," Tyler remarked after studying the encampment's activities. "Those are Soviet marines and that makes sense. Why would the invasion commander have third class soldiers guarding him? Over to the right of the main body is another BTR with five soldiers standing guard. Then to their rear about twenty feet is another post with marines." Lowering his glasses he looked at James. "Taking out that camp won't be easy. I count thirty marines on guard at overlapping positions."

"I estimate there are at least eighty troops down there." James said. "That sound about right to you?"

"Yeah," the master sergeant replied. His glasses were pressed against his eyes while studying the encampment. "Judging from that brisk activity around the radio truck they're sending messages now. Sure would like to know what they're sending and to whom."

"They're obviously planning to spend some time there. The bastards are setting up tents." Timothy replied after counting ten canvas tents erected in the middle of their camp. "I also count six heavy machine gun placements in strategic positions." He was silent for a few moments. "That would be a heavy position to over run, James, especially with the few men we have."

"What do you suggest we do then?"

"Very quietly get the hell out of here."

A marine sent scouting the region came back a few minutes later. He had wrapped around his face a cloth to keep the wind from pounding tiny sooty debris into his flesh. He trotted over to James and saluted. The winds were gaining strength while lightning flashes came more frequent. The marine bundled in heavy winter clothes and gloves made him appear heavier than he was. While one marine kept a close watch on the Russian camp, Timothy and Tyler joined James to hear their scout's report. The other marines departing the safety of their vehicles established security perimeters in case the Soviets attacked. It was like standing in a sandstorm, but instead of sand there were tiny sooty debris pounding the flesh like hundreds of needles. Nobody ignored that strange feeling within the air's chill.

"What did you find out?" James asked.

"The road leading into the mountains is unguarded. But we do have a small out post about one mile from here. I counted only four Russian soldiers who aren't the brightest kids on the block. I came across four sectors that had recently seen fighting. Other than those we have a clear path to the lodge."

"Were they wearing any insignia above the sleeve red star?" Tyler asked.

The marine thought about it then shook his head. "Not that I remember."

James looked at his sergeant. "What difference does it make?" he asked.

"Those marines down there with the general have another insignia above their red stars. From here it's too far to see exactly what it is. But they're probably some elite formation. Those soldiers you seen are probably regular army who got separated from their regiment." Tyler shrugged. "I can't think of one reason why the Soviets would want an out post up here."

"Well, reason or no reason," James speculated. "We got to get pass that patrol. So let's figure out how without causing noises that would alert the general down there."

*   *   *

Leaving their Shoets behind the marines set out on the short brisk walk to where their scout had found the isolated patrol. Even when using their night goggles it was a slow walk. The blowing sooty debris caused difficulty in seeing very far ahead. The flying dirt bit into their exposed flesh like tiny needles. But this didn't discourage the vengeful marines. For thirty minutes they carefully made their way through the burned out forest by climbing over rough terrain. The going was rough even for well conditioned bodies. It was a toss which was the worst, the howling biting winds or walking through the sooty layers that rose up in billowing clouds.

Soon James held up his hand signaling a halt. Their scout came trotting back. After that the marines slowly crept through the darkness to where the enemy had established an outpost. Two canvas tents were noisily flapping in the winds. One soldier trying to cook something in a pot sitting in the fire was having his share of troubles. Another soldier was pissing nearby while laughing at something another had said. James saw the third soldier sitting in a tent doing something with his uniform jacket. James looked at his men and signaled they were to use only their knives. They acknowledged his signal a prisoner was to be taken.

Minutes later four Ten Delta marines crept closer to the unsuspecting camp. They carried their weapons strapped to the backs while ugly jagged knives were carried in hand. The men's faces were firm with determination to kill Russians. While the others waited in the shadows the strike team disappeared into the murkiness. Stopping at the out post's edge the marines evaluated the situation. Two soldiers were seated around a small campfire eating food from the pot and drinking cheap Mexican wine. Their chattering revealed no fears of being compromised. The third soldier was eating a piece of stale black bread while pissing on the ground. When the Americans stormed from the shadows, he quickly dropped the bread and put his hands in the air. His limp penis hung like a wet noodle. By the time James and the others arrived the soldiers around the fire were dead.

The tall soldier, probably a poor farmer from Siberia's backwoods, was roughly tied to a tree trunk. His mouth was taped close. While the Americans examined their wallets and pockets for documents his fears were widely expressed. His dark colored penis still hung from his unbuttoned pants. Any other time James would have found the scene amusing, but not today. They were on a tight schedule and this little sortie was costing time. The Russian's large face was rather ugly from its pock marks and several days' growth of a shabby black beard.

"Learn anything useful?" James questioned.

"Not much. He's part of the 97th Infantry Division dropped off five days ago by the amphibious ship. Three companies under the command of Captain Ivan Pros . . . oh hell I can't pronounce those Russian names. Too many damned Ss and Is." Dropping plastic wrapping torn from a small box, he removed the clear tube then inserted a syringe into its bottle's rubber cap. "Chatterbox always said this stuff never failed." After filling the syringe he lightly tapped the tube with his finger and smiled broadly. "You might as well relax for a few minutes. This stuff takes five minutes to work."

James nodded and walked away from the fire to look about. His marines were in defensive positions listening for signs of trouble. Another trotted back to report the general's camp settling down hadn't sent patrols out. That was good news, but the darkening skies were not. He wondered how Major Thomas was handling the situation on Vandenberg? Looking over his shoulder James seen the mountain's heights and hoped the others had reached the hunting lodge. He thought of Savannah in a different manner than when first meeting her. Thinking about another woman other than his dead wife should have bothered him, but it didn't. Further thoughts on the issue were interrupted when the soldier administering that truth serum called his name. Walking to the tree he waited for the marine to explain what he had discovered.

"His name is Peter Mekhlis and before the war he worked at Kavkazsky's."

"What's that?"

"It's a popular restaurant that was on 25 Nevsky Prospekt in Leningrad. He worked there as cook. The name was changed back to St. Petersburg after the Soviet Union collapsed, but Kossier changed it back to Leningrad." He shrugged. "Crazy, huh?"

"Interesting," James grunted. "But what about his regiment and what are they doing up here? I really don't give a damn what he did before the war."

"Yes sir, I'm sorry. It's just that this stuff makes a person talk about funny things. You have to work your way to the questions that is important." The marine looked over his shoulder. The Russian was hanging limp against the rope binding his bloodied body to the tree. "His regiment from the 97th was supposed to secure the regions south of Riverside to San Diego and establish static positions."

"What happened? Why are they up here many miles from their objective?"

"Everything went wrong according to him. Their regiment was cut off from their armor support and logistics. His captain was a stupid fool from Moscow who thought he knew everything, but according to our friend there the only thing he knew was how to blow gas through his ass."

"So where is the regiment now?"

"They were cut to pieces by rebels . . . I believe that was what he was trying to say."

"Are there any other patrols or outposts up here?"

"He doesn't know if there is. When we caught them they were making plans to get back to their lines in Canada." The marine frowned then said. "He doesn't know how far that is."

The lieutenant walked a few feet away and studied the general area where the Russian command group was camping. "How far away is the lodge?"

"Maybe another one hour if we don't run into interference."

Timothy rushed up. "That ain't gonna happen. We got tanks coming our way. Six of the bastards with infantry support!" James ran with the chief to a low knoll giving them a view of the sloping terrain that faded into burnt woody regions. "I don't know where in the hell they came from."

"They must be that armor formation we couldn't find." James groaned while appraising the situation. Though it was a gray heavy overcast it was easy to see the rumbling steel monsters grinding their way up the inclining terrain. There were at least four hundred infantrymen on their flanks. "The soldiers are Soviet Marines and heavily armed. Chief, I think we got a problem."

When the first shell came storming over their heads and exploded the chief grumbled. "What was your first clue?"

"Let's get the hell out of here!" James shouted. "Get the men loaded . . ."

Before he finished a screaming shell hit one transport blowing it to bits. As scraps of hot metal fell among the withdrawing Americans, another explosion took out some marines still in their trenches. The second armored vehicles burst into flames. Giving the order to withdraw James wasn't sure where they would go. A quick glance at the approaching tanks he knew it didn't really matter where just as long as they escaped the tightening jaws of this trap. The heavy weapons their enemy possessed were ripping gaps in James' small command. Their desperate flight on foot soon became slow while dodging falling cannon shells that were exploding all around them. When several Russians boldly charged from their inland flank, James whirled about and let loose with short bursts. With that threat eliminated another one popped up.

"Chief," James shouted above the screaming incoming shells. "Radio Thomas and let him what's going on. Tell him the enemy still has tank columns in the hills. Give him our coordinates." Ducking as sprouting geysers of dirt and debris dropped among their ranks, he mumbled. "Not that it'll do any good for us."

*   *   *

Major Thomas was addressing his problems of surrendering Russians when informed Lieutenant Blackmore was trapped in the Santa Inez Mountains. Asking for a map he quickly studied their coordinates before calling over another officer. Behind him sooty dust was raised as landing Chinook helicopters disembarked infantrymen. Lying off shore were two American destroyers monitoring the subdued hostile situation on the devastated air force base.

The saluting junior lieutenant with 101st Airborne arm badges was anxious to get into battle though none was evident around there.

"We have a bunch of marines trapped in the Inez Mountains. It seems Blackmore ran into a hornets' nest of tanks and they're kicking his butt. Take some men and a couple of helicopters and eliminate their problems."

*   *   *

James was having his share of troubles when it became obvious fleeing was out of the question. Thick crusty terrain created by the past fires made it near impossible to run fast. Seeing no other course of action he ordered his men to dig in and fight it out. A quick scan down the hill showed the tanks had for some reason halted. But their infantrymen weren't stopping. After spreading out the platoons began their hostile approach up the hill. After digging into the soft soil the American marines set up their opposition against the Russians. For the time being the howling winds had died down, but the hazy grayness still shrouded the wasted terrain like a cemetery.

James watched the Russians inching their way up the 30 degree slopes. They were still not in range. "Cocky bastards aren't they?" he said.

"Soviet Marines have always been arrogant as hell." the chief mumbled from the hole they were sharing.

"What do we have in the way of weapons?"

"We definitely don't have anything heavy. A few automatics and some laser rifles. We have three boxes of grenades that were divided among the men." The chief thoughtfully watched the cautious Soviets moving up the hill. All around them were burnt tree trunks that looked like forgotten tombstones. "We probably can fight off two charges, but after that they'll over run our positions."

"It looks like it." James said. "And there's nothing we can do to stop that many soldiers or tanks." He forced a weak smile. "But you got to admit Ten Delta ran a good track. We sure as hell kick some Russians butts."

"Yeah that we sure did. I wonder if history will even remember that we accomplished the impossible out here . . . probably not." He was solemnly silent for a while. "Right now I could stand a good slug of that whiskey we had back at Ten Delta." the chief grumbled while lining up several grenades along the hole's rim.

James uneasily laughed. "Hell with slugs I could stand a whole damned bottle." For a few moments he indifferently watched those soldiers climbing the incline. "Do you know what I miss the most?"

"What's that?"

"That I didn't try to know Savannah better than I did."

"She's a good woman, James."

He slowly nodded. "That's the strange thing about facing death in the face. You begin to see things a lot differently. I was too busy fighting a war to see my second chance at love glaring me in the face."

"We were all too busy doing that." Timothy replied. "The soldiers are stopping their advance. I wonder why?"

"Because the tanks are about to soften our positions," James anxiously said. Whirling about he shouted to prepare for incoming shells.

CHAPTER THIRTY-TWO

With falling darkness the Mexicans attacked the hunting lodge. Expecting an easy target the bandits were surprised at the stubborn defenses they encountered. Though few in number Savannah had skillfully arranged their defenses so it appeared there were more of them. Earl was alone among some rocks with a Stinger launcher. He was able to take out two of their three transports before throwing aside the now useless rocket weapon. With a Dragunova rifle picked up from a dead bandit he kept up a fierce fight until it too was empty.

Running to another position Earl ran into a bandit armed with the deadly Russian rifle. Three rapid squeezed shots from his Dragunova rifle caught Earl squarely in the arm. After he painfully pulled himself up from the dirt that sniper was nowhere around. A cold chill sluggishly moved through the wounded envoy's body. Snipers were chosen for their determination and brutal disrespect for lives, especially if the opposition was his sworn enemy. Earl stood still while slowly appraising the rolling burnt out terrain. There were too many places a sniper could hide.

The envoy's good hand removed his combat knife then crept through the smelly terrain until reaching that first burning vehicle. Its fierce heat warmed his face. His thoughts remained cold and single-minded in purpose. Down the hill and some miles away he could hear another battle going on. He gave little thought to who was engaging Russian tanks. They had their own problems up here. His boots crunched the hard soil in a ravine he was cautiously passing through. Above him the skies were darker and clinging to that strange smell. His arm wounds were tied with a dirty rag that kept the blood from flowing. In several places around the lodge Earl heard gunfire as his comrades fought off the Mexican bandits. Fortunately, the Mexicans weren't battle veterans so they were making some serious blunders in their night attack. But for the time being what the others were doing wasn't his concern. He was stalking a lonely sniper.

When the bandit rushed from concealment, Earl barely had time to duck the man's swinging knife. He fell against the burning truck then quickly leaped to his feet with a scream. The white hot metal had burned deep into his right shoulder. The pain was immense. When the Mexican charged again Earl rolled over missing the thrusting knife. Each time the civilian made a physical move his burns sent hot flashes of pain charging through his body. The bandit was good with the knife and Earl had trouble missing his thrusts. Maybe because he was slow this saved his life. For a split second the Mexican let his guard down and Earl took advantage. Kicking out the envoy knocked the man to his feet. Before he could leap up Earl drove his knife deep into the chest. His enemy didn't scream, but merely stared bewilderedly at the wound's spurting blood before tumbling over.

Earl hesitated a few moments before finding the sniper's dropped rifle. Then he crawled back into the rocks affording a better view of the struggle going on around the lodge. The Samazaryadnaya Vintovka Dragunova rifle was Russia's standard issue for their snipers. He wondered how the Mexican came into its possession. Using full powered 7.62x54mm rimmed cartridges a trained sniper could take out a slow walking man at 800 meters. Snuggling into a shooting position Earl looked through the built-in Metalscope infrared tracking device. He took careful aim and fired. A bandit in the semi-darkness never knew where the bullet came from that ended his life. In the following few minutes Earl brought down seven more bandits. By the time the Mexicans realized there was a sniper in the rocks and investigated Earl had crept away.

It required dodging shadows before Earl reached where Savannah and two more marines were fiercely fighting off charging bandits. When another Mexican ran from the shadows firing his automatic weapon, Earl swung up the Dragunova and fired. The bullet caught that running soldier in the forehead. Finding the gunfire too deadly the bandits pulled back into the darkness. Savannah knew they weren't fleeing, but only regrouping. Savannah had seen Earl running from the rocks and leaped among the rocks where they were fighting. The man sure could get around when he wanted to.

After flopping down alongside the major Earl grinned. "Sure are persistent bastards, aren't they." His face and hands were black from soot while blood stained the shoulder bandage. After a few seconds looking about the defenses where she had fought, he wondered how they had held the battered site. There were lots of bodies scattered about the rocks. "How many men did you lose?"

"A couple." Savannah after reloading her two weapons sighed. "They'll be back."

Earl nodded. "I'm sure they will." He gestured down the burnt terrain. "We aren't the only ones fighting. I heard tanks firing a few minutes ago." He checked the sniper rifle then laid it aside. "Any idea who that is fighting?"

"Nope, it could be anybody considering the situation out here."

One marine after unsnapping his belt canteen handed it to Earl. "Drink some of this. It'll make hair grow on your chest." When the envoy drank the whiskey and nearly choked the corporal smiled. "See I told you it would grow hair on your chest." Snapping the canteen back on his web belt, the marine turned back watching the darkness for threats.

Though the marines had night enhancers and their enemy didn't odds was still against them. When their violence stopped the defenders could hear that vicious roar from that distant battle. There were lots of heavy calibers firing. Savannah frowned when realizing those were the tanks James was unable to find yesterday. While Earl rewrapped his wound, Savannah recommended they use the darkness and find another place.

In their camouflages it was easy moving around in the darkness without been seen. They repositioned their firing lines among some rocks overlooking the lodge. When the enemy returned they would be caught in a vicious cross fire. With no other option the lodge defenders impatiently waited until the next murderous charge stormed from that darkness cloaking the Santa Inez Mountains.

*   *   *

The battle down the mountain was heated and slowly turning against James' small group of fighters. After a savage cannon barrage the tanks jerked into motion and slowly rumbled up the incline. None of Ten Delta's marines needed to be told their enemy was throwing everything they had at them. While the tanks were firing the general arrived with his command to join in the fighting.

One young marine sweated while jamming in another magazine into his hot rifle. The enemy was everywhere below his posting and when he killed one there seemed to be twenty more taking that man's place. Russian soldiers were running toward his isolated position firing their weapons like crazy. This marine did not see faces. In battle nobody had faces. Snapping in his last magazine he prepared for their assault. His M16 assault rifle fired until clicking on an empty chamber.

The young marine from Houston, Texas saw those grenades silently hurling through the icy night. His lips moved in loud condemnations on the invading Russians while one blast after another devastated the foxhole. His body was lifted into the air by the explosions then savagely thrown against nearby rocks. As enemy soldiers raced over his twisted bloodied body the war for him was over.

Having seen the attack Timothy yelled. "Hanson is gone! Our right flank is exposed!"

James didn't acknowledge as his attention was glued on those six tanks slowly rumbling over the burnt terrain. Crashing toppled trees didn't slow their progress. Their long cannons menacingly rotated while heavy machine guns supported their advancing troops. With all the gunfire and explosions this area had become a nightmare to the few Americans contesting their approach.

"Hold this area!" James shouted while climbing out of the hole. "I'll try plugging the flank!" Not giving the chief a chance to argue he ran into the darkness.

Unexpectedly meeting a squad of Russians creeping through the murkiness James quickly mowed them down. Picking up a Gail shoulder fired rocket launcher he had to be satisfied with only two reloads. He also found a canvas bag of grenades dropped by a fallen soldier. Running cautiously further into the darkness he stopped not far from where the Texan died fighting. Falling behind some rocks he rapidly appraised his situation. Having no night enhancers the Soviets were slowly moving through the darkness. Hearing a roaring engine the lieutenant peeked over the rocks. The general's command BTR was struggling over burnt tree trunks while twenty hunched over soldiers walked alongside. They had to be eliminated before coming up from the rear and destroying his trapped marines.

Charging the rocket launcher James lifted it and fired without aiming. The high explosive warhead was with a hit-to-kill fuse. During its short flight James muttered a short prayer for success then quickly reloaded. The micro-processor guidance system took the flaming shaft straight to the BTR. A Russian officer standing in that BTR saw the oncoming threat and yelled a warning, but he was too late. Amidst a thunderous explosion the vehicle was reduced to burning metal with its screaming soldiers trapped inside the burning hell. That explosion had caught many soldiers in its death grip.

Abandoning his position James ran like hell through the night. With the Gail he may be able to slow one tank from rumbling over their positions. Close to where his marines were savagely fighting the invading Russians, James dived to the ground as bullets switched the soil about his feet. He had run into another encircling squad of Soviets. Dropping the Gail the lieutenant fought a five minute battle against odds that should have seen his demise.

After capturing a heavy machine gun, Chatterbox walked his bullets back and forth across stubborn enemy formations that wouldn't stop advancing. Blood soaked the black soot. Twisted pieces of bloody flesh flew about like grotesque parts from Hell. Chatterbox fired magazine after magazine into the thinning ranks, but they kept coming. By now he had stopped worrying about the fears numbing his senses. His motions were automatic. Kill Russians and kill more Russians dominated his actions. Even though accomplishing some amazing victories the last few days, Chatterbox knew this engagement wouldn't be in their favor. Running out of munitions the staff sergeant pushed over the machine gun and leaping from the foxhole ran through the night to where other marines were fighting. That was a good move. Seconds after he departed a dull explosion sounded in the hole. Dropping behind some rocks he caught a rifle thrown to him by a marine who seen he was unarmed. From his new position Chatterbox saw several dead marines in their foxholes. Their numbers were rapidly dwindling.

Though they had managed to kill many infantrymen, James knew those few tanks posed their greatest threat. And all they had to challenge their presence was one Gail reload. In the last minutes strong winds had returned while the skies were ripped by darting lightning streaks. Brilliant lightning bolts illuminating the general area cast a strange glow over the violence. Kossier's marines were determined to quash the Americans regardless of their losses. With all the explosions erupting on that higher ground where James' marines desperately fought, it appeared the earth was remolding its surfaces. The lieutenant frequently had to hug the foxhole when grenades tumbled through the night. And above this nightmarish eruption could be heard the cries of dying men. Firing his automatic rifle James brought down several Russians. His real interest was on a tank slowly clawing at the loose dirt while climbing.

*   *   *

When the Mexicans renewed their attacks Earl squatting behind some rocks watched the violence. Soils around the hunting lodge smelled terribly of acidly smoke and burnt human flesh. But this didn't bother the Presidential envoy patiently waiting until a bunch of bandits came within shooting range. He could hear the exploding grenades and rapid chattering of machine guns as Savannah's marines fought back the Mexicans. Even though presently holding the heights those advantages would change when their munitions ran low.

Savannah's clothing was torn and dirty from close quarter fighting, but her spirit was still flushed with a determination to win. Scattered around her rocky defenses were numerous bodies. With a lull in the charges she quickly took inventory of her ammo and wasn't surprised it was getting low. The marine major unclipped her last four grenades and laid them within reach. The rapid lightning cast a frightening glow across the land while providing unrestricted visual command around them. At one time she was sure this was a beautiful serene area, but not now. Savannah compared their surroundings with a scene from some dreadful horrible movie. Some feet away Barnes lay sprawled in a hole. She wondered what Earl would do since the scientist died during one of the Mexicans' many charges. The woman thoughtfully glanced at the ugly skies and shrugged after a few moments. Did it really matter now? She was doubtful if anybody would live to see the coming of another day.

Somebody yelled. "Here they come again!"

The rapid chattering of machine guns and exploding grenades harshly broke the brief silence as Mexican bandits stormed across open ground with blazing guns. Not understanding Spanish Savannah didn't know what they were shouting, but she was sure the political slogans didn't favor their position.

When two bandits suddenly darted in front of her she fired and brought one down. The other jumped into her hole with a jagged knife. She grabbed the blade before he could maneuver and plunged it through his chest. Kicking the man aside she returned to her close quarters fighting. Though the enemy's numbers were sharply reduced they still outnumbered the Americans. Seeing Earl was about to be over run she leaped from her hole and ran towards him firing her assault weapon all the while. This crazy woman's charge threw the bandits' confidence into the gully and they broke. But not before throwing a grenade at Earl's feet. Savannah yelled a warning but it was too late. The explosion ripped the scientist into shreds. Halting long enough to jam a reload into her weapon, the major then continued chasing the frightened bandits from the area.

When the gunfire stopped Corporal Butterworth found the major wrapping her wounds. The few surviving marines left their battered positions and walked among the dead that seemed to be everywhere. Then the solemn task of collecting their dead and attending the wounded began. The corporal went about rifling the bandits' pockets. No Mexican flags were found, but lots of stolen jewelry was discovered. After Savannah did her final casualty count she accompanied the corporal about the grounds. The more they looked the more it became amazing how such a powerful force was wiped out by their small numbers.

When finding a headless corpse wearing four Naval Academy rings, the corporal tried removing them. When this didn't work he chopped off the fingers. After examining the rings he angrily looked up. "This one belonged to the naval lieutenant commanding our radar station at San Diego."

"Then the Mexicans destroyed the station?" Savannah dubiously suggested.

He shook his head. "I don't think these bastards are that smart. Instead, I bet they looted their bodies after the Soviets killed the men."

Standing in the winds she thoughtfully listened to the distant sounds of battle. "That fight is still going on hot and heavy. Somebody is kicking somebody's butt real bad." When told the bandits were preparing to charge again she angrily groaned.

*   *   *

Savannah's speculation was right on the button. Now reduced to only a few men manning the collapsing defenses, James people were indeed getting their butts kicked. After a short lull in the fighting the Soviets resumed their savage attacks. Timothy had crawled to the battered right flank hoping to stop its cave in after their men there were slaughtered. It didn't take long to realize their opposition was elite troops. Two of those six tanks having detoured from the rest were slowly clawing their way up the slopes. All the while their cannons kept firing. Accompanying the metal monsters were large numbers of well disciplined troops. Diving behind some large rocks to escape flying bullets as numerous as bunches of angry bees, the chief began firing at soldiers topping the crest.

There were too many Soviets coming over the knoll's crest so Timothy ran further up the hill while bullets whizzed all around him. Hearing his name called the chief turned and ran to the rocks where James and his surviving marines gathered for a last ditch stand. Timothy counted only six men. The marines uncomfortably greeted their petty officer and turned back to watching the Soviets slowly climbing the hill. Timothy noticed James was calmly regarding the dead end situation.

"Well, chief, it looks as if the end is near." the lieutenant replied.

"Sort of looks that way." after checking his rifle for reloads the chief mumbled. "Damn, I only got two reloads and that's it."

"You're better off than me."

The trapped men squatted behind their rocky concealment silently observing the enemy's thunderous activity. The formations halting their steady approach suddenly seemed unsure of their objective. There were no longer screaming slogans or the rumbling of tank tracks stinging the air. The marines looked at one another in bewilderment when the tanks began pulling back with their infantrymen following. James cautiously looked about but saw nothing that would prompt this withdrawal. When the first explosion sounded the startled marines jumped. Then quickly on the heels of that blast another eruption of flames fell among the retreating soldiers. It was then smiles appeared on the battle weary marines' faces. They were hearing the familiar sounds of airborne Chinooks rushing into the battle zone. Near exhausted from their fighting didn't stopped the Americans from breaking into cheering when a Chinook landed within running distance. The whirling blades sent thick clouds of sooty dust flying about the area. The second helicopter continued harassing the retreating Soviets. Their Hellfire missiles inflicted heavy casualties and blasted three of the tanks into burning debris. After hauling the men aboard the helicopter thundered back into the skies inbound to the hunting lodge.

"That was close," James yelled to be heard.

The army lieutenant nodded with a smile. "Major Thomas said the army needed to pull some pussy ass jarheads out of a jam."

After laughing, Ten Delta's commanding officer replied. "No argument to that. What about the situation at Vandenberg?"

"That campaign has closed down. We took three hundred odd prisoners including ten senior officers. Two divisions of marines and infantrymen were landed off Santa Barbara earlier today and have moved inland engaging scattered Soviet units. For all intent and purposes Kossier's invasions plans for California have ended on a sour note."

"What about the rest of his invasion force?" Accepting the can of beer the lieutenant nodded his thanks. Fighting in that soot created a tremendous thirst.

"The space station reported his remaining four warships turned back for friendly ports right after the amphibious ship sunk." After glancing about making certain the other marines had beer he then continued. "We have unconfirmed reports from Russia that Kossier is fighting to remain in power. I guess too many generals and admirals were dissatisfied with how he was running the war."

"What about my people who fled to the hunting lodge?"

"We're heading there now."

James was quiet for a few moments. "Maybe this damned war will end soon." He mumbled.

"Maybe, there are strong rumors circulating in Russia that they may sue for a truce."

Timothy came back frowning from the cockpit. "All right, marines, listen up. Lock and load we have a battle going on at the lodge."

There was no hesitation on their part as the few men quickly checked their weapons. Their soot smeared faces were solemnly ready to fight another battle. But this one was different than the others. They were riding to the rescue of fellow marines. As the giant helicopter roared through the darkness their impatience was soon evident. The chief visited the cockpit for an update and soon came back and sat alongside the lieutenant. Except for the roar of those General Electric engines there was no sound generated inside. In the last few hours these men had witnessed their numbers sharply reduced. If they could help it there would be no further casualties.

"Do you think it was worth our losses?" the chief skeptically asked.

"We're alive so I guess it was in a way."

The petty officer slowly nodded. "Maybe?" He was silent for a few moments. "Do you remember all of those discussions we had the last few months?"

"Yeah, they were rather philosophically. Now I only see bloodshed and hear the screams of our wounded." James grumbled. "I don't think I ever will forget these last few days."

"With compassion and understanding you will." the chief remarked with a thin smile. After James looked his way he added. "Give her a chance. You may be surprise how a woman's tender touch can soothe even the worse nightmares."

James shook his head. "I swear you'll determine to see me matched with Savannah."

"When this is all over, my friend, you'll need somebody at your side to make it through the nightmares we still face. Don't turn away the one person who really loves you. You will need all the kindness in this wasted terrified world to mend your torn emotions. Take my word for it."

The co-pilot came back and loudly announced. "We're about there. Load and lock and get ready to rock and roll, marines. Even from here we can see the flashing of guns and exploding shells."

CHAPTER THIRTY-THREE

When the Mexican bandits brought up their armored vehicles, Savannah knew they couldn't hold off another full charge. Corporal Butterworth had disappeared with their last Stinger and three reloads. Quickly looking about evaluating their grim situation, she found nothing offering encouragement. The corporal had warned her not to fall into the bandits' hands alive. He didn't explain and she didn't need him to. The entire area became a hellish nightmare while enemy armor laid down a steady barrage of devastating explosions. The chilly air was saturated with drifting soot and smoke. Thunderous explosions shook the ground. She watched a Soviet PSZH-IV ram through burnt trees and clawed its way over rocks. Ten Delta's handful of survivors now scattered among the rocky crags viciously fought back the charging bandits. For a moment the major wondered where Butterworth was. When an explosion a few feet away hurled splintered rocks and dirt down on her, she hugged the ground for a few seconds then continued fighting.

When gunfire made her position too dangerous to remain, she scrambled into a nearby ravine and continued firing at the charging bandits. The winding ditch was carved out years ago when rain waters rushed down the slopes. It was barely deep enough to shield her body if she kept down. Laying out the few grenades she had left, the major jammed another banana clip into her weapon and waited until four hunched over bandits came her way. Three of her men were trapped when the armored car's coaxial machine gun turned their rocky concealment into a living hell of flying rocky chips. One marine jumping up tried fleeing but was instantly cut down. The other two finding the little spot too deadly crawled away only to be blown to bits by two exploding shells.

Ignoring his hellish surroundings, the corporal crawled around the fighting to an elevated spot providing a good view of the unfolding devastation and bloodshed. Butterworth only wasted a few moments evaluating the situation. He watched the bandits' noisy armored car crunching over that rocky area where the major and her few men fought their last desperate standoff. He knew something about the Czechoslovak-designed BTR-152. Its quad of 12.7mm M53 DshKM machine guns with a cyclic fire of 600 rounds per minute was wasting Ten Delta's feeble defenses. He knew that machine had to be decommissioned. The driver had lowered his shuttle visional block. That meant he couldn't fire a missile inside the vehicle. Its 13.5mm armor plating sloping at 35' gave the car fairly good protection. Only for a few seconds did he analyzed the dangers if exposing himself.

The tiny light was blinking on his Stinger meaning it was ready for firing. Time was running out for the defenders. It was now or never if he expected to save them. With a soft grunt he quickly stood while bringing the shoulder-fired launcher up for firing. He watched with indifference as the Stinger shot away with a flaming tail. The vehicle exploded with flames shooting out both sides. Bandits caught in the open were roasted. This turn of the events caused the remaining Mexicans to reconsider their approach.

The hesitation on their part prompt Savannah's marines to jump up and charge their dwindling ranks. Their furious charge broke the Mexicans' attack and they started fleeing in all directions. That was when the Chinook landed to disembark marines and soldiers who joined in the fighting the last Mexican charge that quickly collapsed. The corporal happy with his shot was about to join in the new fighting when a wounded Mexican took him out with one bullet to the forehead.

Savannah, Tyler, and James stood on a rocky knoll silently watching Timothy move about the area checking their wounded. Reinforcing troops rounded up surviving Mexicans for transport to POW camps once the helicopters arrived. The increasing winds were spreading sooty debris and smoke around in crazy patterns. Savannah watched the BTR furiously burn while its flames whipped around in the howling winds. Above them the gray and ugly skies gave further reason to be gloomy even thought they were alive and well.

James looked at Savannah and asked. "With Earl and Barnes dead what will become of that rocket firing?"

"That's out of the question. They were the only two who could do it. But it wouldn't have mattered if they were alive or not. Thomas said the rocket they needed was damaged too badly to use."

"What about the other rockets that was to be fired?"

"I don't know about them."

James briefly studied the rolling black clouds. "Then what do we do about these weather changes. They aren't getting any better."

Savannah frowned. "I guess it's up to God now."

"I don't think mankind is too high on God's list."

Savannah felt something softly touch her cheek then another. Wiping them away she cried out it was rain drops. About that time the skies exploded with lightning and shook from the deep throated thundering. The deluge of rain came quickly. Though nobody knew it at that time the rain would continue for days cleansing the skies of their burdening sooty debris. Nobody ran for cover from the falling raindrops but jumped around with released joy. James whirled about and grabbing Savannah kissed her with no objections.

The war started abruptly with a heavy hand of death and ended with a bloody climax staggering mankind's emotions. Throughout the devastated world rain poured down and battered civilizations rejoiced over this second chance given them.

The End